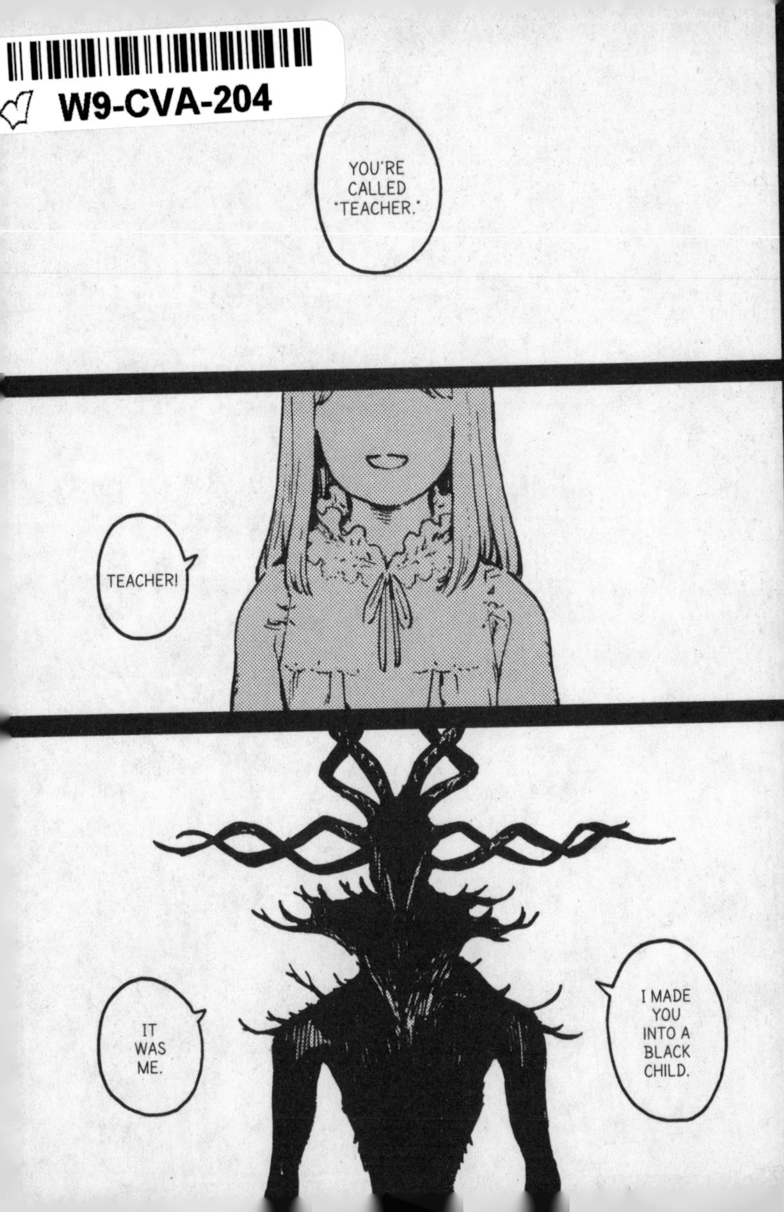
YOU'RE CALLED "TEACHER."
TEACHER!
I MADE YOU INTO A BLACK CHILD.
IT WAS ME.

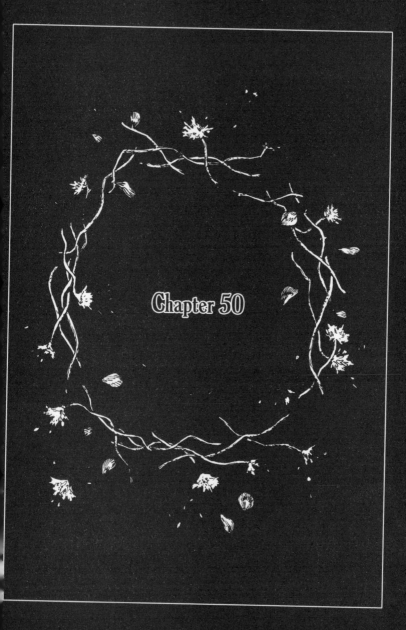

Chapter 50

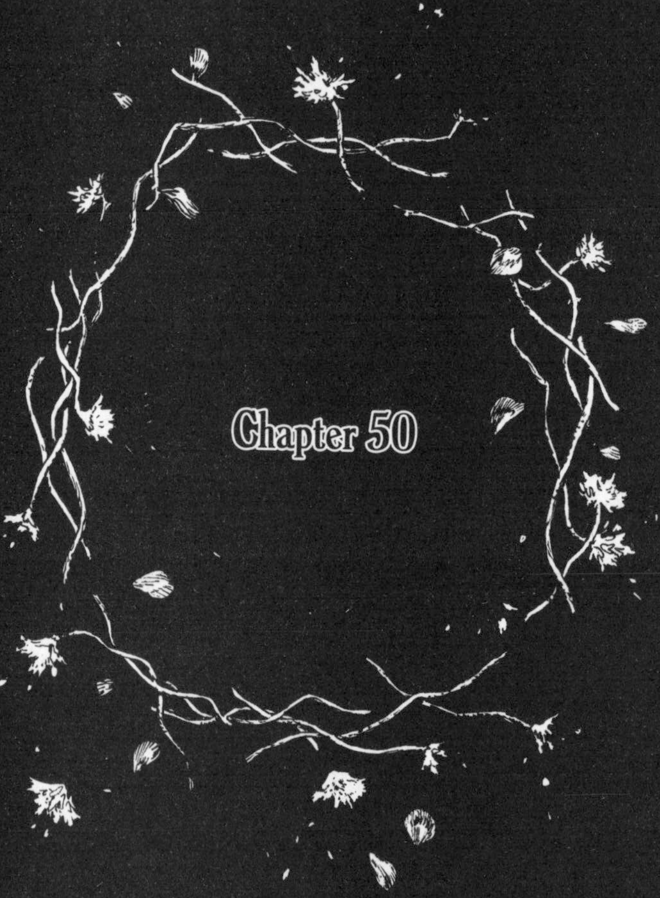

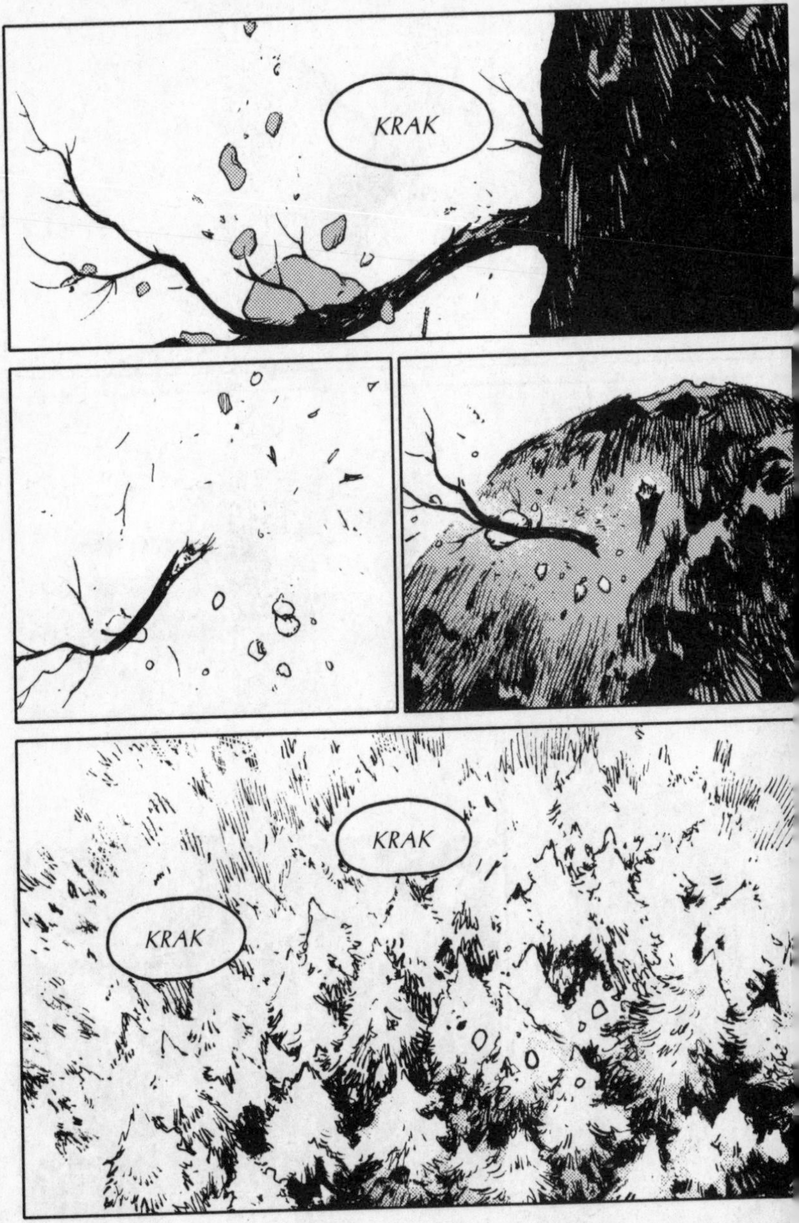
KRAK
KRAK
KRAK

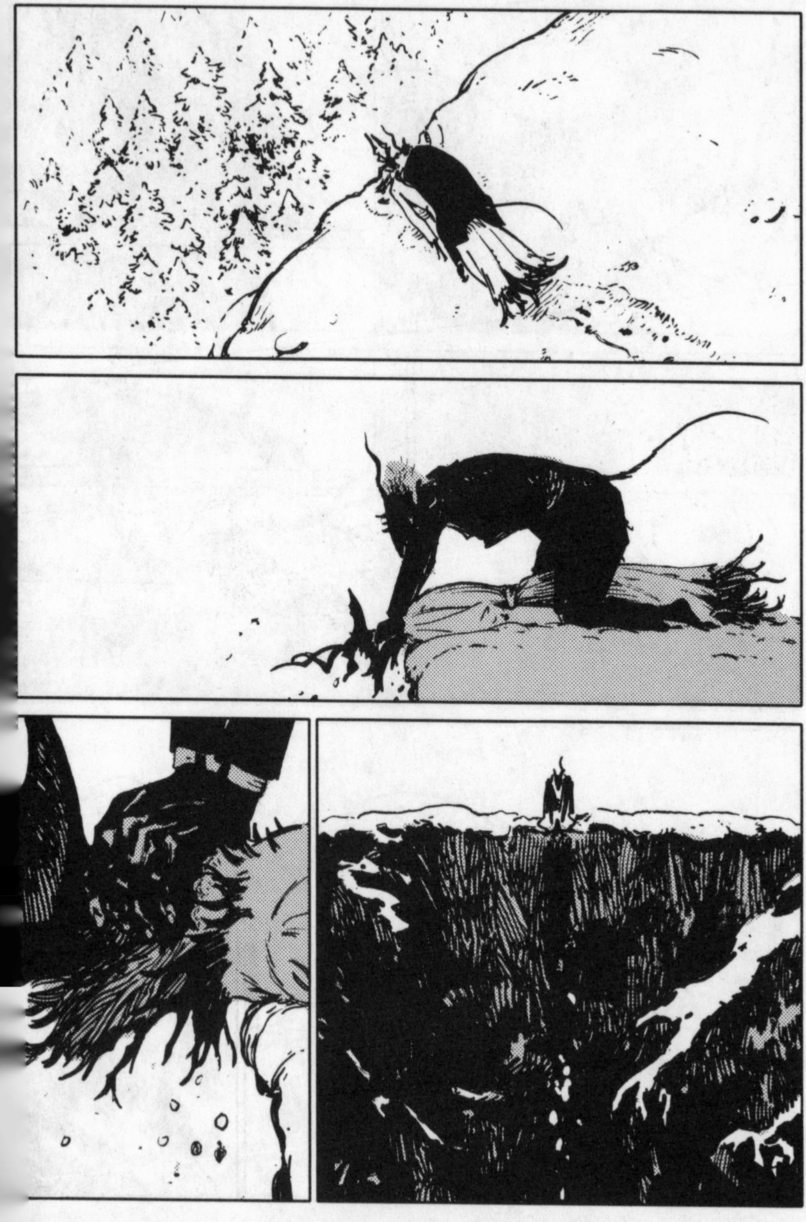

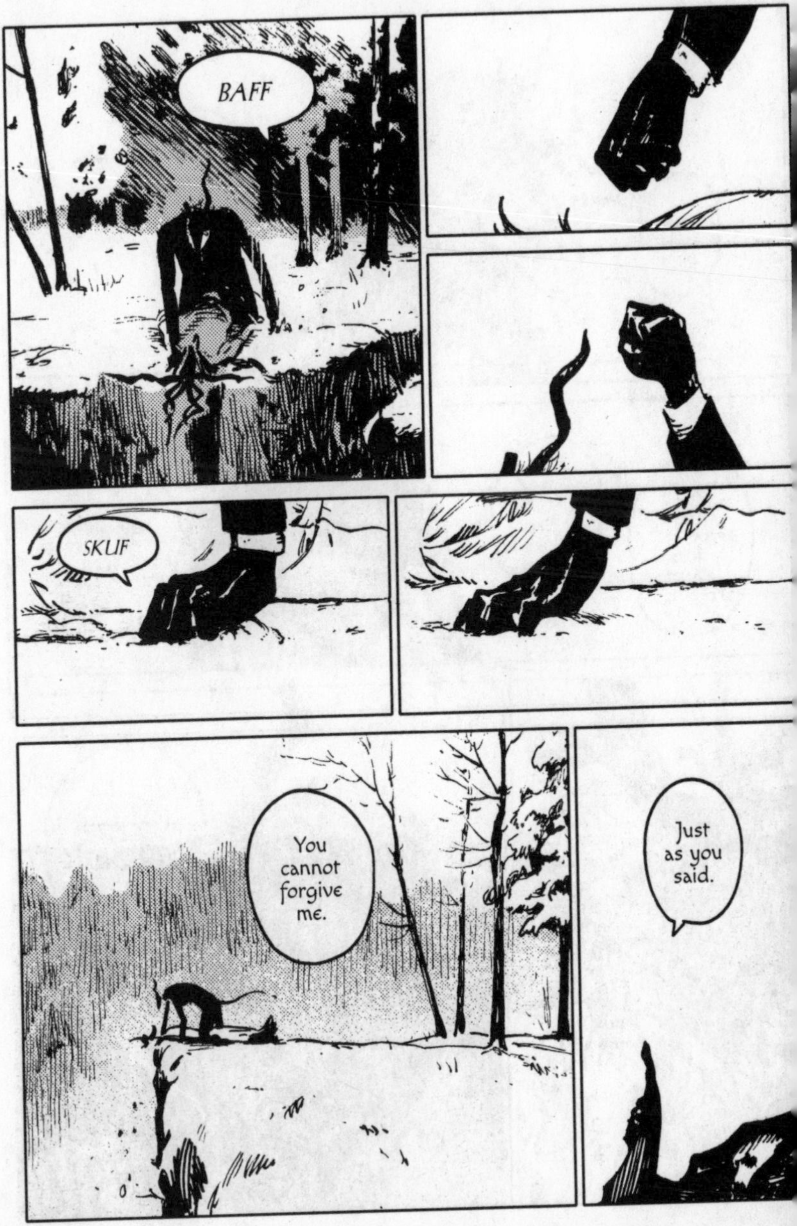
BAFF
SKUF
Just as you said.
You cannot forgive me.

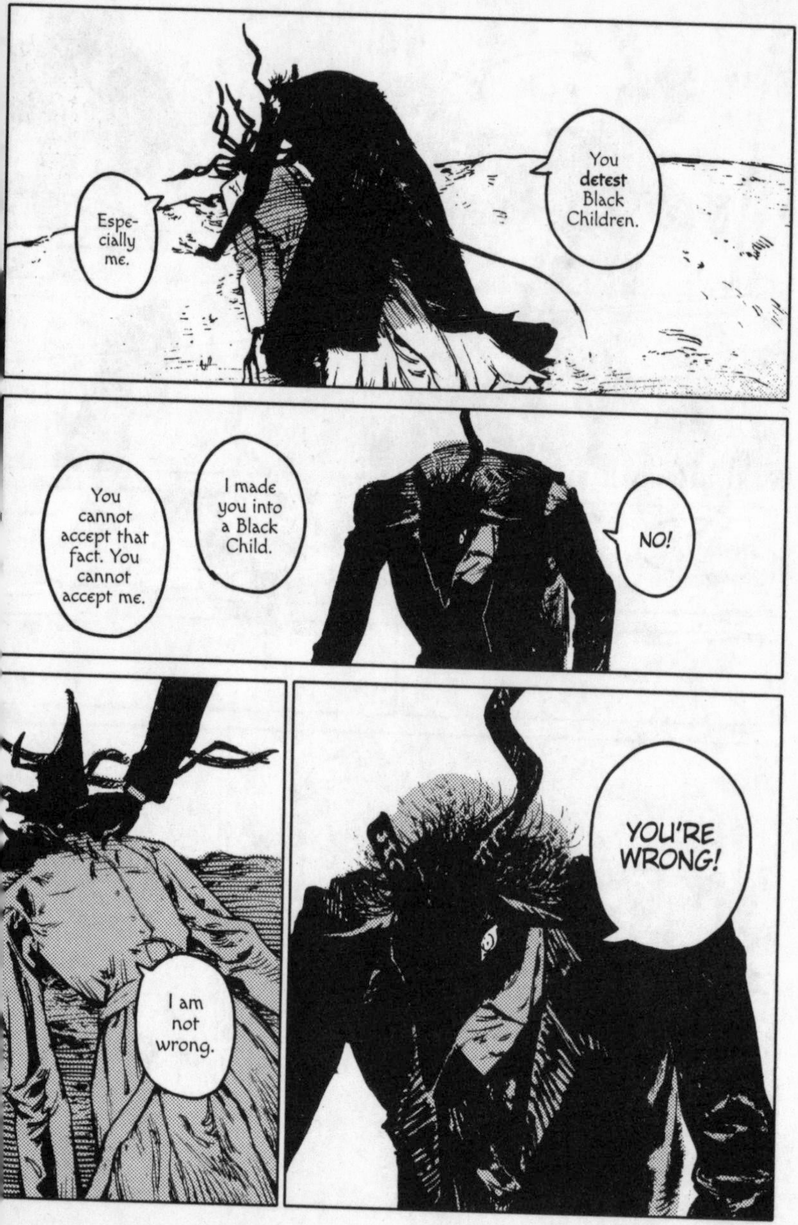
You detest Black Children.
Espe-cially me.
NO!
I made you into a Black Child.
You cannot accept that fact. You cannot accept me.
YOU'RE WRONG!
I am not wrong.

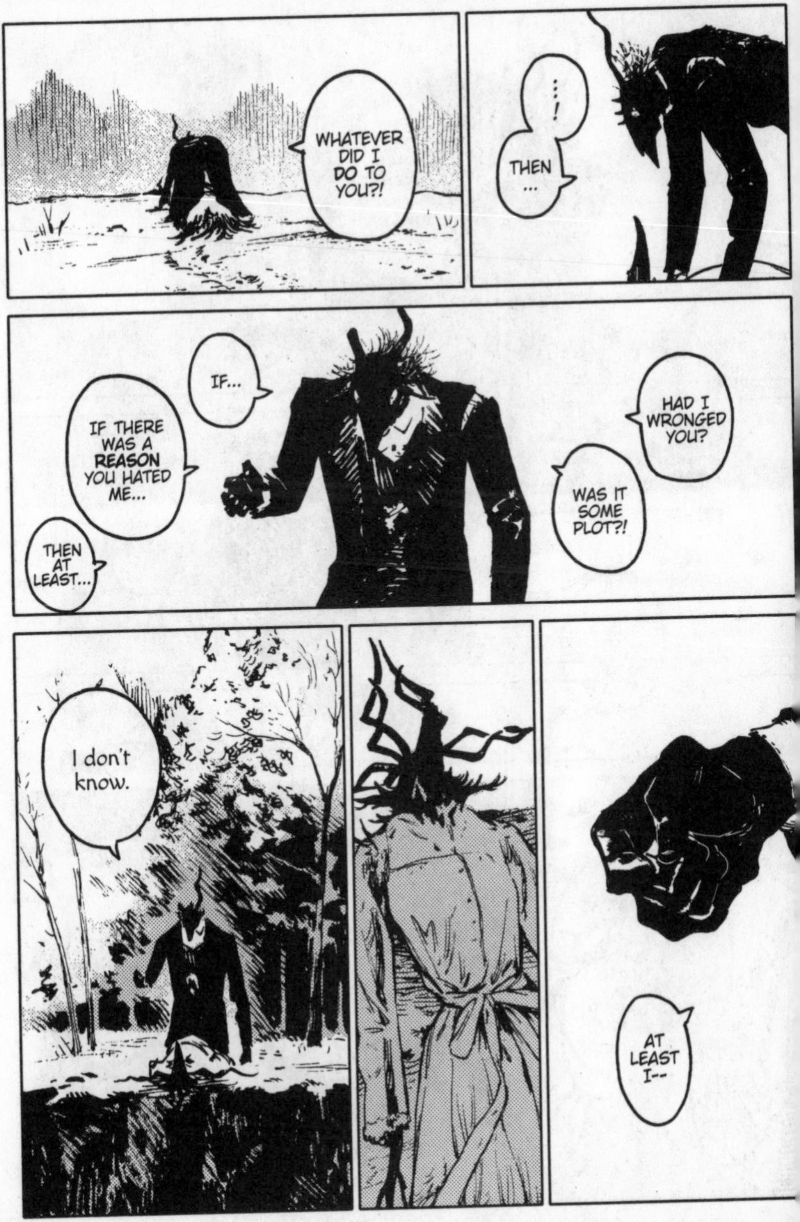
…!
THEN …
WHATEVER DID I DO TO YOU?!
HAD I WRONGED YOU?
WAS IT SOME PLOT?!
IF…
IF THERE WAS A REASON YOU HATED ME…
THEN AT LEAST…
AT LEAST I--
I don't know.

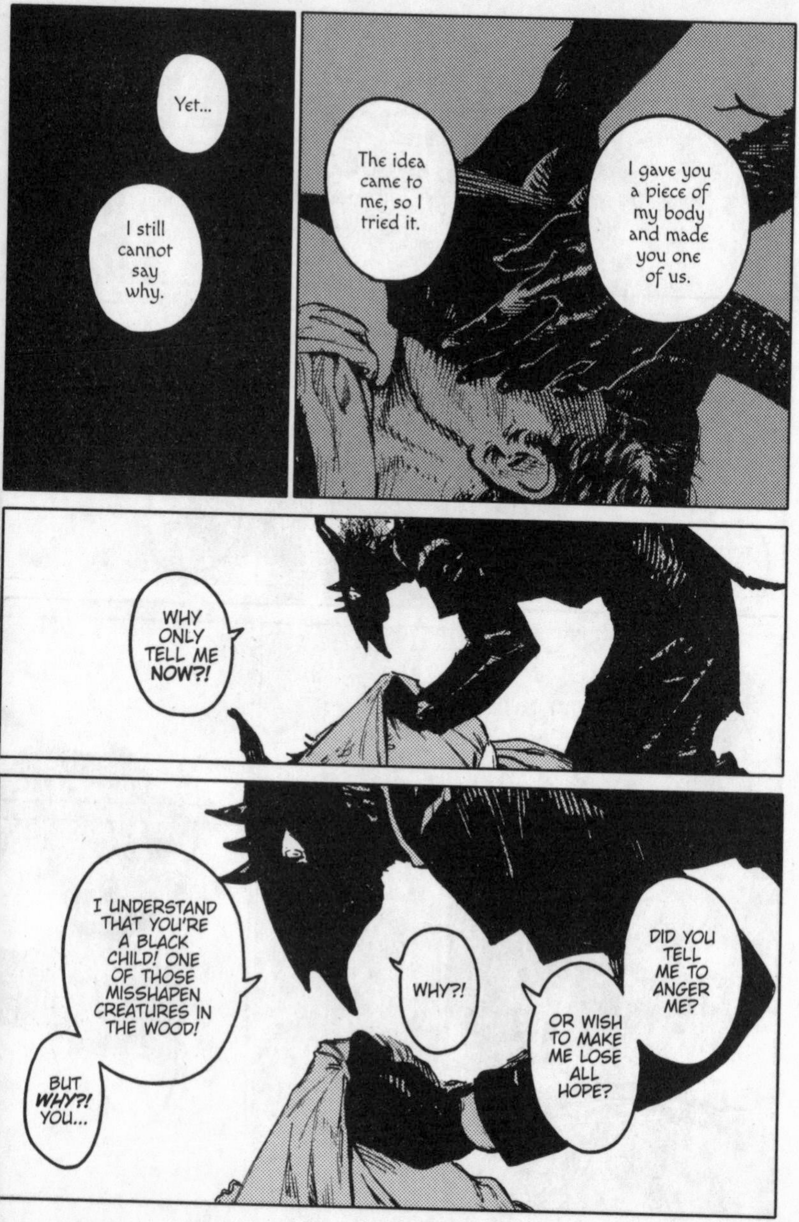
I gave you a piece of my body and made you one of us.
The idea came to me, so I tried it.
Yet...
I still cannot say why.
WHY ONLY TELL ME NOW?!
DID YOU TELL ME TO ANGER ME?
OR WISH TO MAKE ME LOSE ALL HOPE?
WHY?!
I UNDERSTAND THAT YOU'RE A BLACK CHILD! ONE OF THOSE MISSHAPEN CREATURES IN THE WOOD!
BUT *WHY?!* YOU...

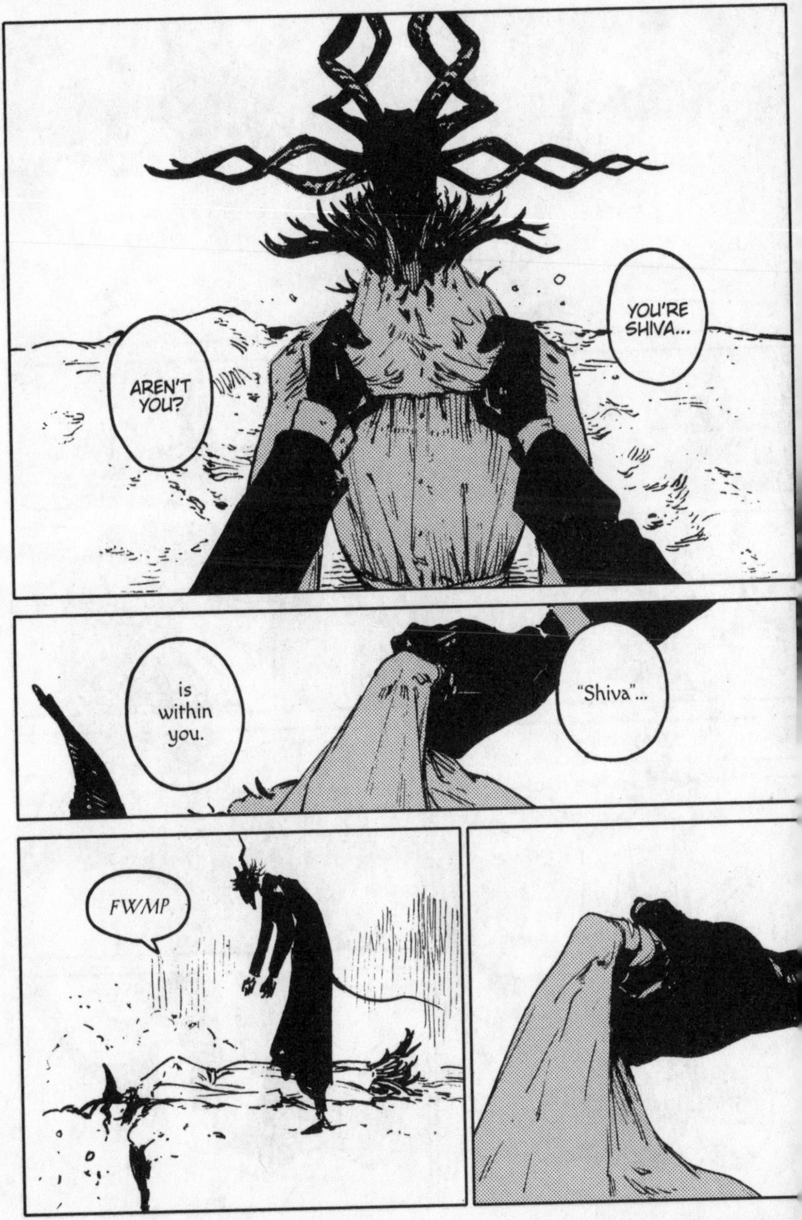
YOU'RE SHIVA...
AREN'T YOU?
"Shiva"...
is within you.
FWMP

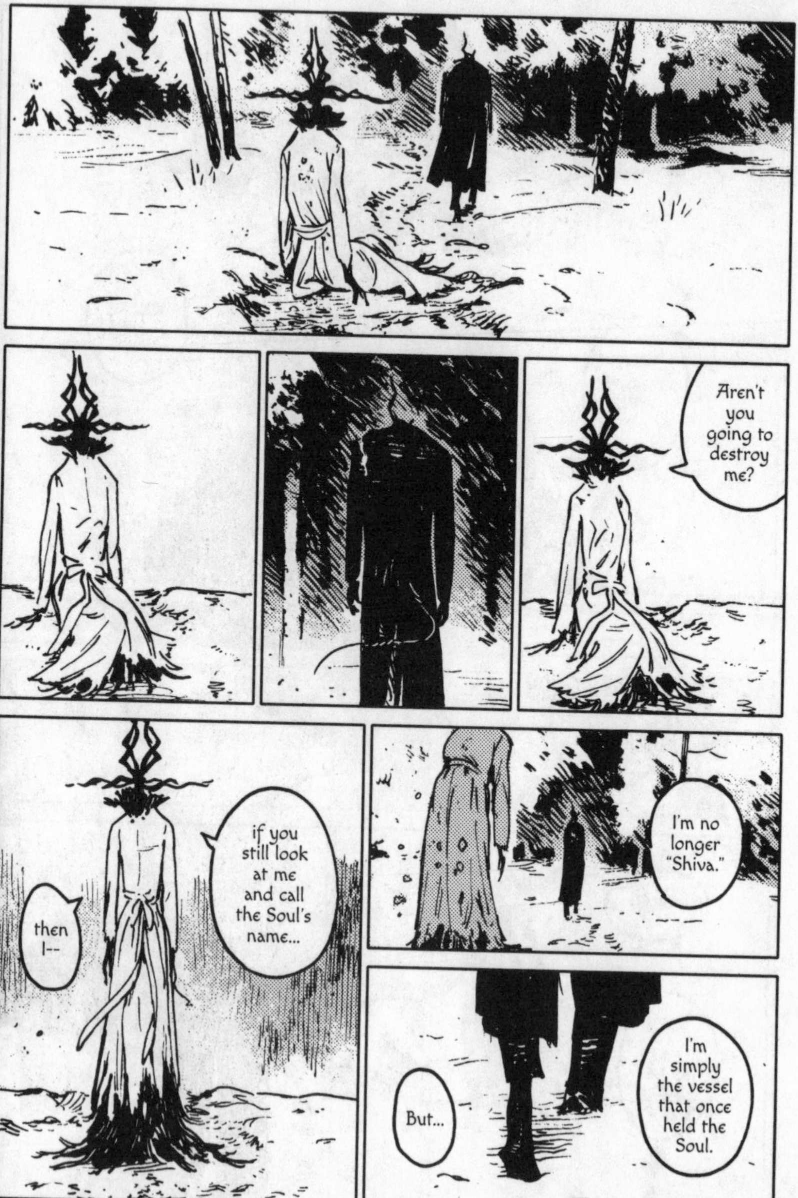
Aren't you going to destroy me?
I'm no longer "Shiva."
I'm simply the vessel that once held the Soul.
But...
if you still look at me and call the Soul's name...
then I--

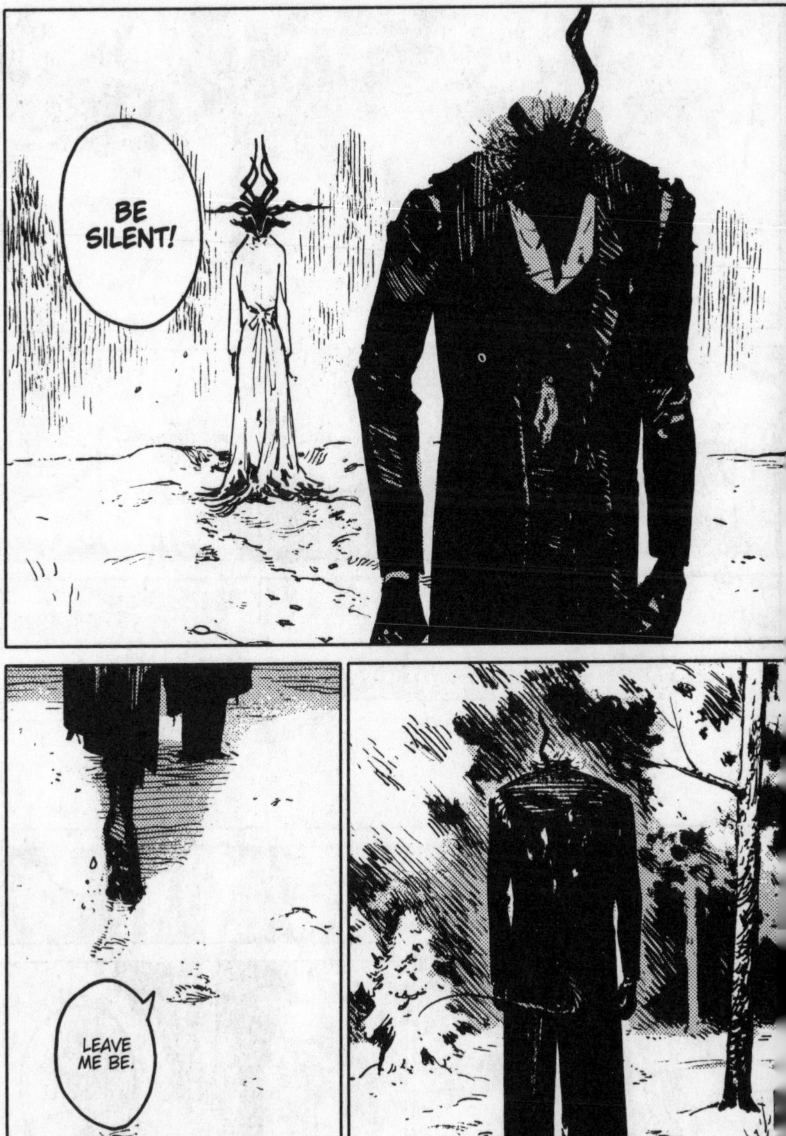
BE SILENT!
LEAVE ME BE.

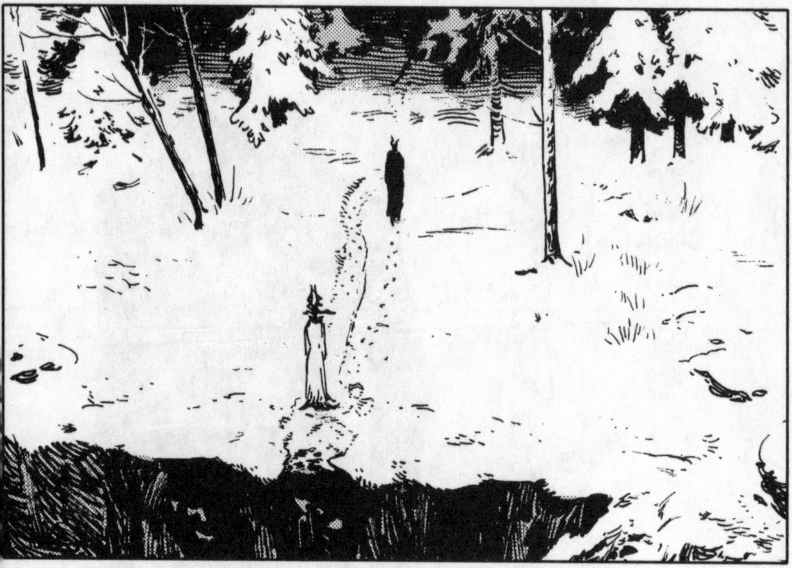
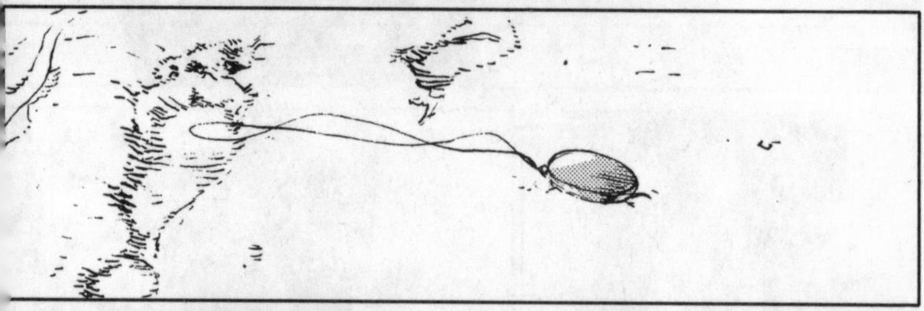
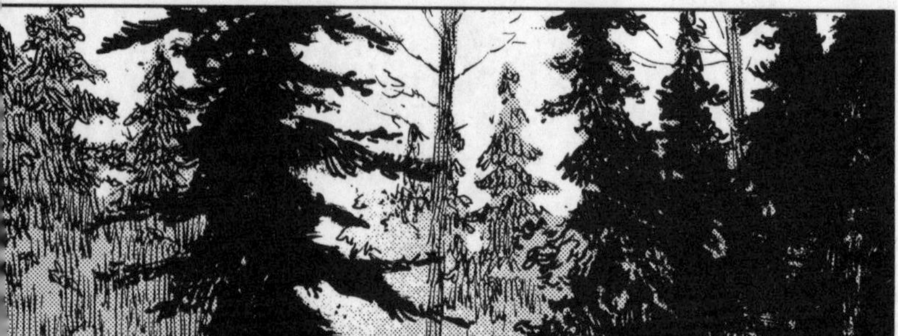

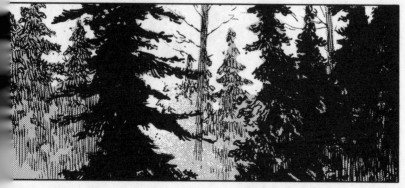

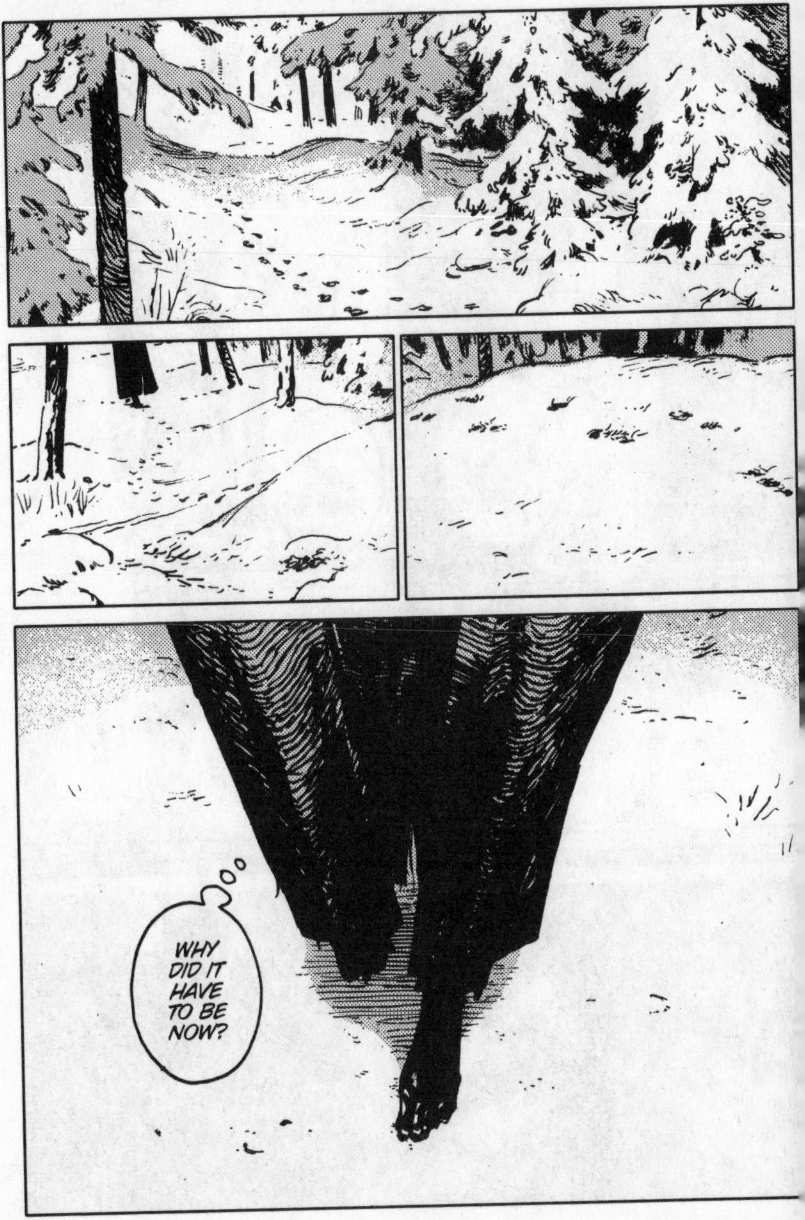
WHY DID IT HAVE TO BE NOW?

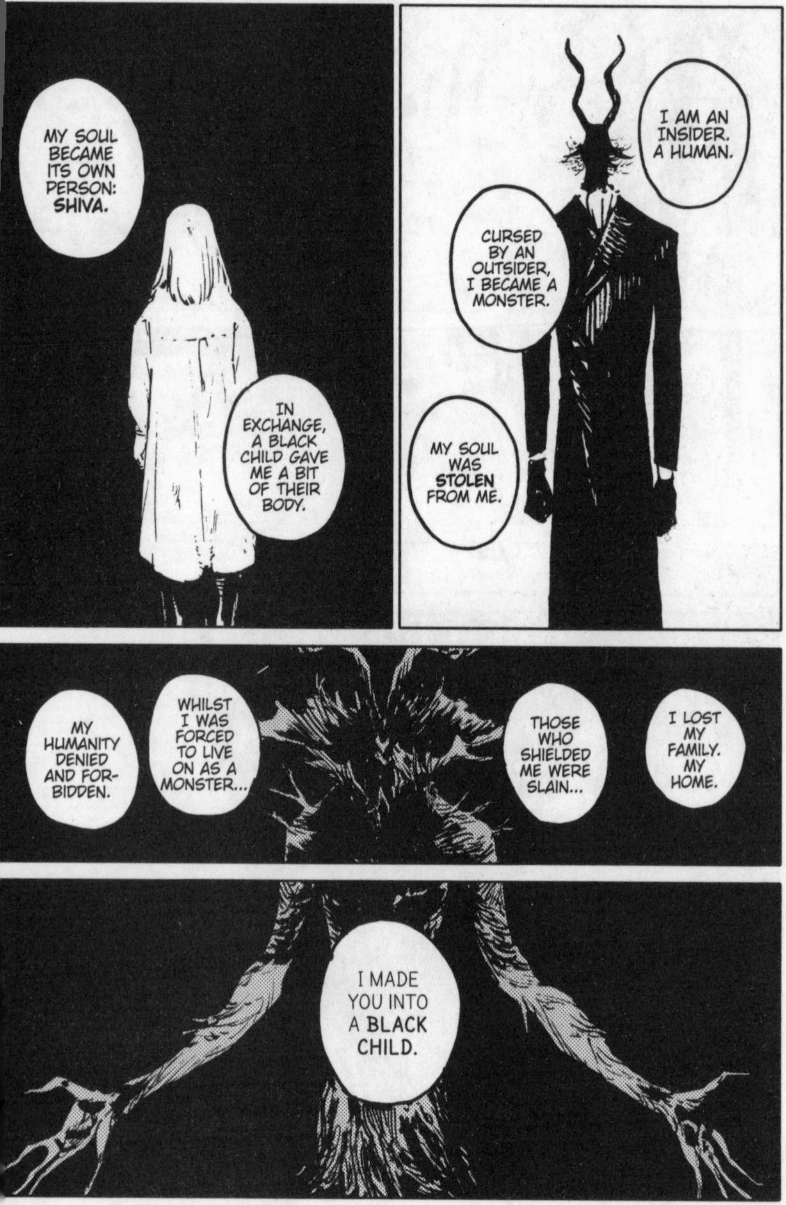

I AM AN INSIDER. A HUMAN.
CURSED BY AN OUTSIDER, I BECAME A MONSTER.
MY SOUL WAS STOLEN FROM ME.
MY SOUL BECAME ITS OWN PERSON: SHIVA.
IN EXCHANGE, A BLACK CHILD GAVE ME A BIT OF THEIR BODY.
I LOST MY FAMILY. MY HOME.
THOSE WHO SHIELDED ME WERE SLAIN...
WHILST I WAS FORCED TO LIVE ON AS A MONSTER...
MY HUMANITY DENIED AND FOR-BIDDEN.
I MADE YOU INTO A BLACK CHILD.

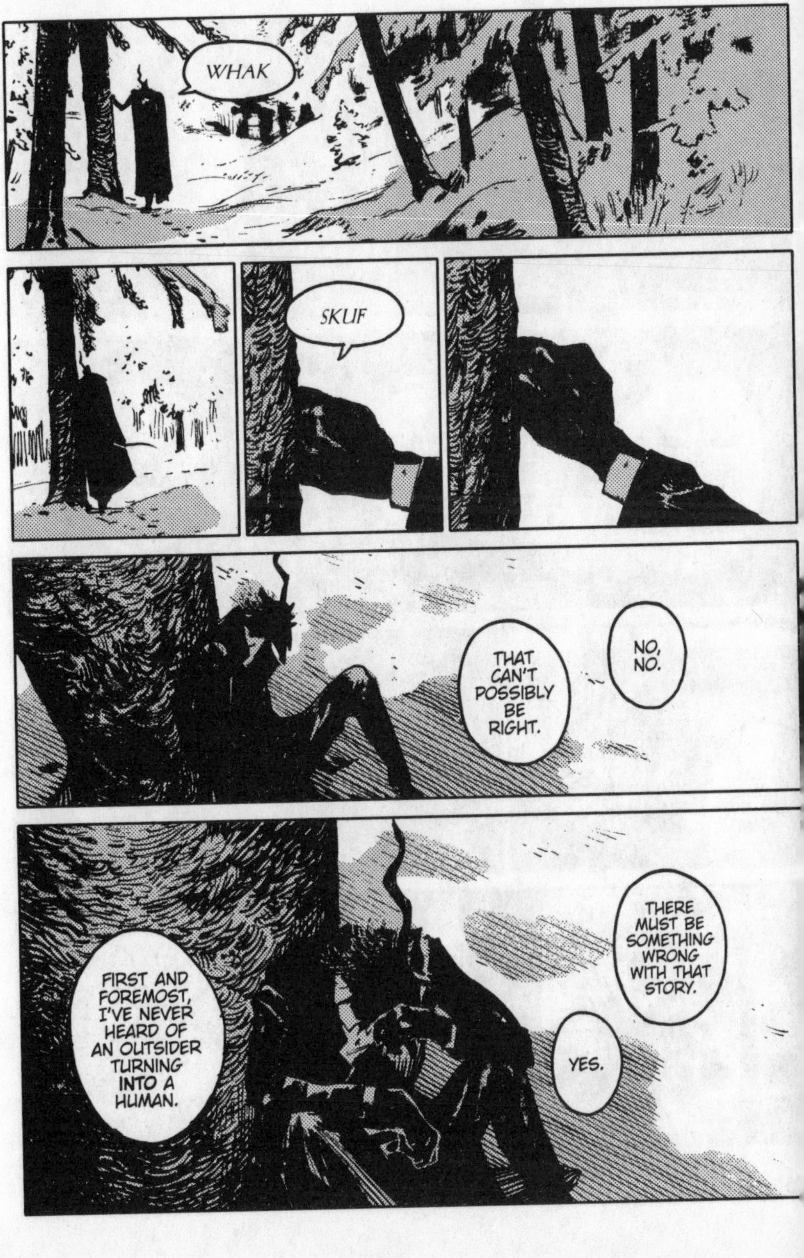
WHAK
SKUF
NO, NO.
THAT CAN'T POSSIBLY BE RIGHT.
THERE MUST BE SOMETHING WRONG WITH THAT STORY.
YES.
FIRST AND FOREMOST, I'VE NEVER HEARD OF AN OUTSIDER TURNING INTO A HUMAN.

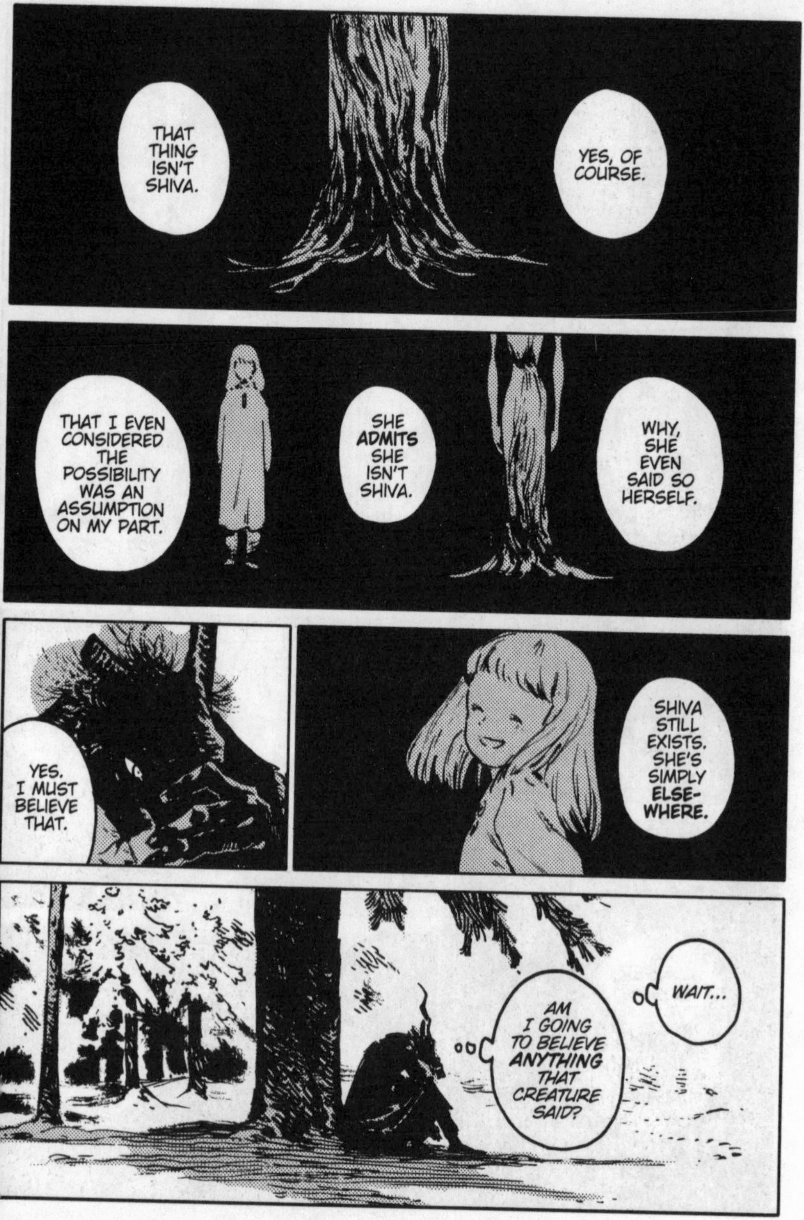
YES, OF COURSE.
THAT THING ISN'T SHIVA.
WHY, SHE EVEN SAID SO HERSELF.
SHE **ADMITS** SHE ISN'T SHIVA.
THAT I EVEN CONSIDERED THE POSSIBILITY WAS AN ASSUMPTION ON MY PART.
SHIVA STILL EXISTS. SHE'S SIMPLY **ELSE-WHERE.**
YES. I MUST BELIEVE THAT.
WAIT...
*AM I GOING TO BELIEVE **ANYTHING** THAT CREATURE SAID?*

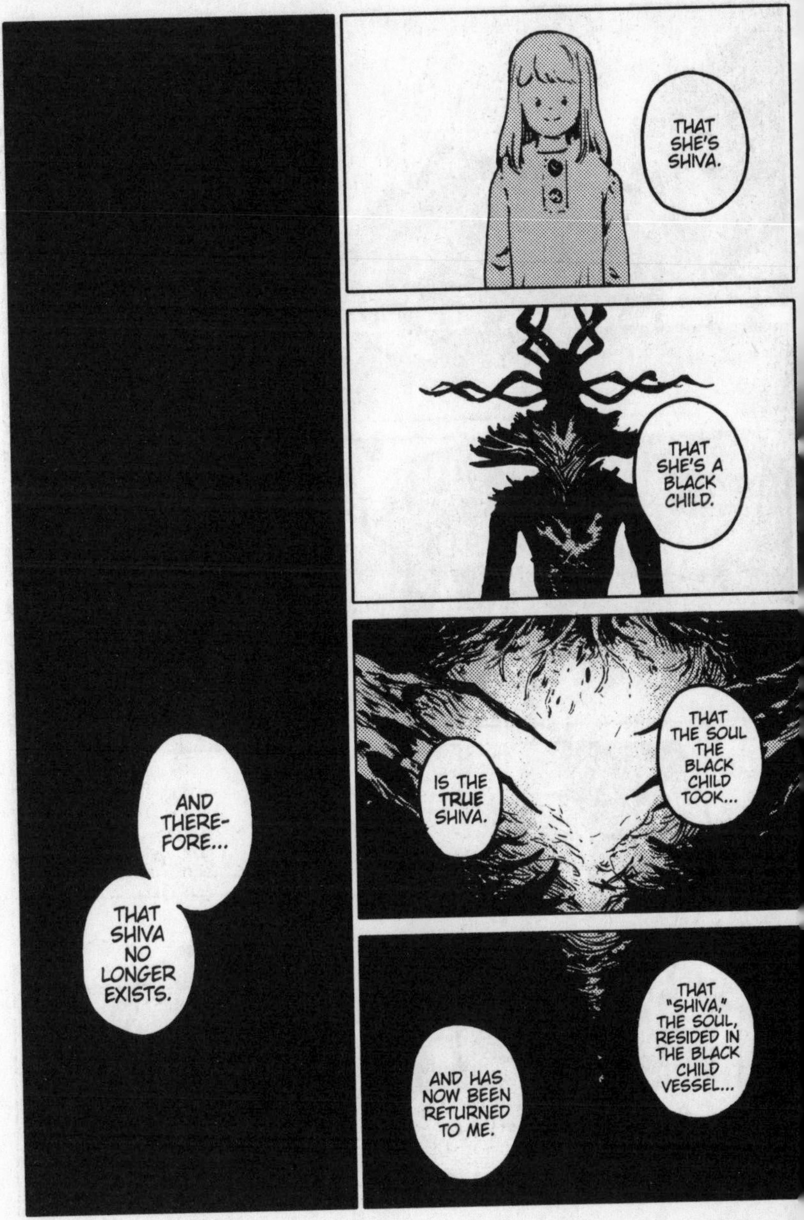
THAT SHE'S SHIVA.
THAT SHE'S A BLACK CHILD.
THAT THE SOUL THE BLACK CHILD TOOK...
IS THE TRUE SHIVA.
THAT "SHIVA," THE SOUL, RESIDED IN THE BLACK CHILD VESSEL...
AND HAS NOW BEEN RETURNED TO ME.
AND THEREFORE...
THAT SHIVA NO LONGER EXISTS.

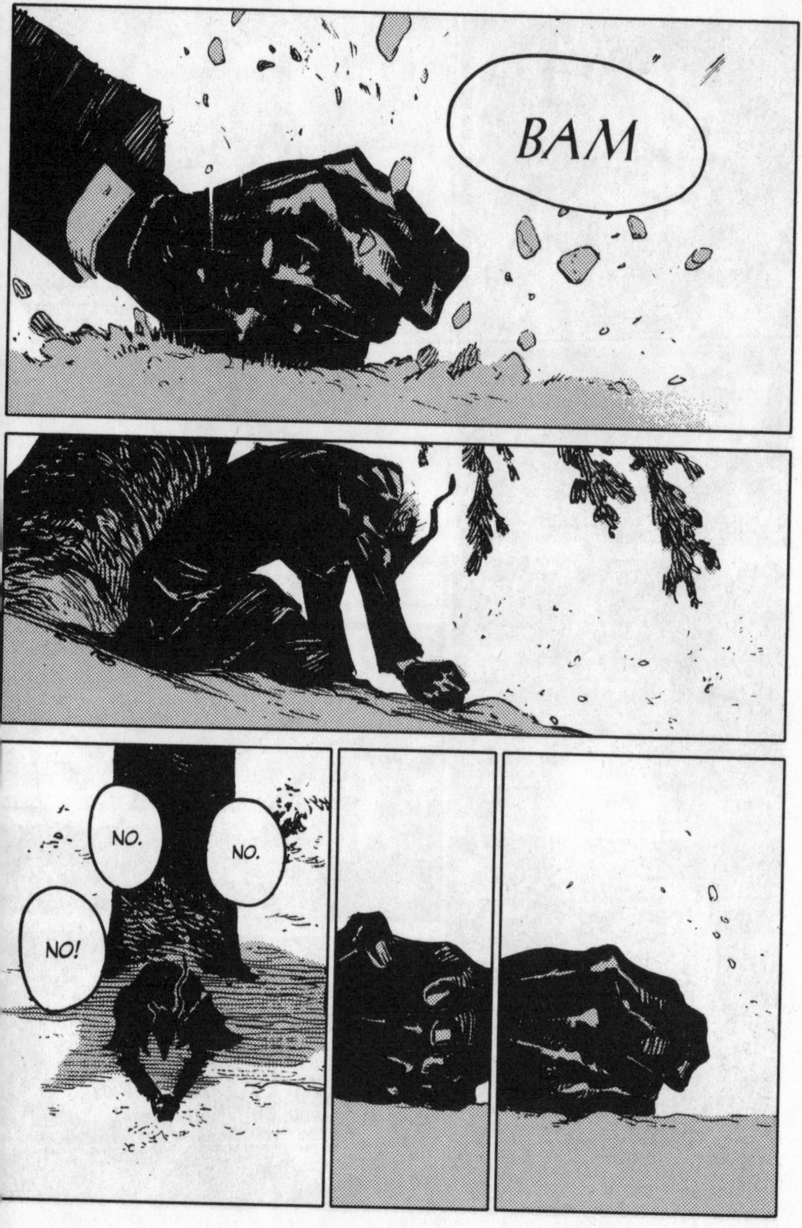
BAM
NO.
NO.
NO!

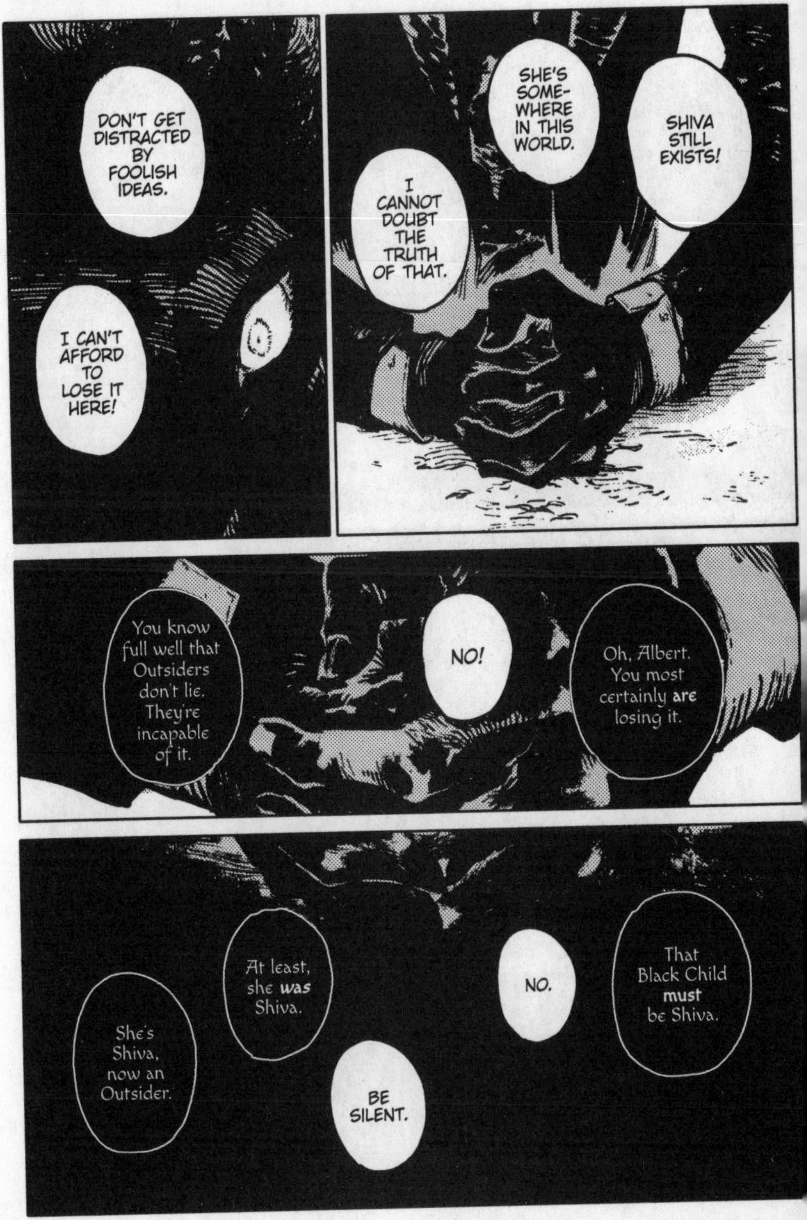
SHIVA STILL EXISTS!
SHE'S SOME-WHERE IN THIS WORLD.
I CANNOT DOUBT THE TRUTH OF THAT.
DON'T GET DISTRACTED BY FOOLISH IDEAS.
I CAN'T AFFORD TO LOSE IT HERE!
Oh, Albert. You most certainly **are** losing it.
NO!
You know full well that Outsiders don't lie. They're incapable of it.
That Black Child **must** be Shiva.
NO.
At least, she **was** Shiva.
BE SILENT.
She's Shiva, now an Outsider.

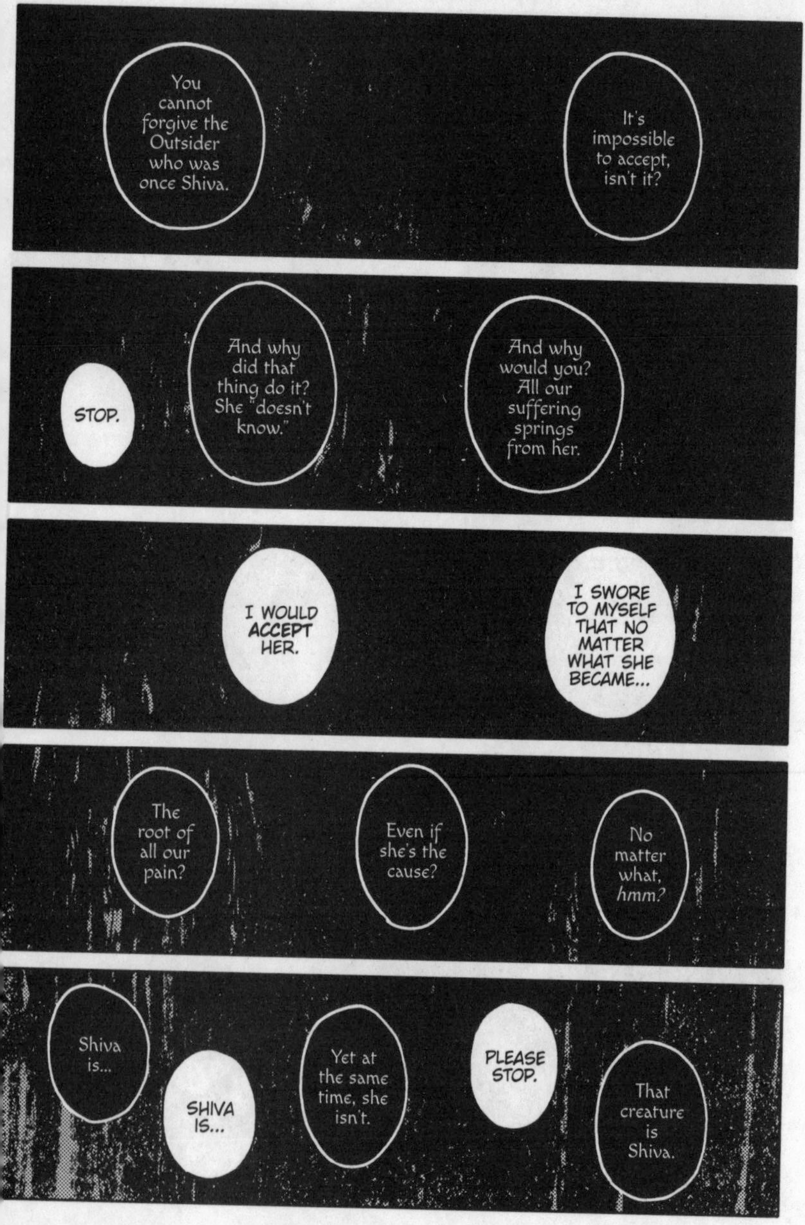

It's impossible to accept, isn't it?
You cannot forgive the Outsider who was once Shiva.
And why would you? All our suffering springs from her.
And why did that thing do it? She "doesn't know."
STOP.
I SWORE TO MYSELF THAT NO MATTER WHAT SHE BECAME...
I WOULD ACCEPT HER.
No matter what, *hmm?*
Even if she's the cause?
The root of all our pain?
That creature is Shiva.
PLEASE STOP.
Yet at the same time, she isn't.
SHIVA IS...
Shiva is...

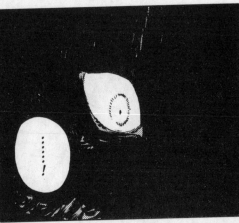

COLD...

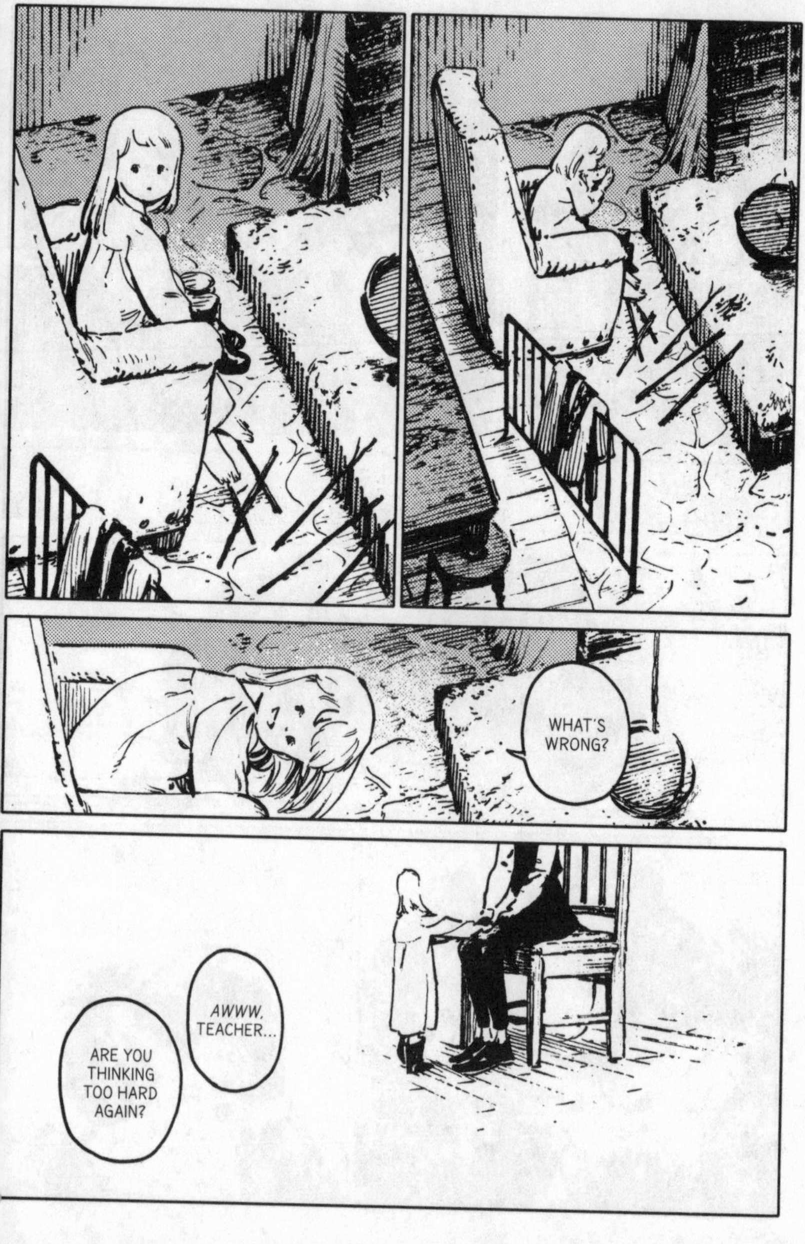
WHAT'S WRONG?
AWWW, TEACHER...
ARE YOU THINKING TOO HARD AGAIN?

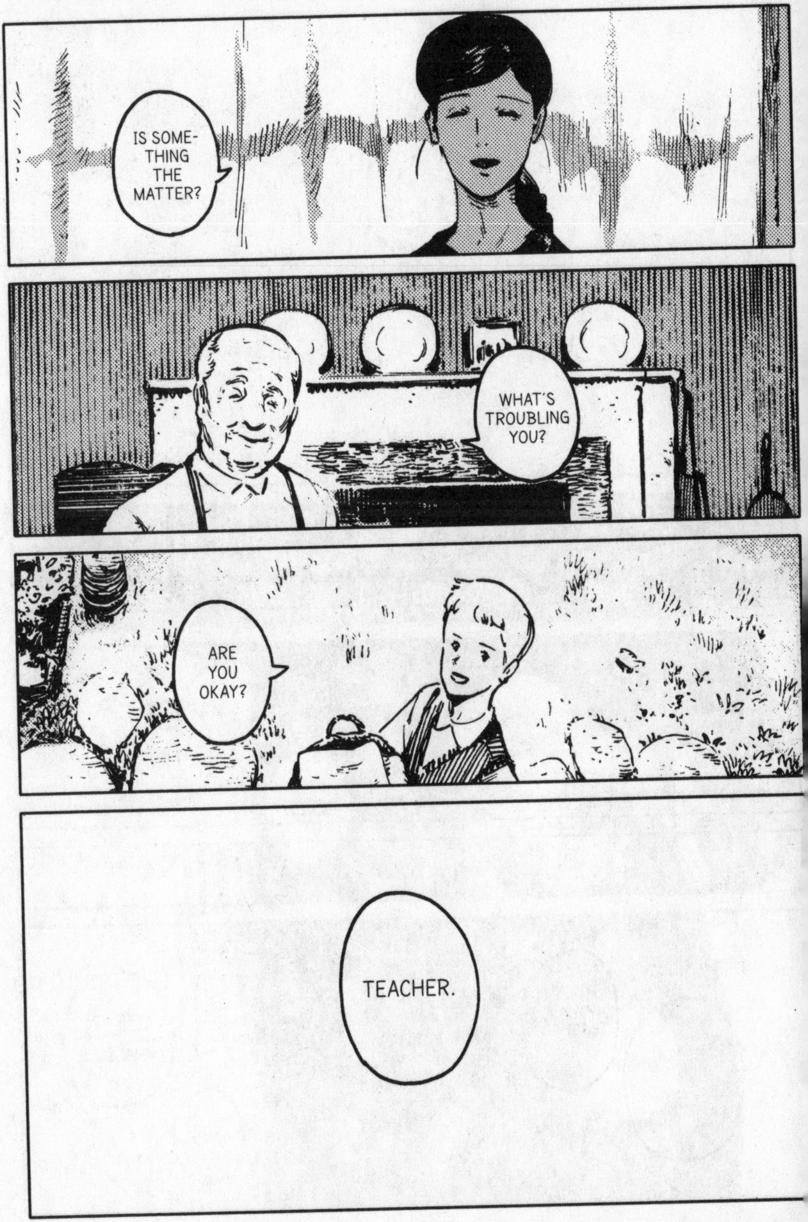
IS SOMETHING THE MATTER?
WHAT'S TROUBLING YOU?
ARE YOU OKAY?
TEACHER.

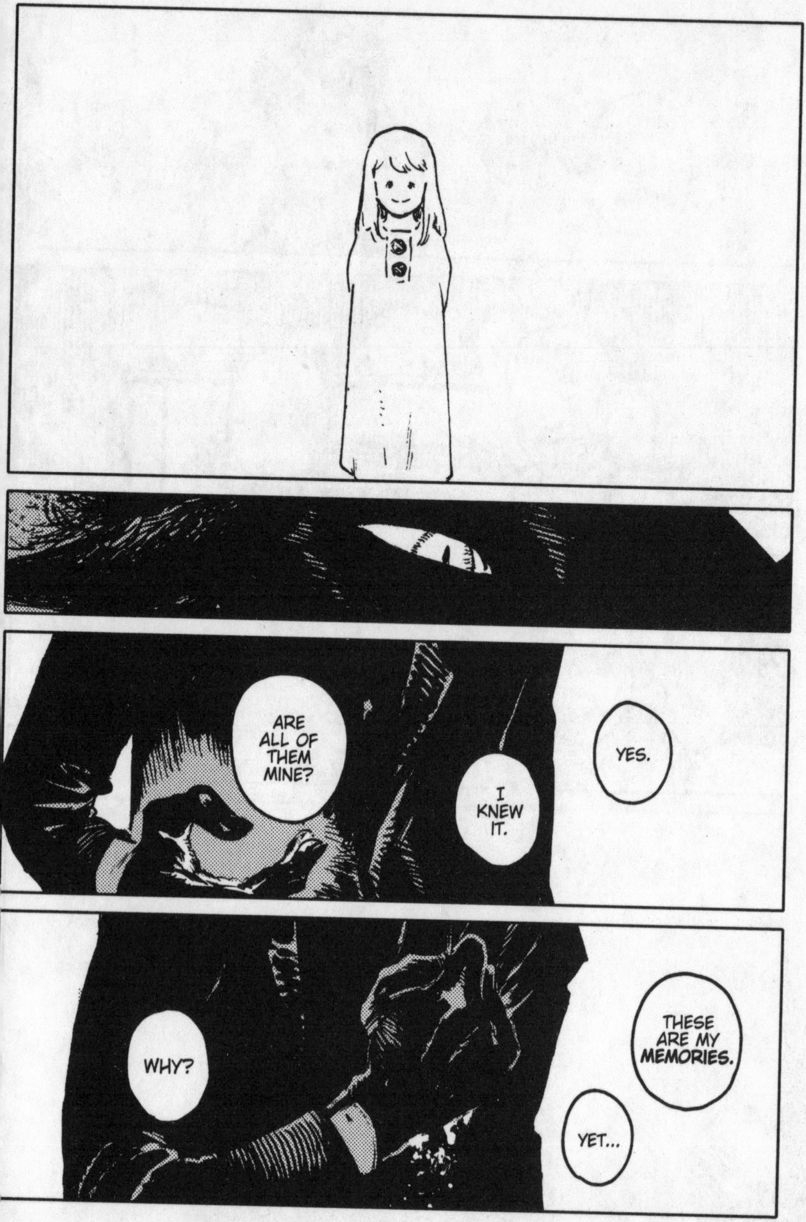
YES.
ARE ALL OF THEM MINE?
I KNEW IT.
THESE ARE MY MEMORIES.
YET...
WHY?

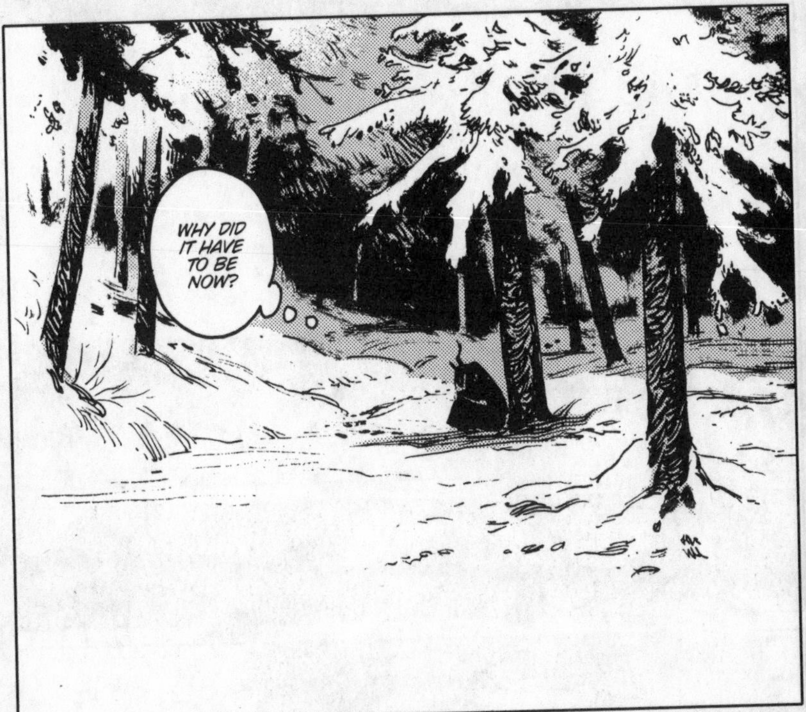
WHY DID IT HAVE TO BE NOW?
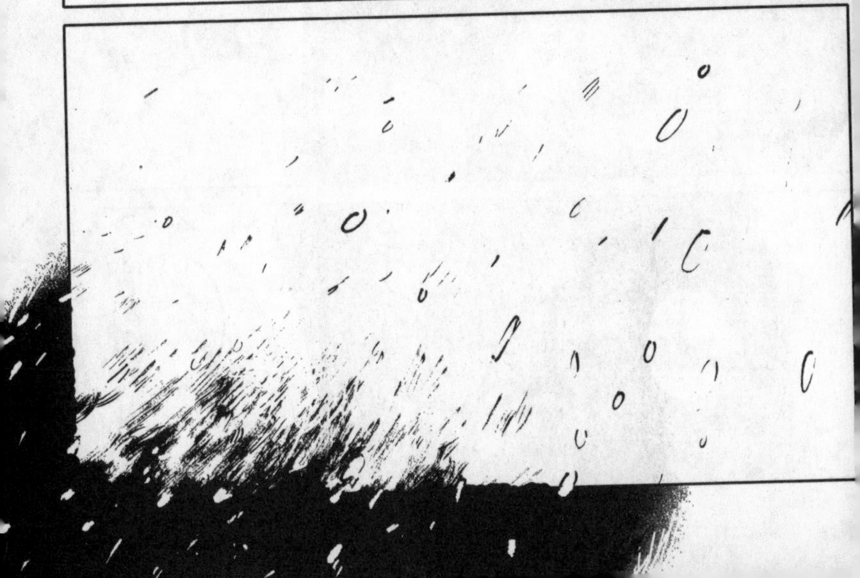

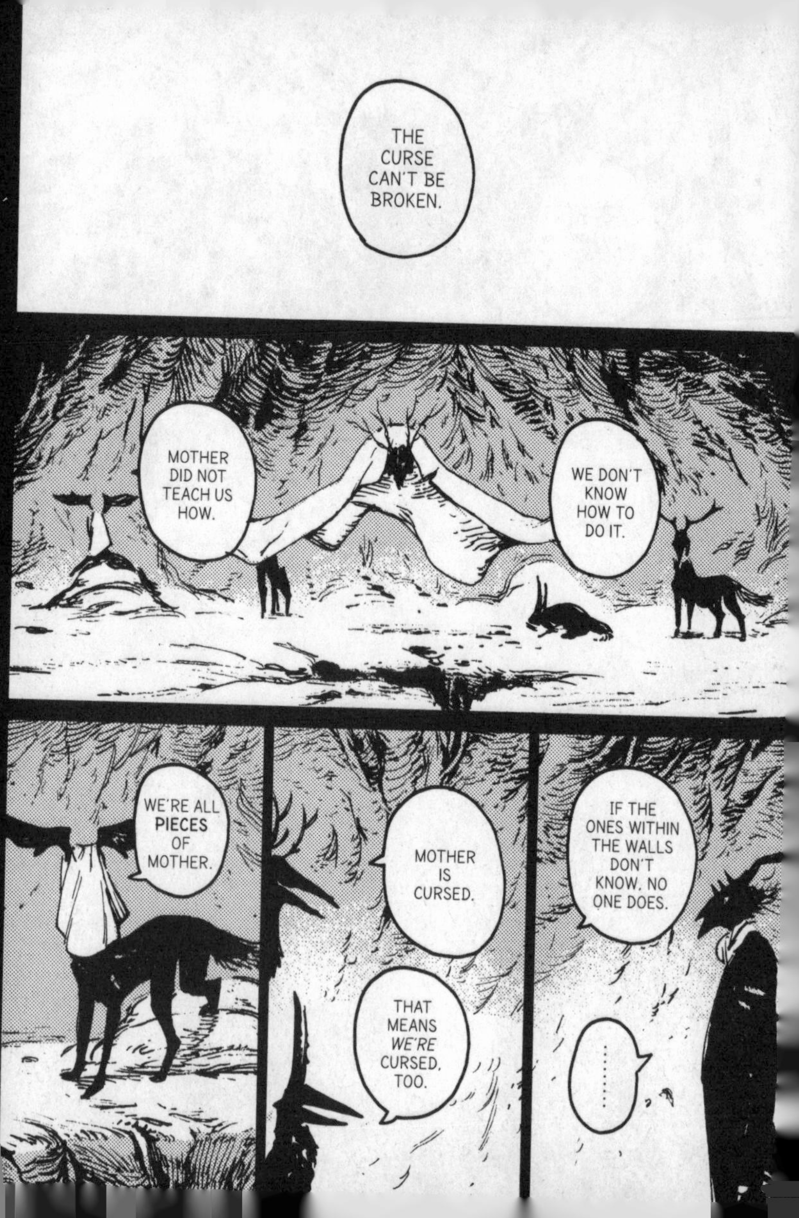
THE CURSE CAN'T BE BROKEN.
WE DON'T KNOW HOW TO DO IT.
MOTHER DID NOT TEACH US HOW.
IF THE ONES WITHIN THE WALLS DON'T KNOW, NO ONE DOES.
....
MOTHER IS CURSED.
THAT MEANS *WE'RE* CURSED, TOO.
WE'RE ALL **PIECES** OF MOTHER.

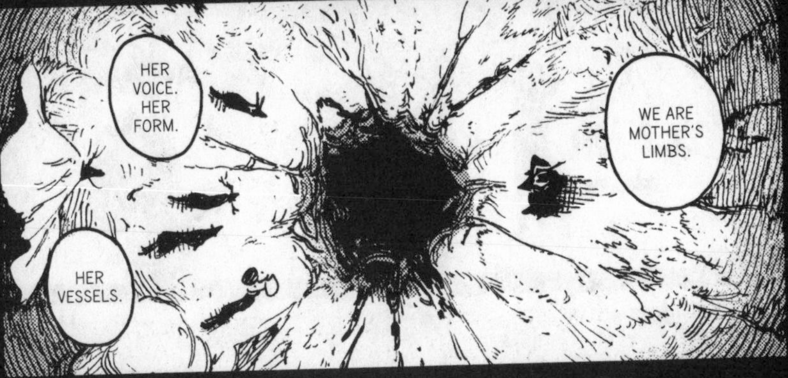
WE ARE MOTHER'S LIMBS.
HER VOICE. HER FORM.
HER VESSELS.
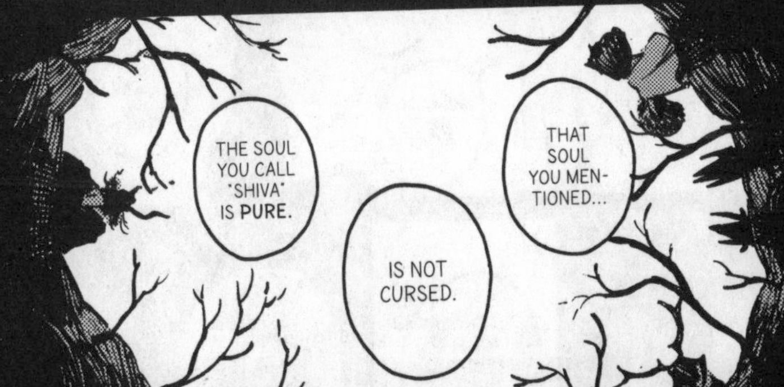
THAT SOUL YOU MENTIONED...
IS NOT CURSED.
THE SOUL YOU CALL "SHIVA" IS **PURE**.
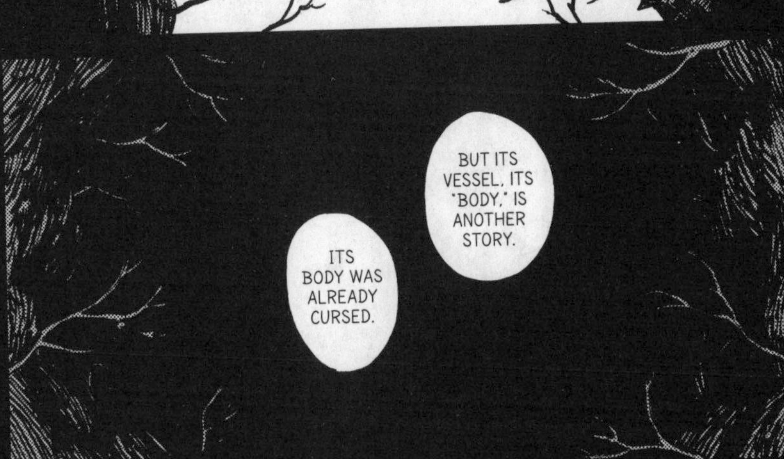
BUT ITS VESSEL, ITS "BODY," IS ANOTHER STORY.
ITS BODY WAS ALREADY CURSED.

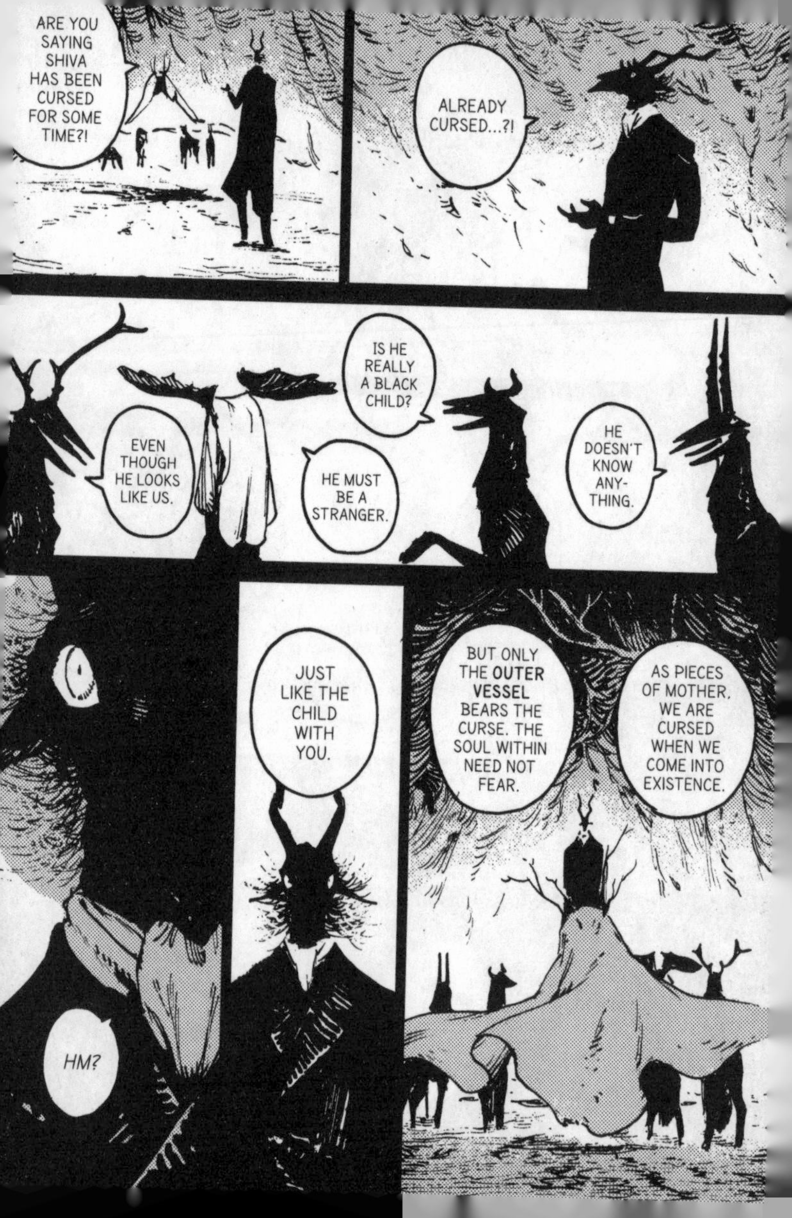

ALREADY CURSED...?!
ARE YOU SAYING SHIVA HAS BEEN CURSED FOR SOME TIME?!
HE DOESN'T KNOW ANYTHING.
IS HE REALLY A BLACK CHILD?
HE MUST BE A STRANGER.
EVEN THOUGH HE LOOKS LIKE US.
AS PIECES OF MOTHER, WE ARE CURSED WHEN WE COME INTO EXISTENCE.
BUT ONLY THE **OUTER VESSEL** BEARS THE CURSE. THE SOUL WITHIN NEED NOT FEAR.
JUST LIKE THE CHILD WITH YOU.
HM?

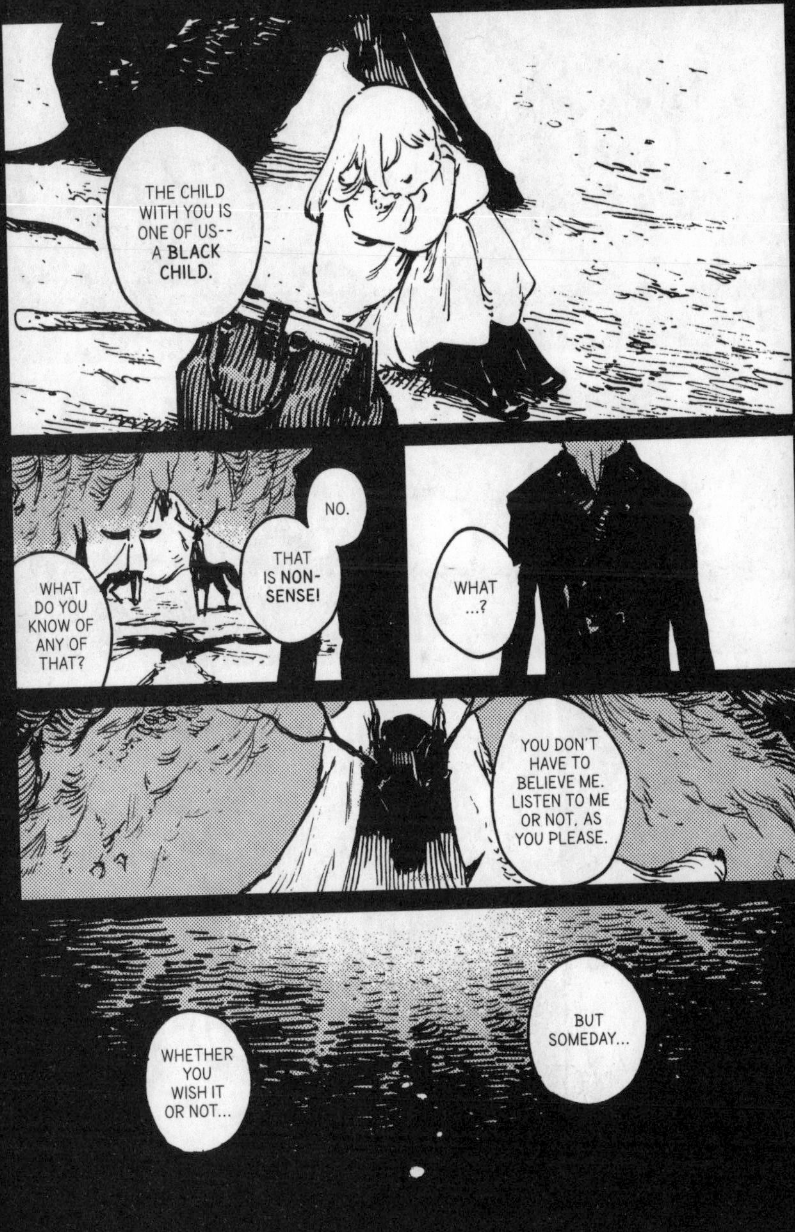
THE CHILD WITH YOU IS ONE OF US-- A BLACK CHILD.
WHAT ...?
NO.
THAT IS NONSENSE!
WHAT DO YOU KNOW OF ANY OF THAT?
YOU DON'T HAVE TO BELIEVE ME. LISTEN TO ME OR NOT, AS YOU PLEASE.
BUT SOMEDAY...
WHETHER YOU WISH IT OR NOT...

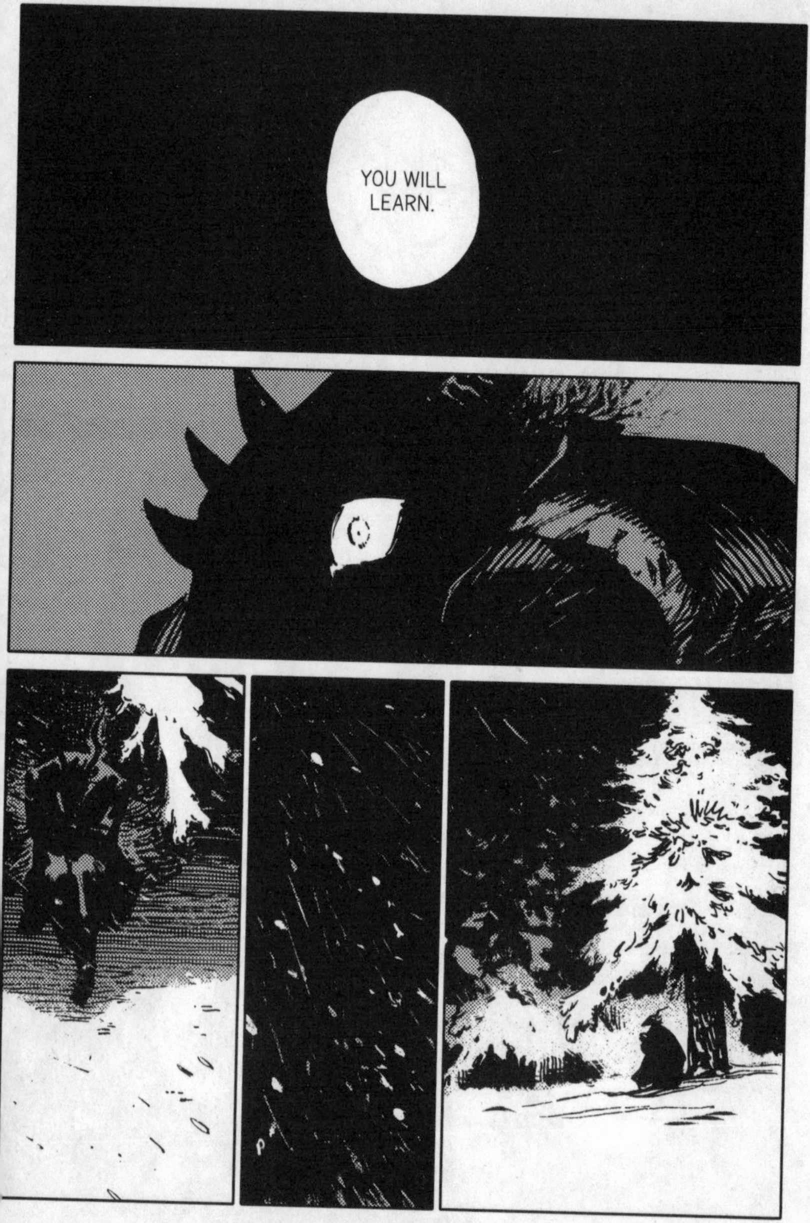
YOU WILL LEARN.

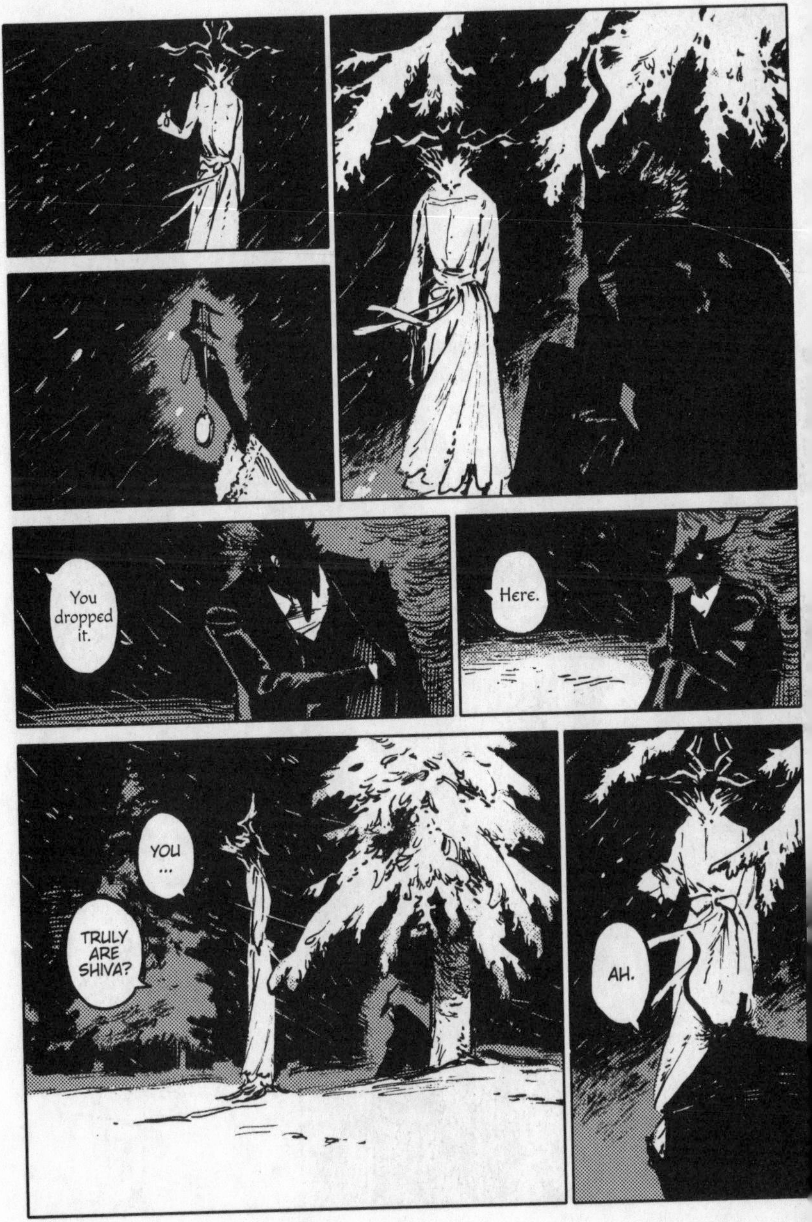
You dropped it.
Here.
YOU ...
TRULY ARE SHIVA?
AH.

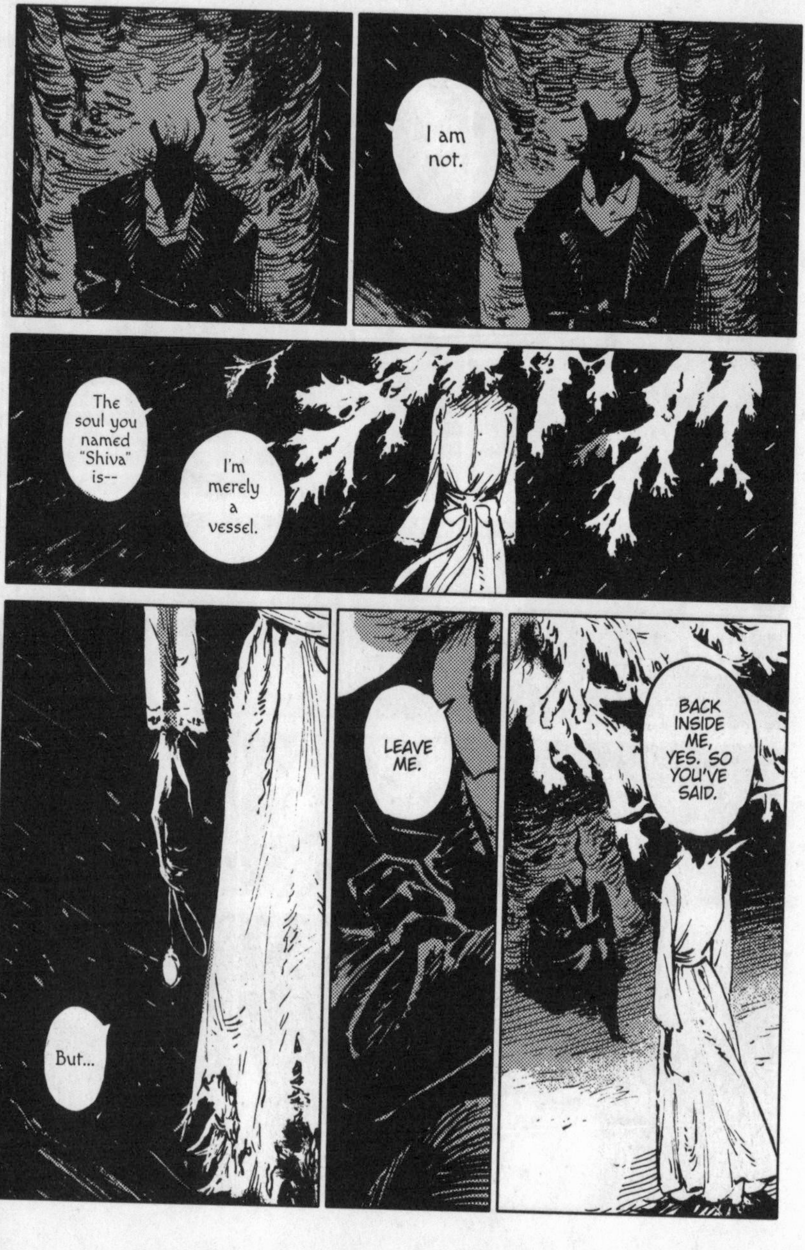
I am not.
I'm merely a vessel.
The soul you named "Shiva" is--
BACK INSIDE ME, YES. SO YOU'VE SAID.
LEAVE ME.
But...

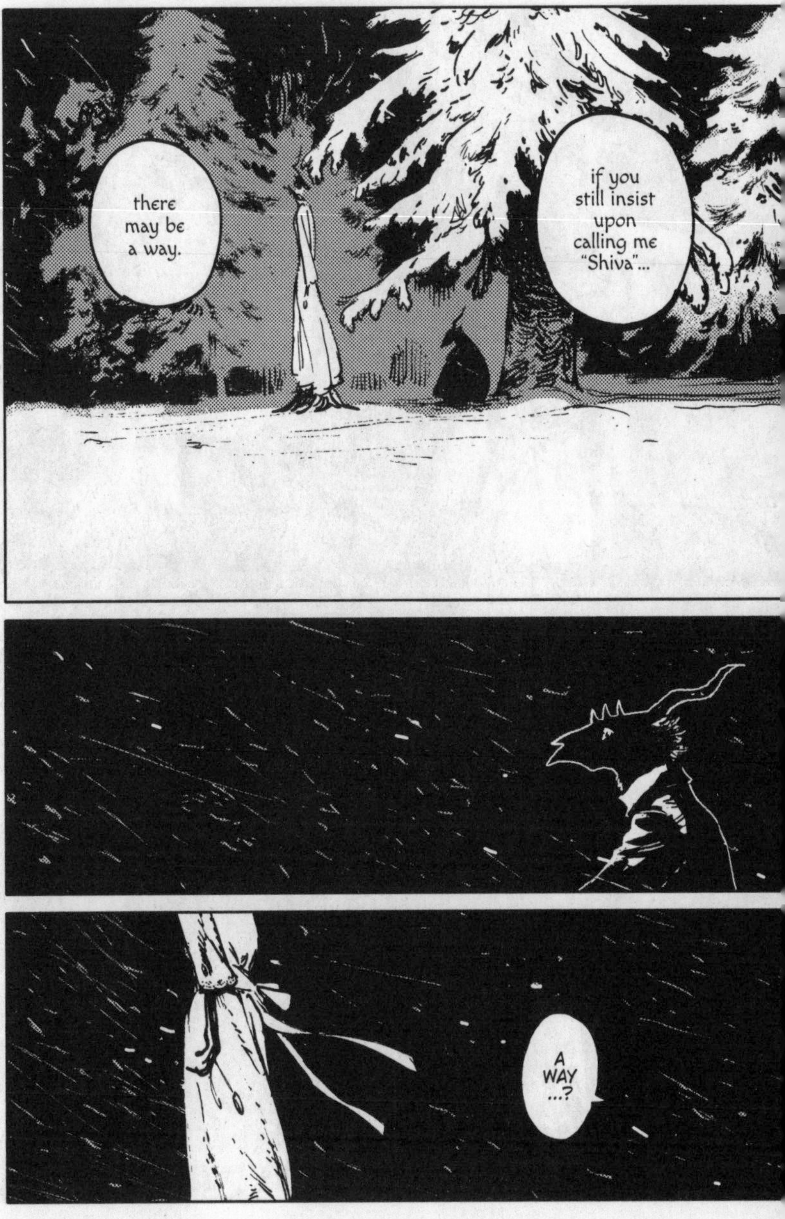
if you still insist upon calling me "Shiva"...
there may be a way.
A WAY ...?

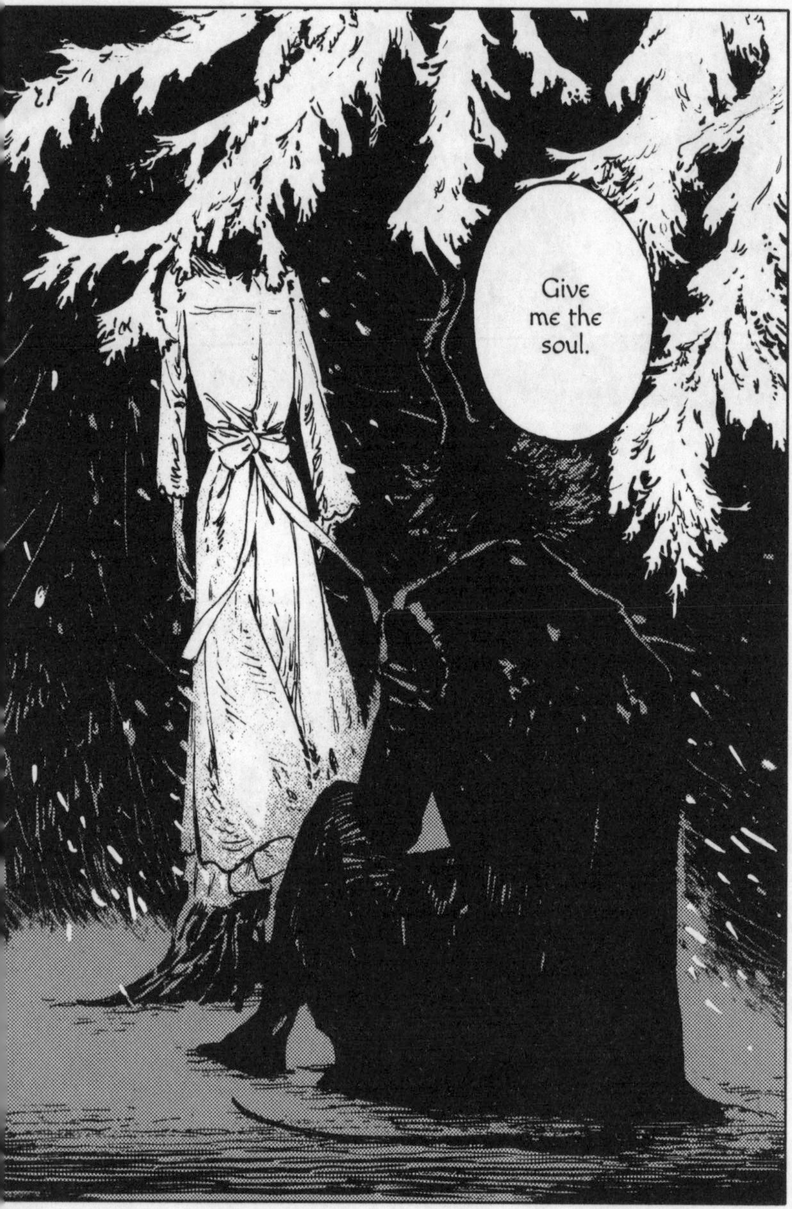
Give me the soul.

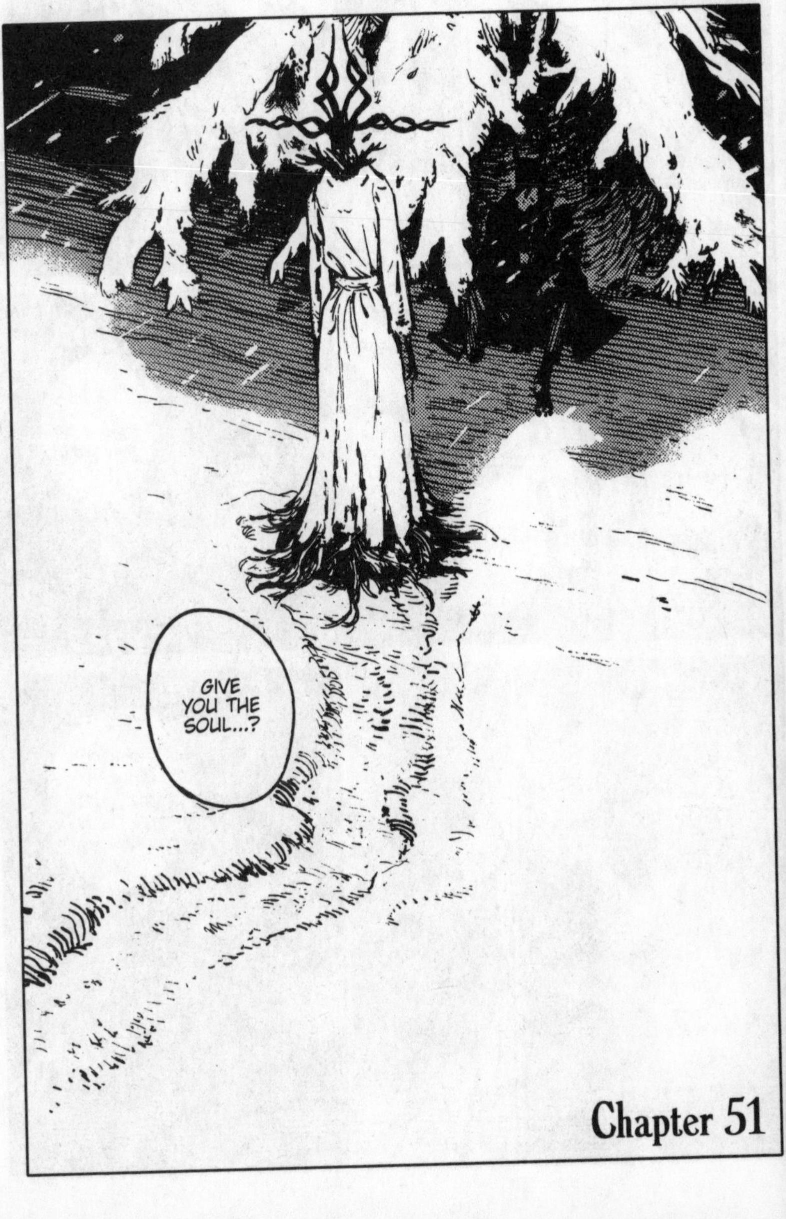
GIVE YOU THE SOUL...?
Chapter 51

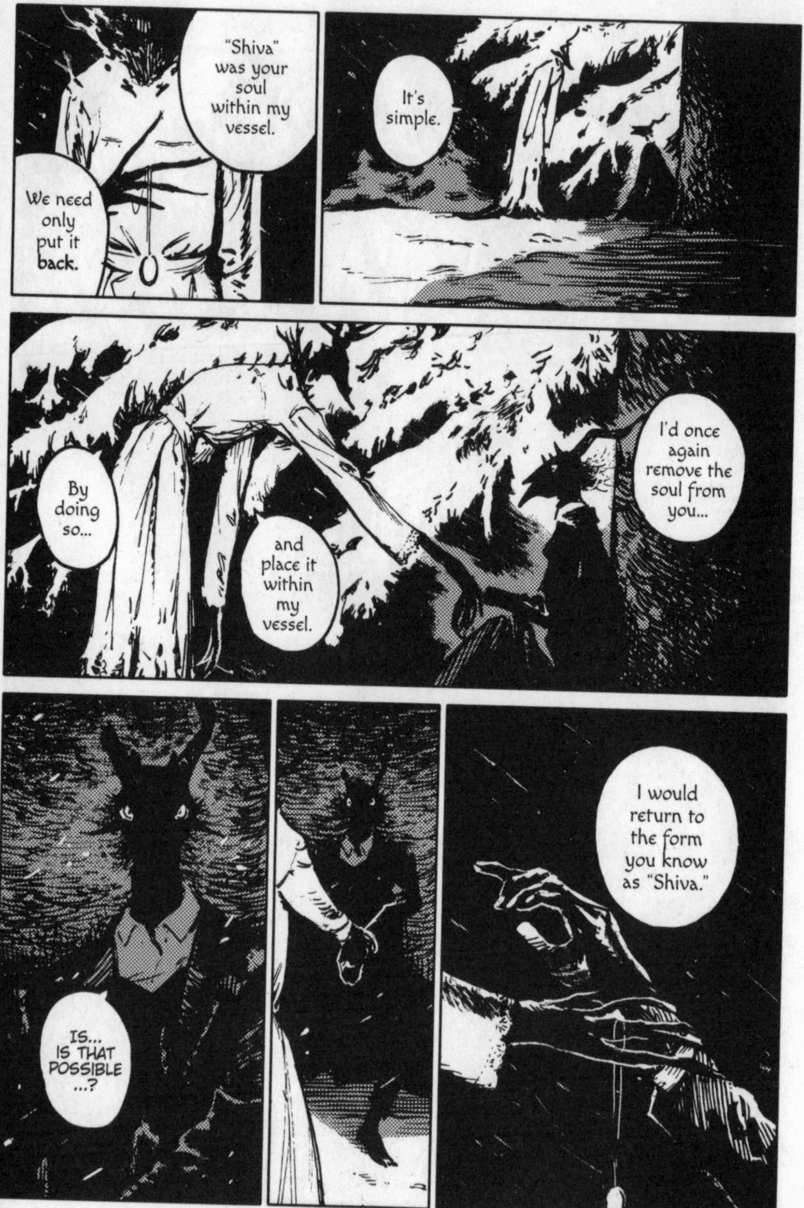
It's simple.
"Shiva" was your soul within my vessel.
We need only put it back.
I'd once again remove the soul from you...
and place it within my vessel.
By doing so...
I would return to the form you know as "Shiva."
IS... IS THAT POSSIBLE ...?

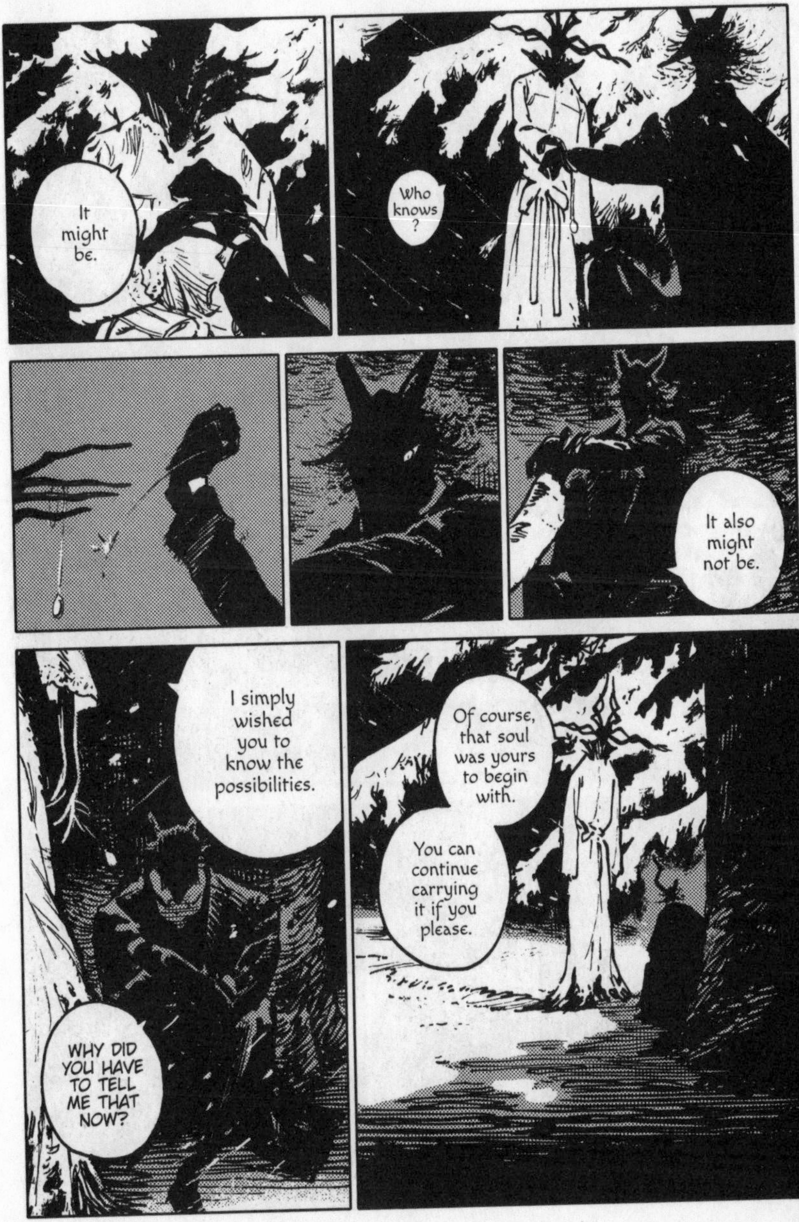
Who knows ?
It might be.
It also might not be.
Of course, that soul was yours to begin with.
You can continue carrying it if you please.
I simply wished you to know the possibilities.
WHY DID YOU HAVE TO TELL ME THAT NOW?

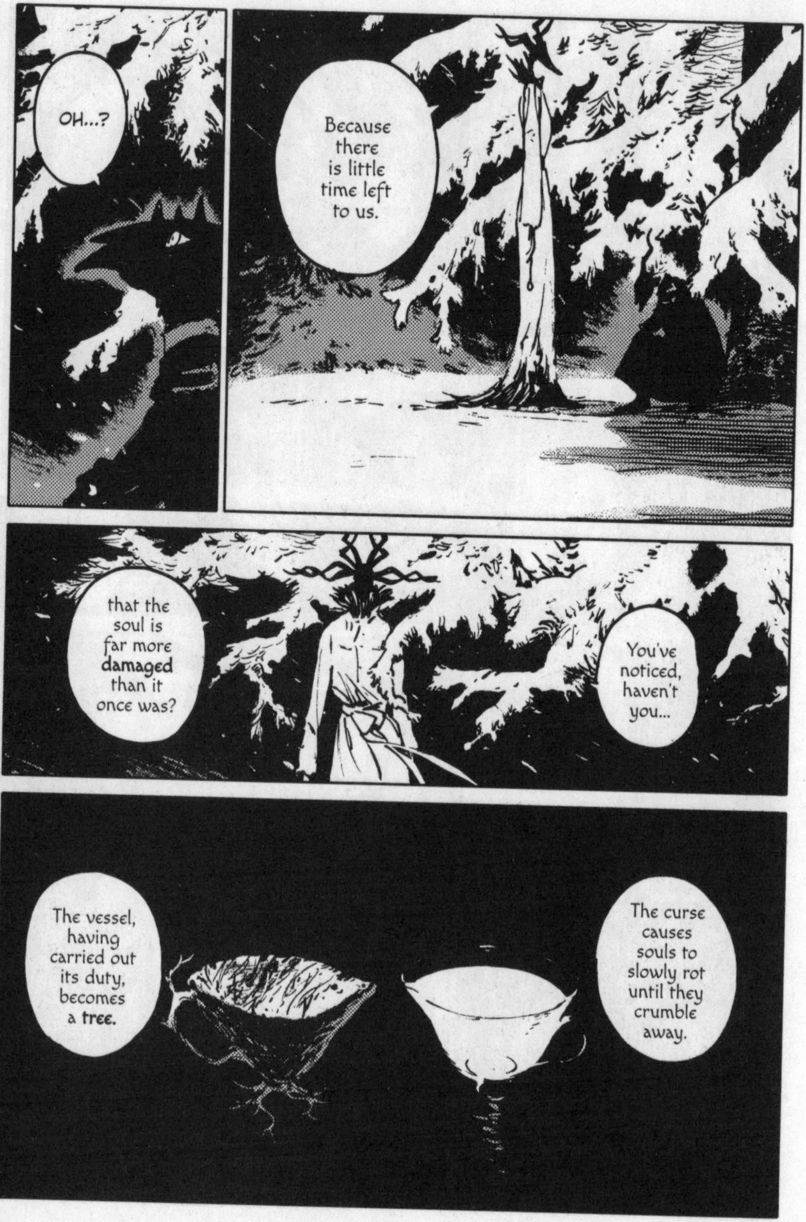
Because there is little time left to us.
OH...?
You've noticed, haven't you...
that the soul is far more **damaged** than it once was?
The curse causes souls to slowly rot until they crumble away.
The vessel, having carried out its duty, becomes a **tree.**

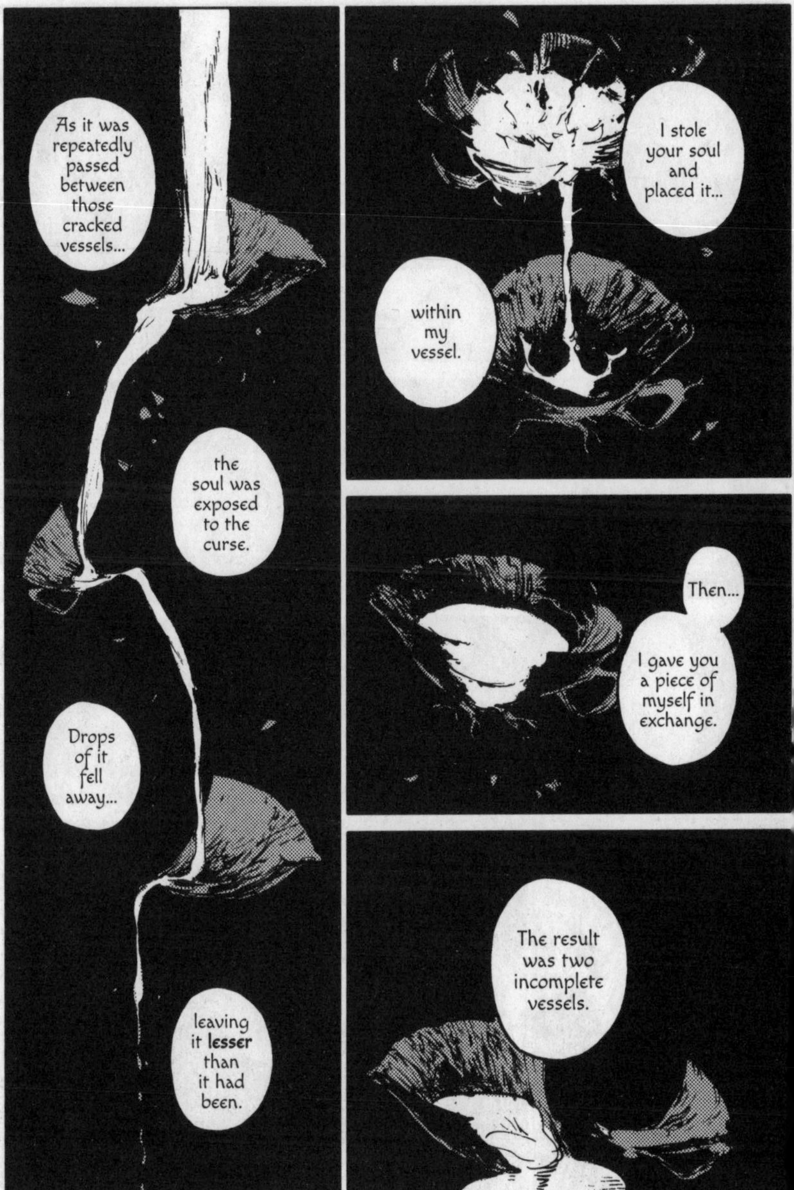
I stole your soul and placed it...
within my vessel.
Then...
I gave you a piece of myself in exchange.
The result was two incomplete vessels.
As it was repeatedly passed between those cracked vessels...
the soul was exposed to the curse.
Drops of it fell away...
leaving it **lesser** than it had been.

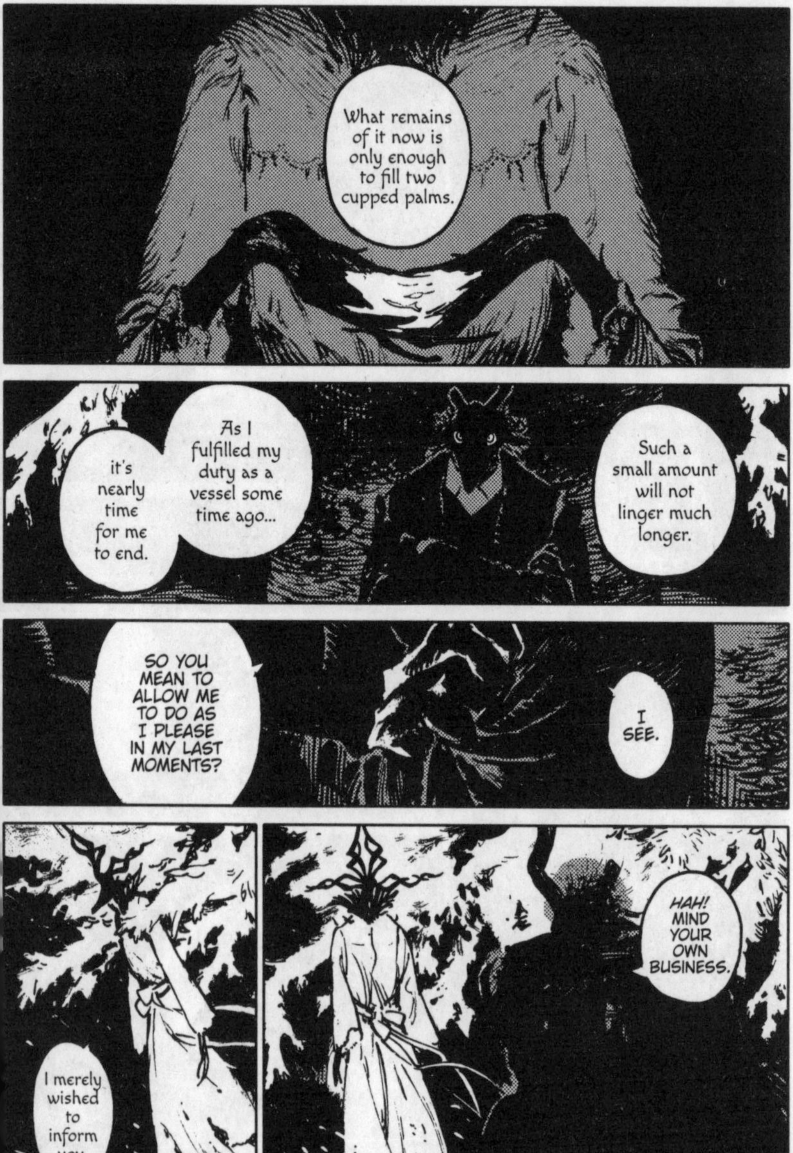
What remains of it now is only enough to fill two cupped palms.
Such a small amount will not linger much longer.
As I fulfilled my duty as a vessel some time ago...
it's nearly time for me to end.
I SEE.
SO YOU MEAN TO ALLOW ME TO DO AS I PLEASE IN MY LAST MOMENTS?
HAH! MIND YOUR OWN BUSINESS.
I merely wished to inform you.

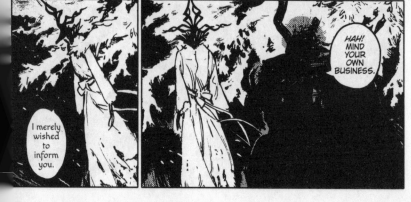

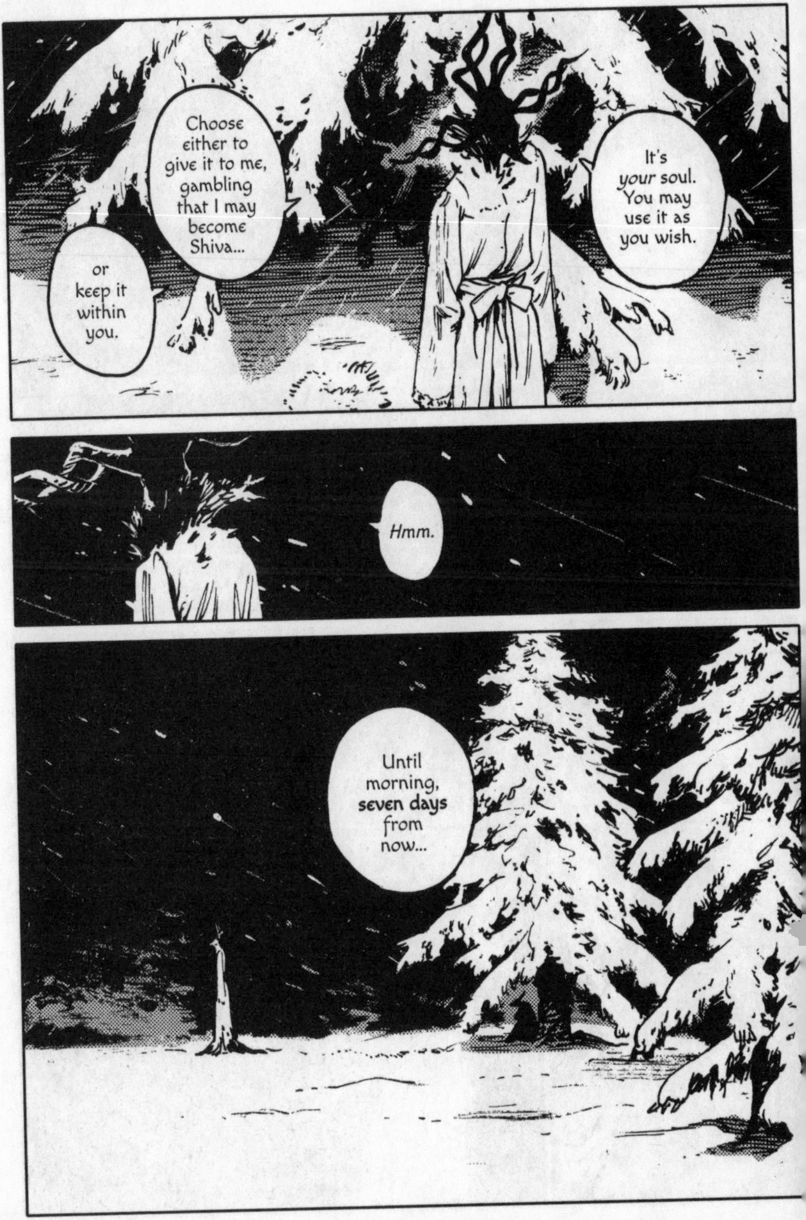
It's *your* soul. You may use it as you wish.
Choose either to give it to me, gambling that I may become Shiva...
or keep it within you.
Hmm.
Until morning, **seven days** from now...

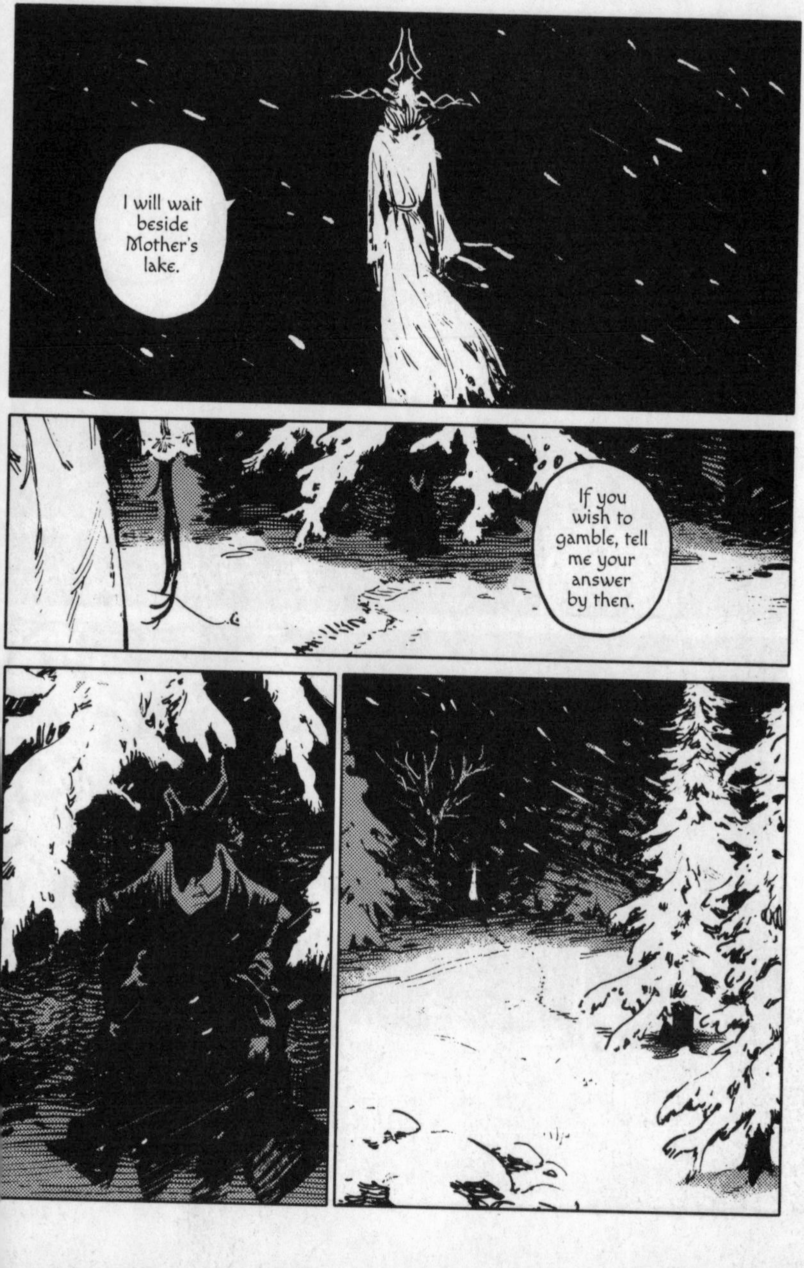
I will wait beside Mother's lake.
If you wish to gamble, tell me your answer by then.

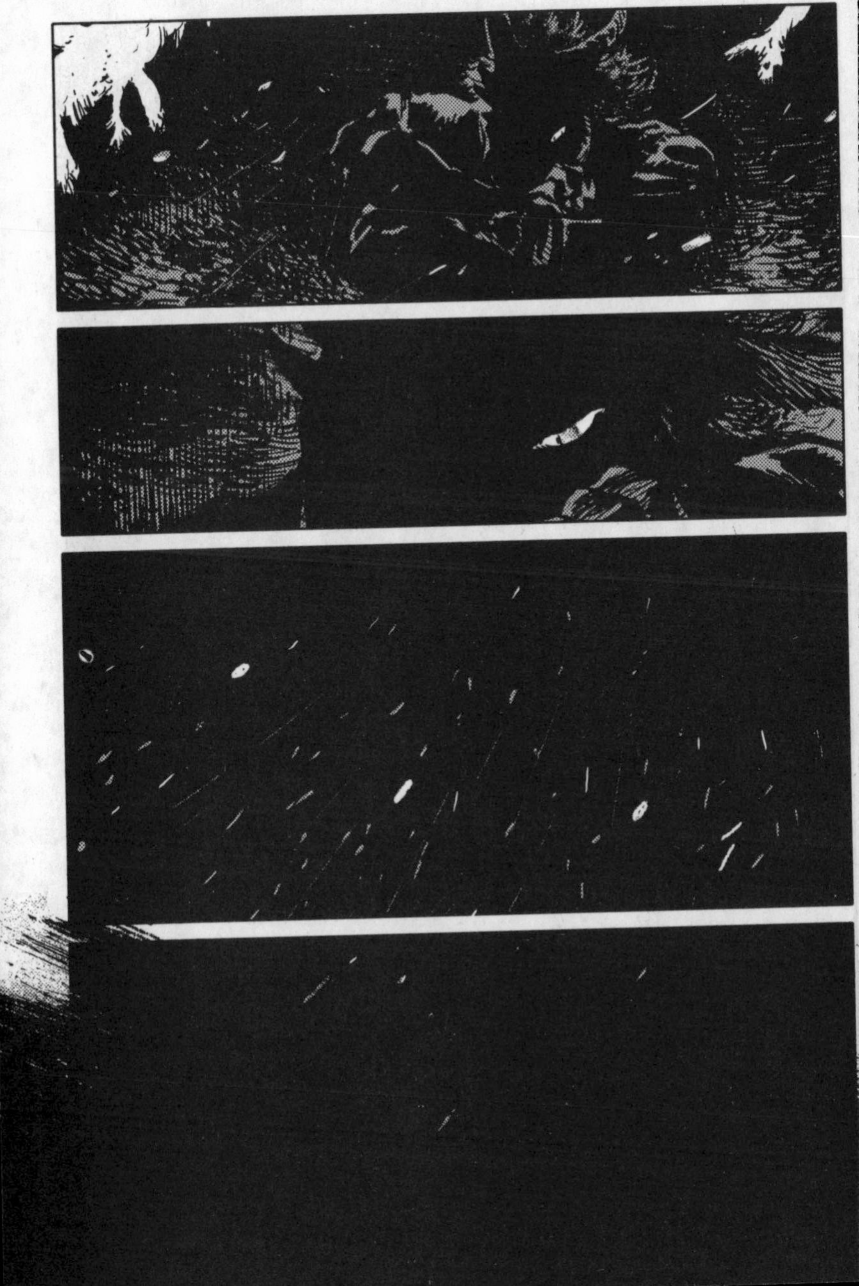

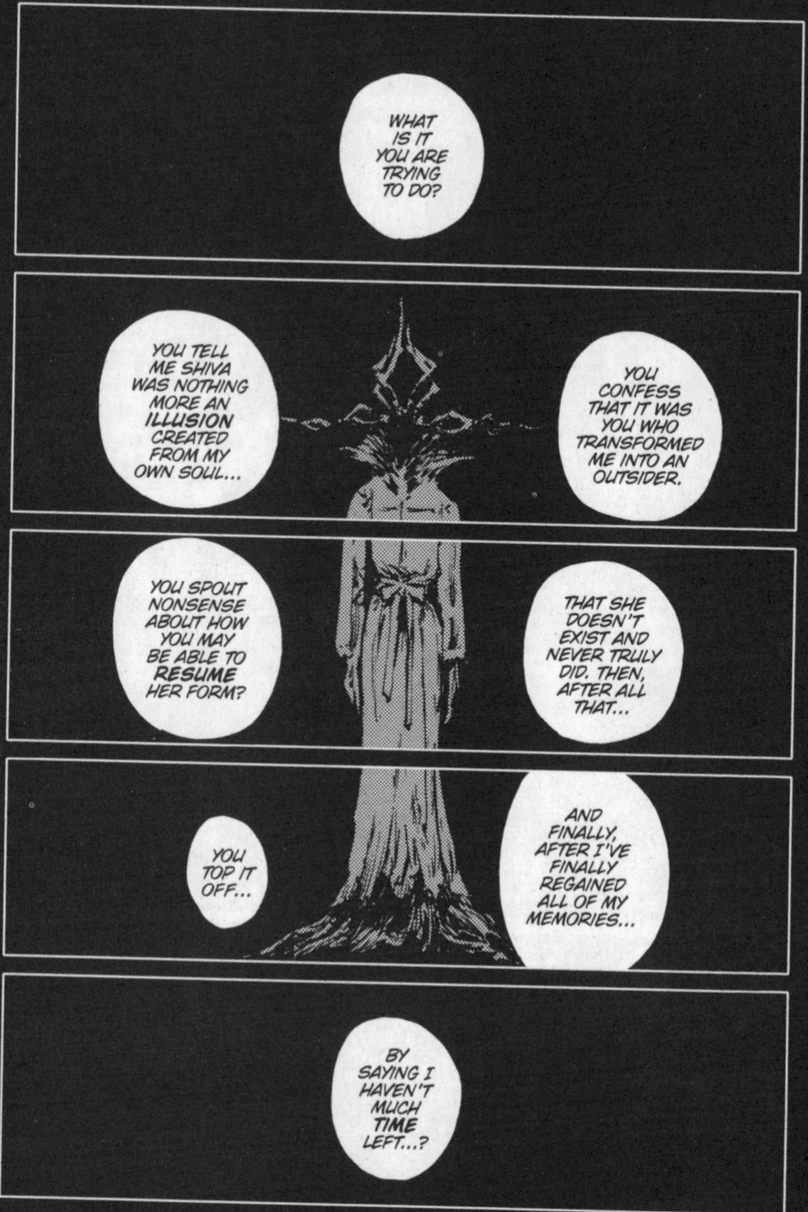
WHAT IS IT YOU ARE TRYING TO DO?
YOU CONFESS THAT IT WAS YOU WHO TRANSFORMED ME INTO AN OUTSIDER.
YOU TELL ME SHIVA WAS NOTHING MORE AN ILLUSION CREATED FROM MY OWN SOUL...
THAT SHE DOESN'T EXIST AND NEVER TRULY DID. THEN, AFTER ALL THAT...
YOU SPOUT NONSENSE ABOUT HOW YOU MAY BE ABLE TO RESUME HER FORM?
AND FINALLY, AFTER I'VE FINALLY REGAINED ALL OF MY MEMORIES...
YOU TOP IT OFF...
BY SAYING I HAVEN'T MUCH TIME LEFT...?

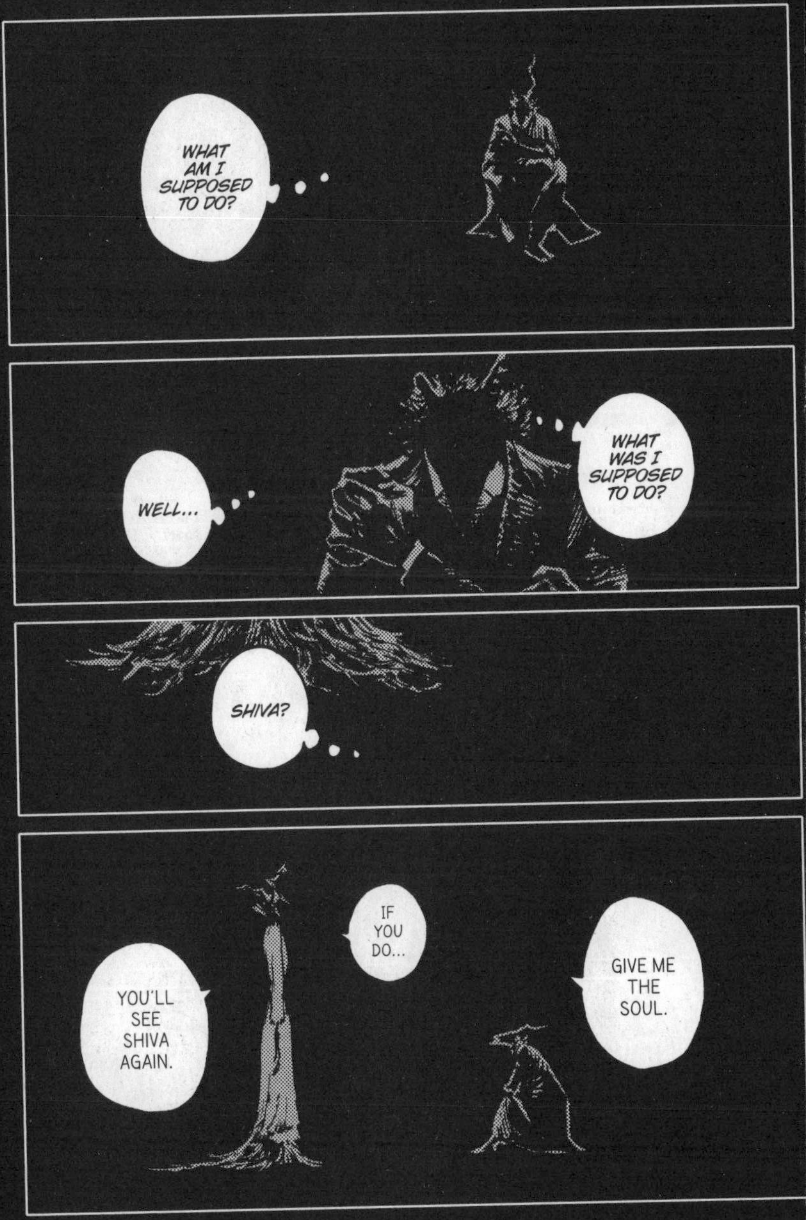
WHAT AM I SUPPOSED TO DO?
WHAT WAS I SUPPOSED TO DO?
WELL...
SHIVA?
GIVE ME THE SOUL.
IF YOU DO...
YOU'LL SEE SHIVA AGAIN.

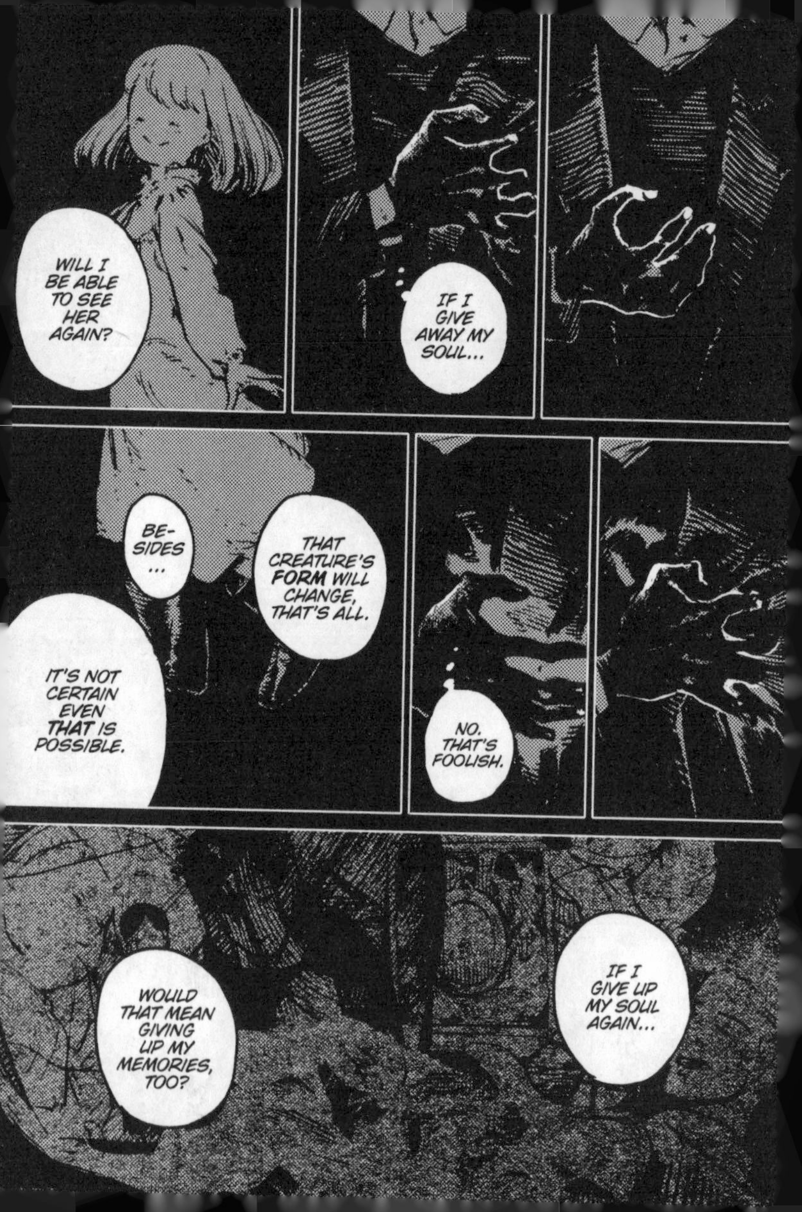
IF I GIVE AWAY MY SOUL...
WILL I BE ABLE TO SEE HER AGAIN?
NO. THAT'S FOOLISH.
THAT CREATURE'S **FORM** WILL CHANGE, THAT'S ALL.
BE-SIDES...
IT'S NOT CERTAIN EVEN **THAT** IS POSSIBLE.
IF I GIVE UP MY SOUL AGAIN...
WOULD THAT MEAN GIVING UP MY MEMORIES, TOO?

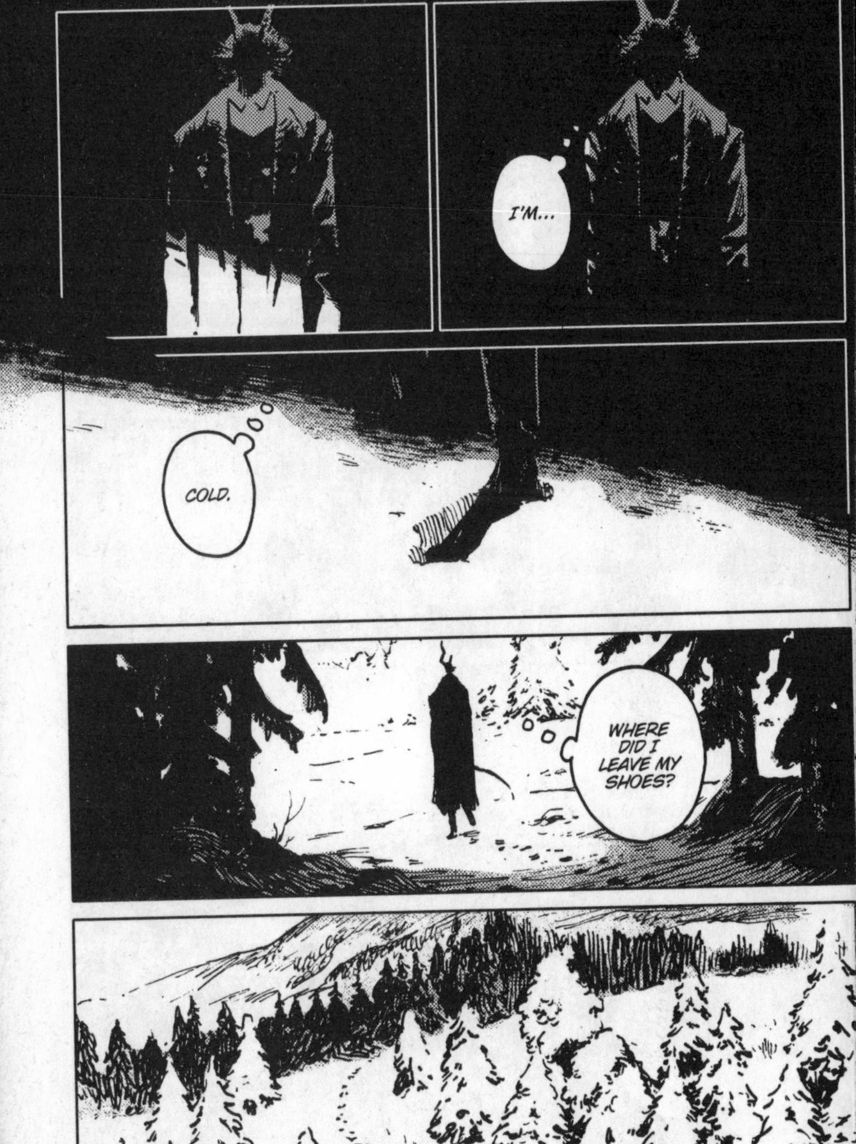
I'M...
COLD.
WHERE DID I LEAVE MY SHOES?

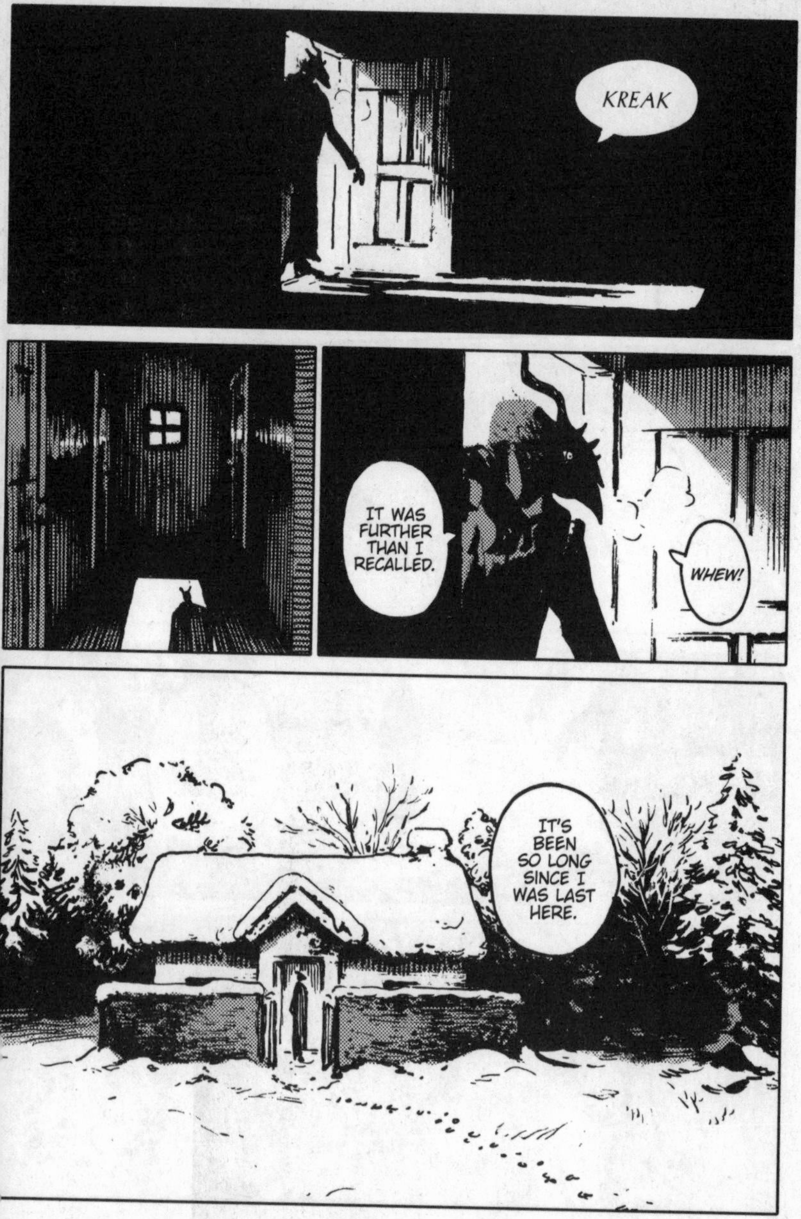
KREAK
WHEW!
IT WAS FURTHER THAN I RECALLED.
IT'S BEEN SO LONG SINCE I WAS LAST HERE.

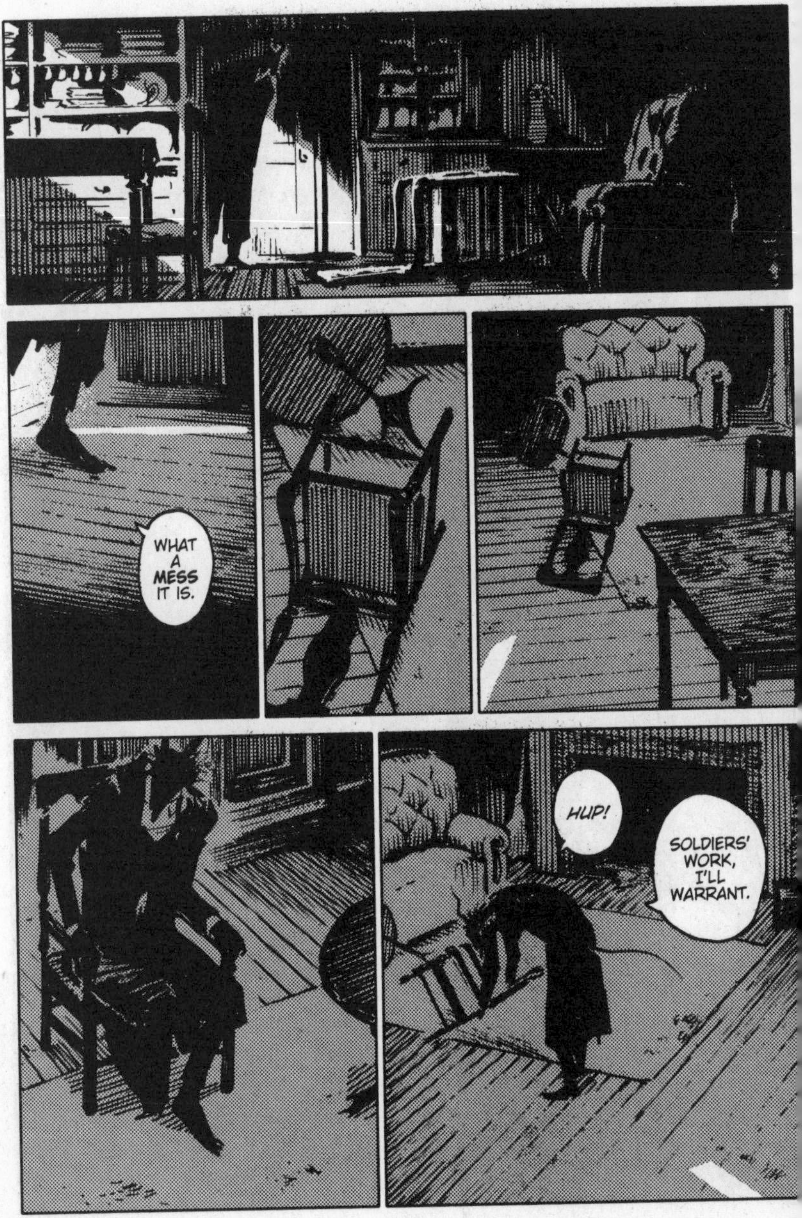
WHAT A MESS IT IS.
HUP!
SOLDIERS' WORK, I'LL WARRANT.

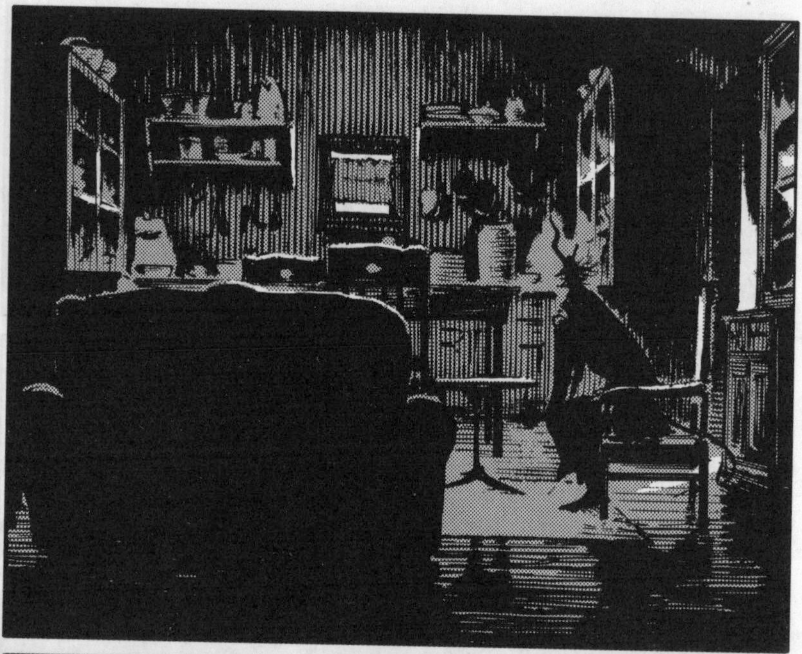

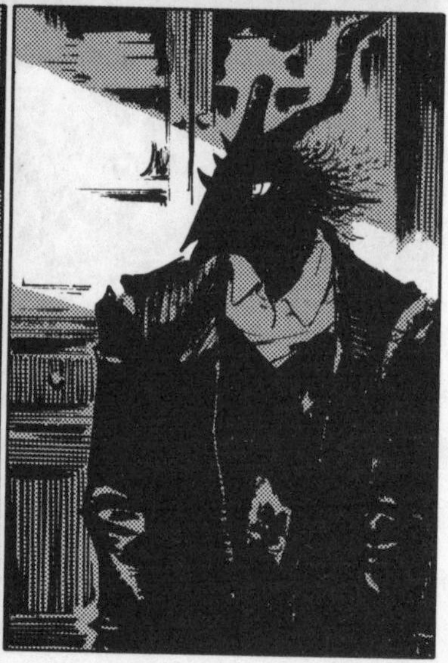

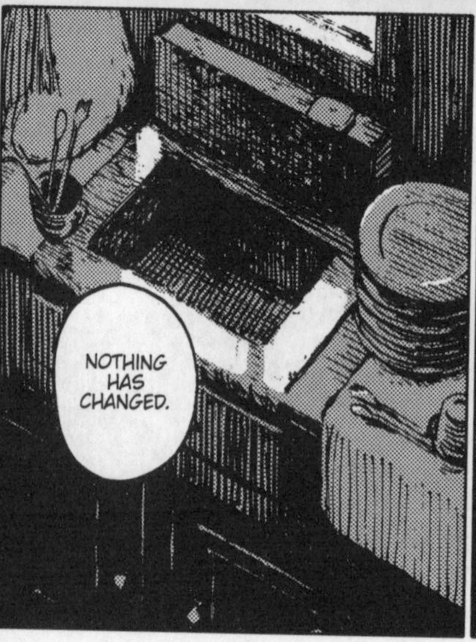
NOTHING HAS CHANGED.

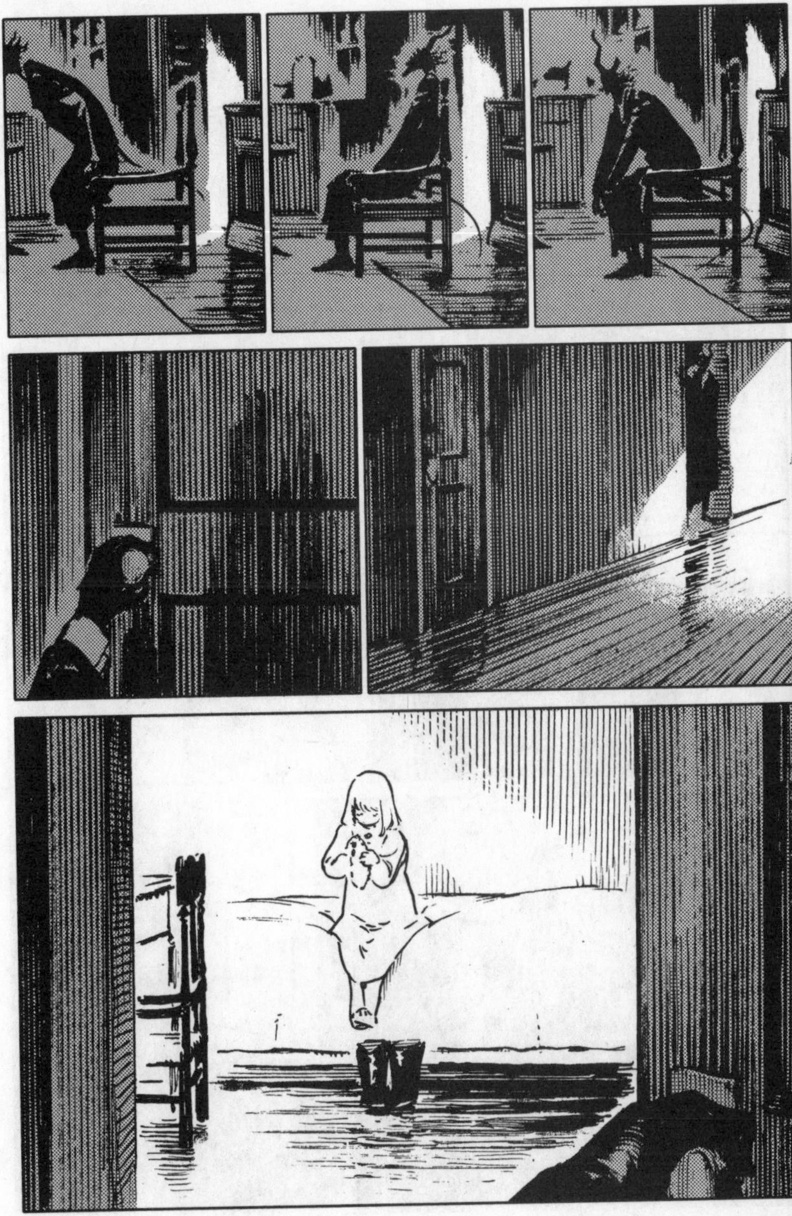

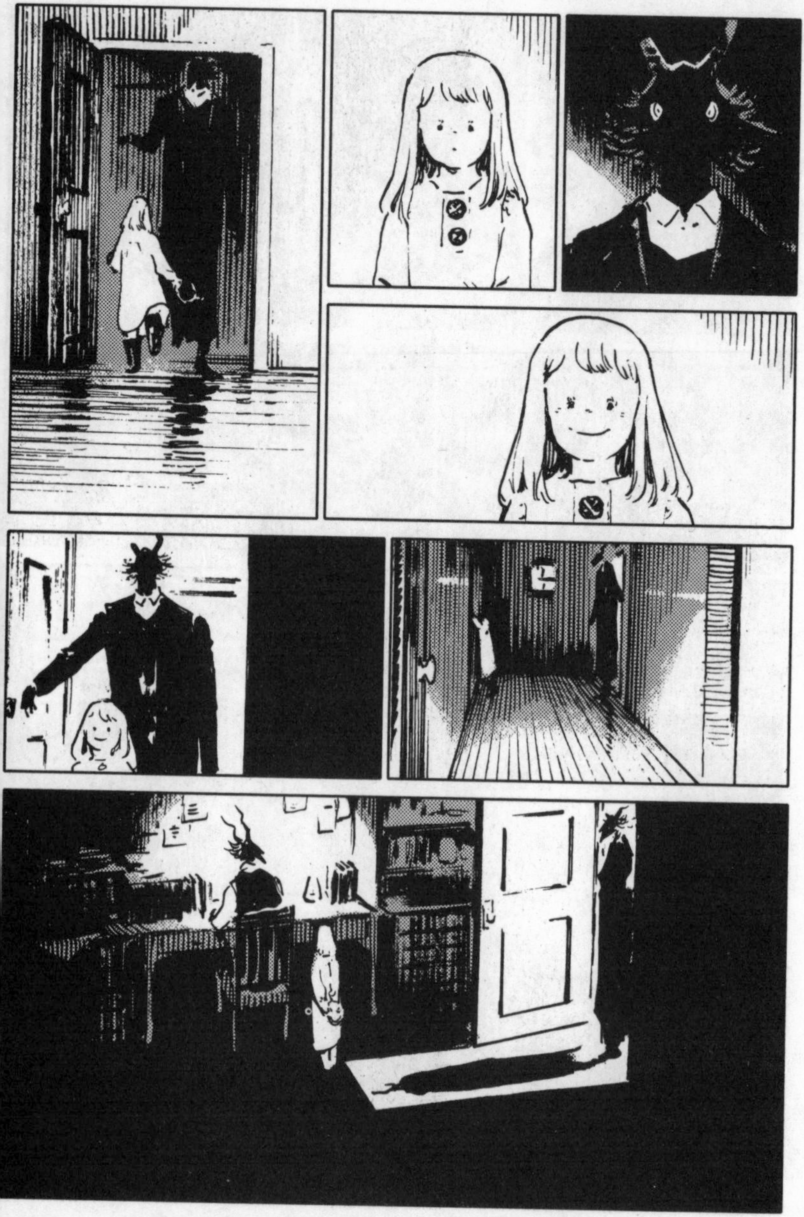

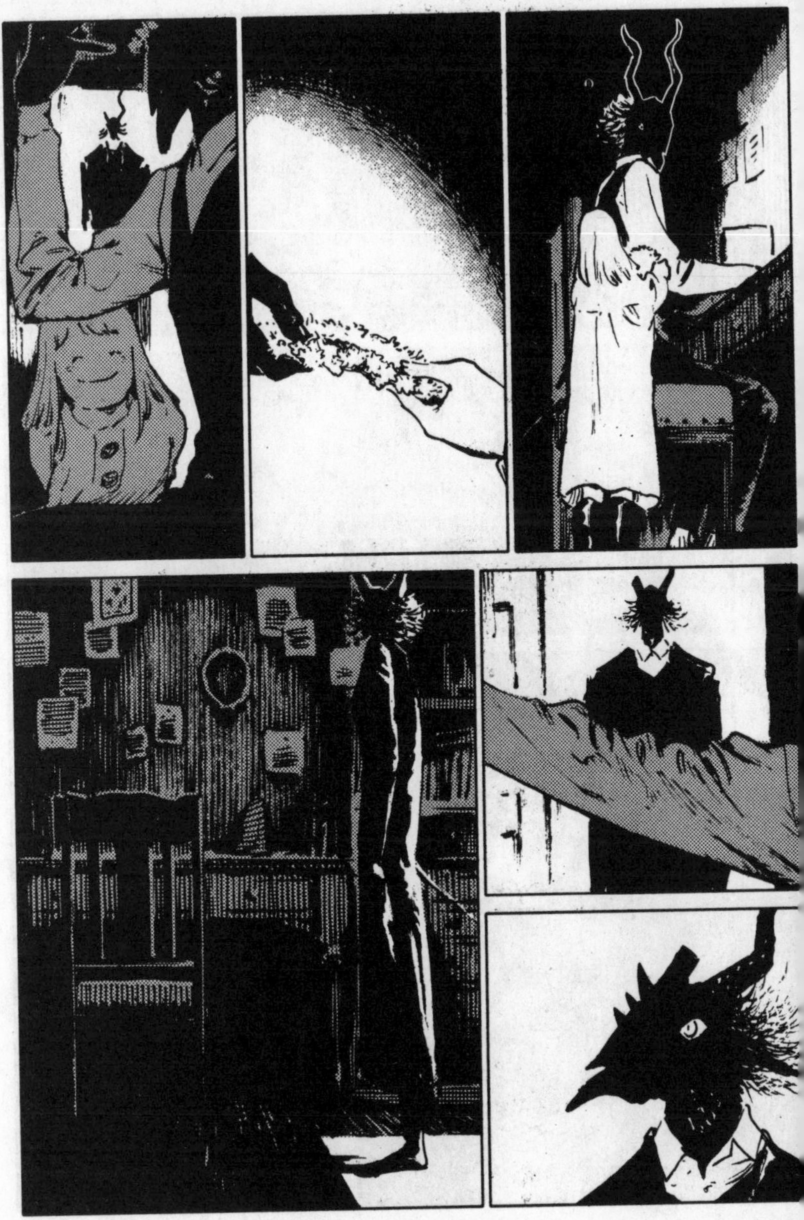

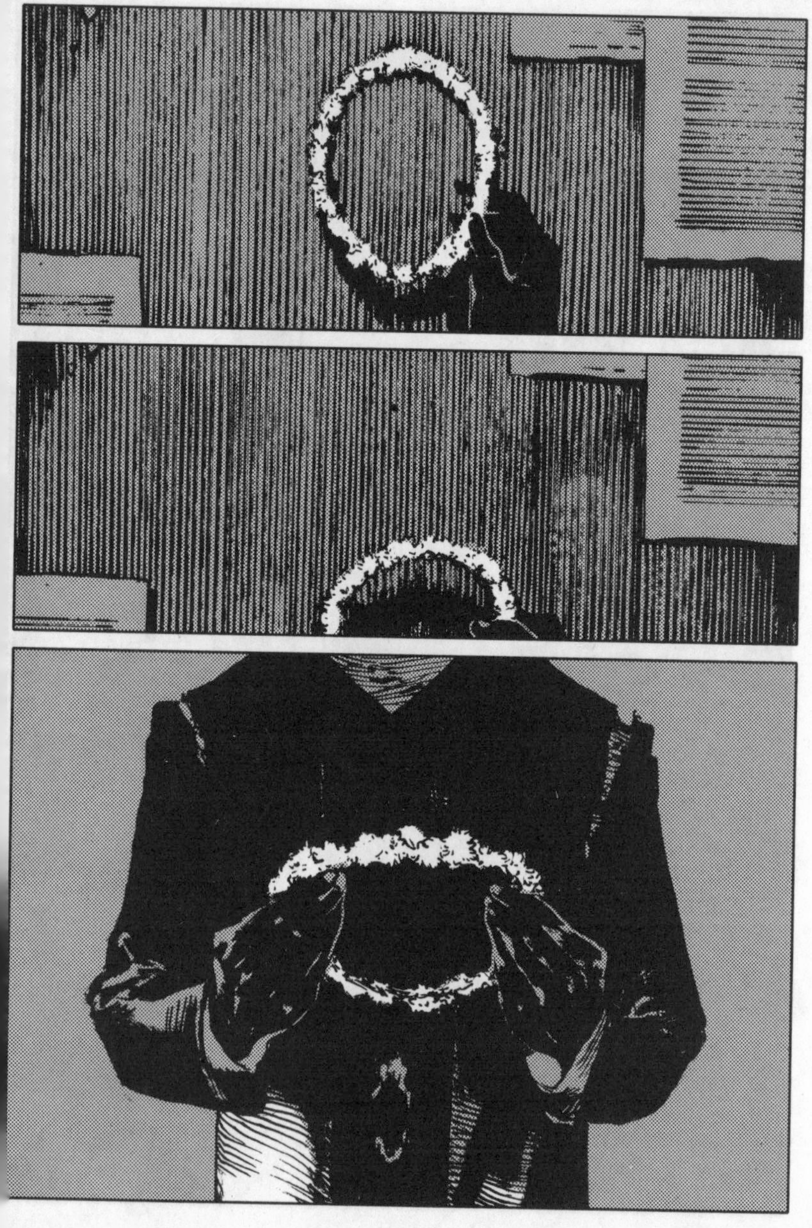

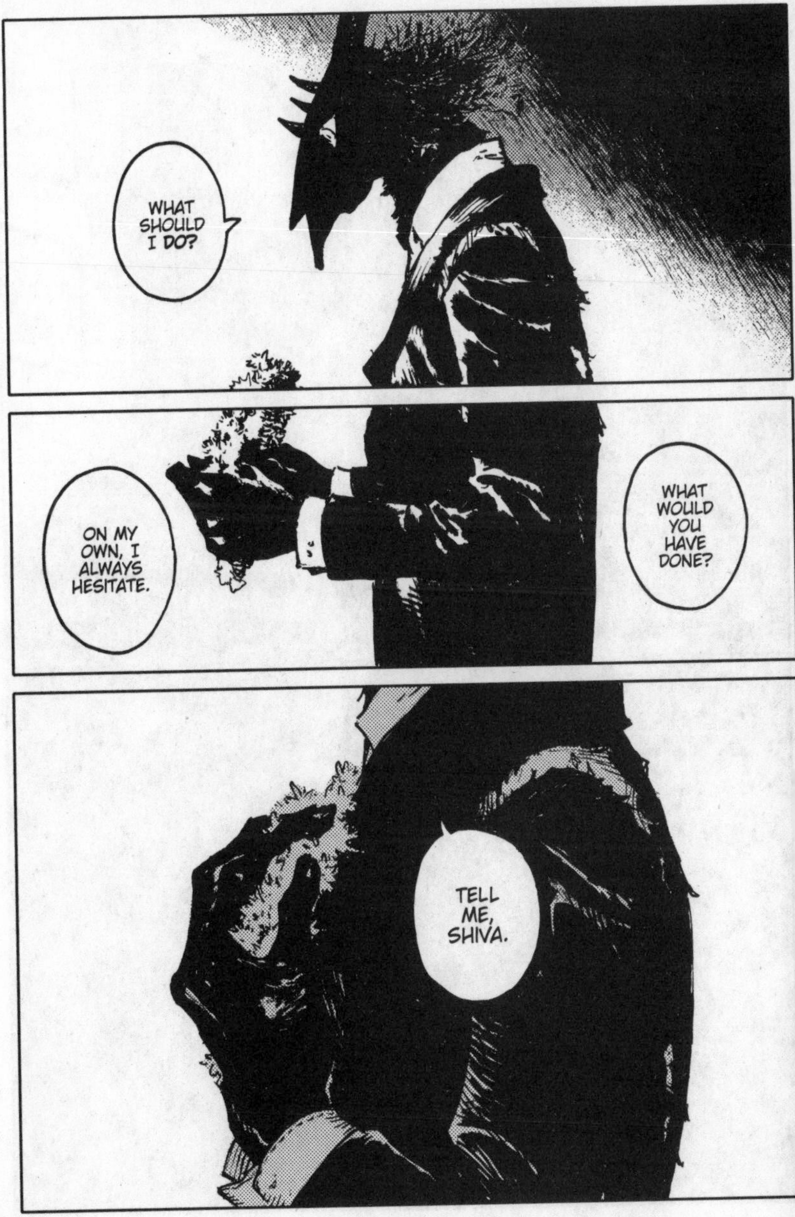
WHAT SHOULD I DO?
WHAT WOULD YOU HAVE DONE?
ON MY OWN, I ALWAYS HESITATE.
TELL ME, SHIVA.

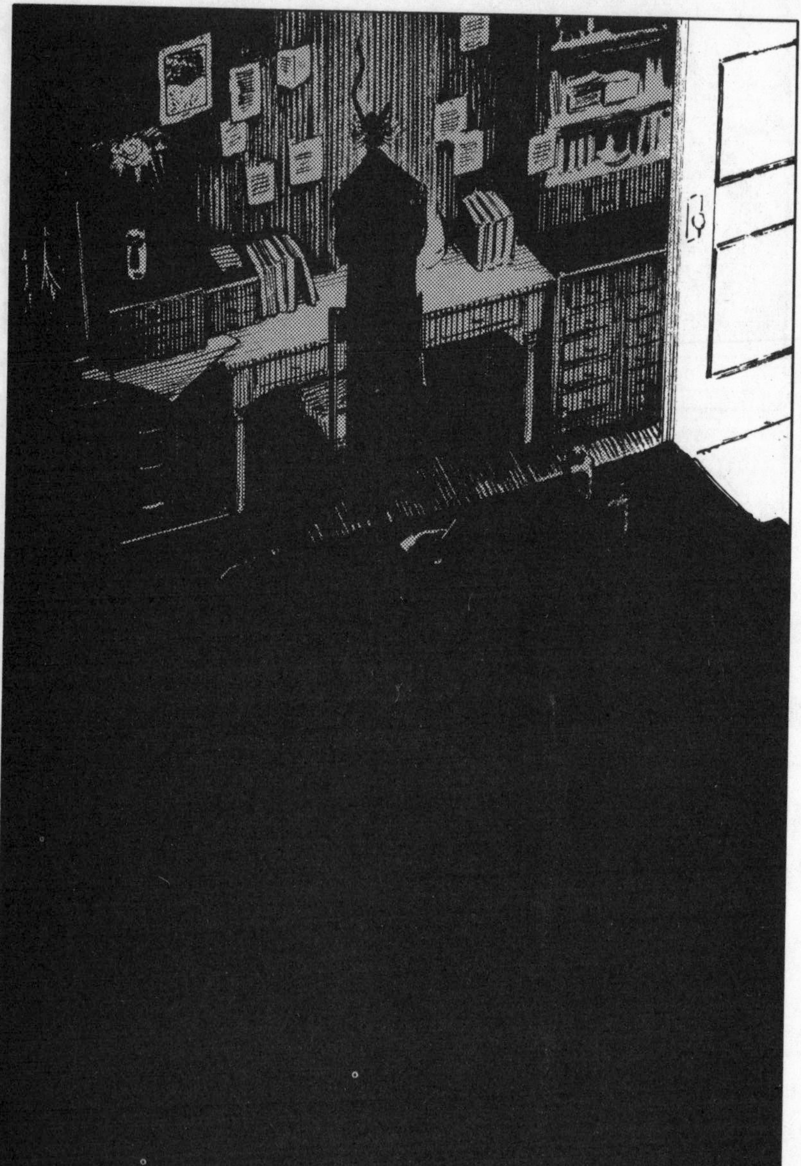

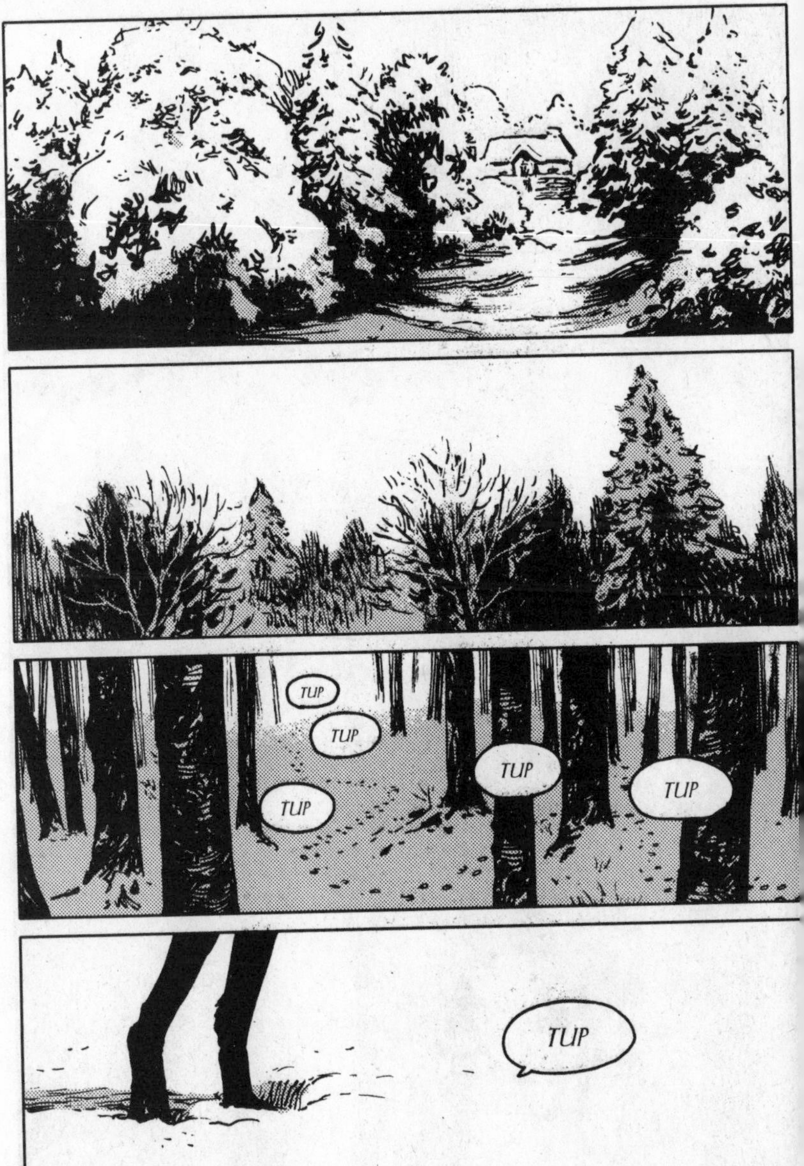
TUP
TUP
TUP
TUP
TUP
TUP

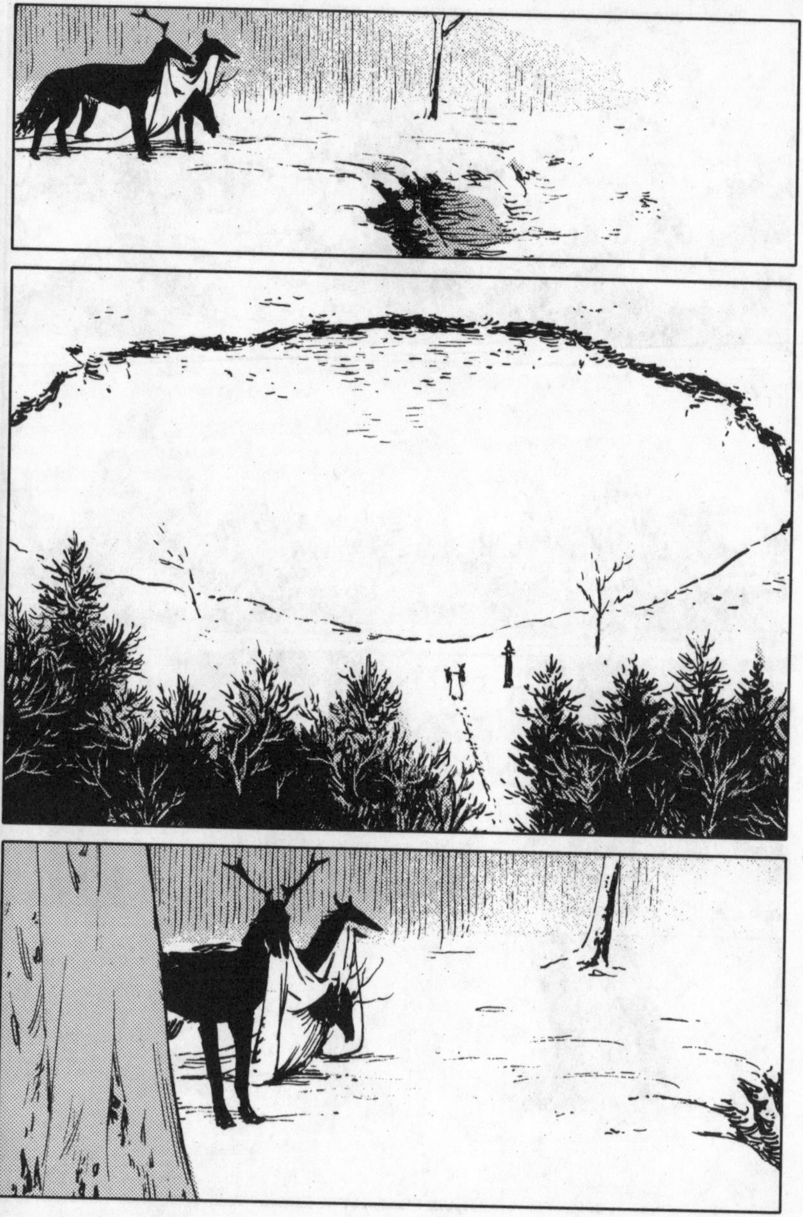

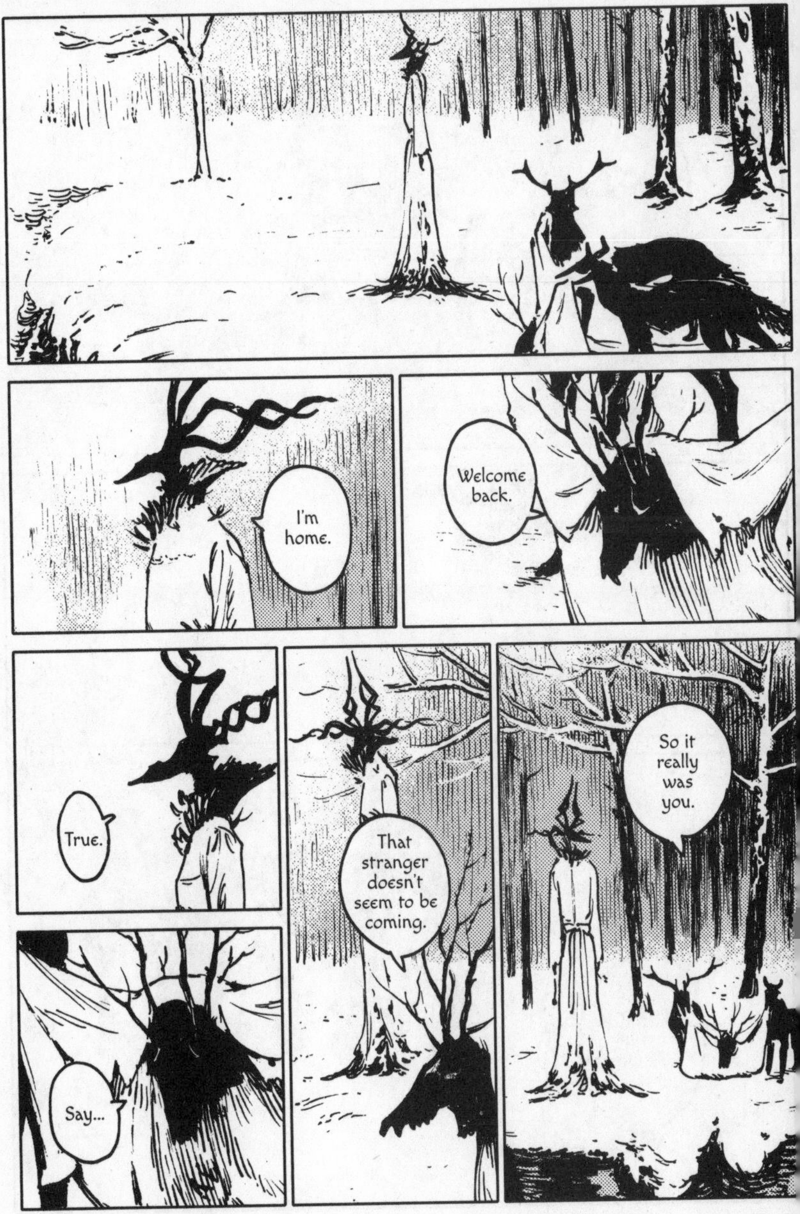
Welcome back.
I'm home.
So it really was you.
That stranger doesn't seem to be coming.
True.
Say...

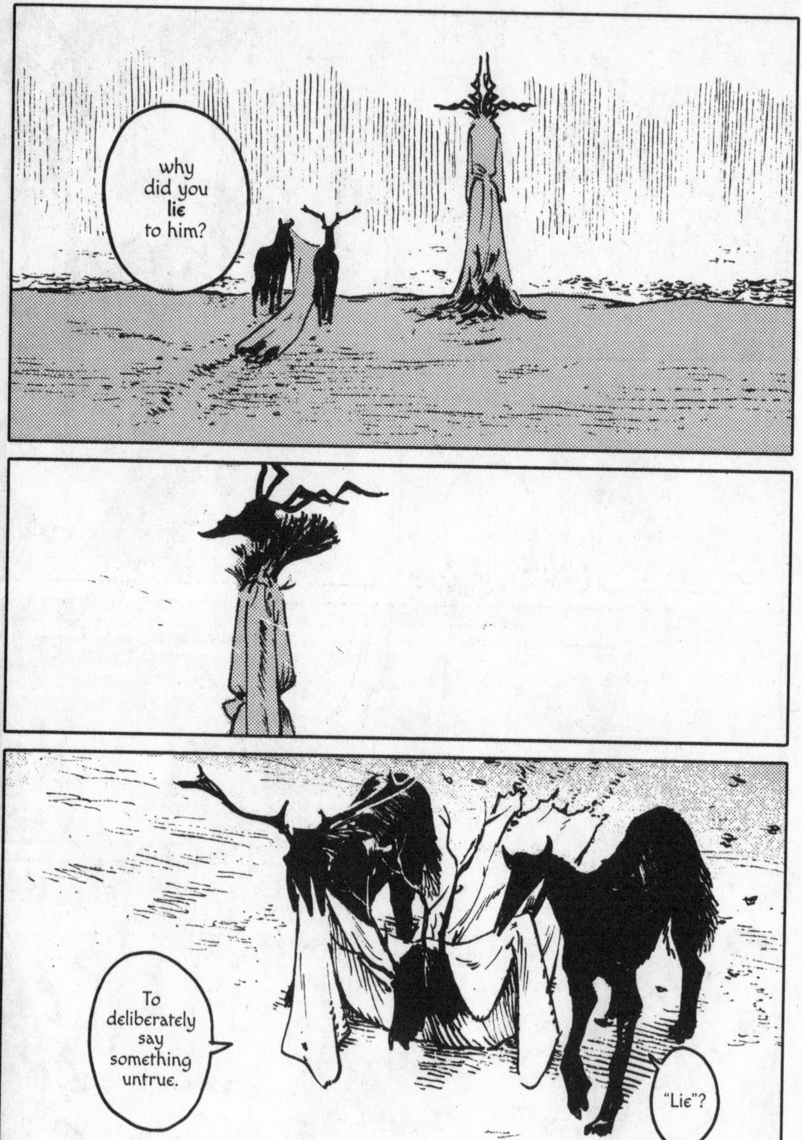
why did you lie to him?
"Lie"?
To deliberately say something untrue.

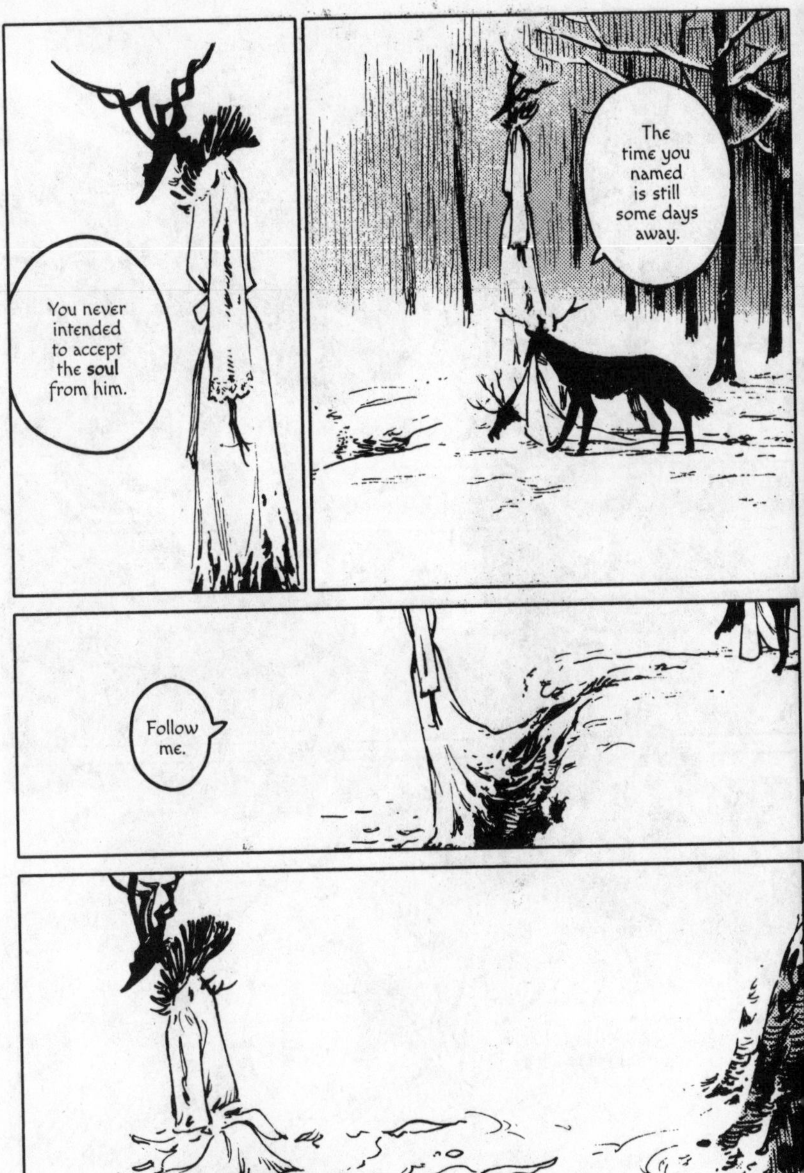
The time you named is still some days away.
You never intended to accept the soul from him.
Follow me.

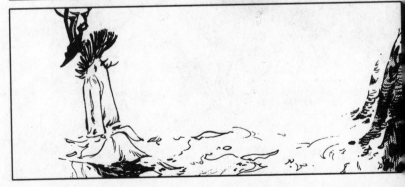

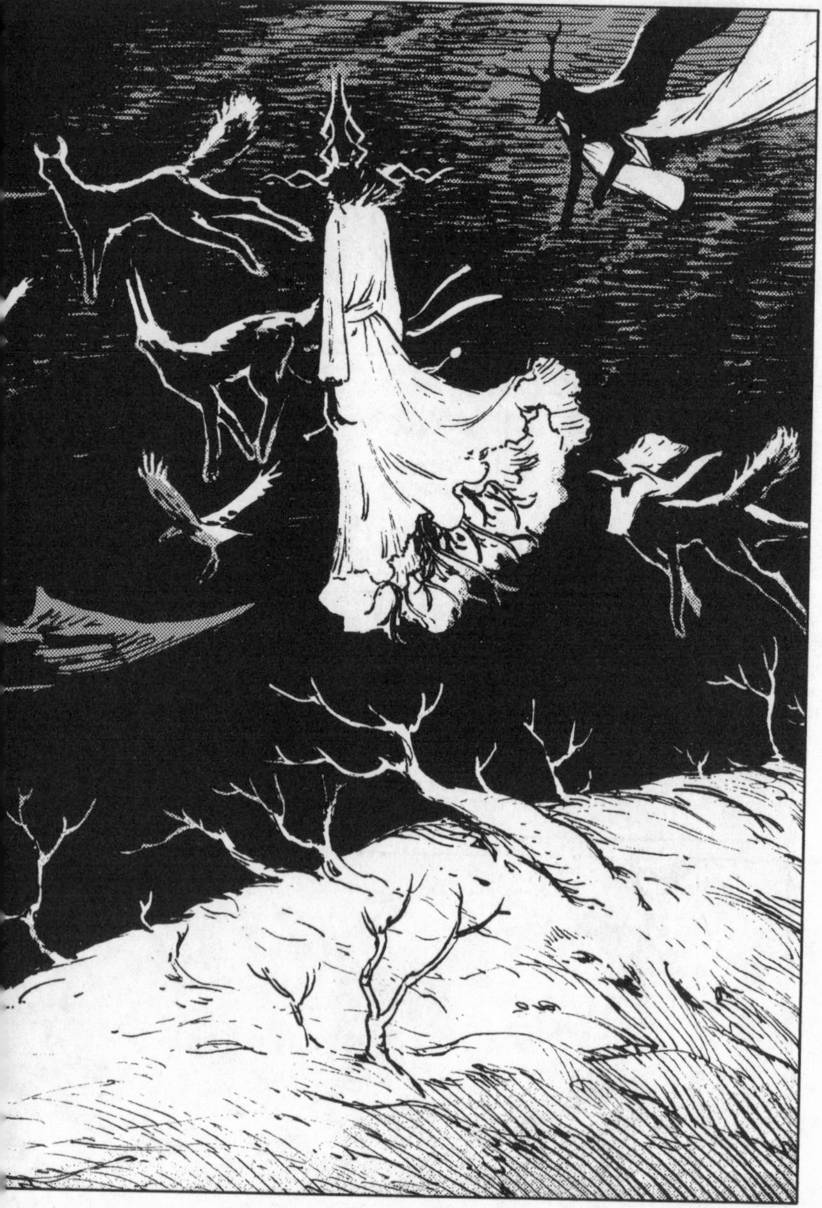

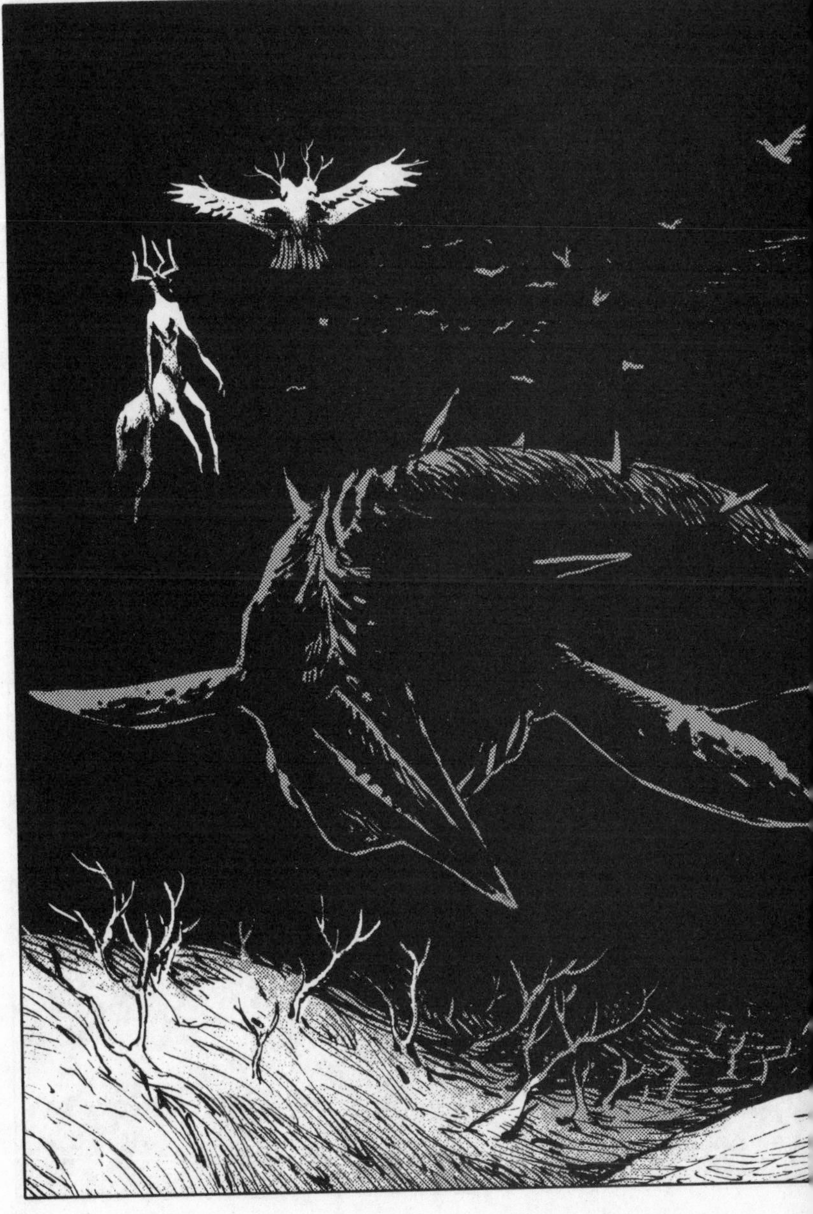

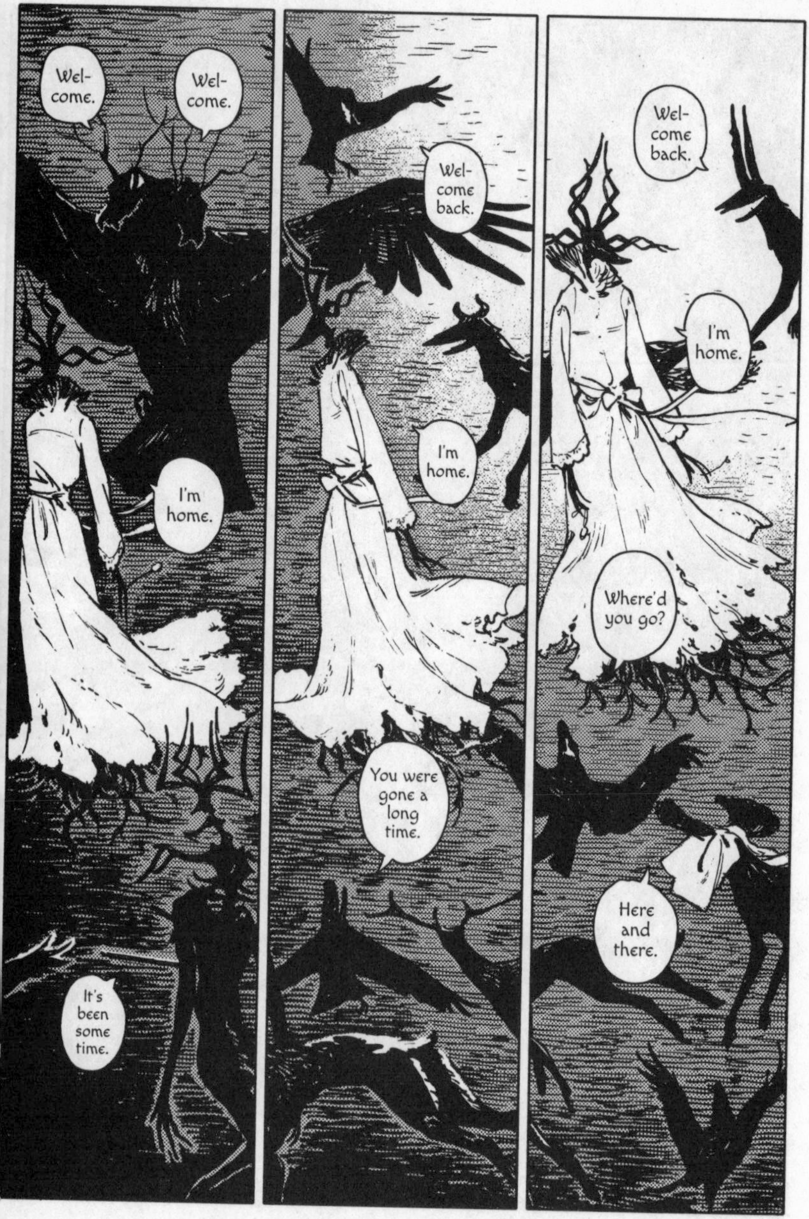
Wel-
come.
Wel-
come.
I'm
home.
It's
been
some
time.
Wel-
come
back.
I'm
home.
You were
gone a
long
time.
Wel-
come
back.
I'm
home.
Where'd
you go?
Here
and
there.

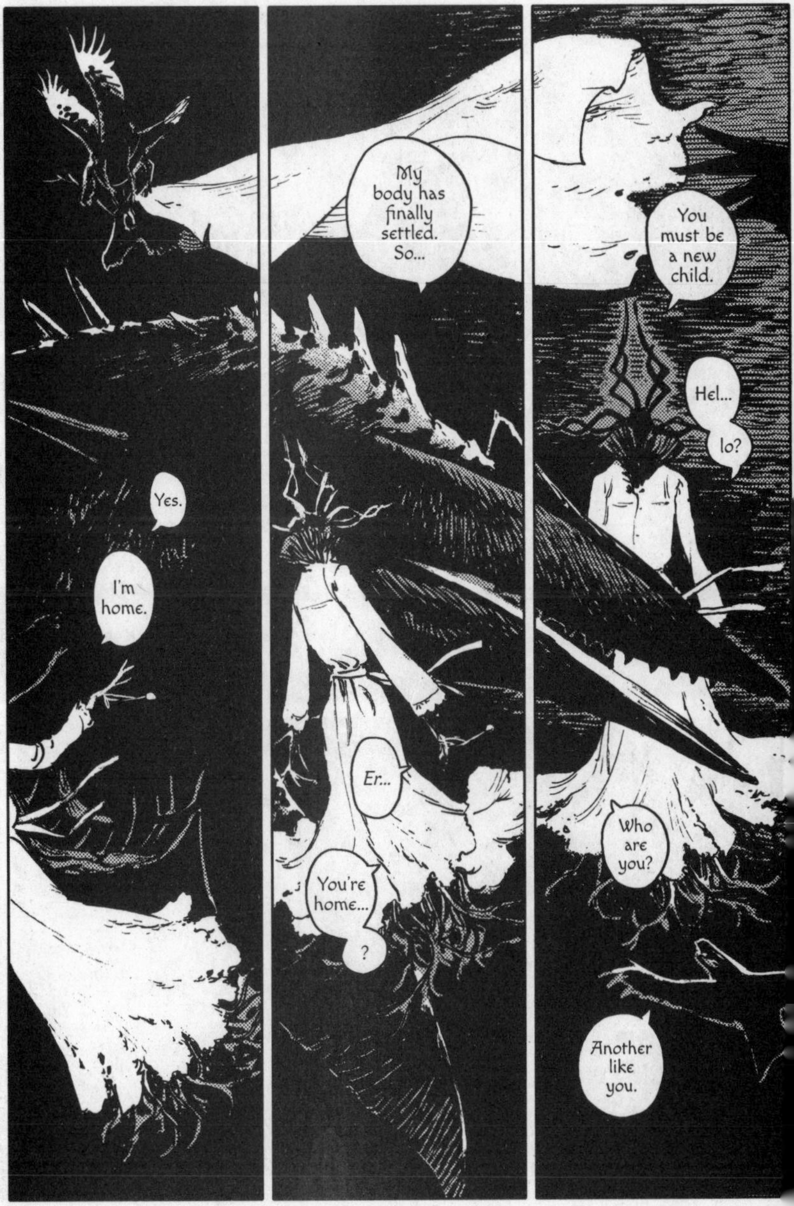
You must be a new child.
Hel...
lo?
Who are you?
Another like you.
My body has finally settled. So...
Er...
You're home...
?
Yes.
I'm home.

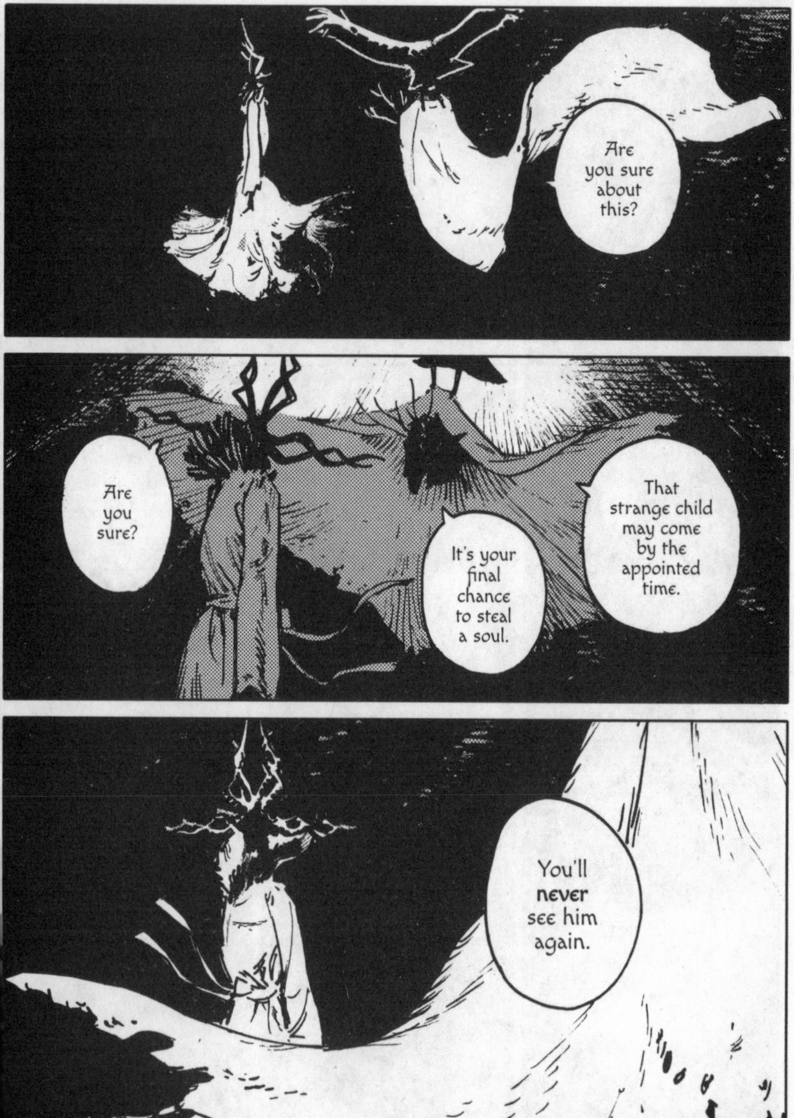
Are you sure about this?
That strange child may come by the appointed time.
It's your final chance to steal a soul.
Are you sure?
You'll **never** see him again.

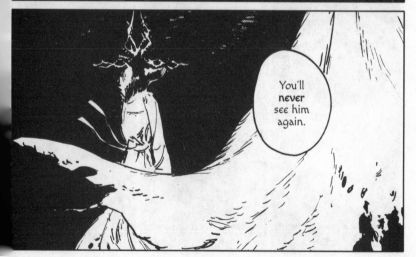

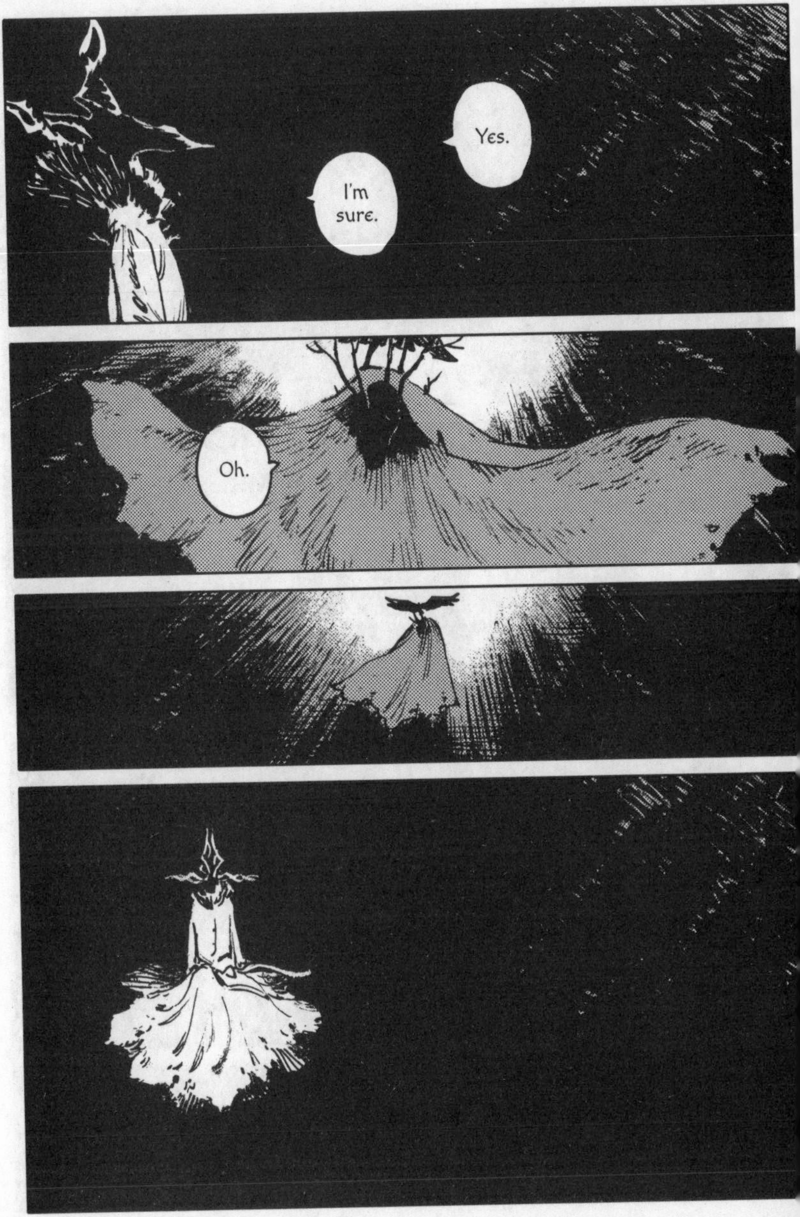
Yes.
I'm sure.
Oh.

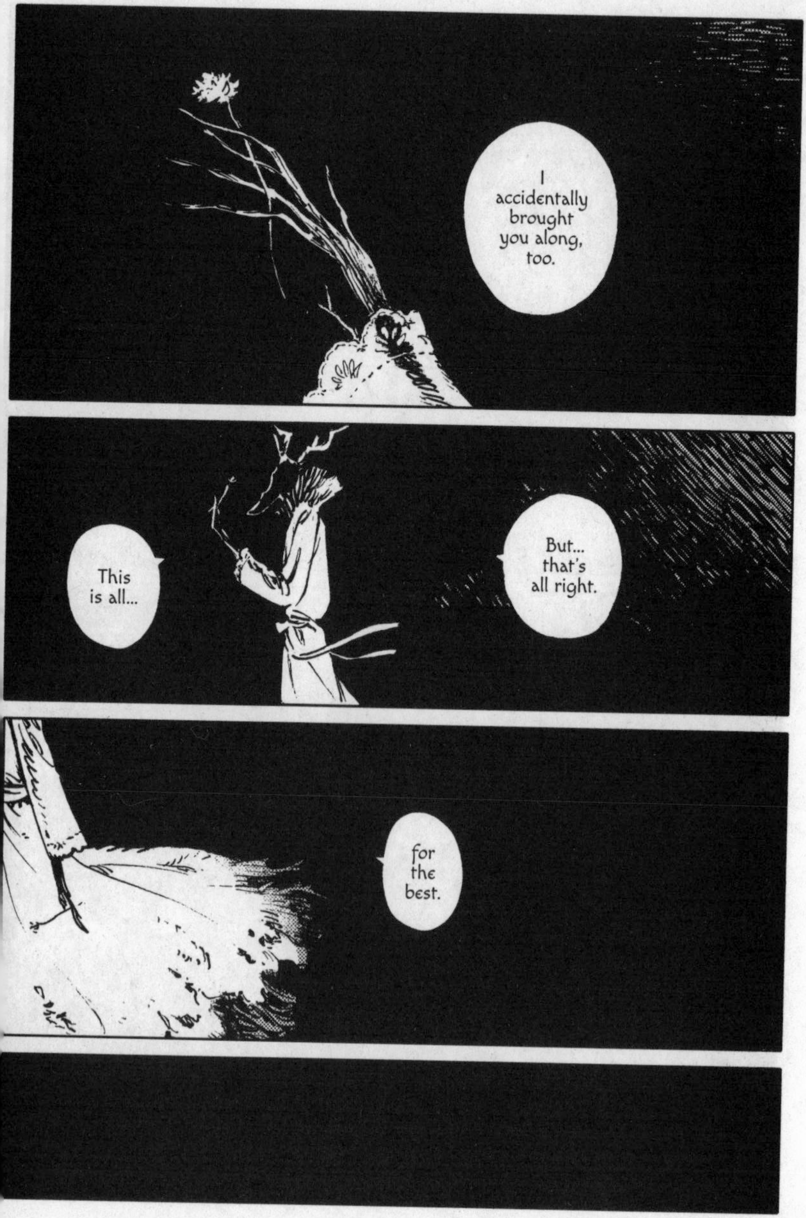
I accidentally brought you along, too.
But... that's all right.
This is all...
for the best.

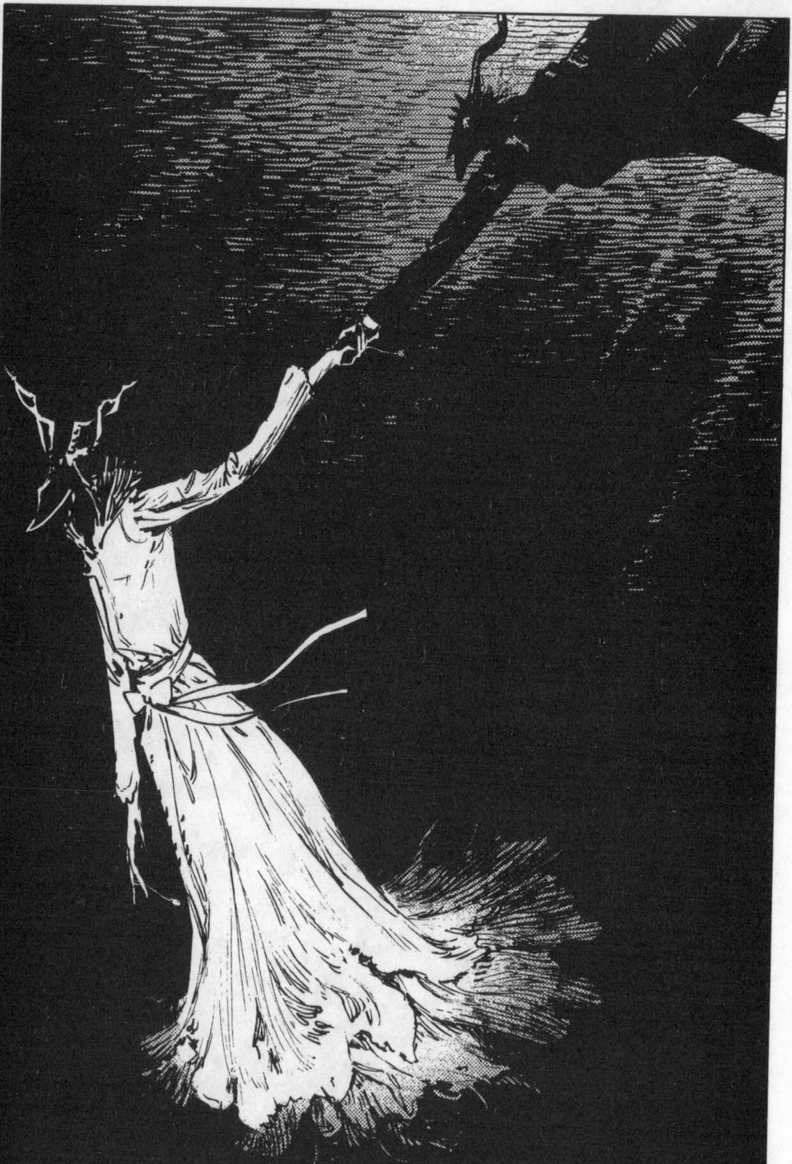

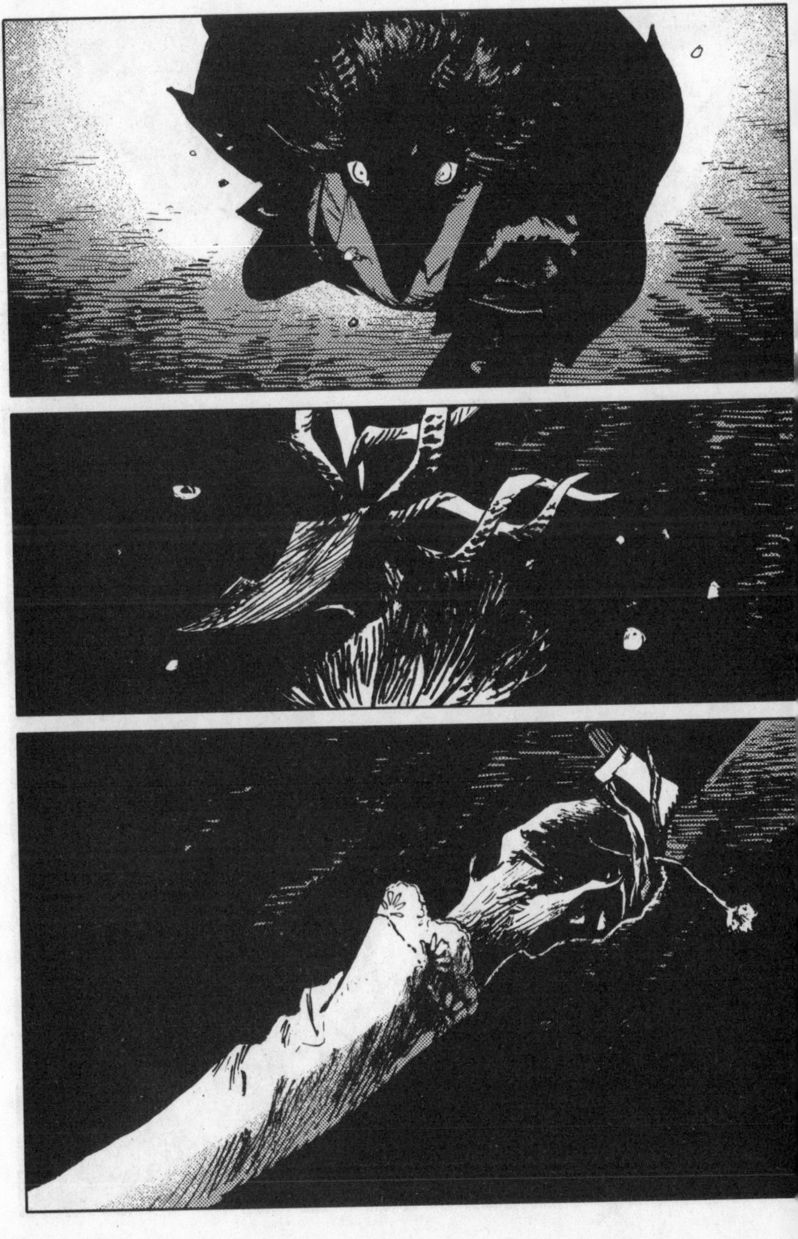

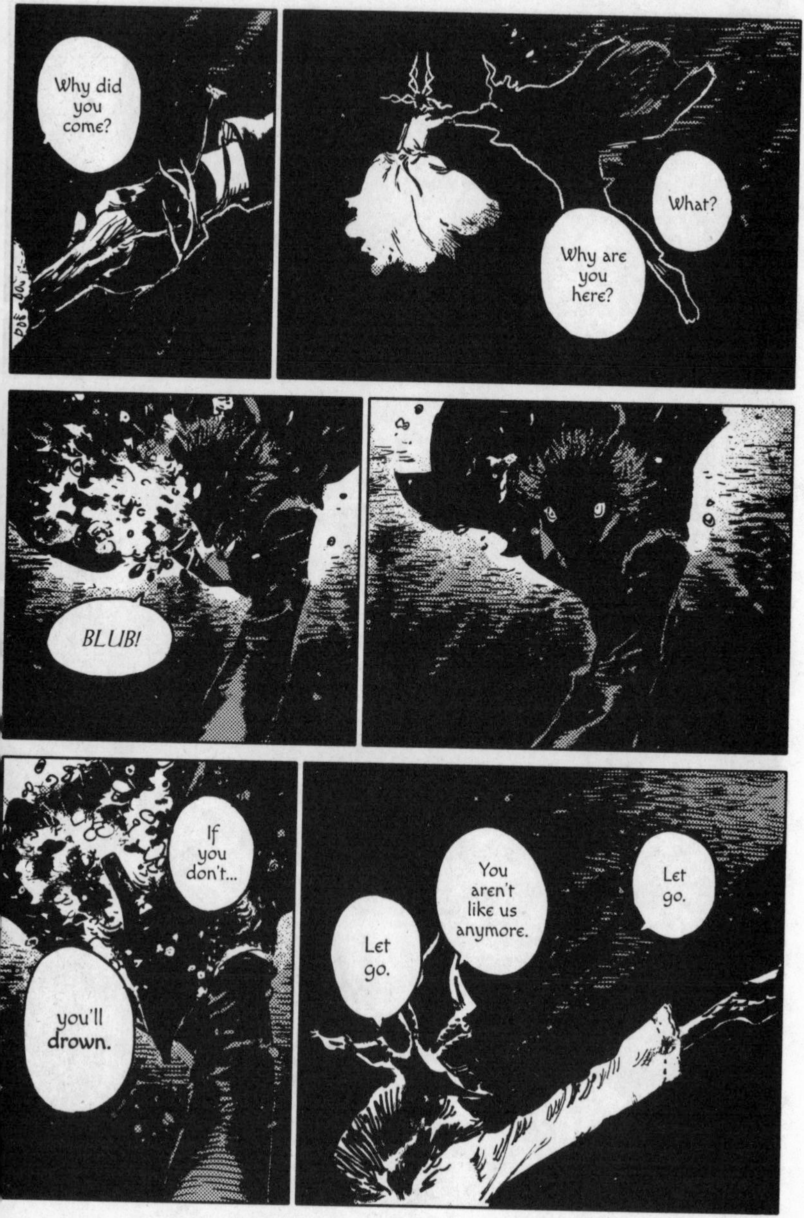
What?
Why are you here?
Why did you come?
BLUB!
Let go.
You aren't like us anymore.
Let go.
If you don't...
you'll drown.

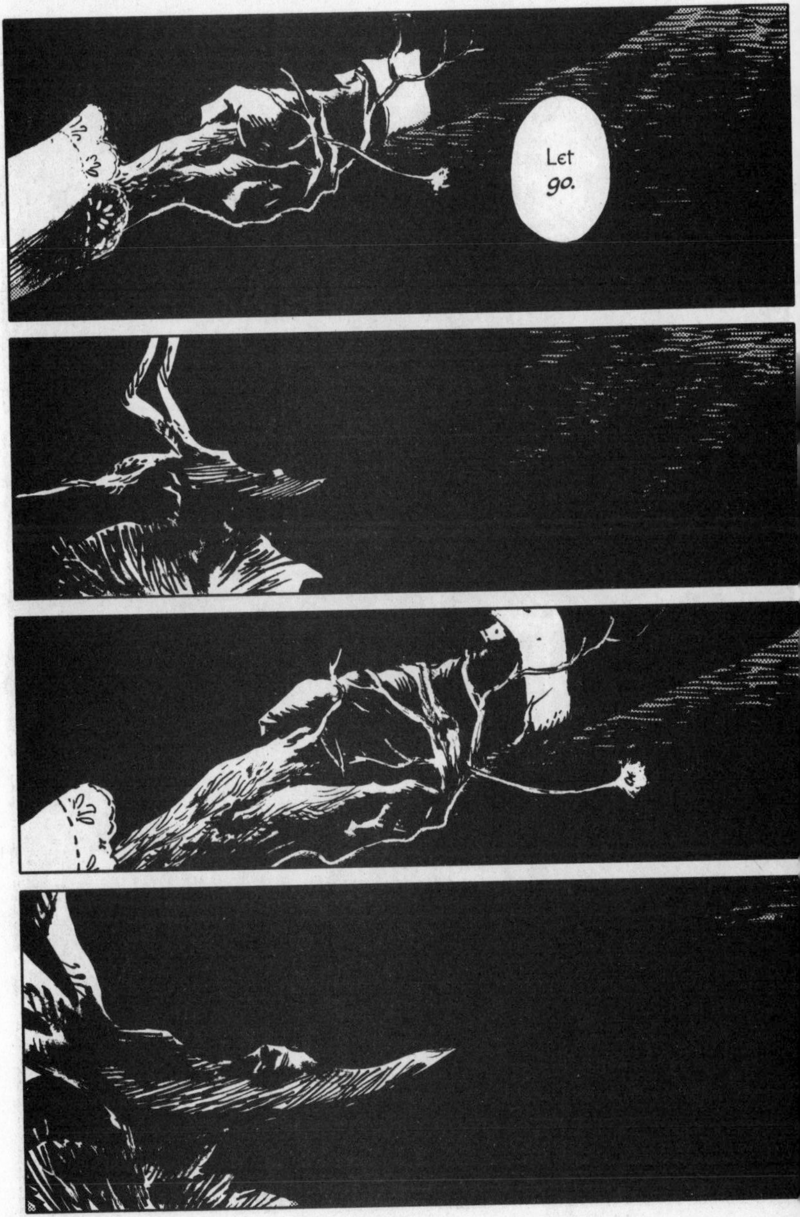
Let
go.

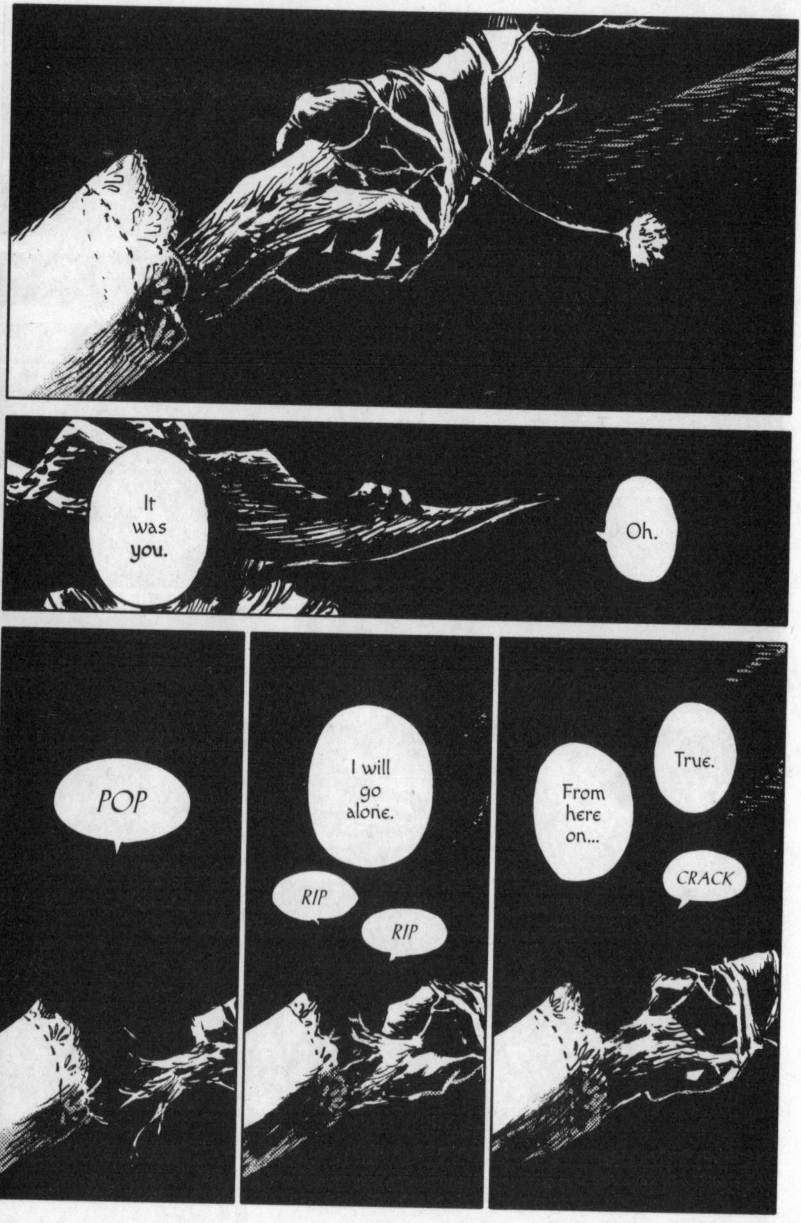
It was you.
Oh.
POP
I will go alone.
RIP
RIP
From here on...
True.
CRACK

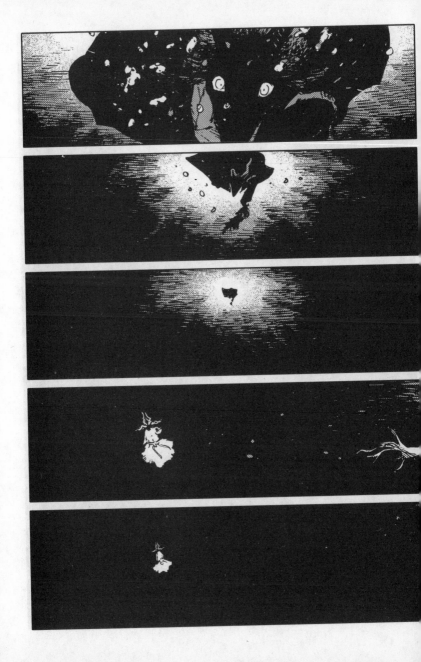

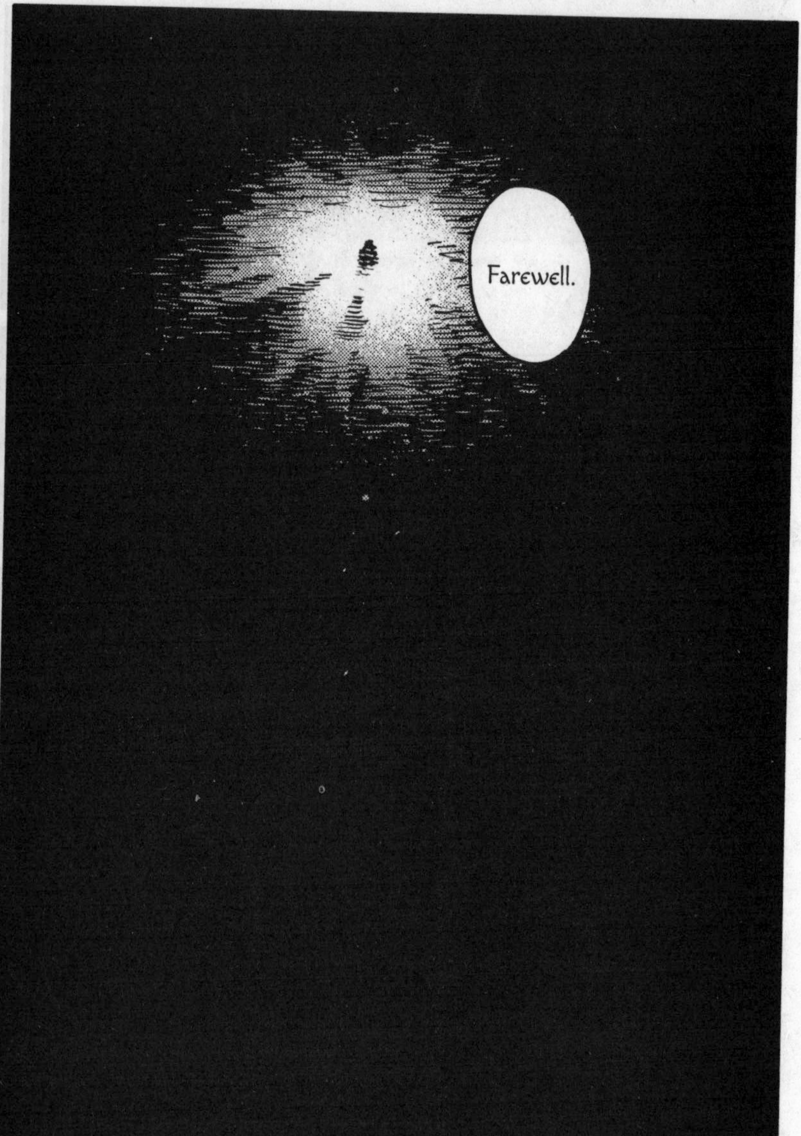
Farewell.

Chapter 52

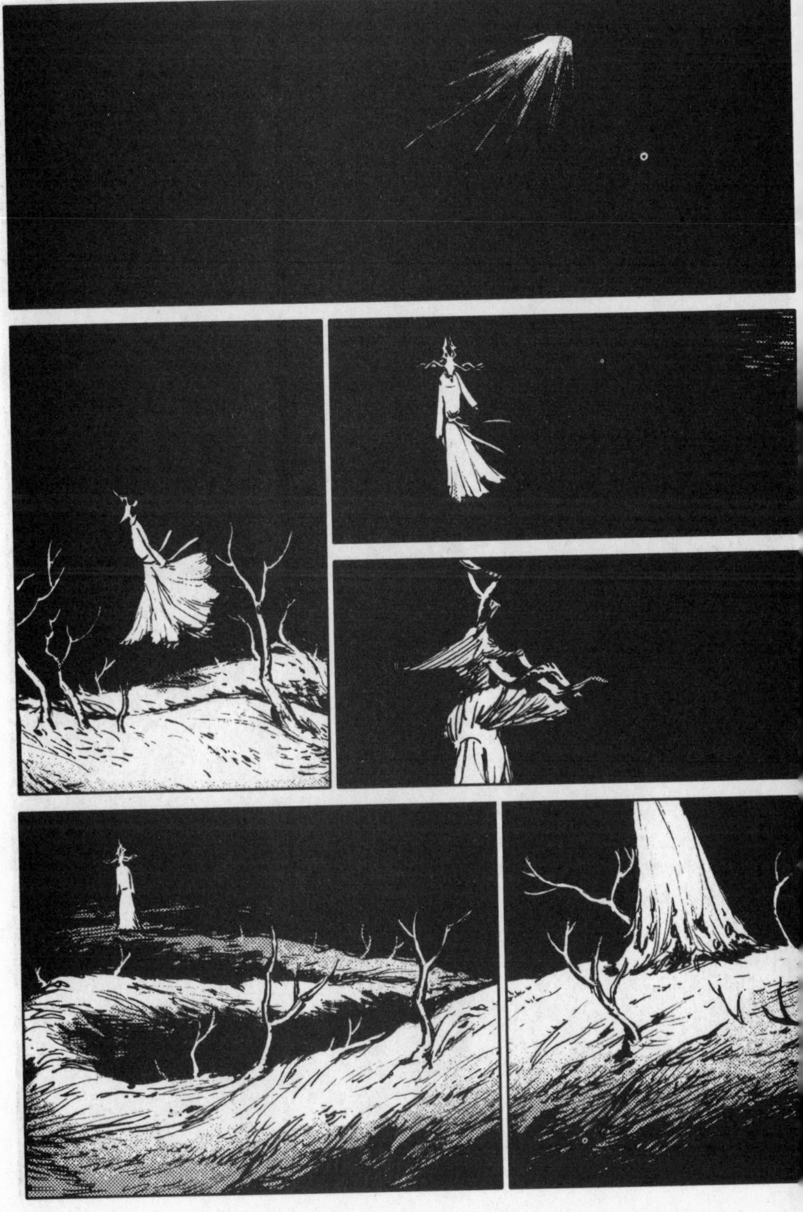

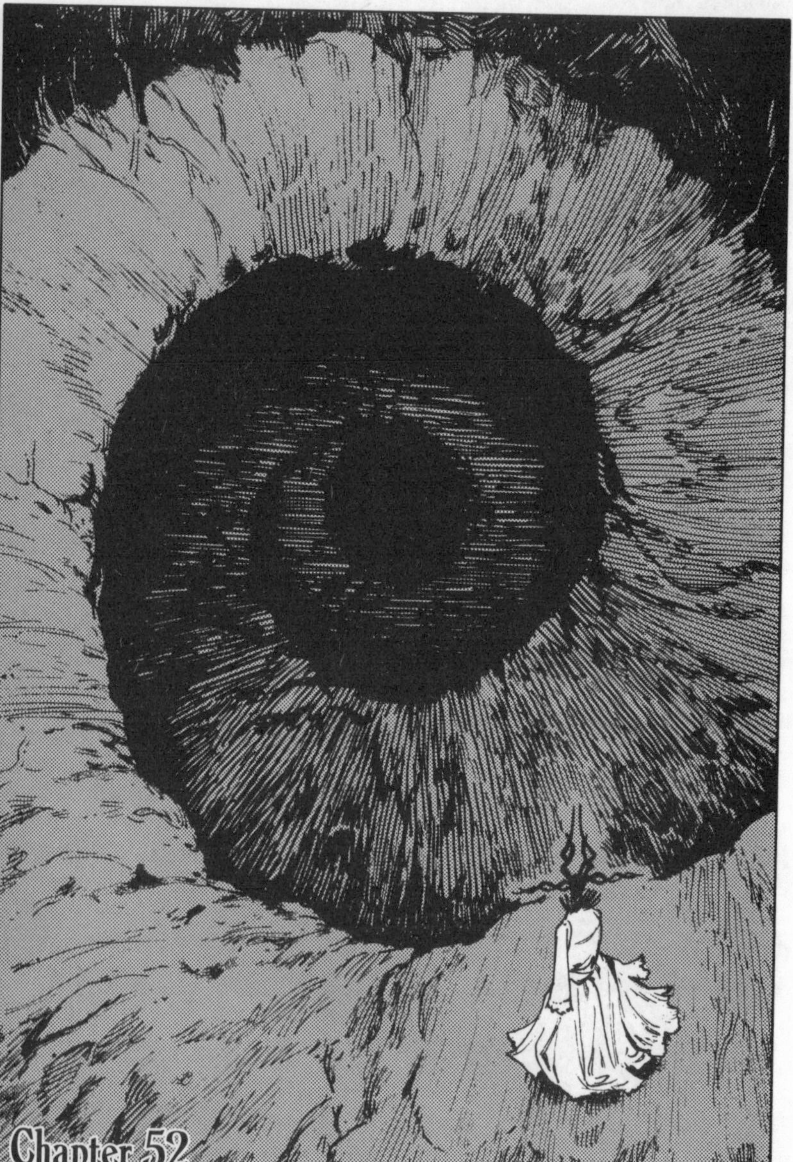
Chapter 52

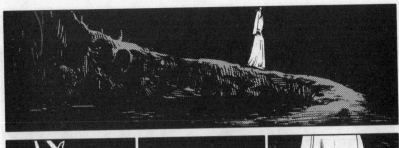

Mother.
I'm back.

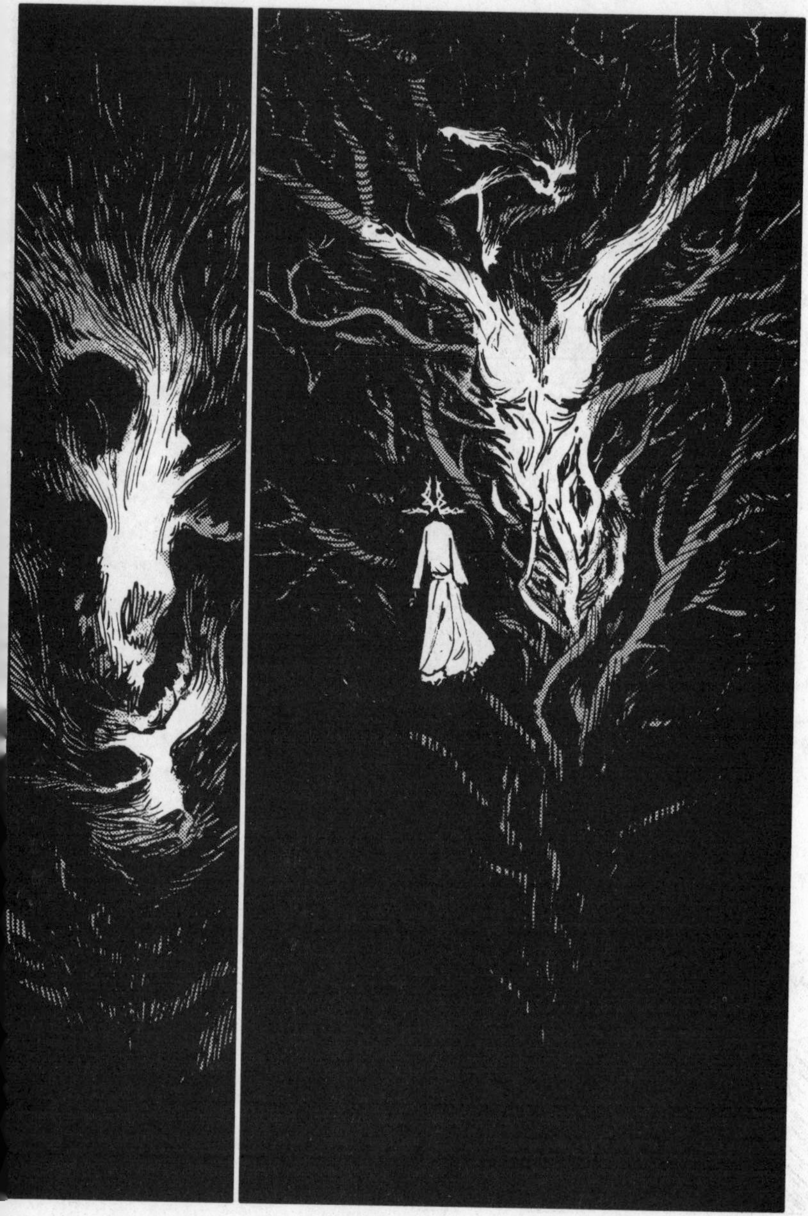

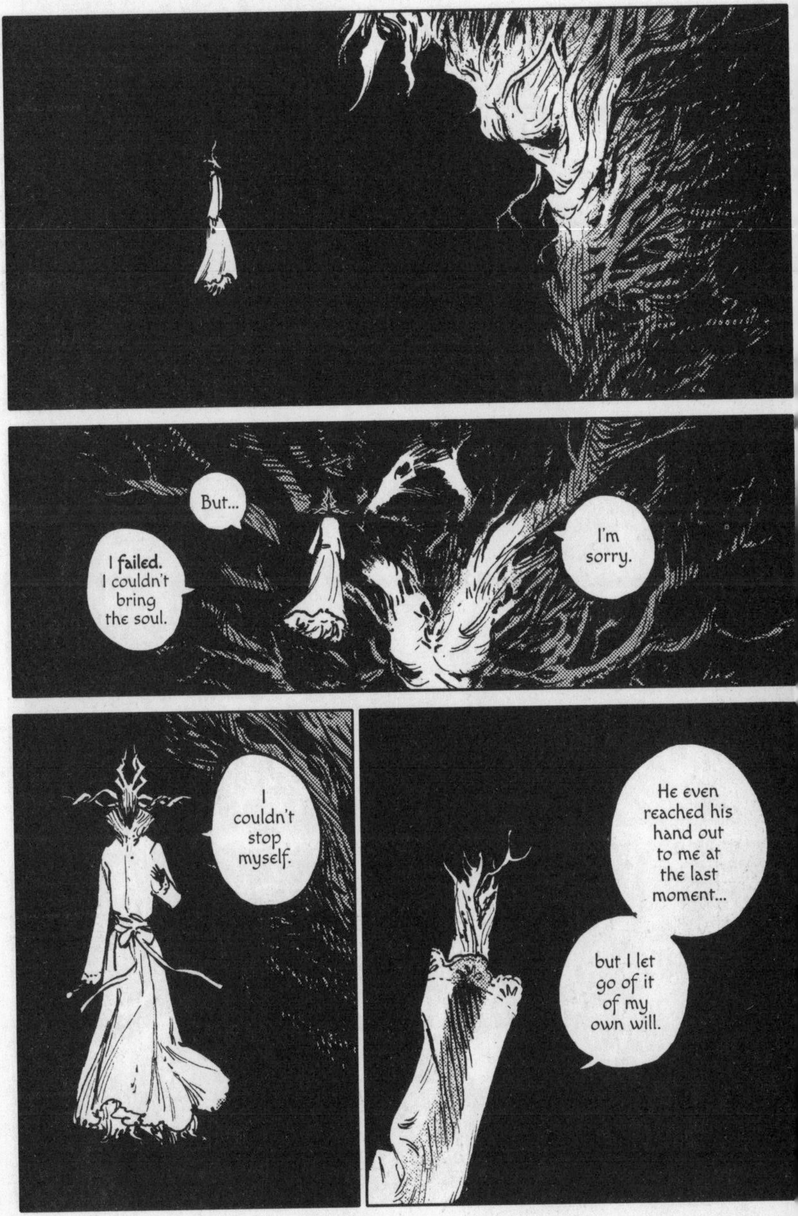
I'm sorry.
But...
I **failed.** I couldn't bring the soul.
He even reached his hand out to me at the last moment...
but I let go of it of my own will.
I couldn't stop myself.

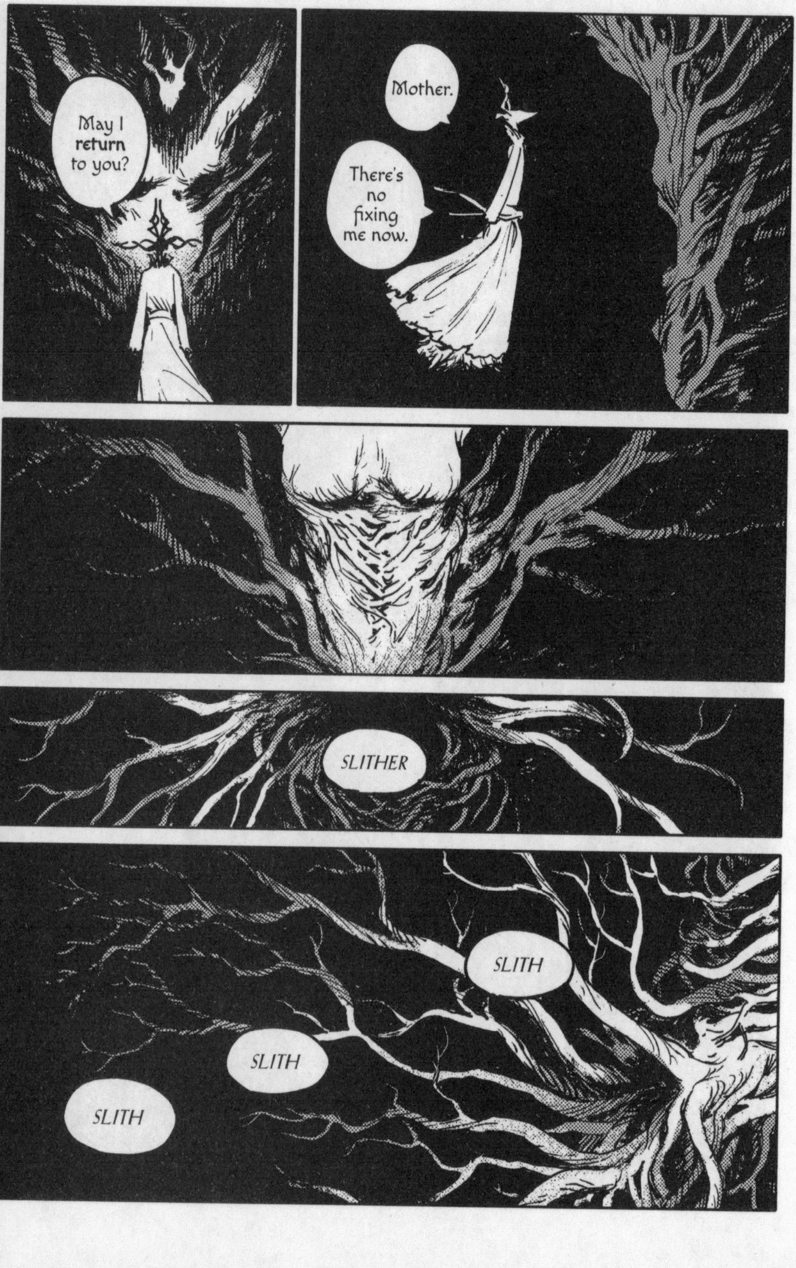
Mother.
There's no fixing me now.
May I return to you?
SLITHER
SLITH
SLITH
SLITH

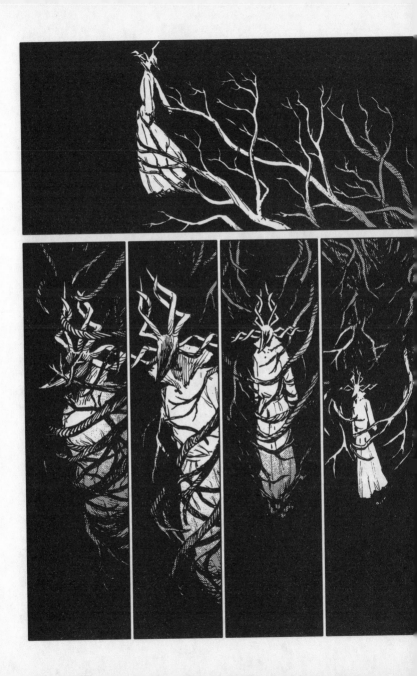

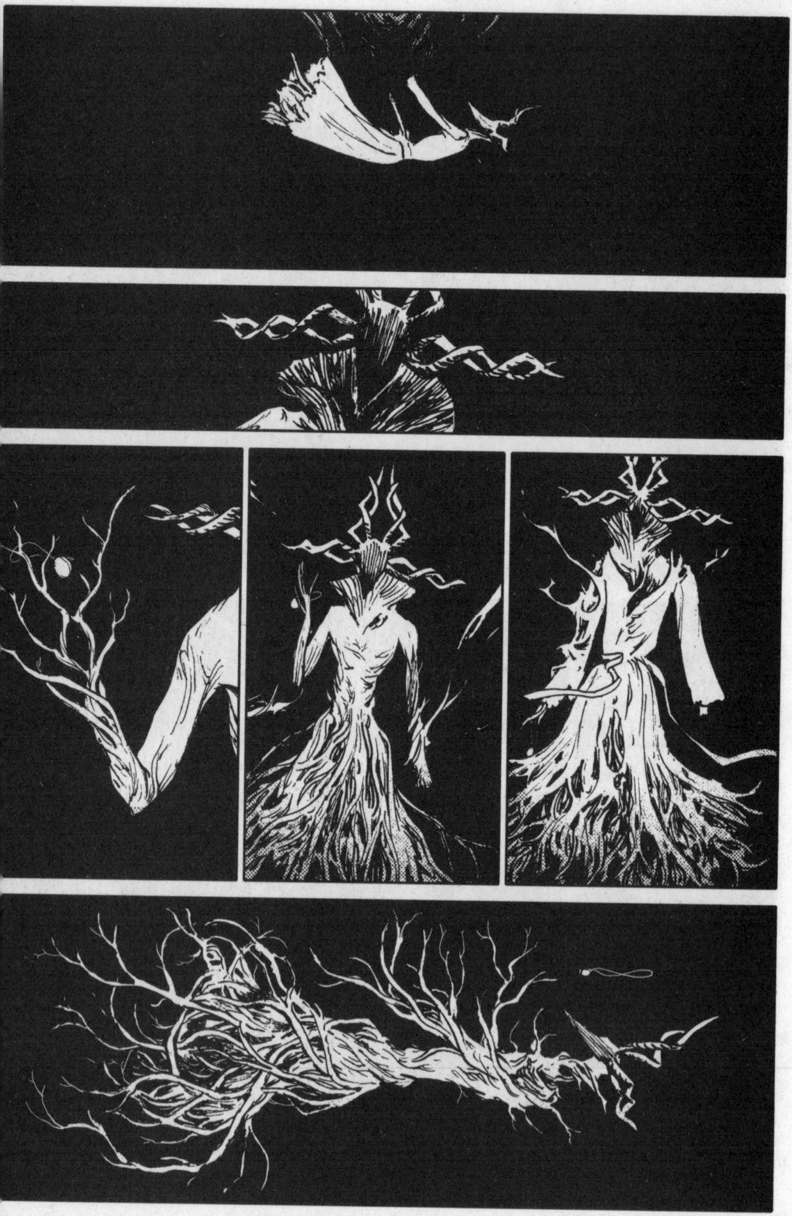

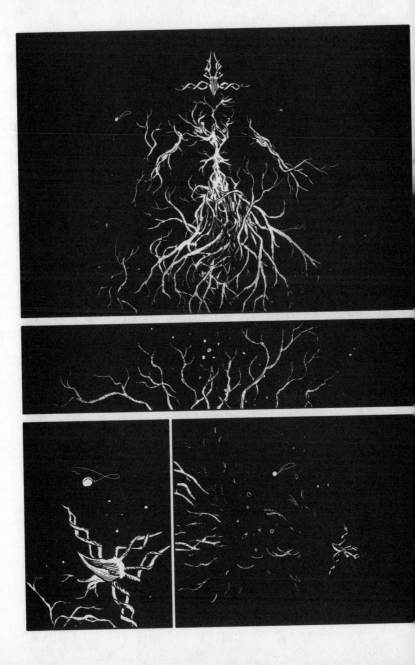

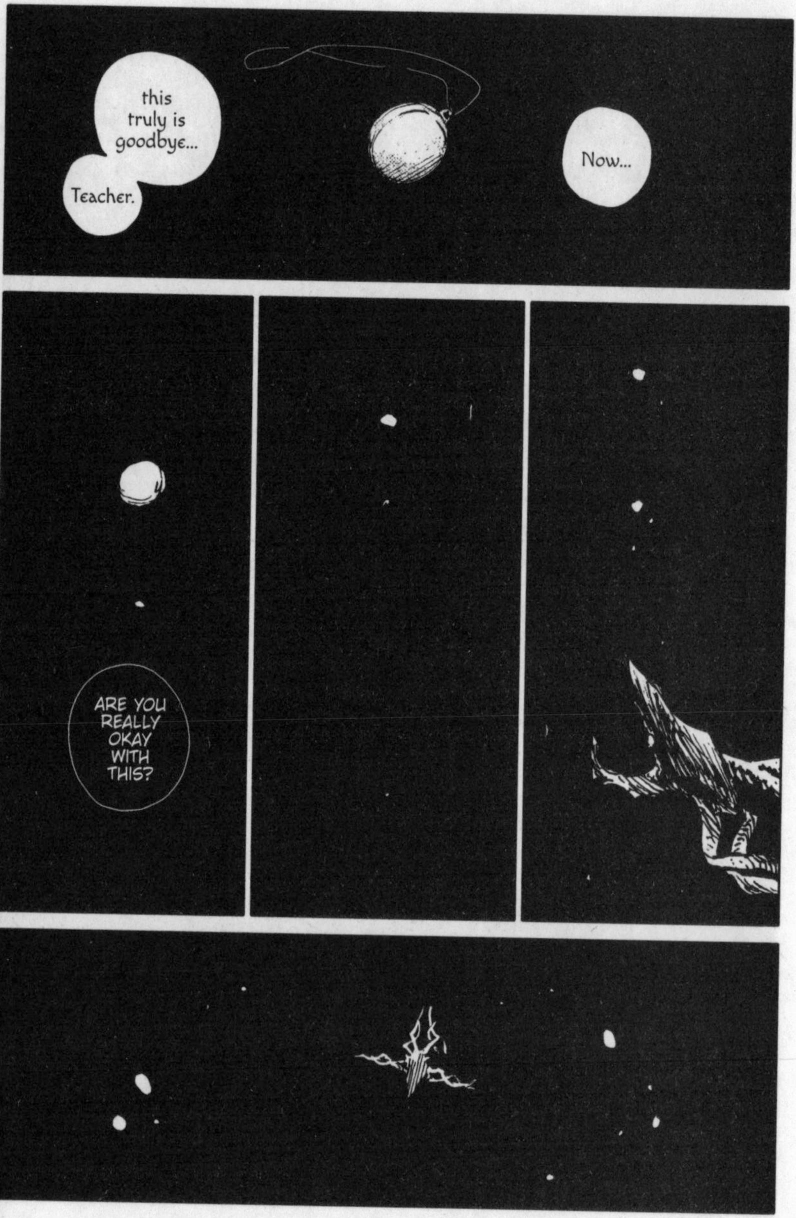
Now...
this truly is goodbye...
Teacher.
ARE YOU REALLY OKAY WITH THIS?

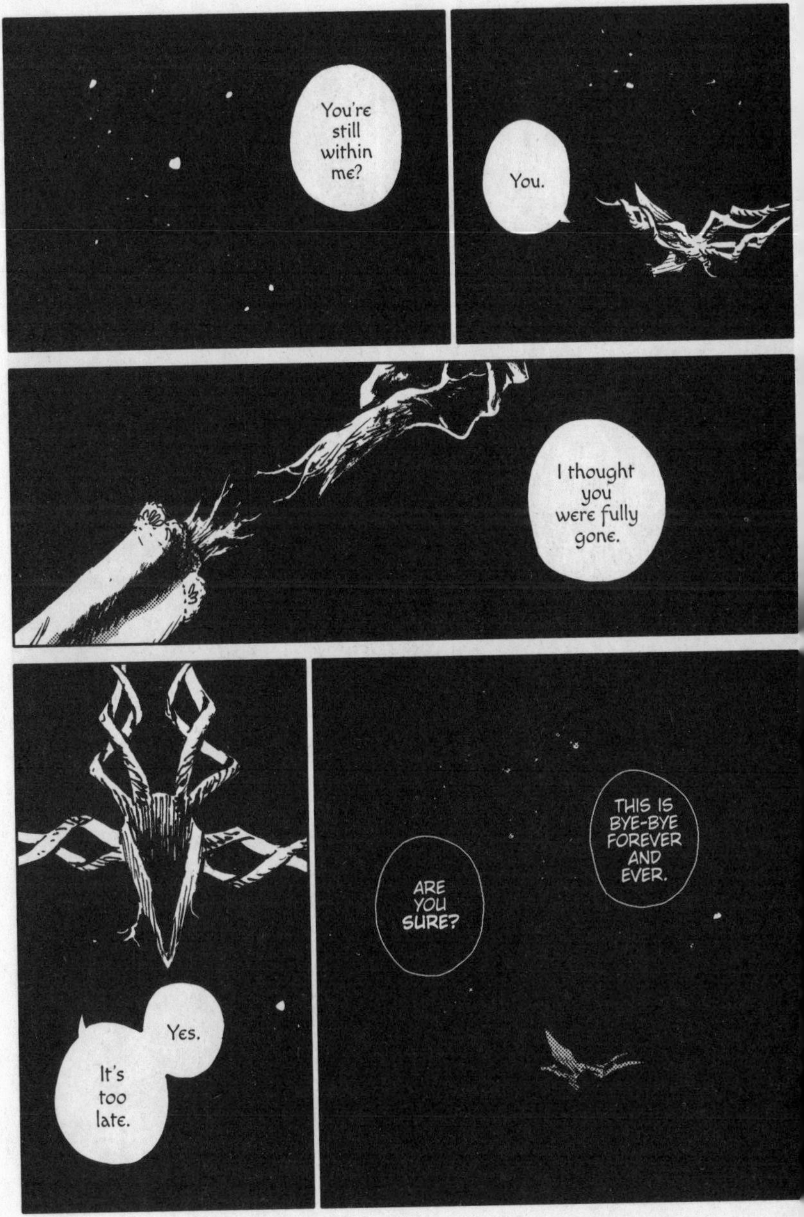
You.
You're still within me?
I thought you were fully gone.
THIS IS BYE-BYE FOREVER AND EVER.
ARE YOU SURE?
Yes.
It's too late.

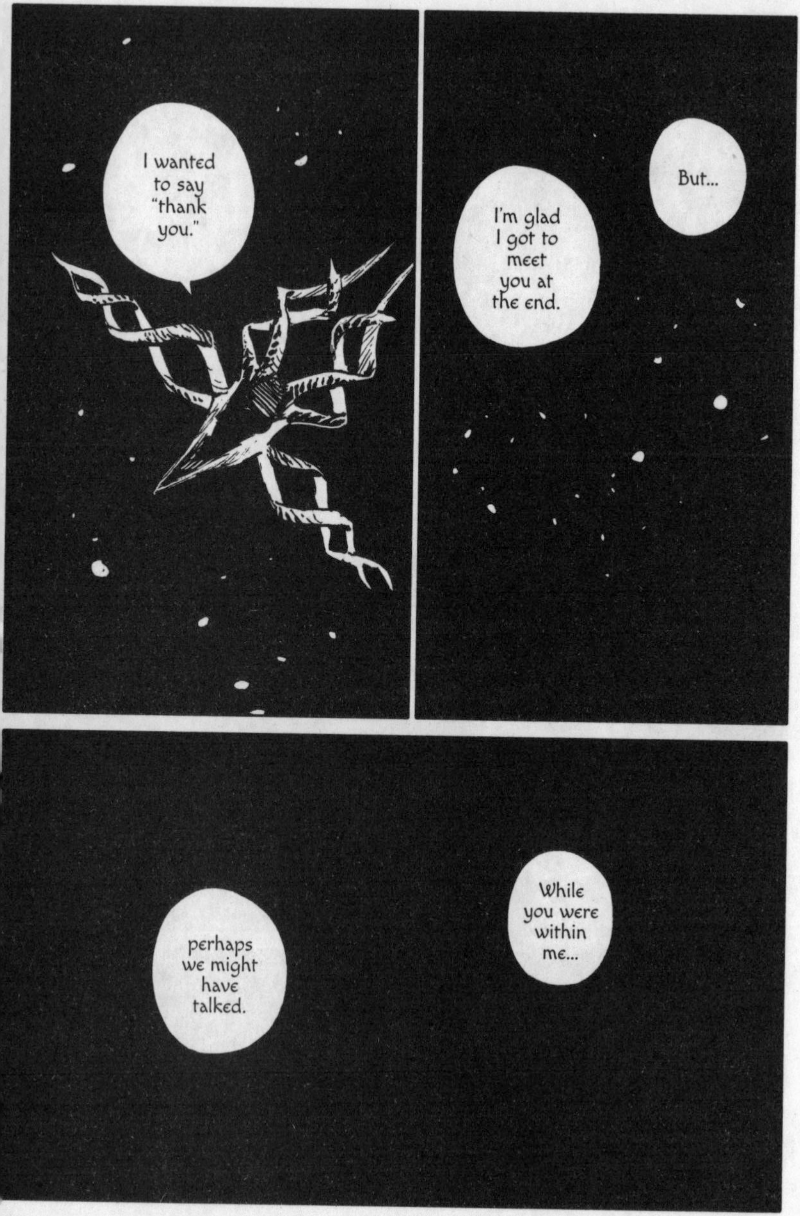
But...
I'm glad I got to meet you at the end.
I wanted to say "thank you."
While you were within me...
perhaps we might have talked.

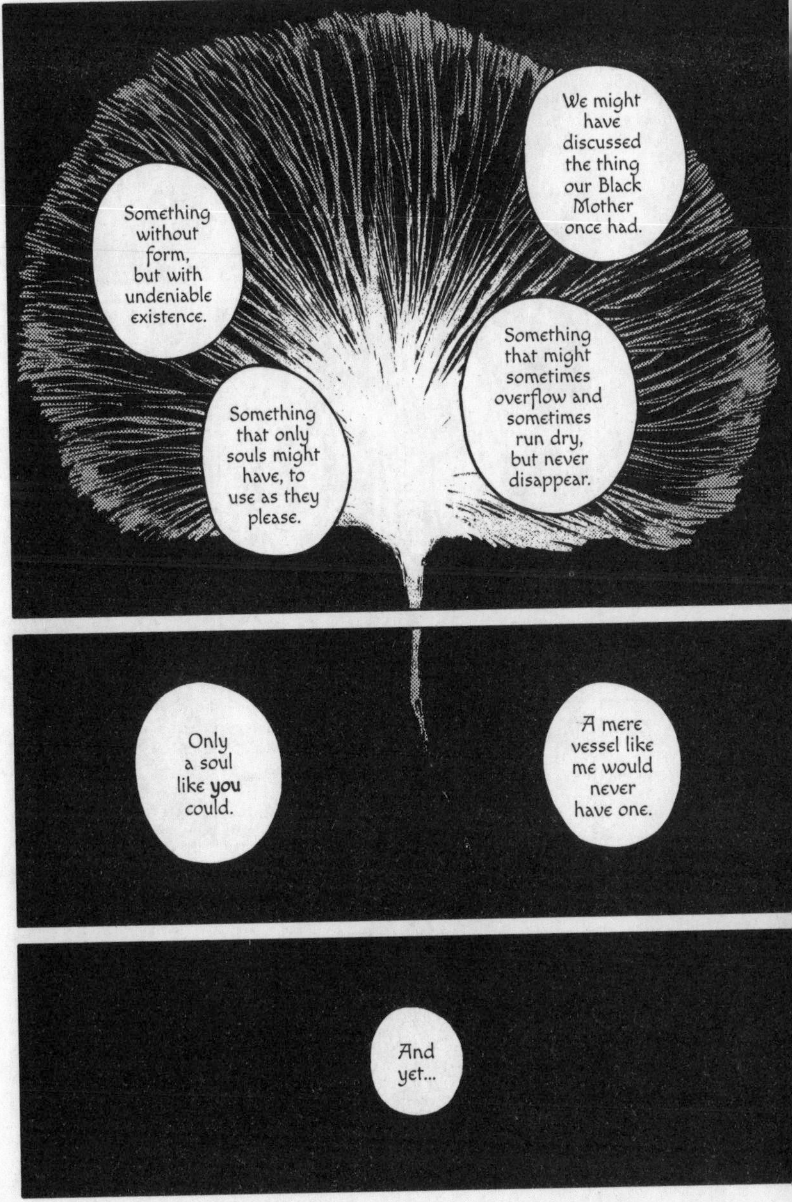
We might have discussed the thing our Black Mother once had.
Something without form, but with undeniable existence.
Something that might sometimes overflow and sometimes run dry, but never disappear.
Something that only souls might have, to use as they please.
A mere vessel like me would never have one.
Only a soul like you could.
And yet...

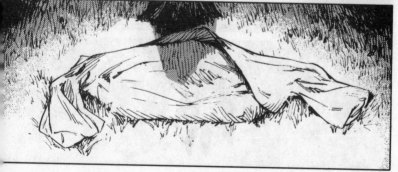

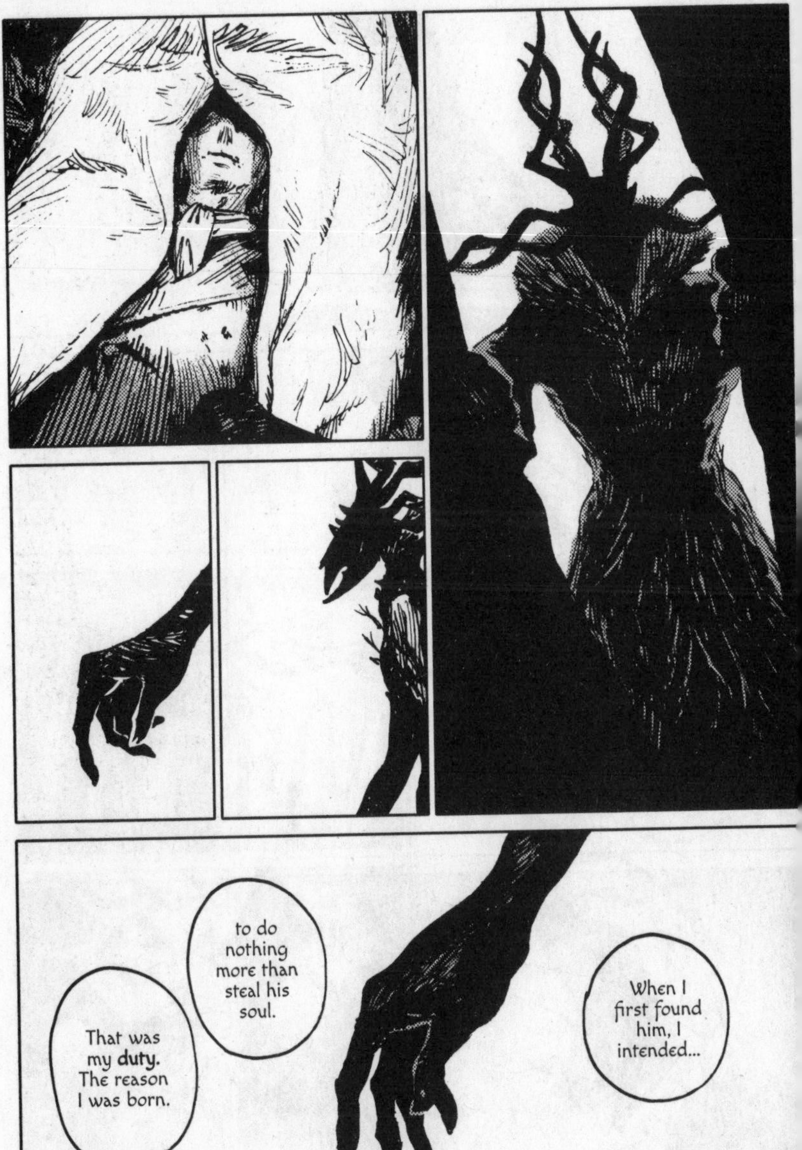
When I first found him, I intended...
to do nothing more than steal his soul.
That was my **duty.** The reason I was born.

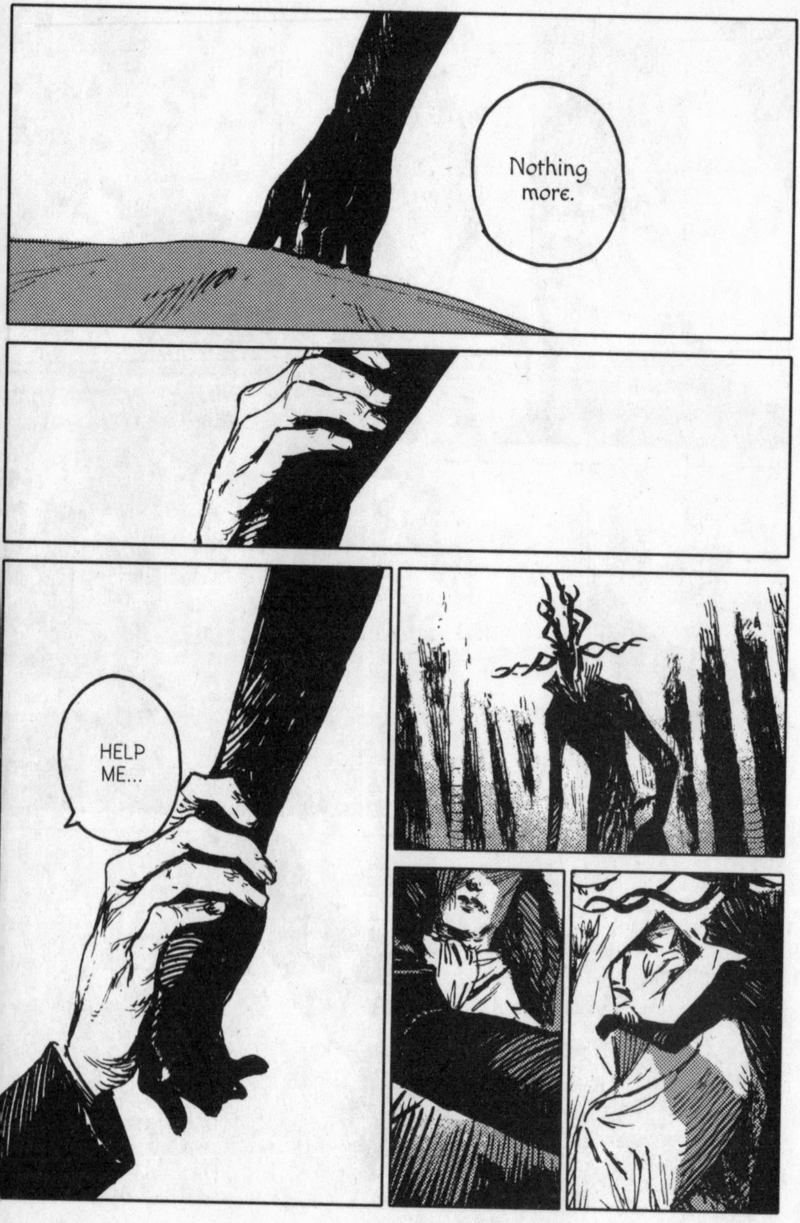
Nothing more.
HELP ME...

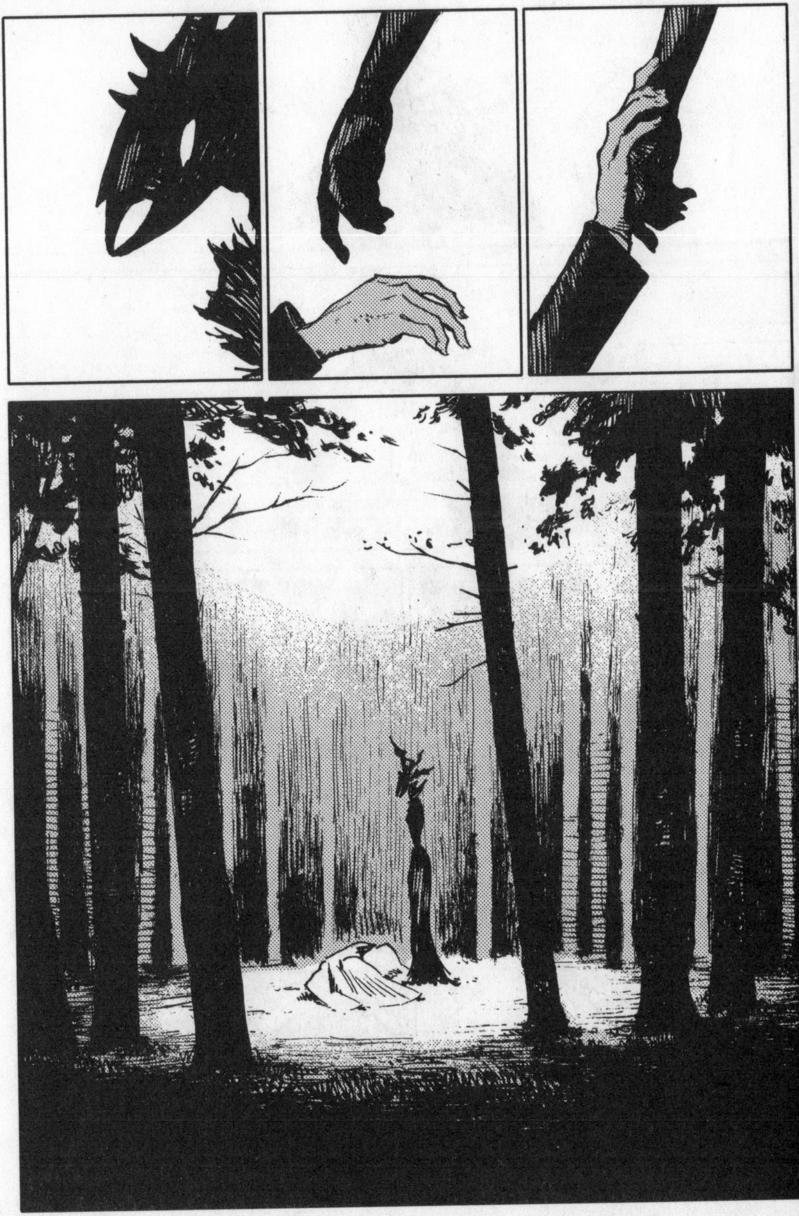

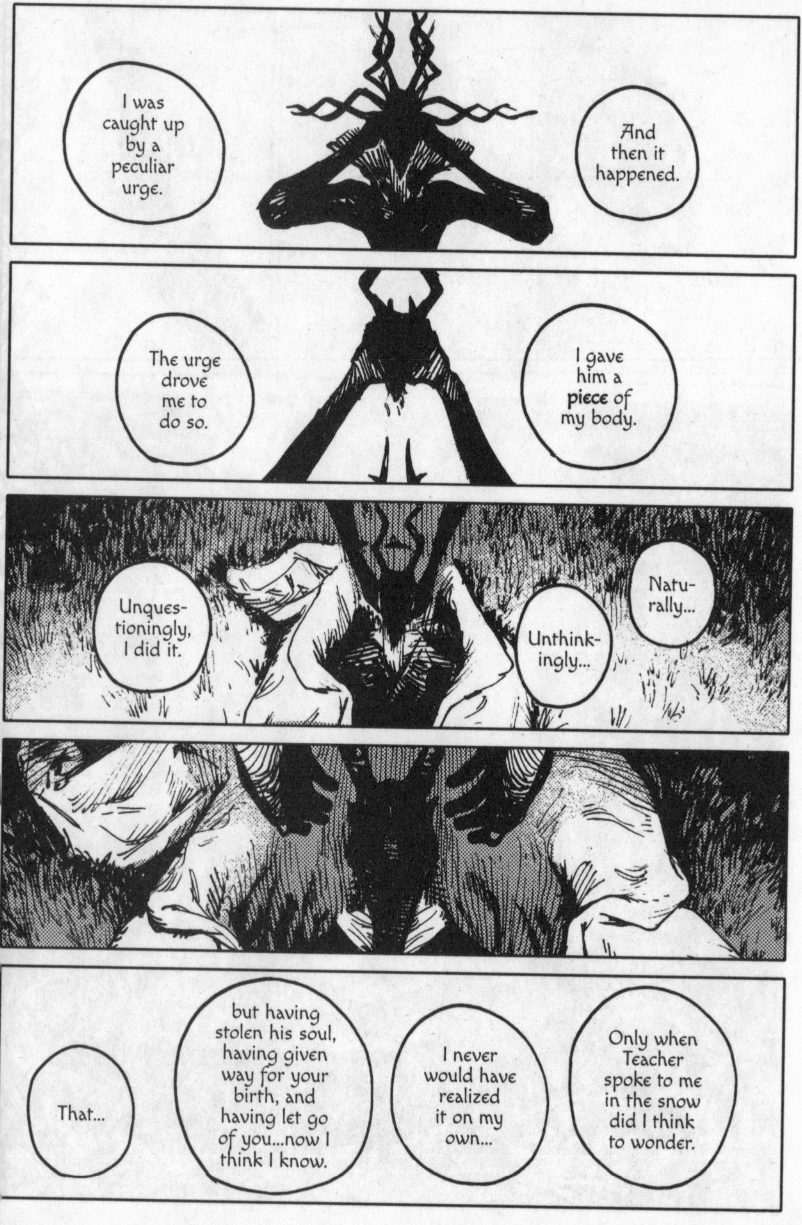
And then it happened.
I was caught up by a peculiar urge.
I gave him a **piece** of my body.
The urge drove me to do so.
Naturally...
Unthinkingly...
Unquestioningly, I did it.
Only when Teacher spoke to me in the snow did I think to wonder.
I never would have realized it on my own...
but having stolen his soul, having given way for your birth, and having let go of you...now I think I know.
That...

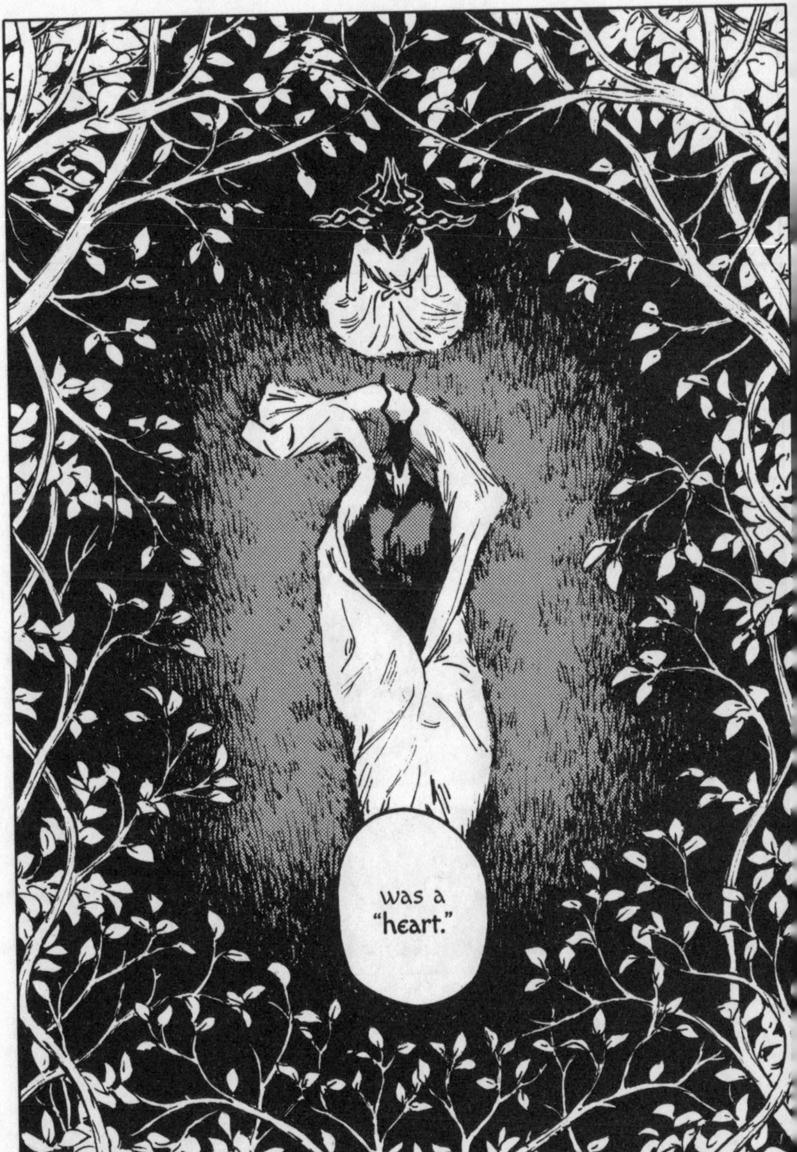
was a "heart."

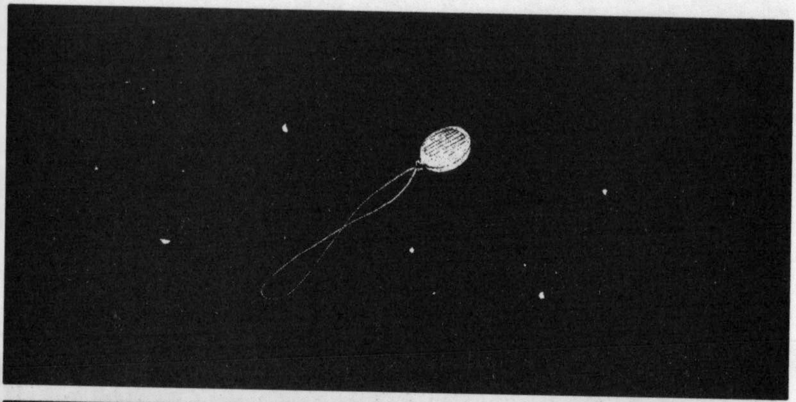
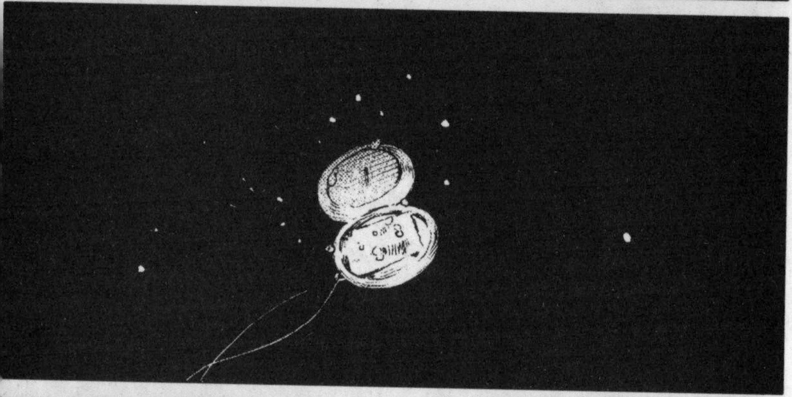
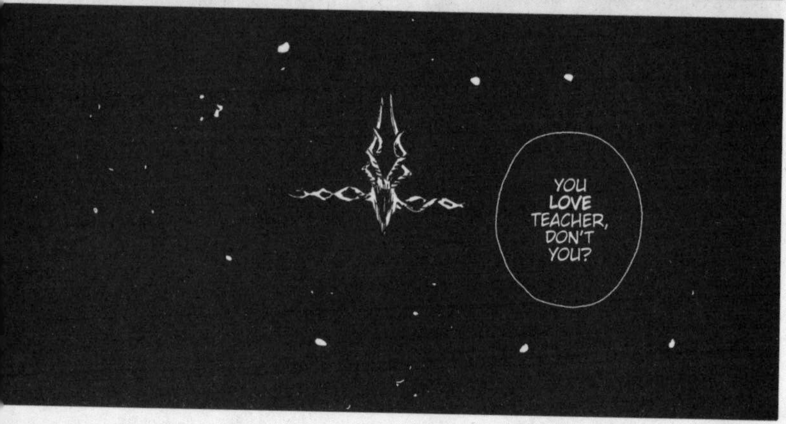
YOU LOVE TEACHER, DON'T YOU?

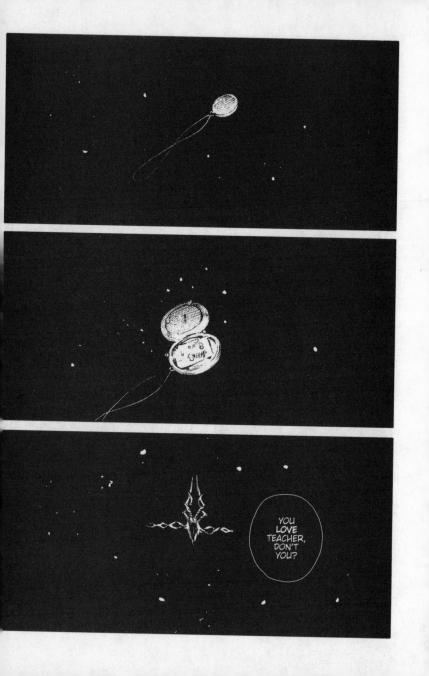

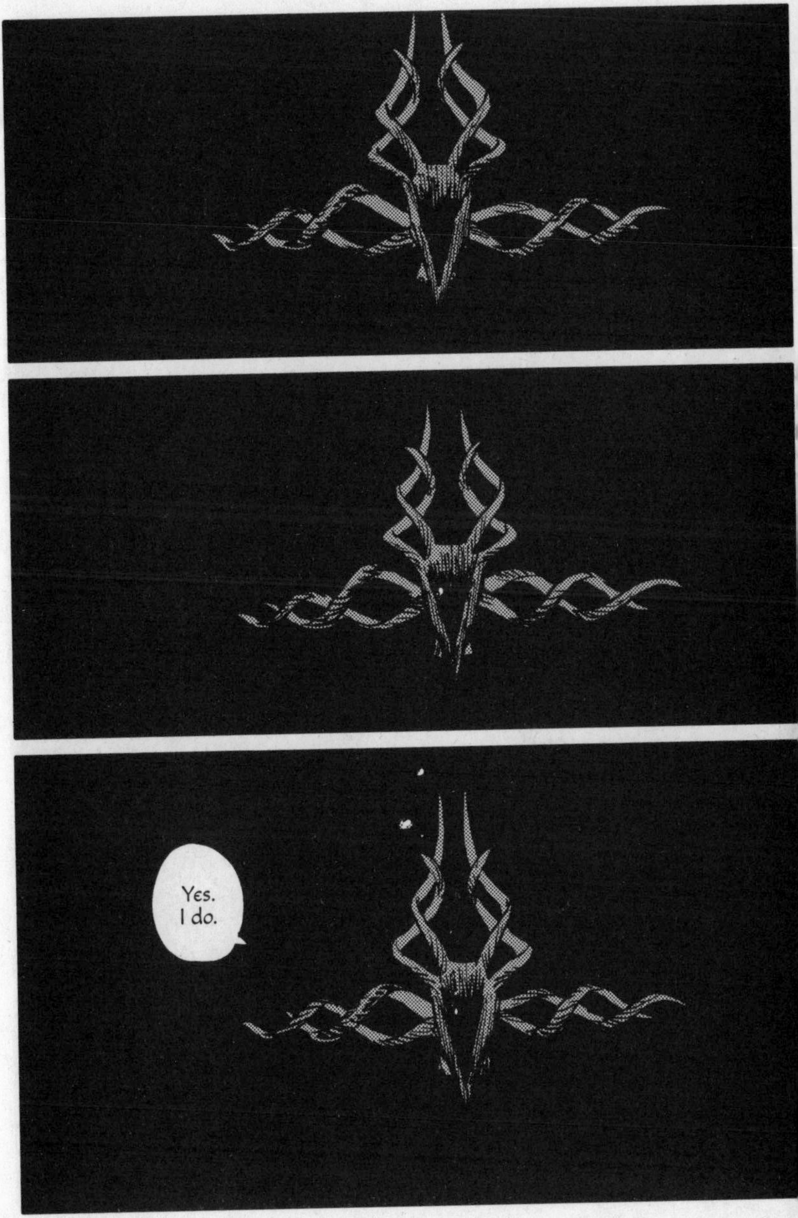
Yes.
I do.

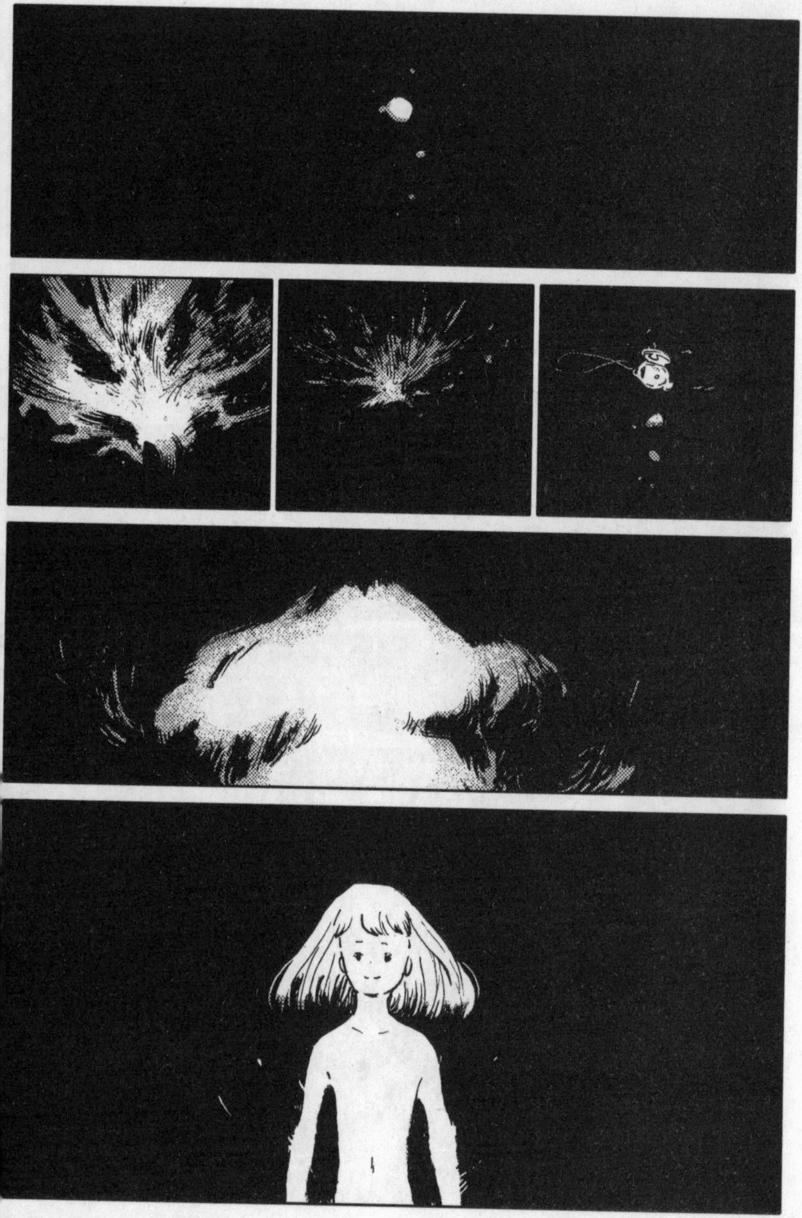

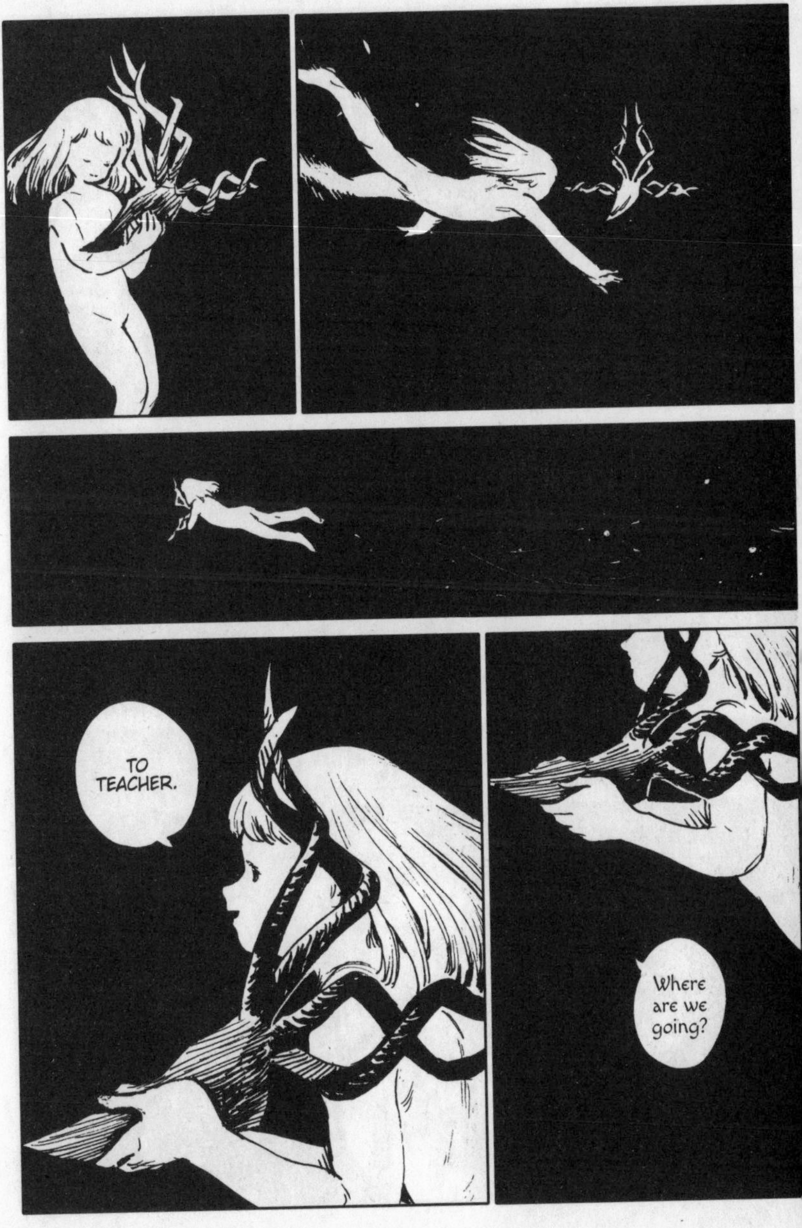
Where are we going?
TO TEACHER.

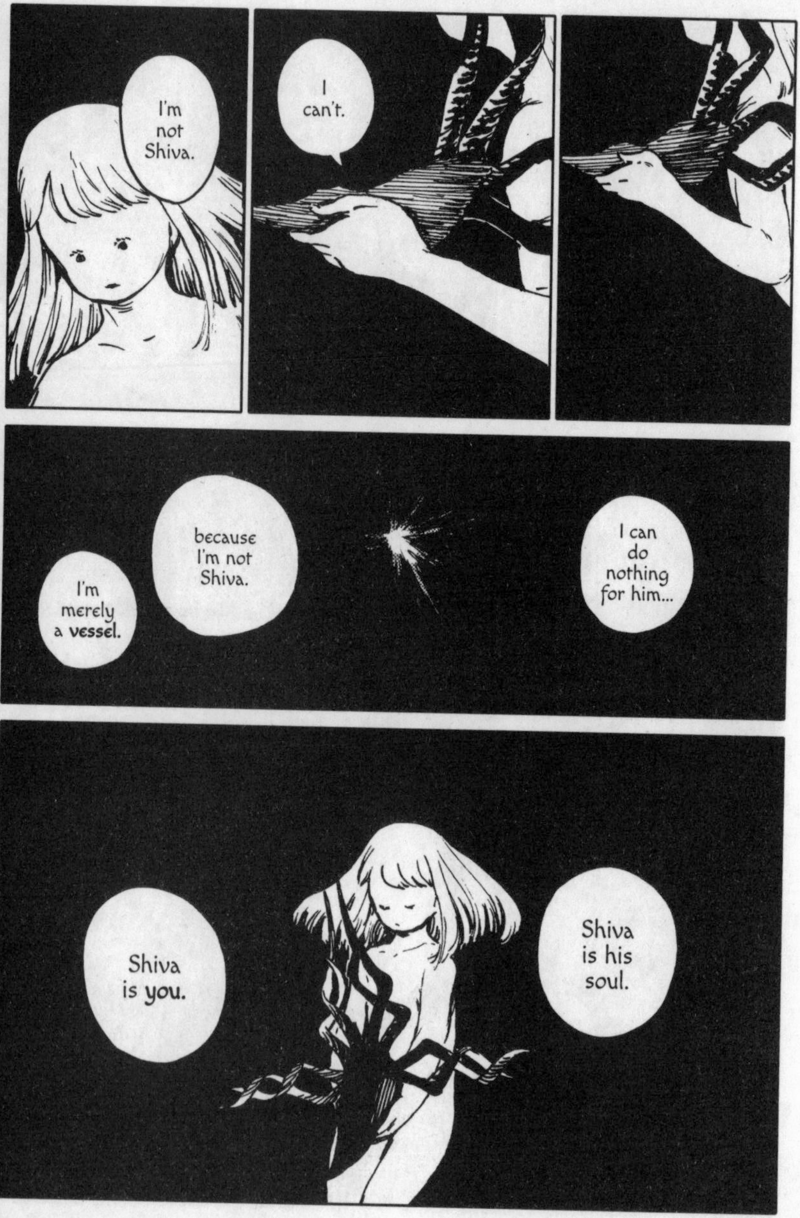
I can't.
I'm not Shiva.
I can do nothing for him...
because I'm not Shiva.
I'm merely a vessel.
Shiva is his soul.
Shiva is you.

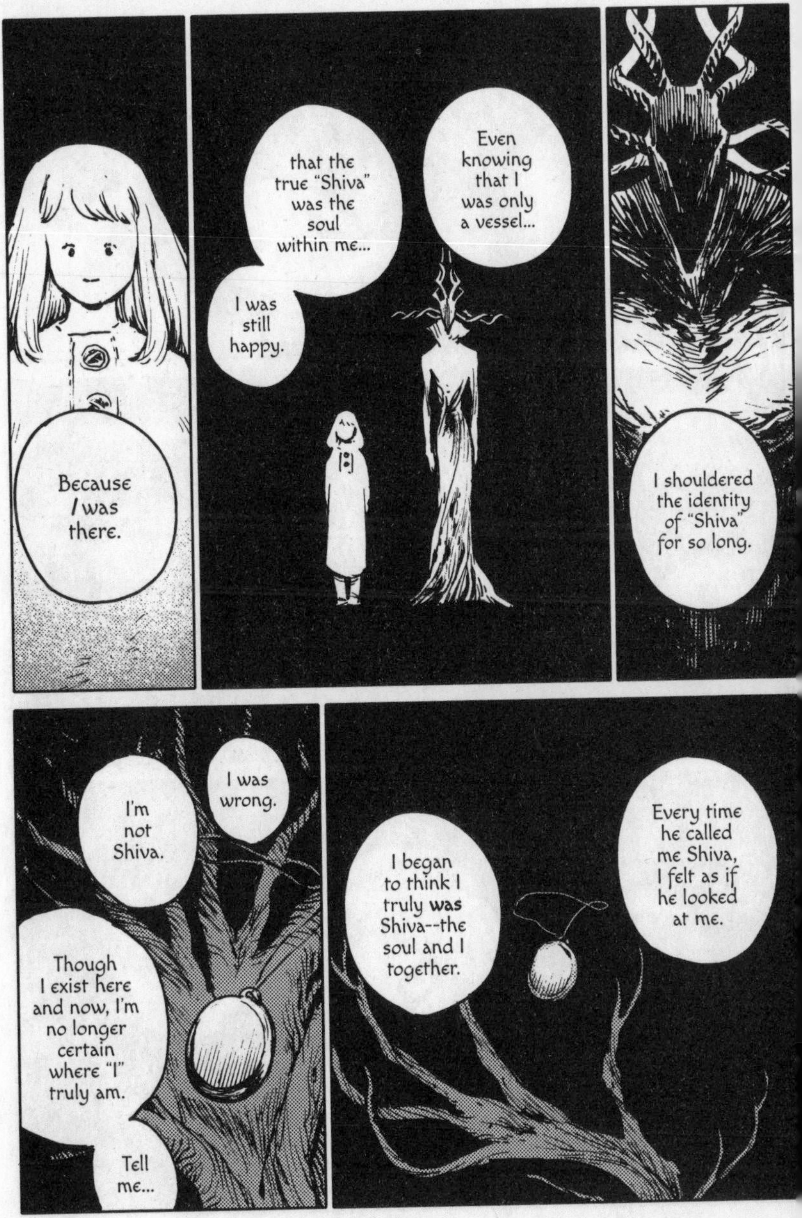
I shouldered the identity of "Shiva" for so long.
Even knowing that I was only a vessel...
that the true "Shiva" was the soul within me...
I was still happy.
Because *I* was there.
Every time he called me Shiva, I felt as if he looked at me.
I began to think I truly **was** Shiva--the soul and I together.
I was wrong.
I'm not Shiva.
Though I exist here and now, I'm no longer certain where "I" truly am.
Tell me...

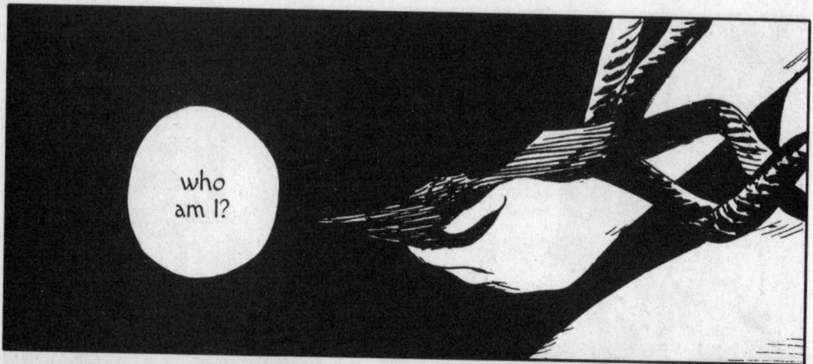
who
am I?
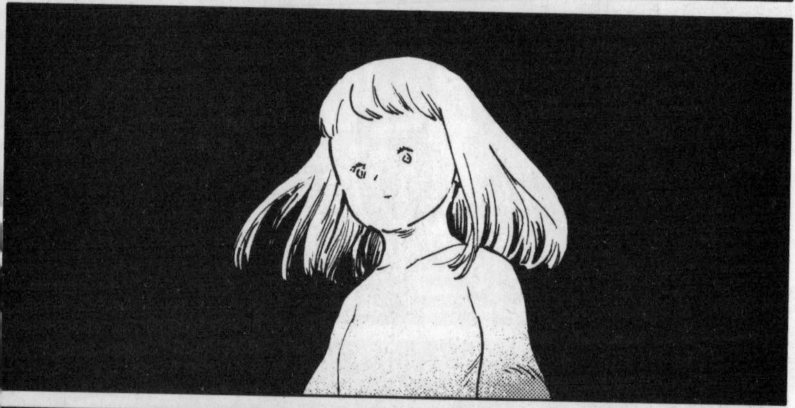
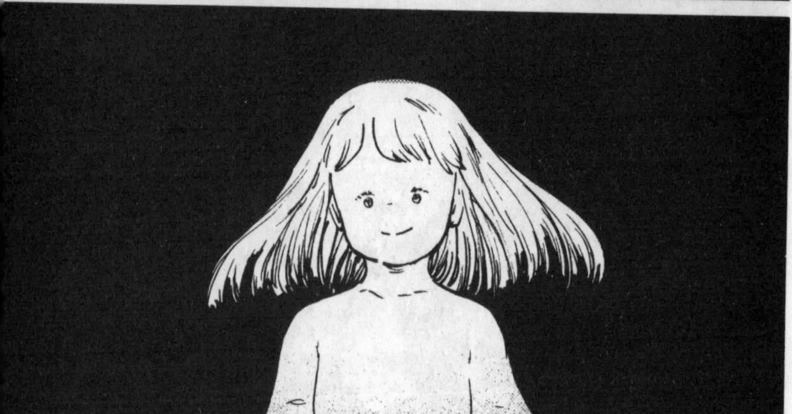

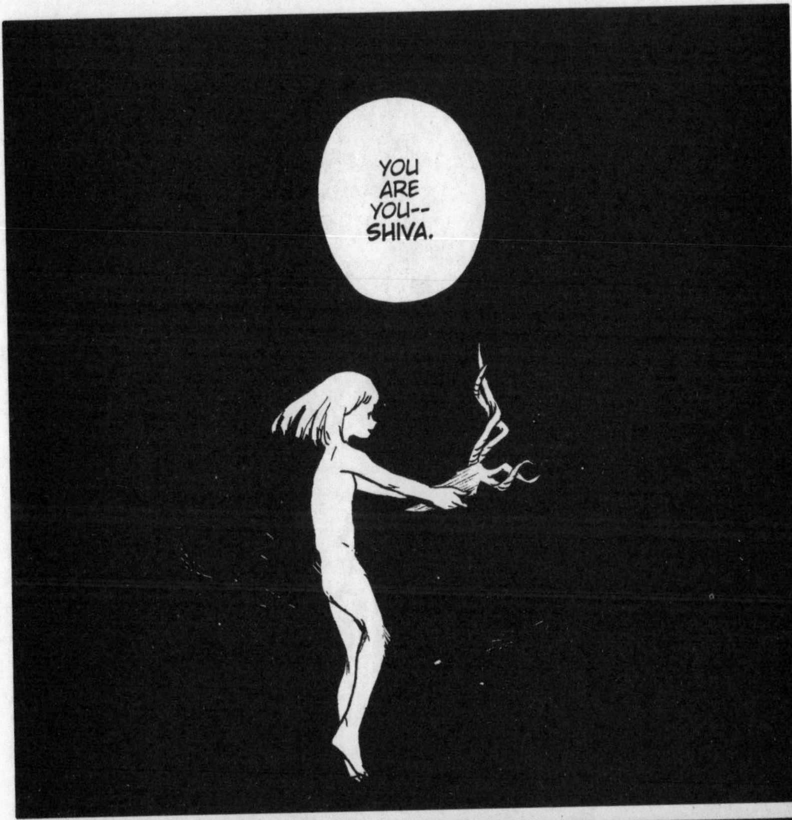
YOU ARE YOU-- SHIVA.
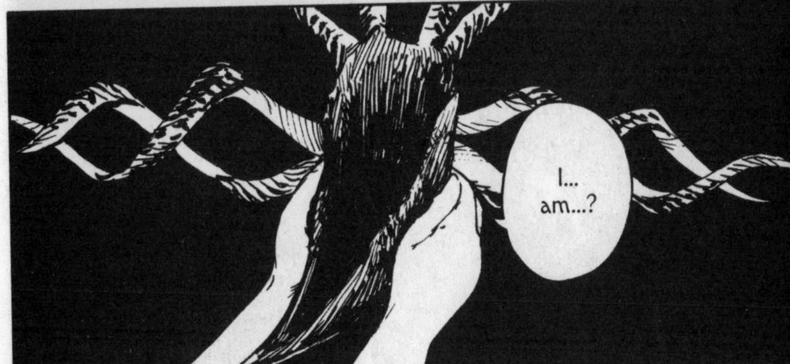
I... am...?

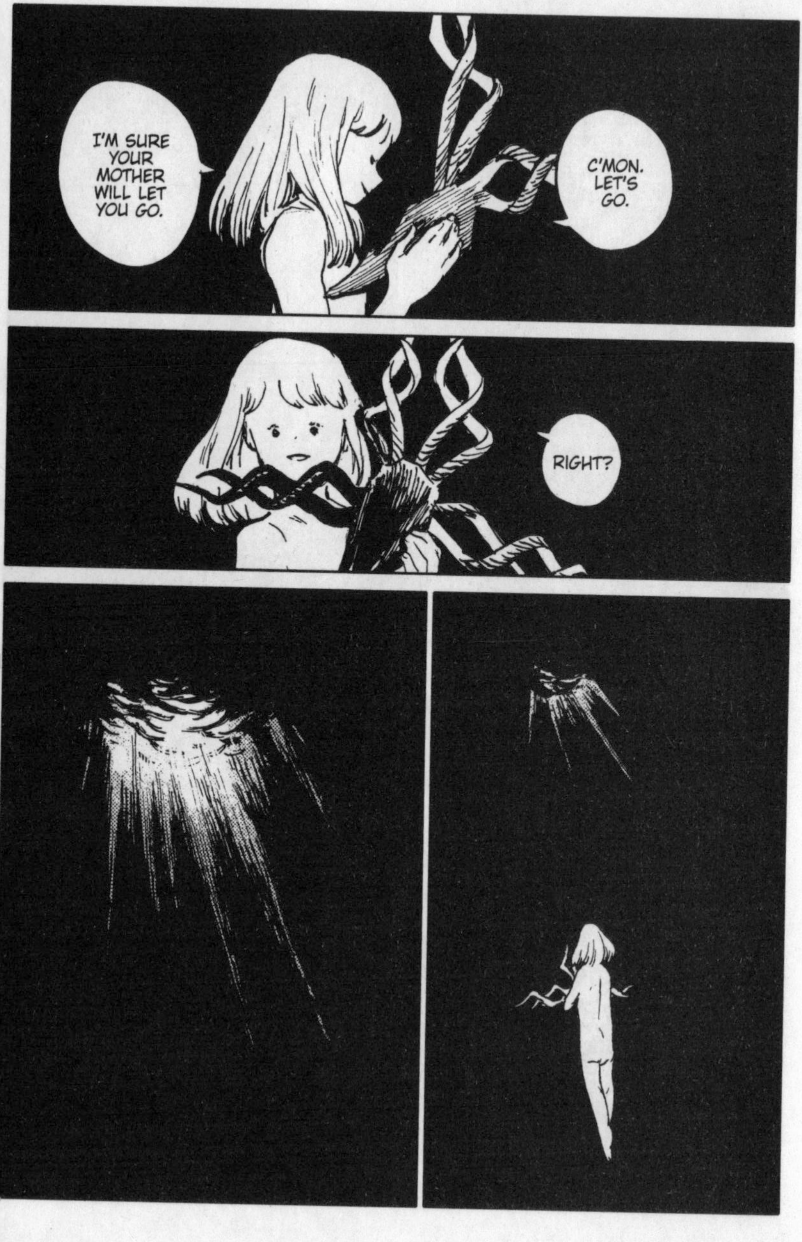
C'MON. LET'S GO.
I'M SURE YOUR MOTHER WILL LET YOU GO.
RIGHT?

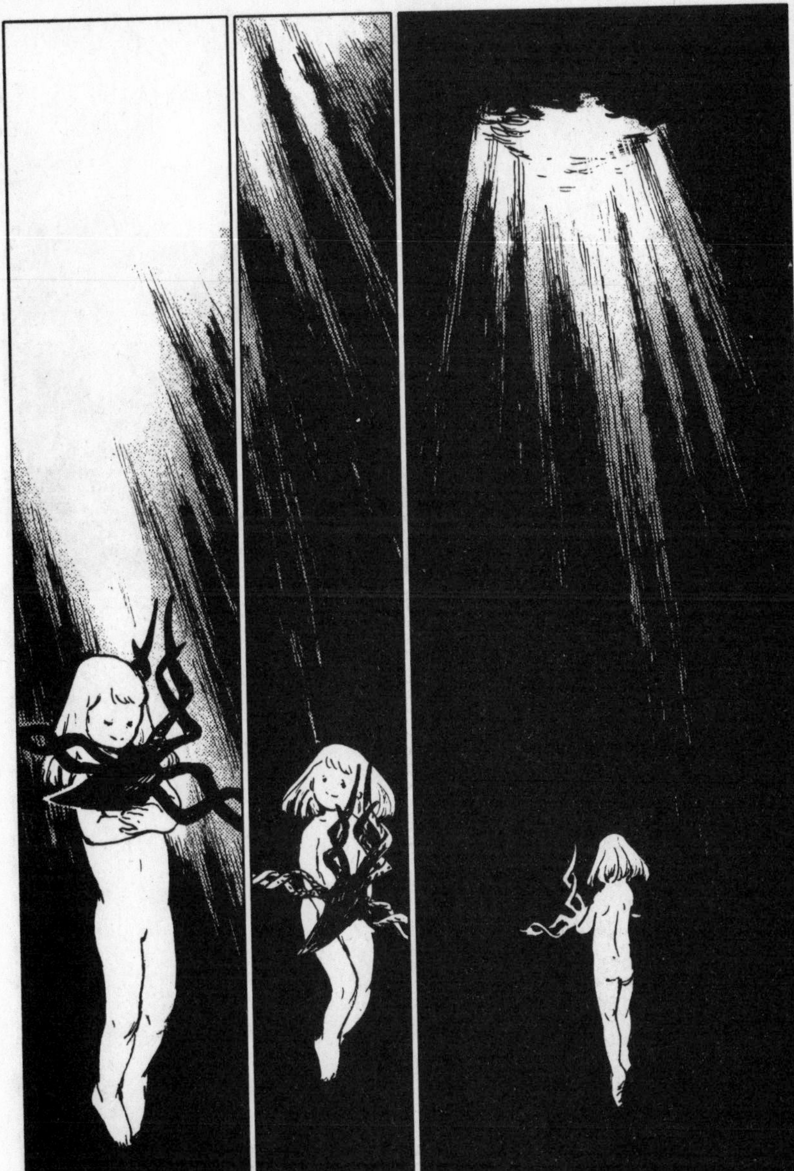

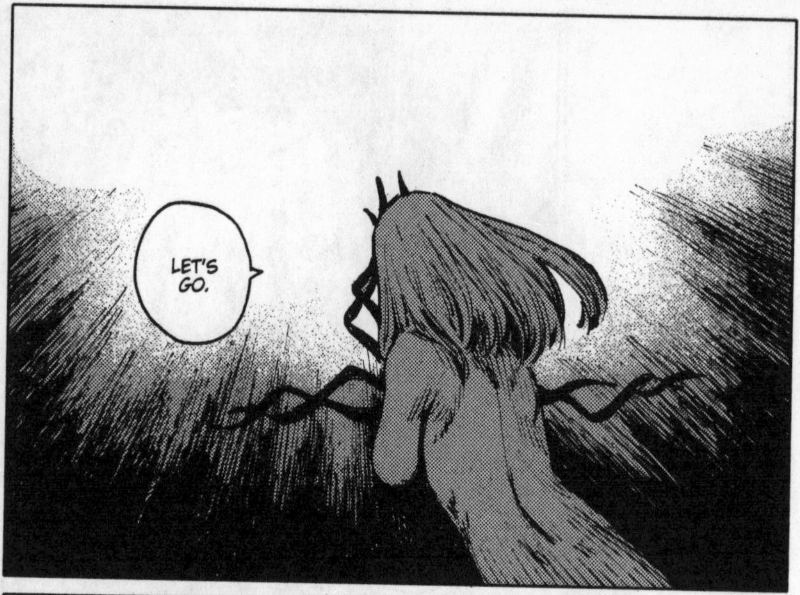
LET'S GO.
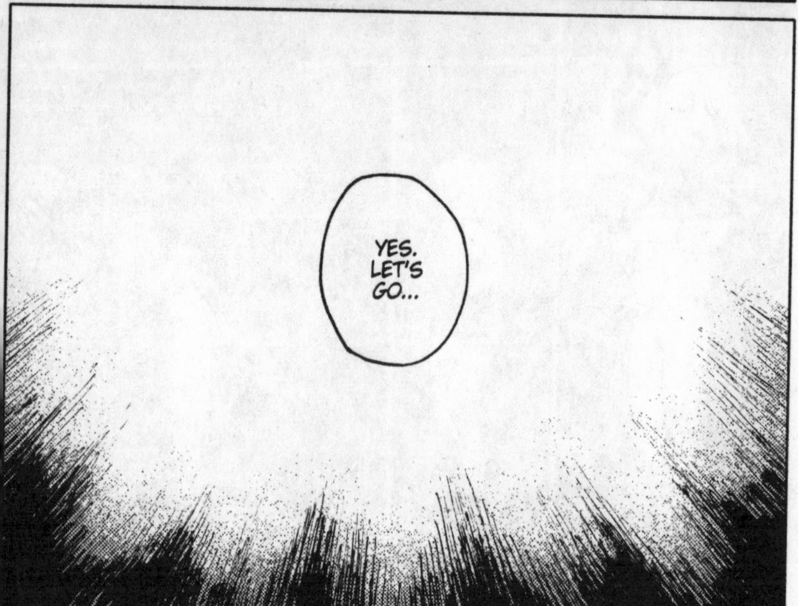
YES. LET'S GO...

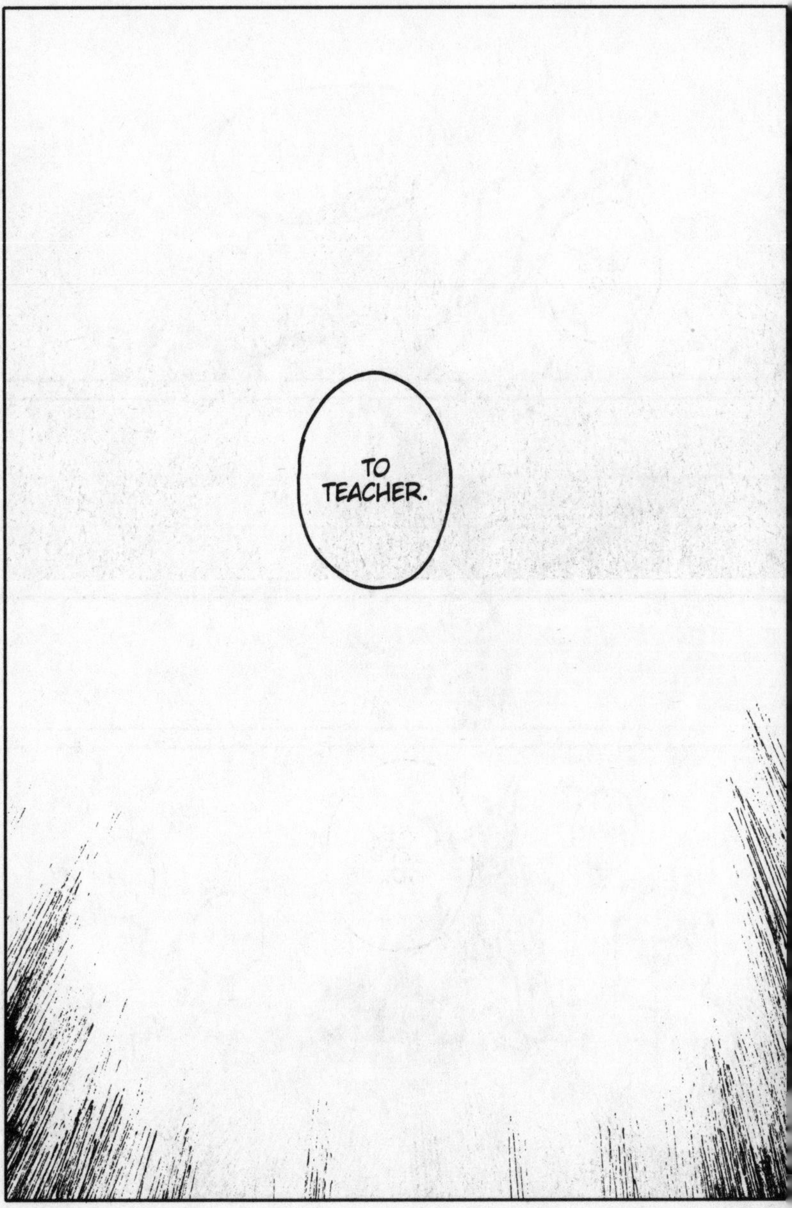
TO TEACHER.

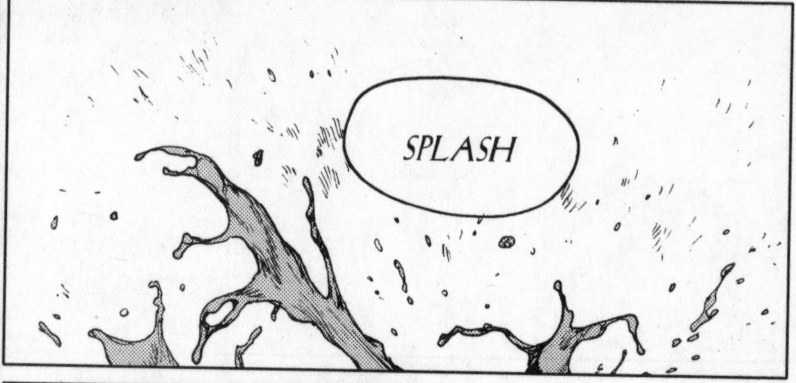
SPLASH
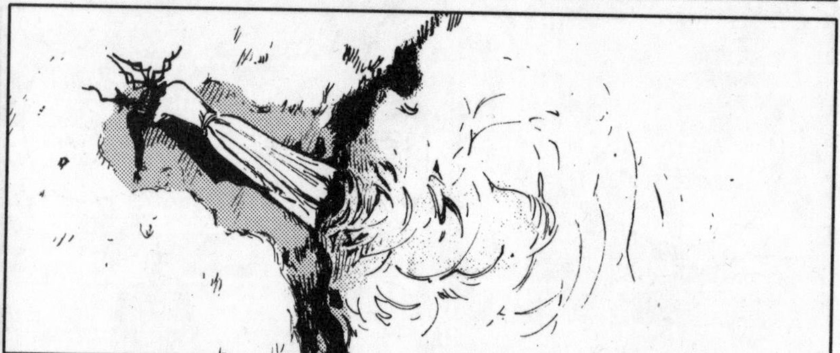
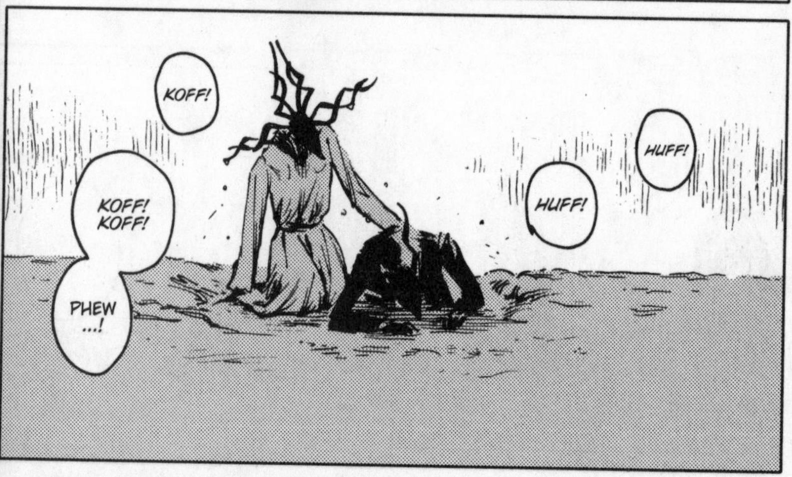
HUFF!
HUFF!
KOFF!
KOFF! KOFF!
PHEW ...!

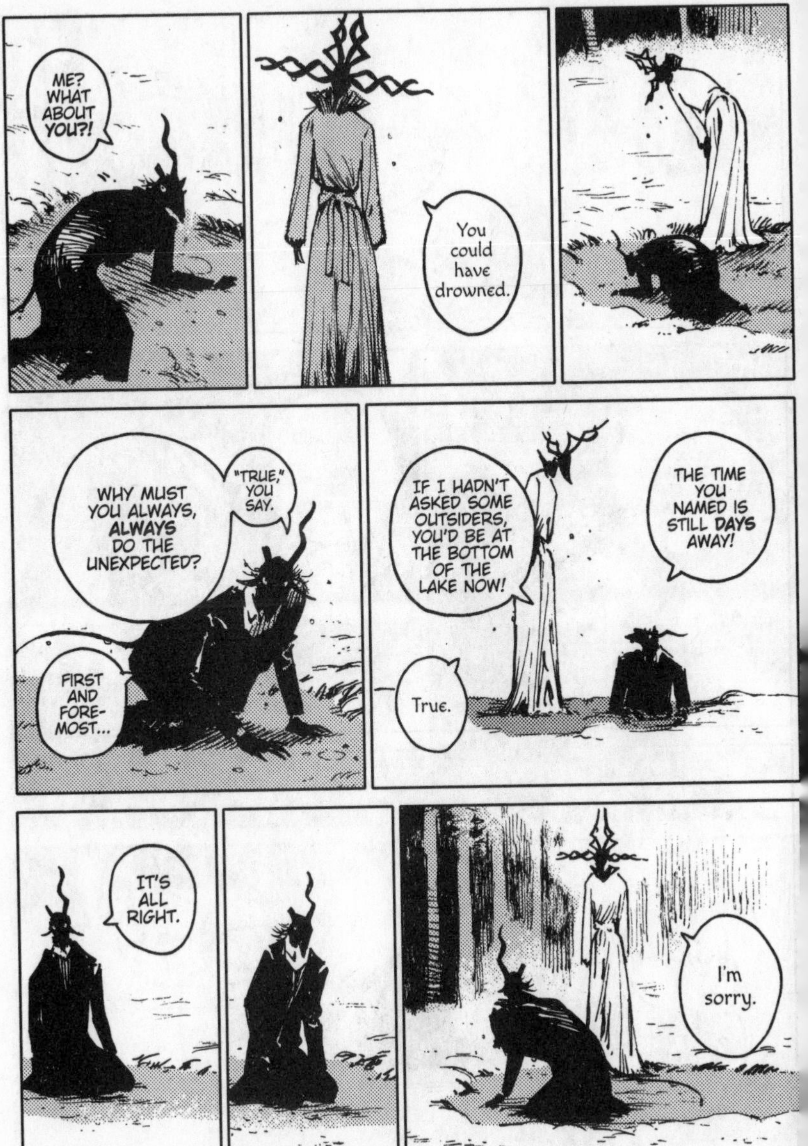
You could have drowned.
ME? WHAT ABOUT YOU?!
THE TIME YOU NAMED IS STILL DAYS AWAY!
IF I HADN'T ASKED SOME OUTSIDERS, YOU'D BE AT THE BOTTOM OF THE LAKE NOW!
True.
"TRUE," YOU SAY.
WHY MUST YOU ALWAYS, ALWAYS DO THE UNEXPECTED?
FIRST AND FORE-MOST...
I'm sorry.
IT'S ALL RIGHT.

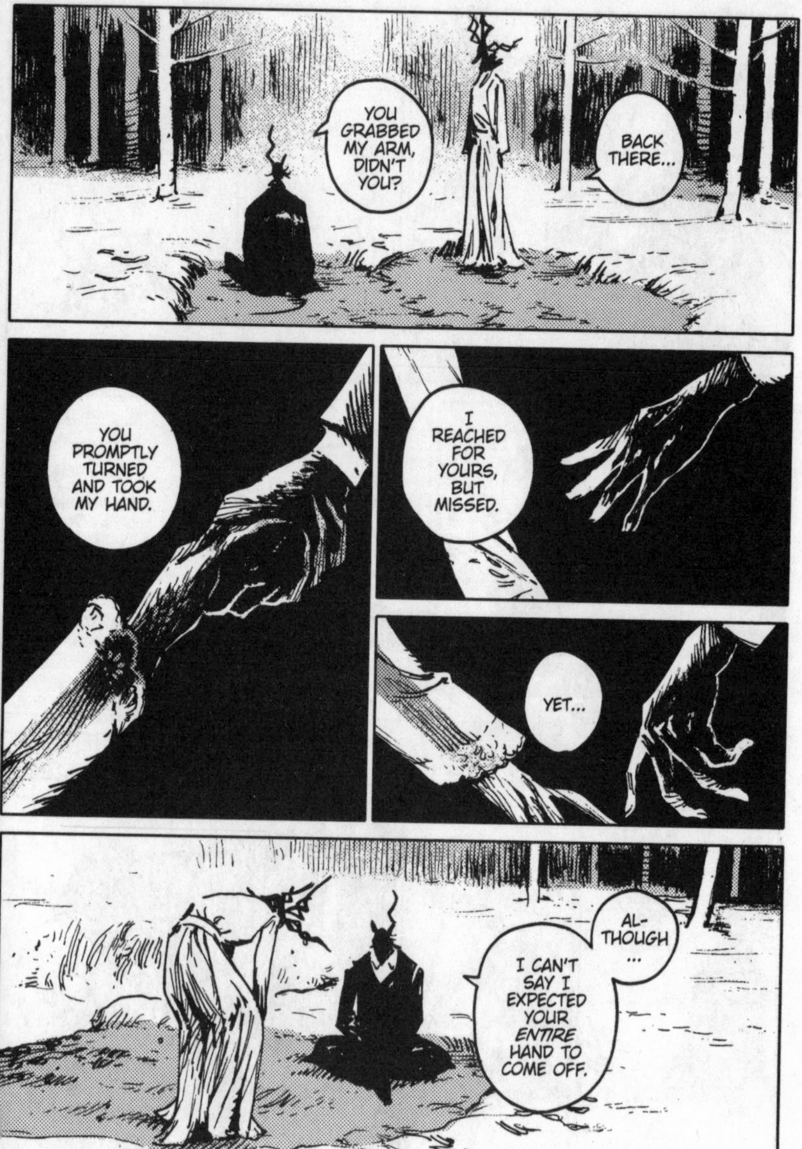
BACK THERE...
YOU GRABBED MY ARM, DIDN'T YOU?
I REACHED FOR YOURS, BUT MISSED.
YET...
YOU PROMPTLY TURNED AND TOOK MY HAND.
AL-THOUGH ...
I CAN'T SAY I EXPECTED YOUR *ENTIRE* HAND TO COME OFF.

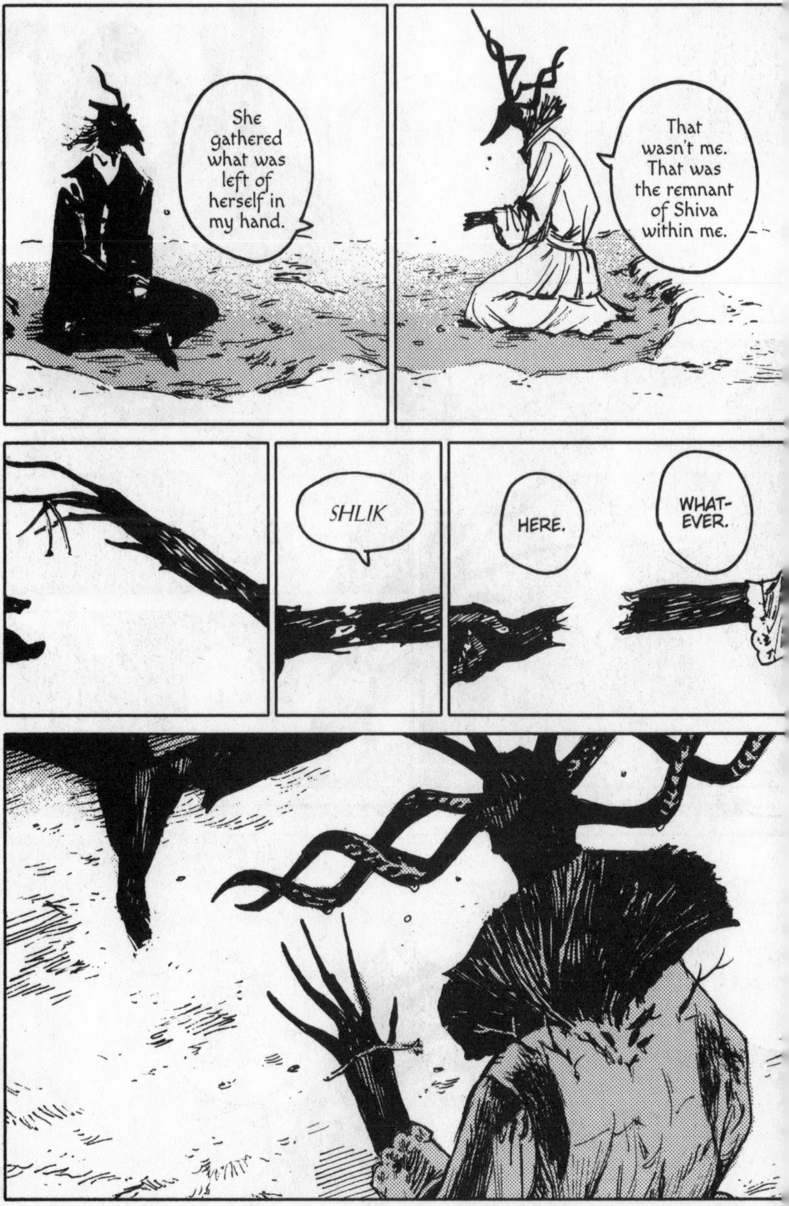
That wasn't me. That was the remnant of Shiva within me.
She gathered what was left of herself in my hand.
WHAT-EVER.
HERE.
SHLIK

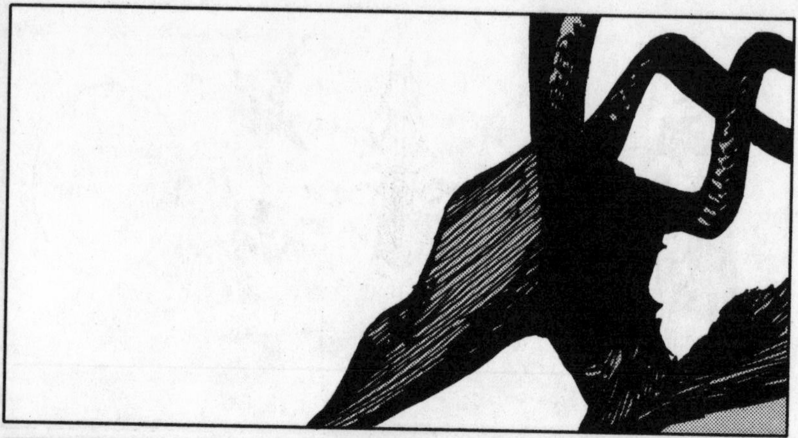
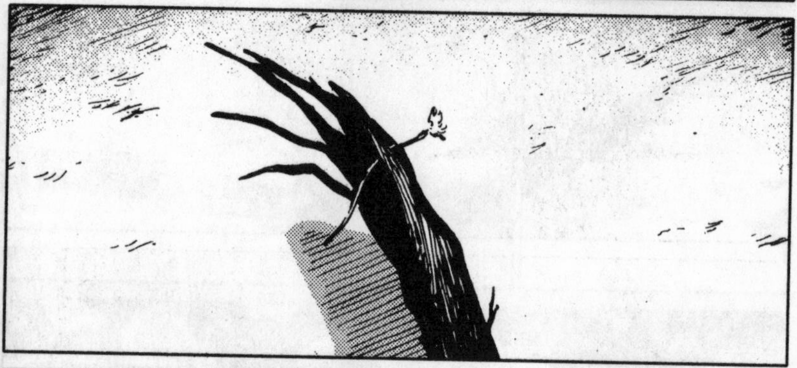
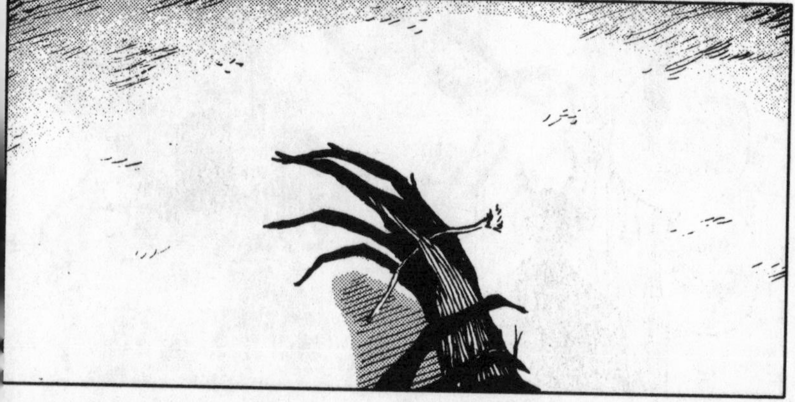

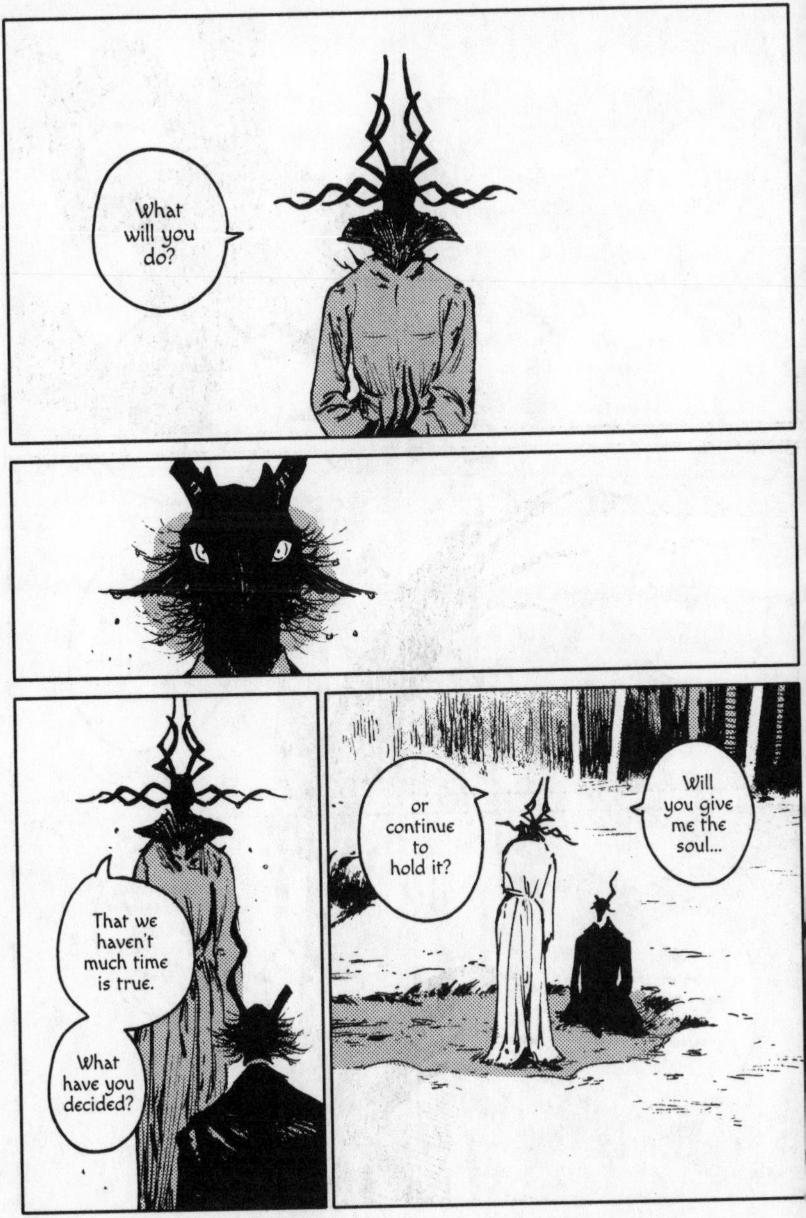
What will you do?
Will you give me the soul...
or continue to hold it?
That we haven't much time is true.
What have you decided?

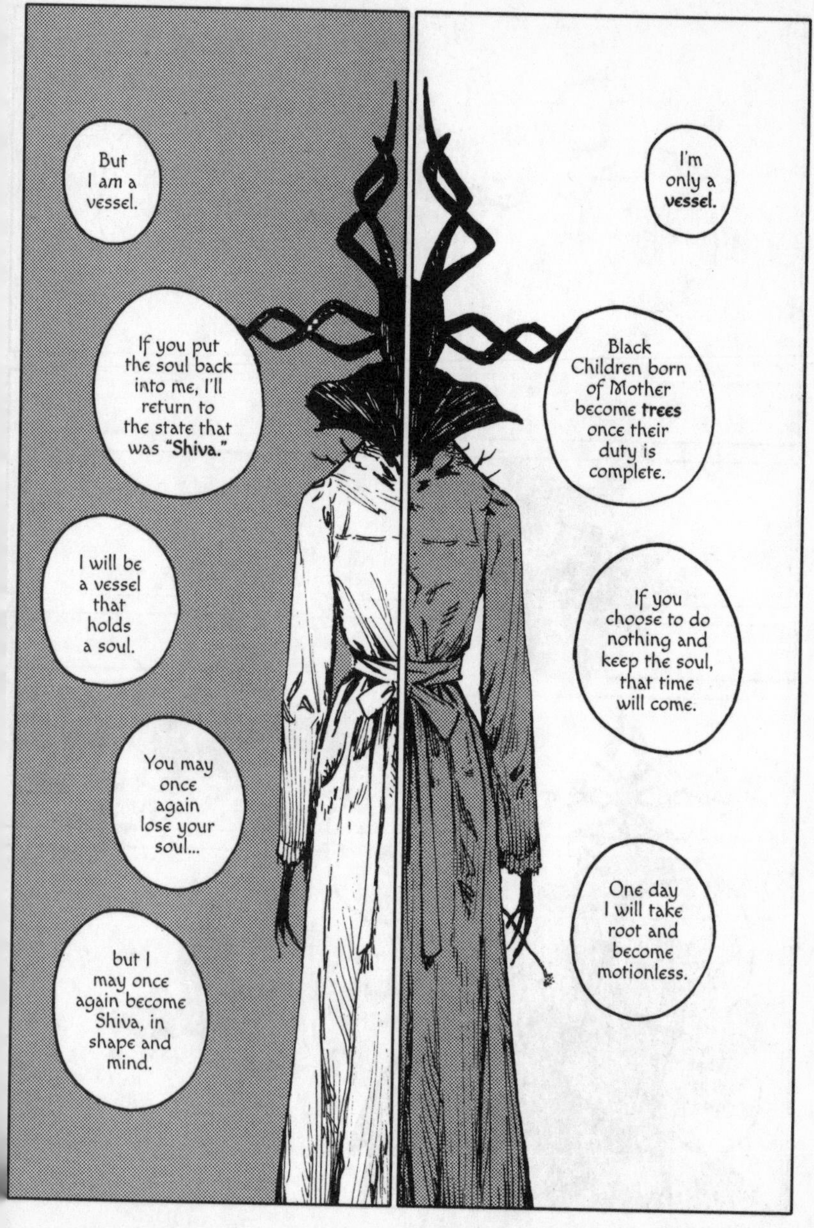
I'm only a vessel.
Black Children born of Mother become trees once their duty is complete.
If you choose to do nothing and keep the soul, that time will come.
One day I will take root and become motionless.
But I am a vessel.
If you put the soul back into me, I'll return to the state that was "Shiva."
I will be a vessel that holds a soul.
You may once again lose your soul...
but I may once again become Shiva, in shape and mind.

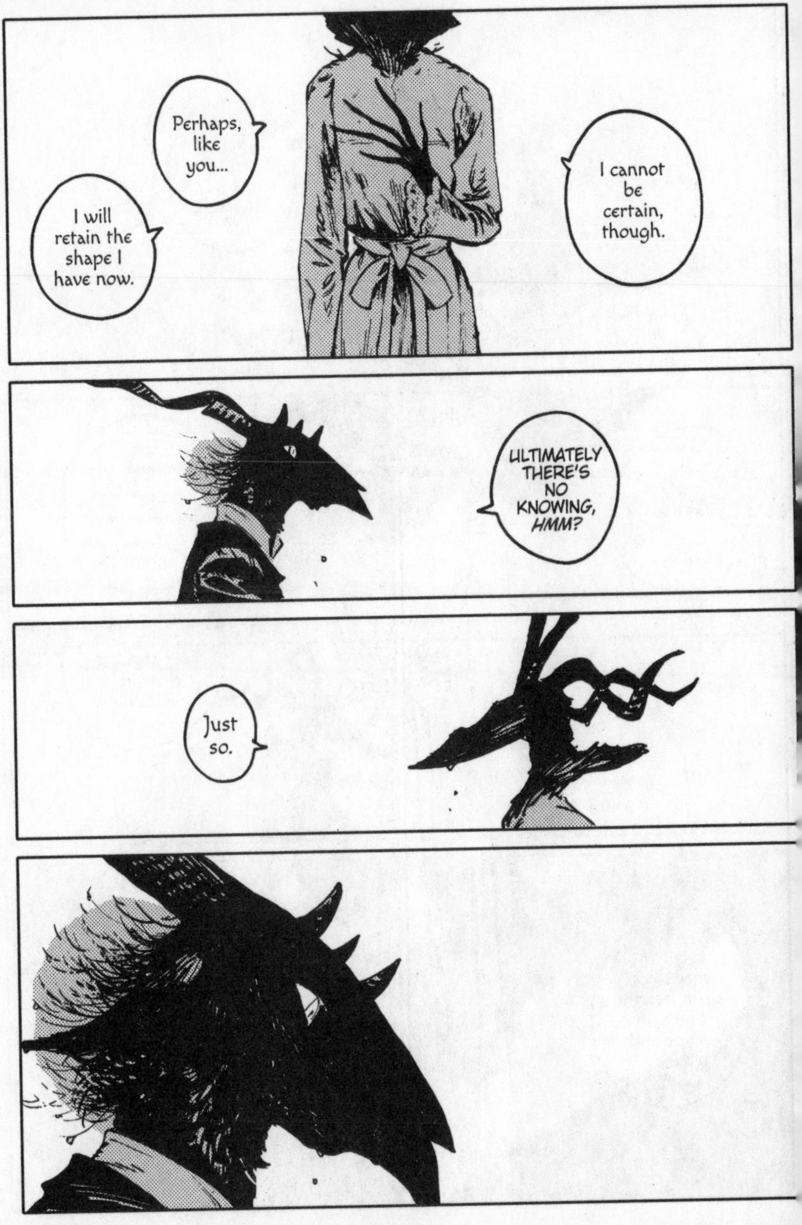
Perhaps, like you...
I will retain the shape I have now.
I cannot be certain, though.
ULTIMATELY THERE'S NO KNOWING, HMM?
Just so.

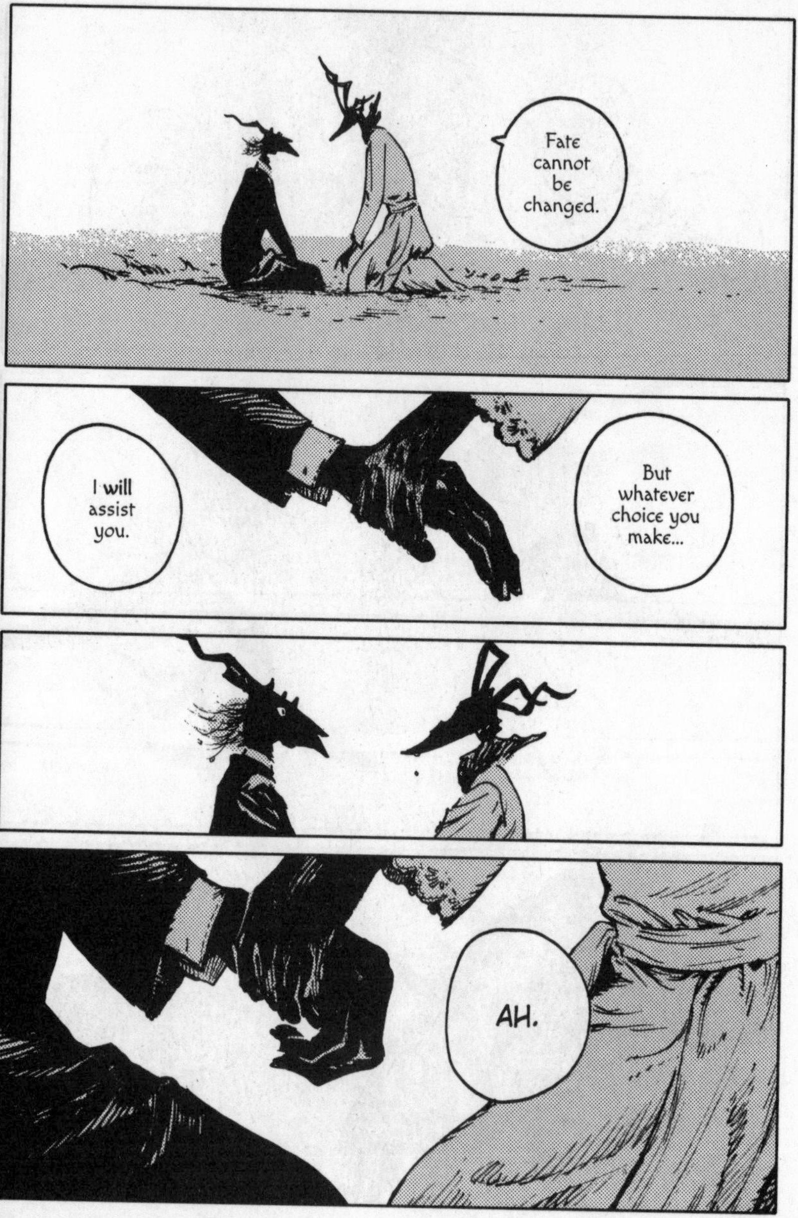
Fate cannot be changed.
But whatever choice you make...
I will assist you.
AH.

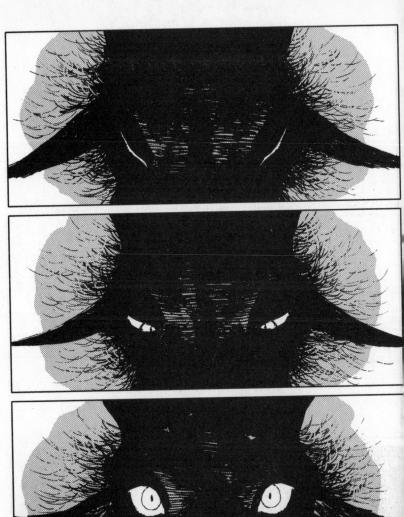

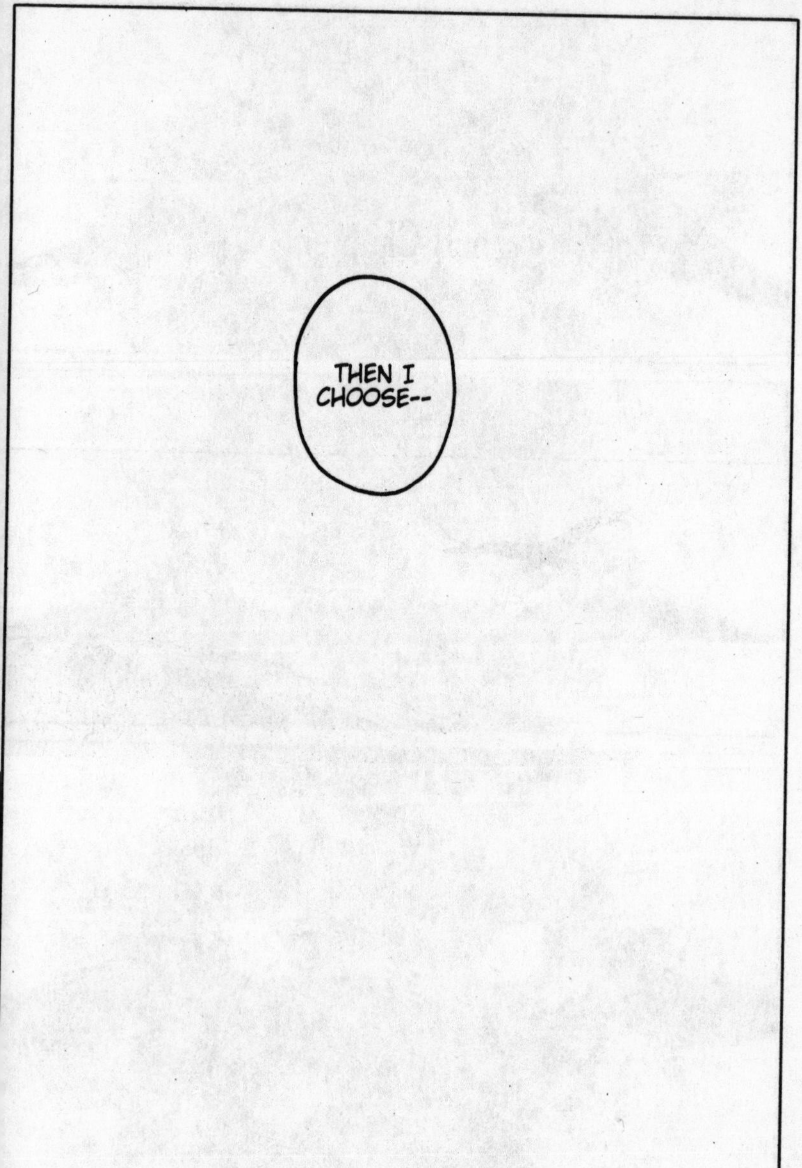
THEN I CHOOSE--

Final Chapter

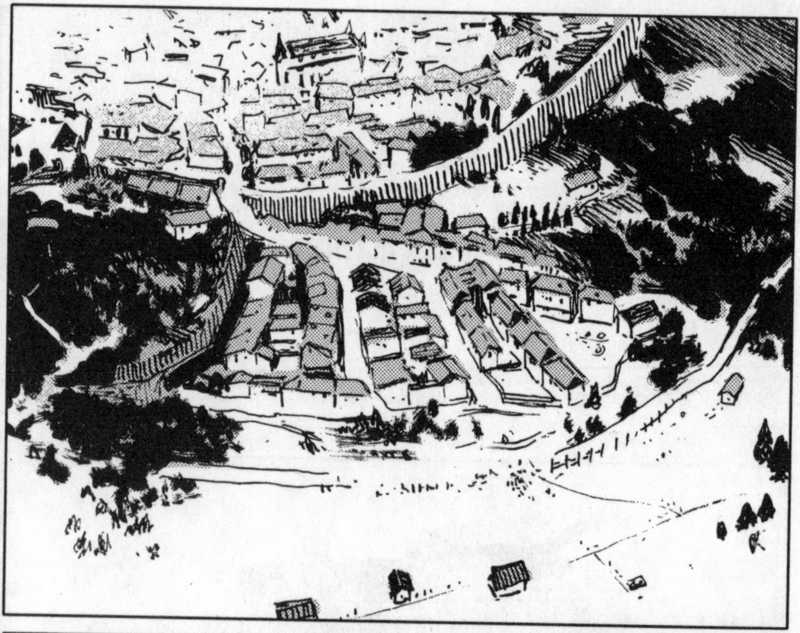
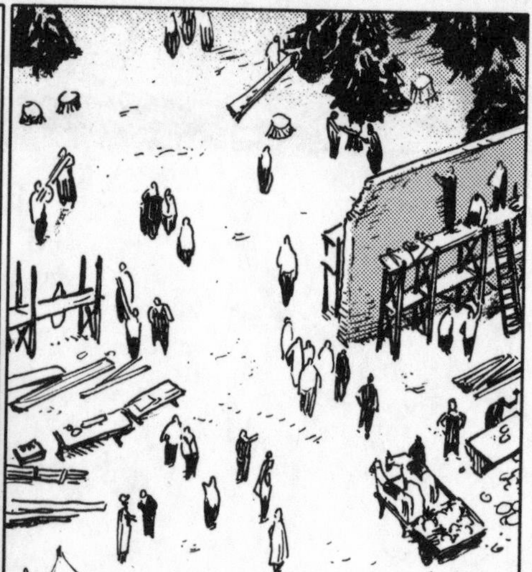
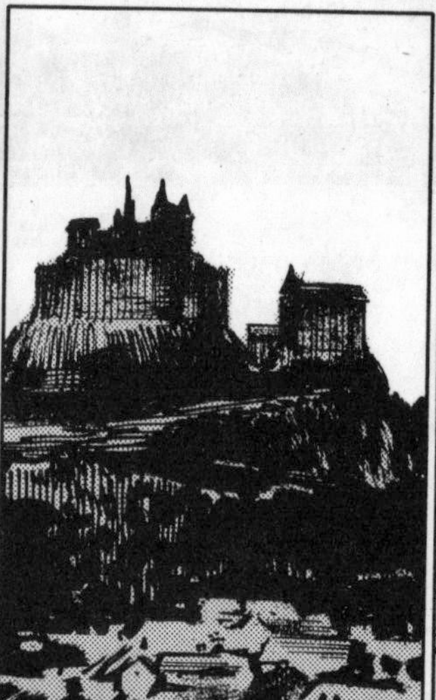

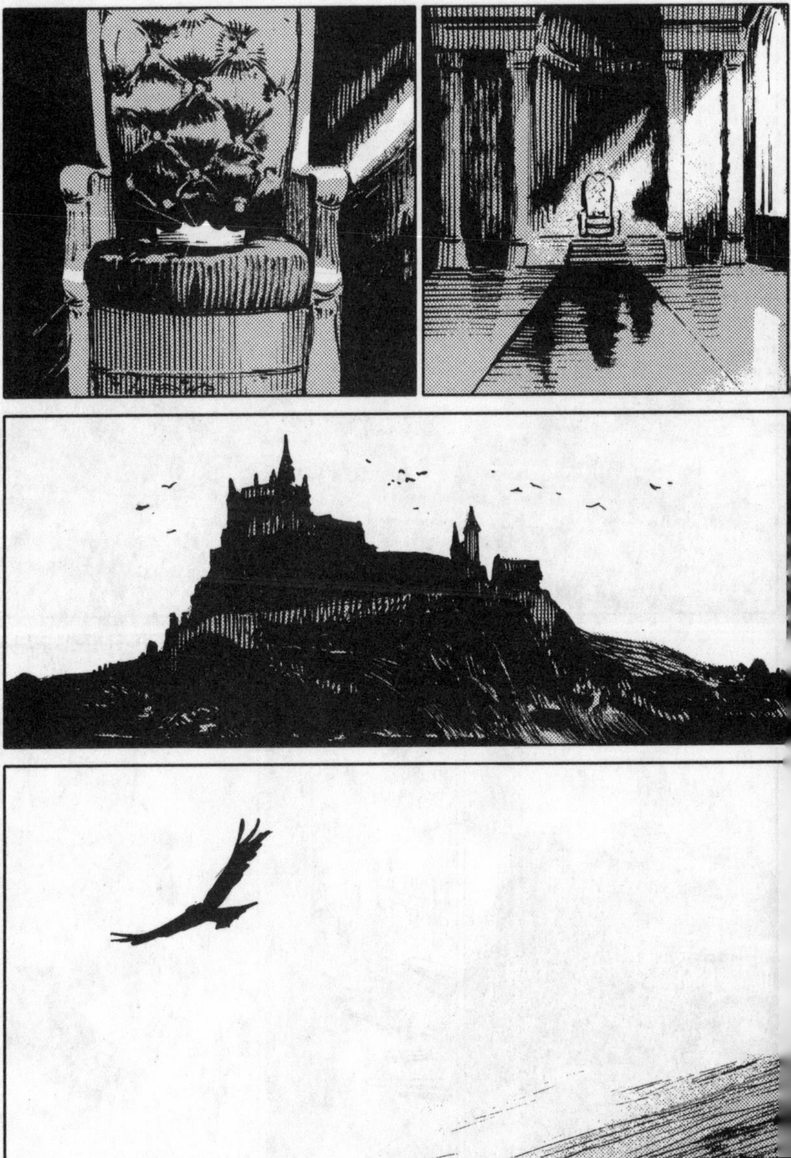

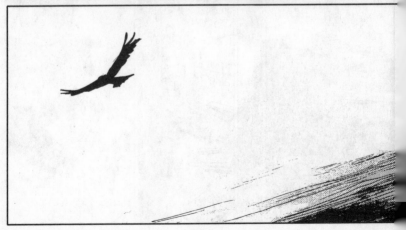

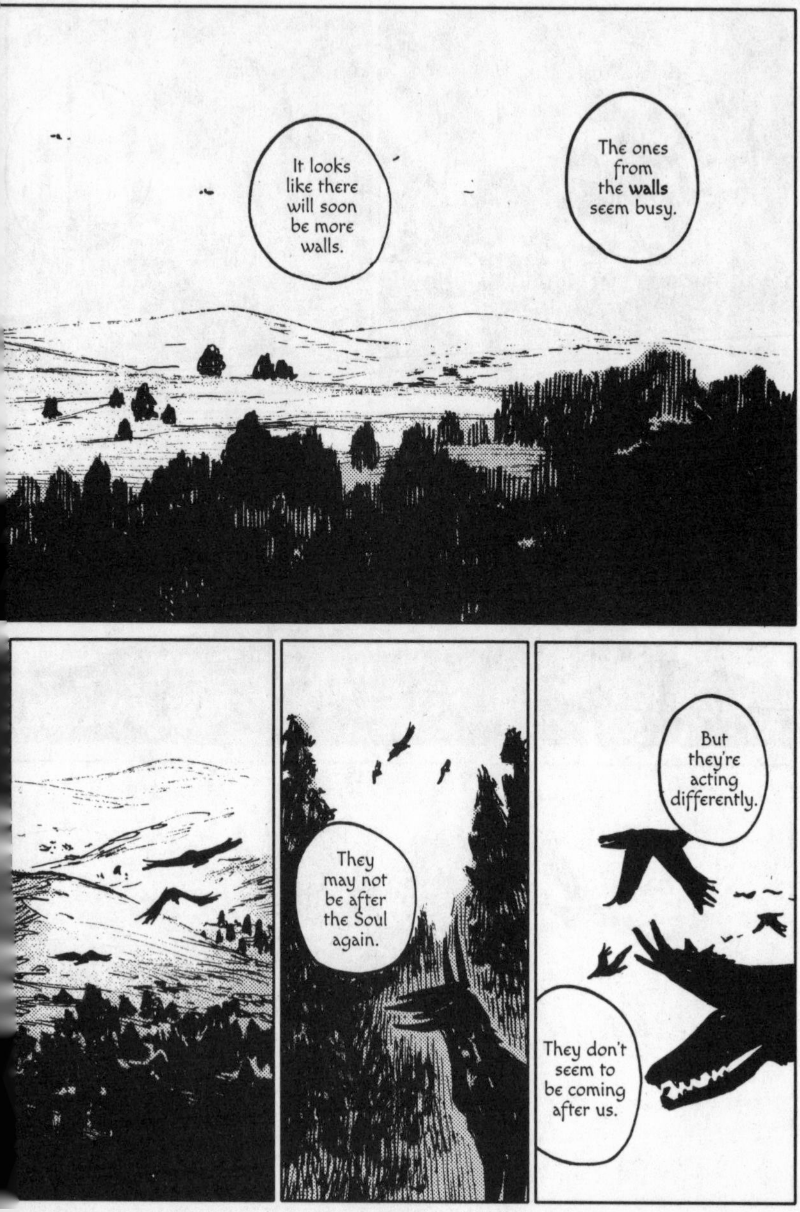
The ones from the **walls** seem busy.
It looks like there will soon be more walls.
But they're acting differently.
They don't seem to be coming after us.
They may not be after the Soul again.

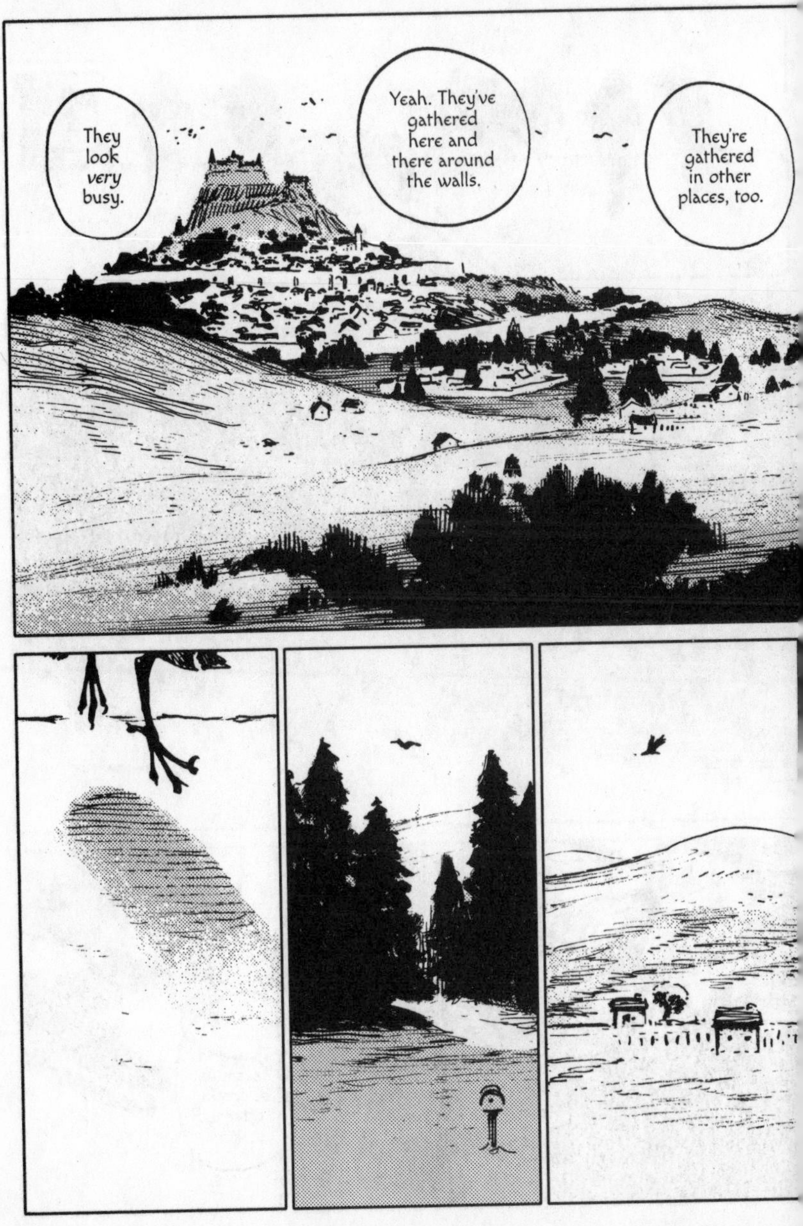
They look *very* busy.
Yeah. They've gathered here and there around the walls.
They're gathered in other places, too.

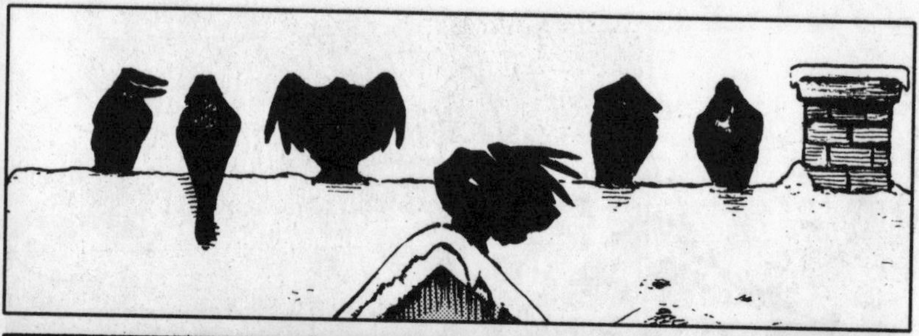
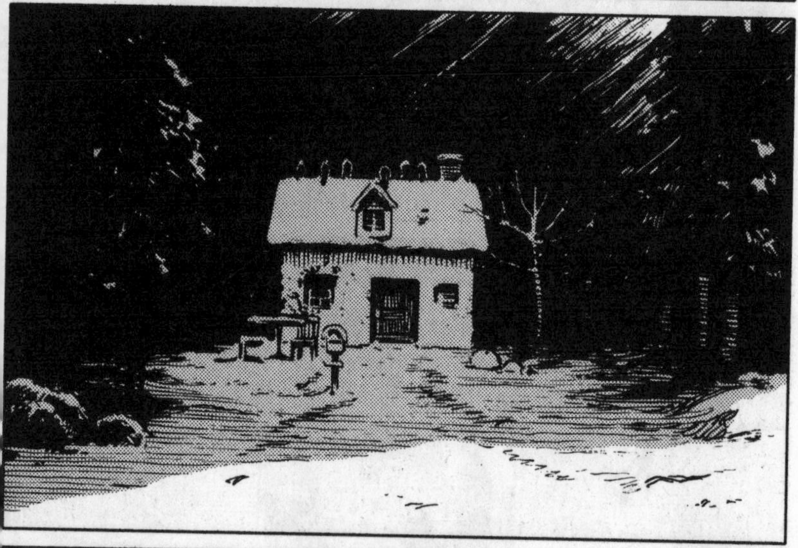
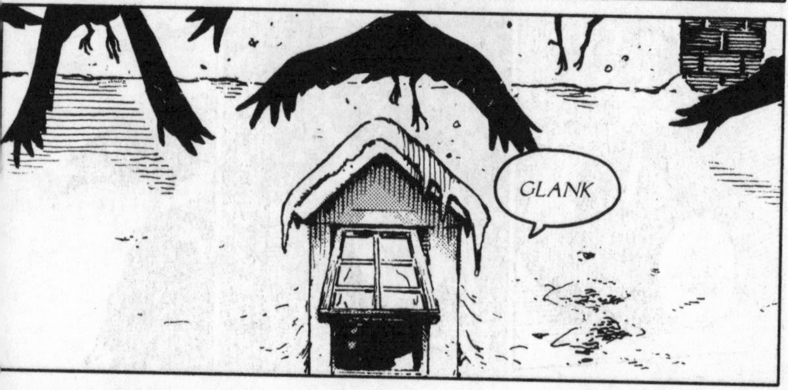
GLANK

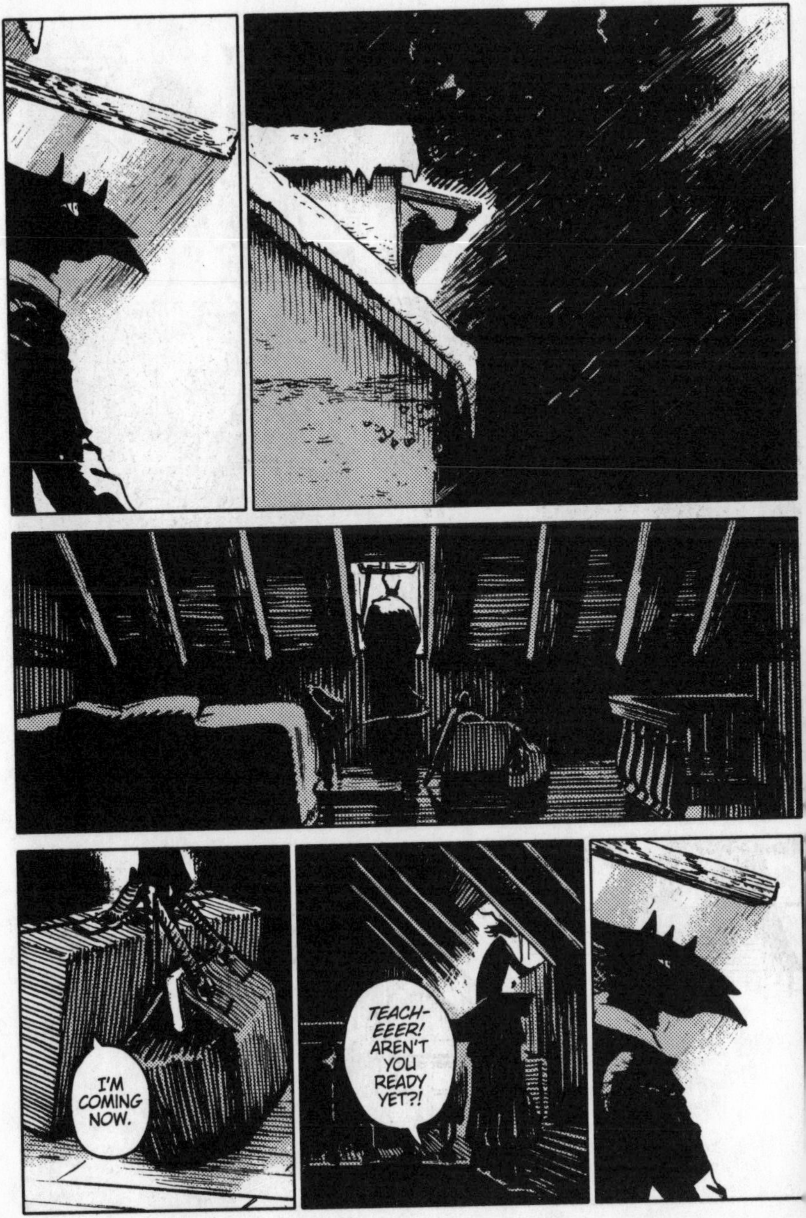
TEACH-EEER! AREN'T YOU READY YET?!
I'M COMING NOW.

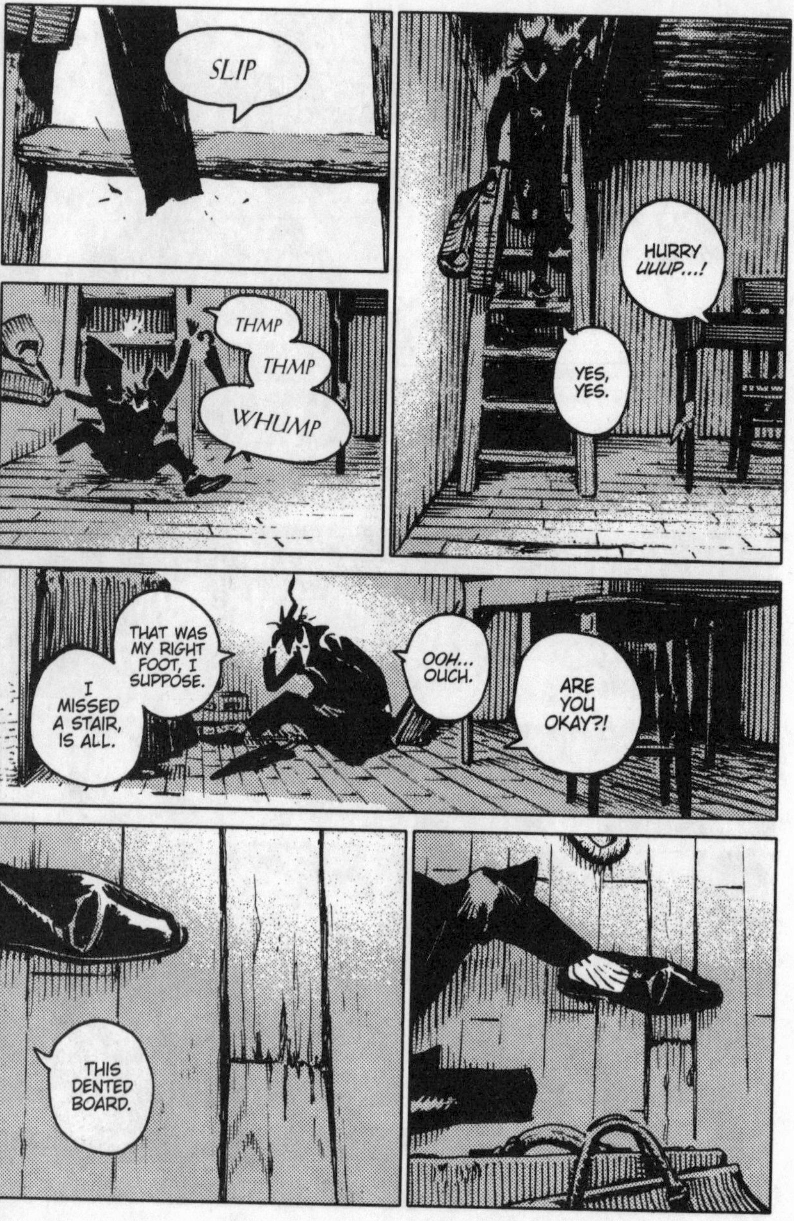
HURRY UUUP...!
YES, YES.
SLIP
THMP
THMP
WHUMP
ARE YOU OKAY?!
OOH... OUCH.
THAT WAS MY RIGHT FOOT, I SUPPOSE.
I MISSED A STAIR, IS ALL.
THIS DENTED BOARD.

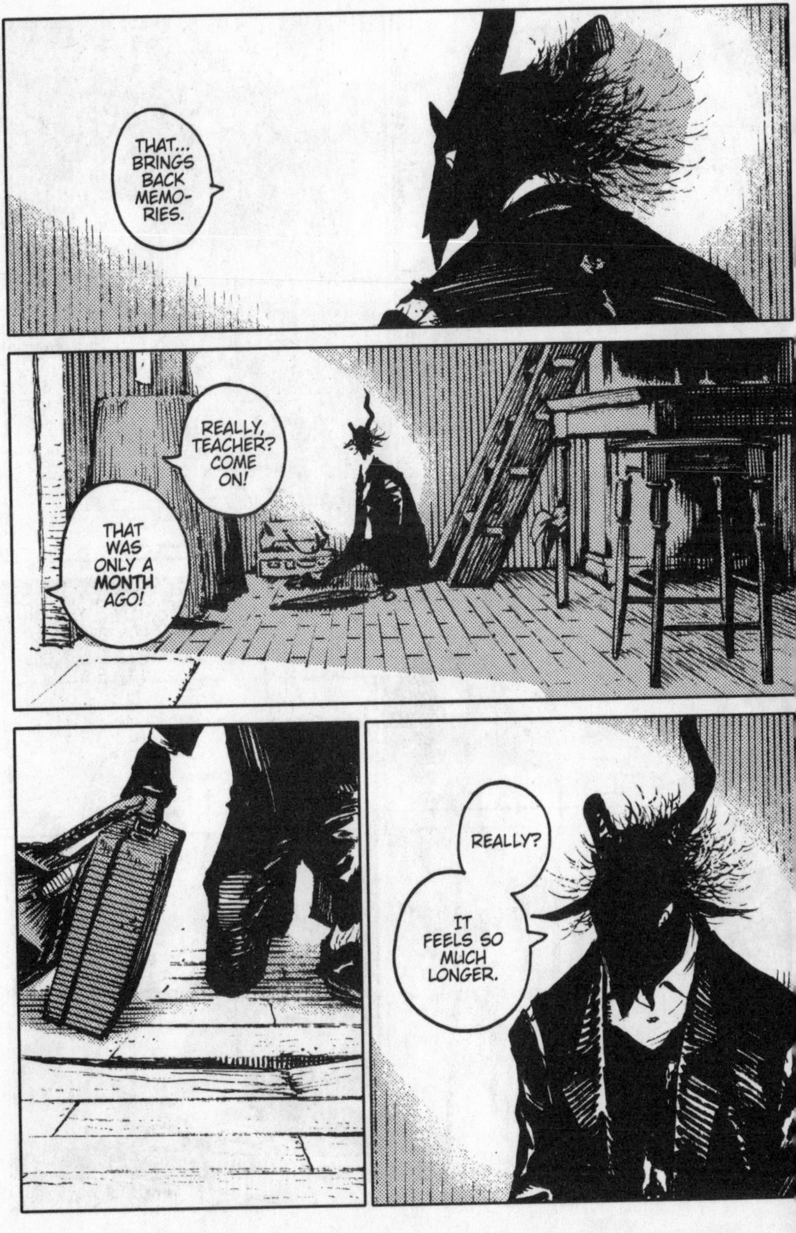
THAT... BRINGS BACK MEMO-RIES.
REALLY, TEACHER? COME ON!
THAT WAS ONLY A MONTH AGO!
REALLY?
IT FEELS SO MUCH LONGER.

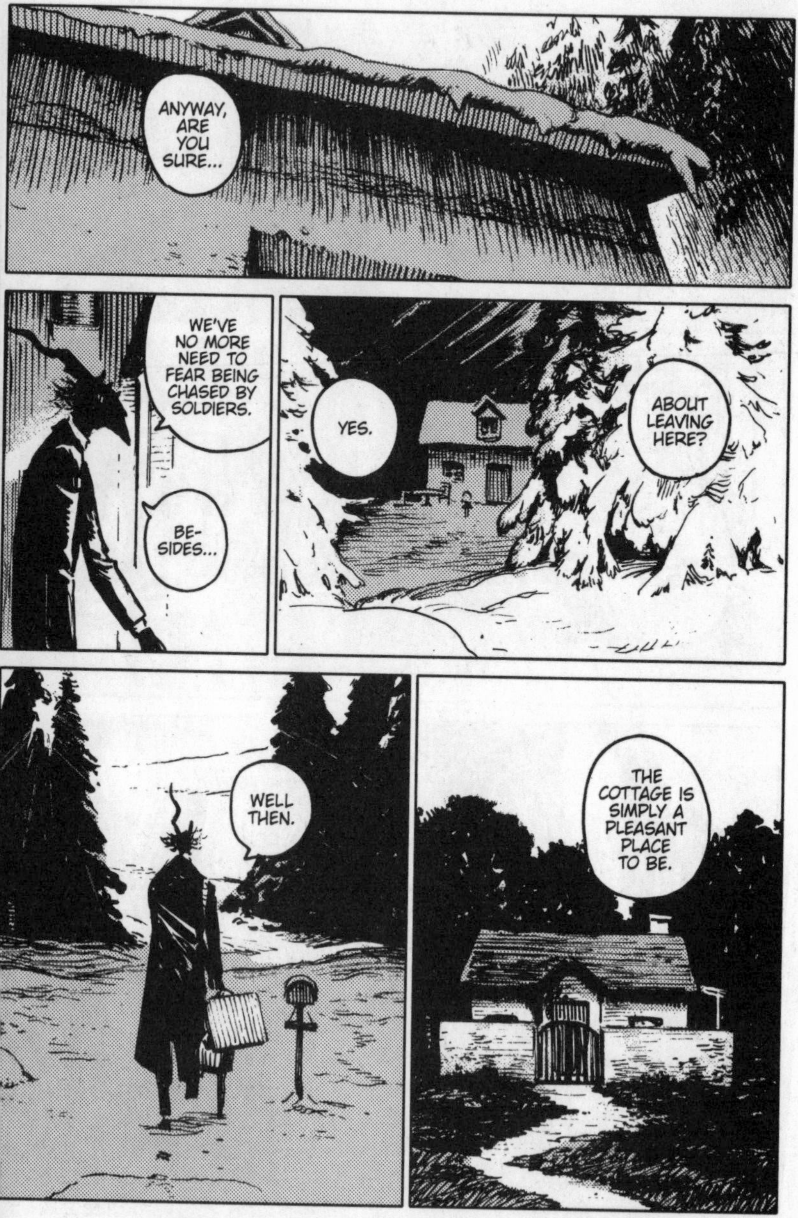
ANYWAY, ARE YOU SURE...
ABOUT LEAVING HERE?
YES.
WE'VE NO MORE NEED TO FEAR BEING CHASED BY SOLDIERS.
BE-SIDES...
THE COTTAGE IS SIMPLY A PLEASANT PLACE TO BE.
WELL THEN.

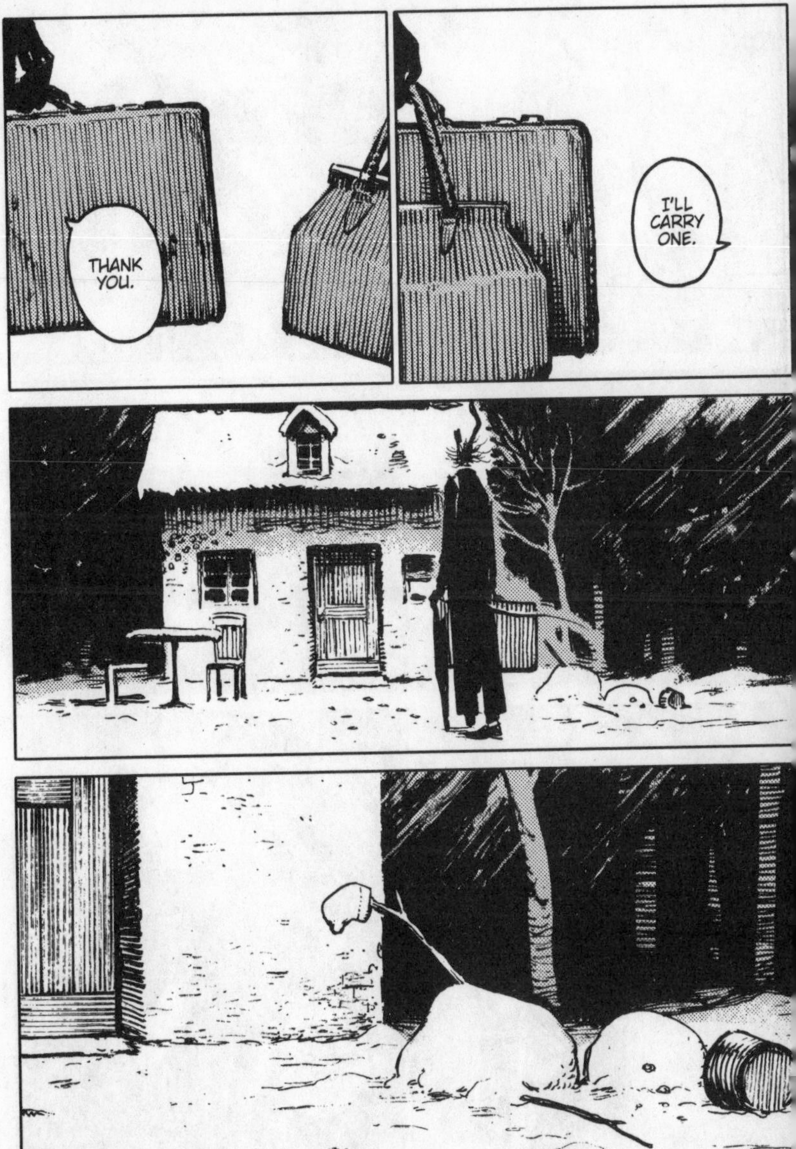
I'LL CARRY ONE.
THANK YOU.

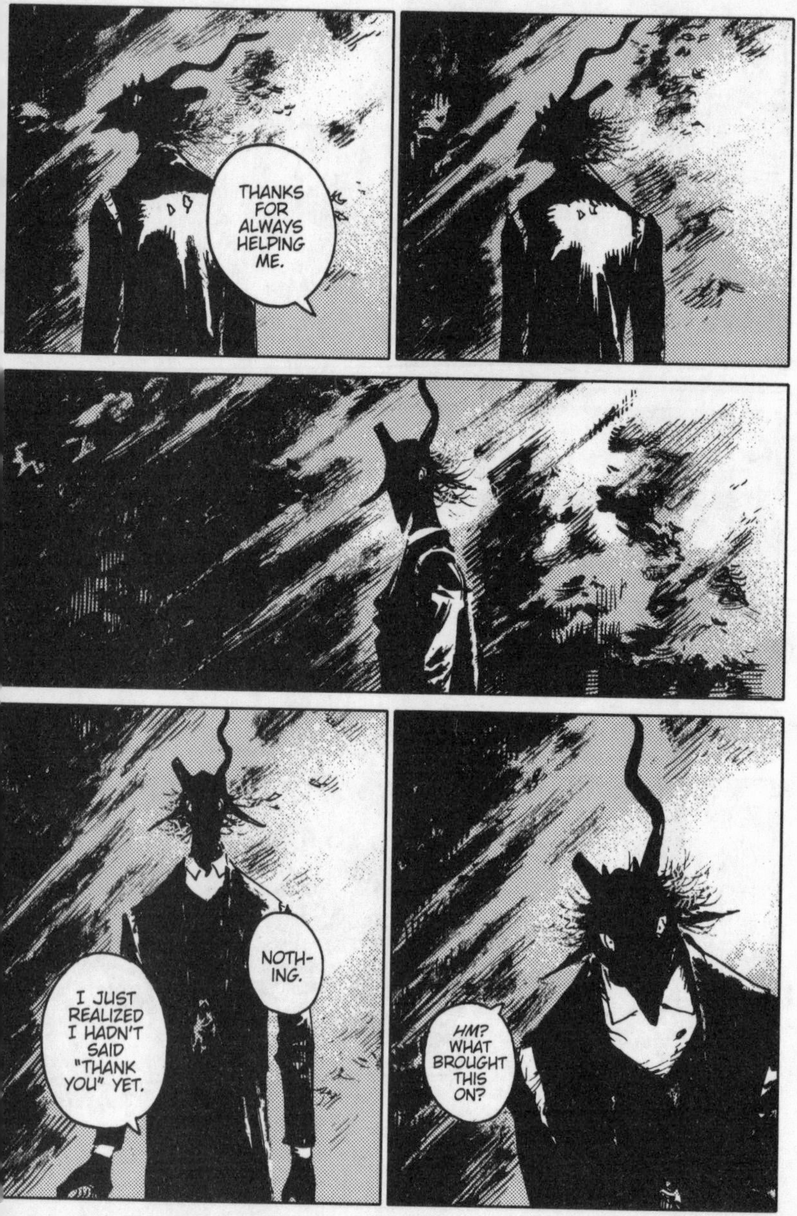
THANKS FOR ALWAYS HELPING ME.
HM? WHAT BROUGHT THIS ON?
NOTH-ING.
I JUST REALIZED I HADN'T SAID "THANK YOU" YET.

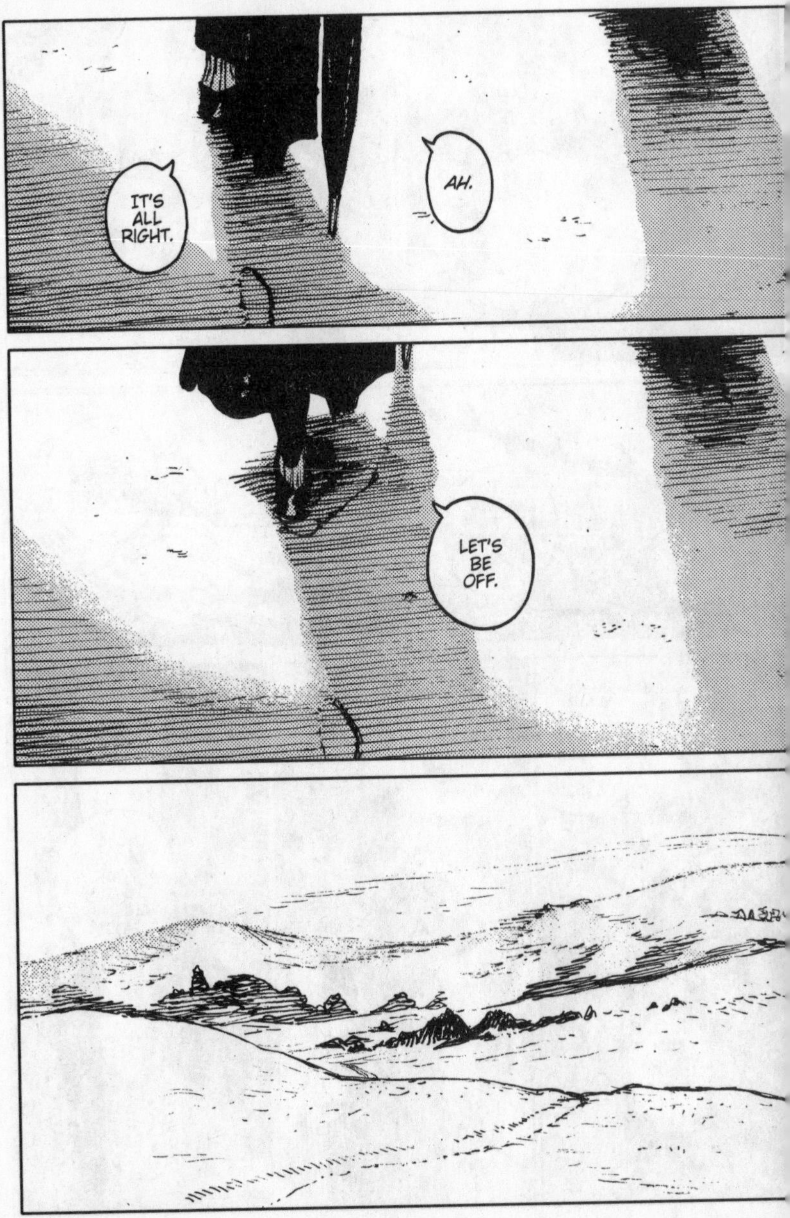
AH.
IT'S ALL RIGHT.
LET'S BE OFF.

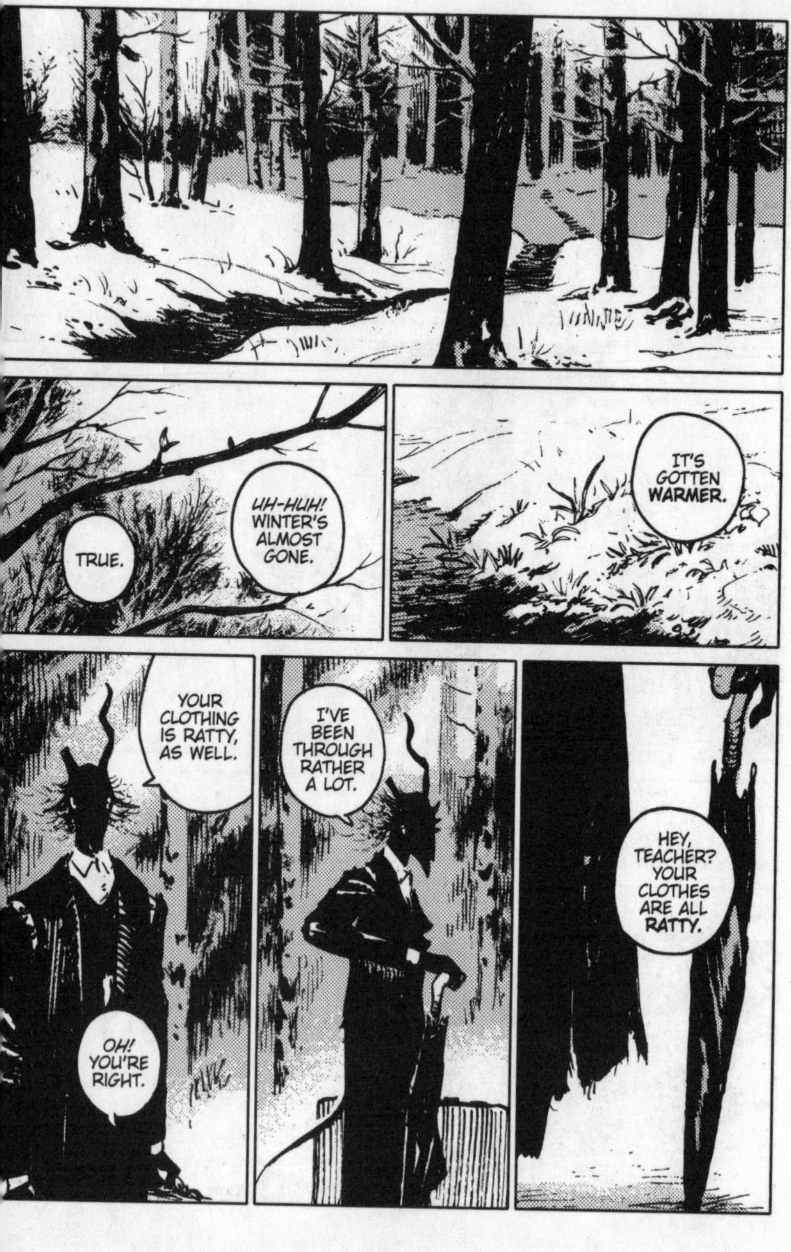
IT'S GOTTEN WARMER.
UH-HUH! WINTER'S ALMOST GONE.
TRUE.
HEY, TEACHER? YOUR CLOTHES ARE ALL RATTY.
I'VE BEEN THROUGH RATHER A LOT.
YOUR CLOTHING IS RATTY, AS WELL.
OH! YOU'RE RIGHT.

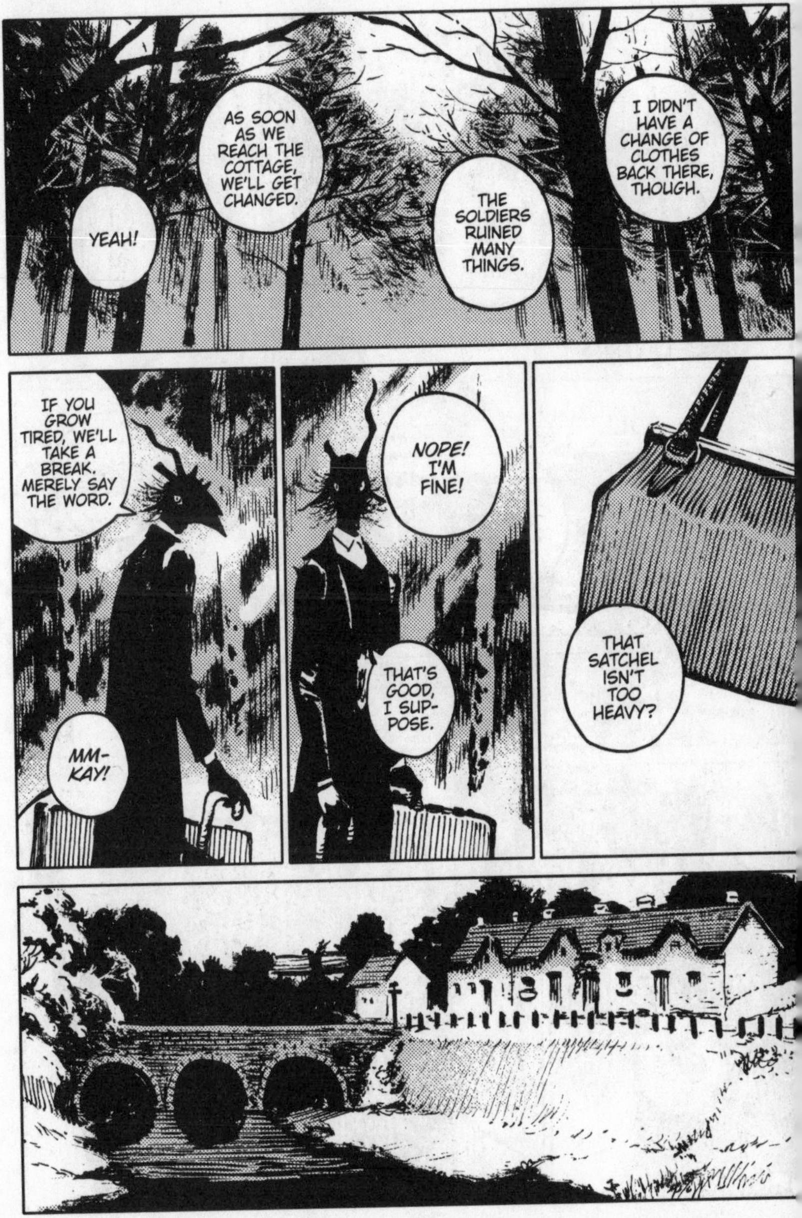
I DIDN'T HAVE A CHANGE OF CLOTHES BACK THERE, THOUGH.
THE SOLDIERS RUINED MANY THINGS.
AS SOON AS WE REACH THE COTTAGE, WE'LL GET CHANGED.
YEAH!
THAT SATCHEL ISN'T TOO HEAVY?
NOPE! I'M FINE!
THAT'S GOOD, I SUP-POSE.
IF YOU GROW TIRED, WE'LL TAKE A BREAK. MERELY SAY THE WORD.
MM-KAY!

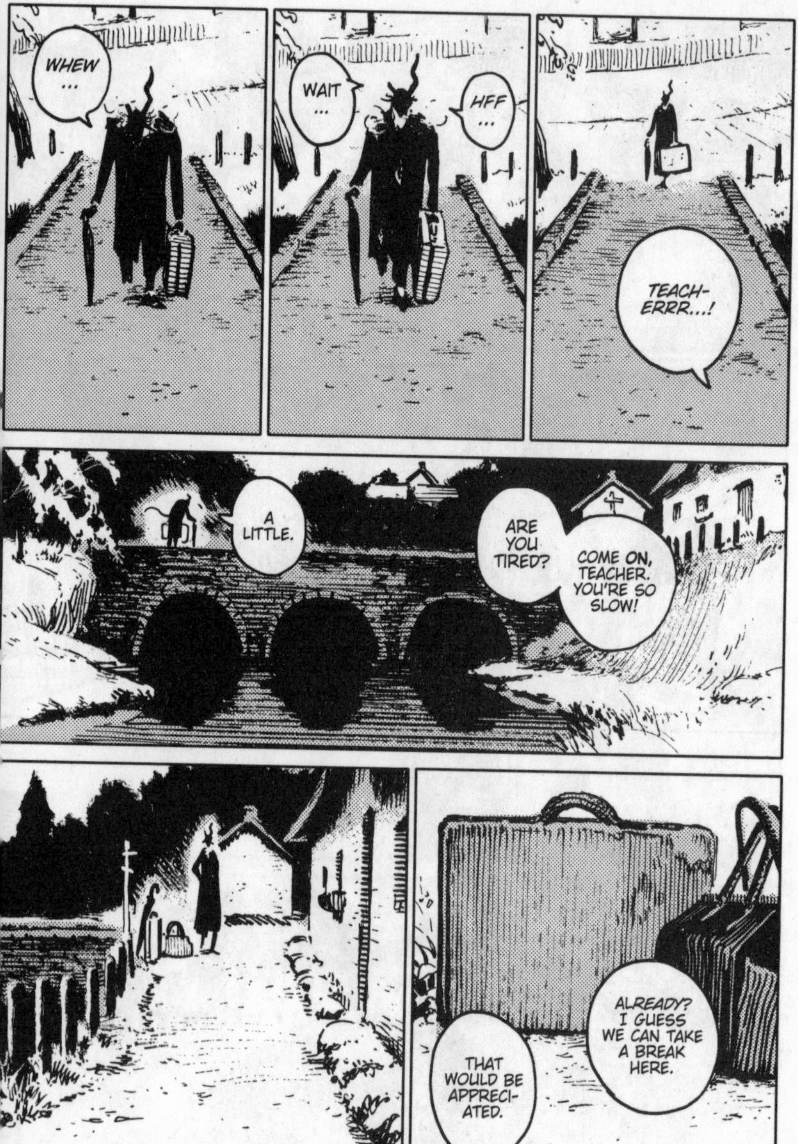
TEACH-ERRR...!
HFF ...
WAIT ...
WHEW ...
COME ON, TEACHER. YOU'RE SO SLOW!
ARE YOU TIRED?
A LITTLE.
ALREADY? I GUESS WE CAN TAKE A BREAK HERE.
THAT WOULD BE APPRECI-ATED.

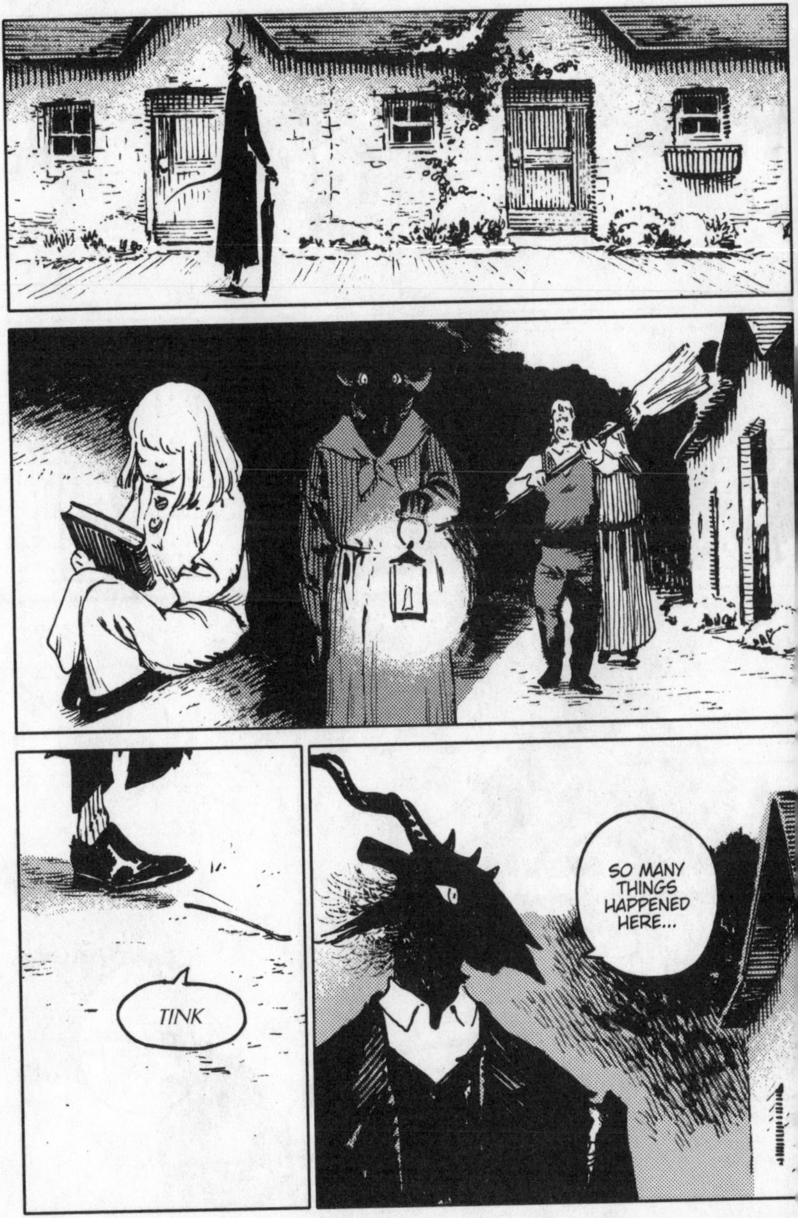
SO MANY THINGS HAPPENED HERE...
TINK

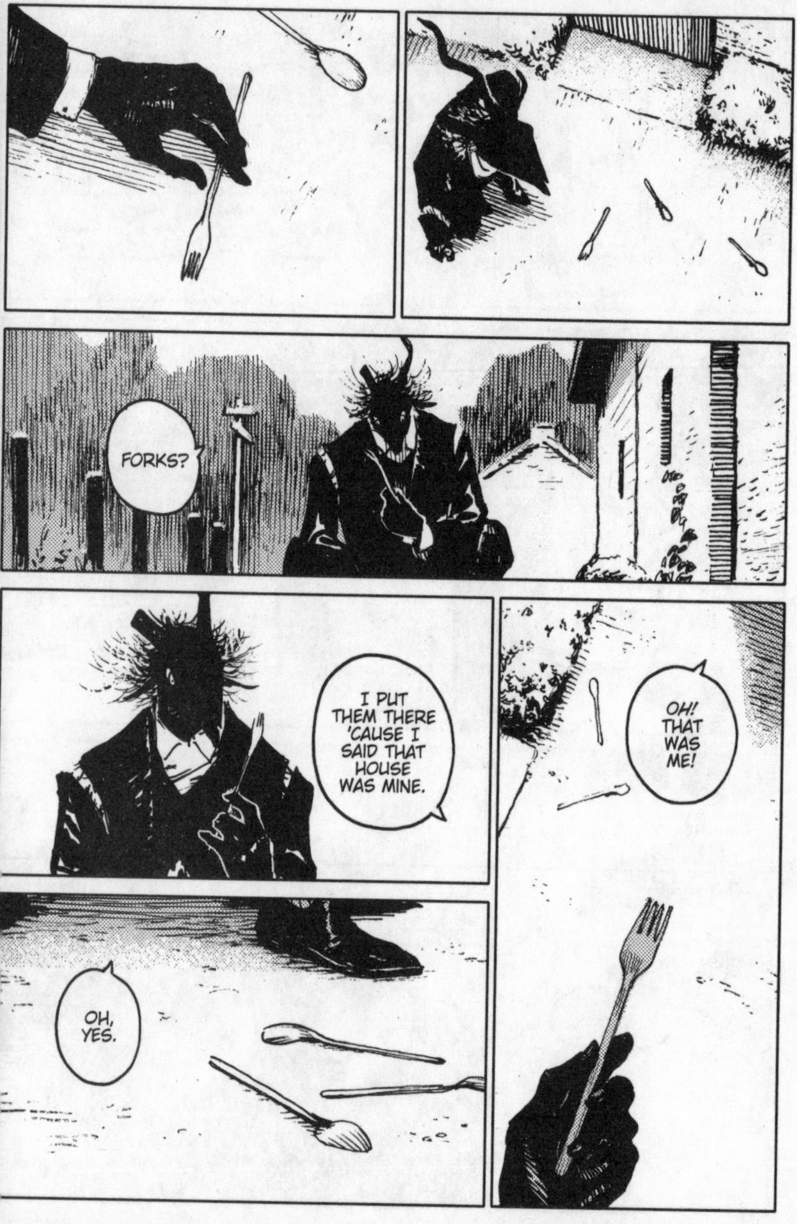
FORKS?
OH! THAT WAS ME!
I PUT THEM THERE 'CAUSE I SAID THAT HOUSE WAS MINE.
OH, YES.

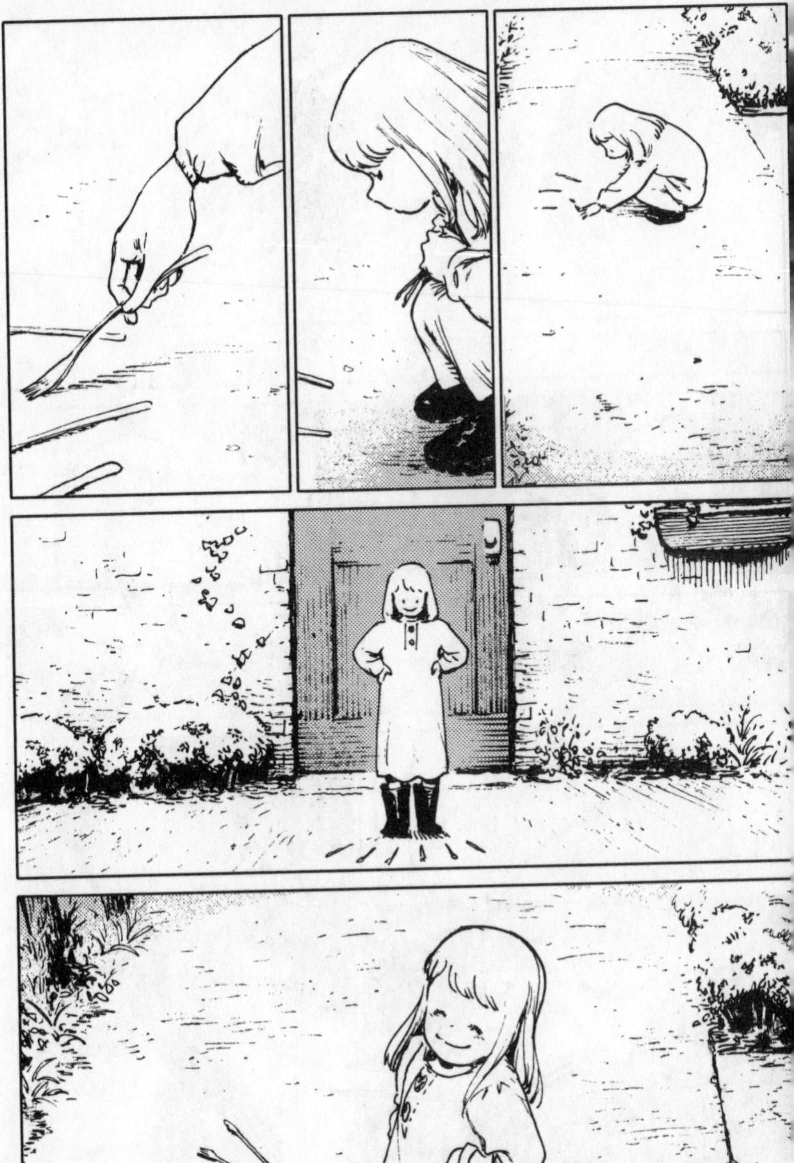

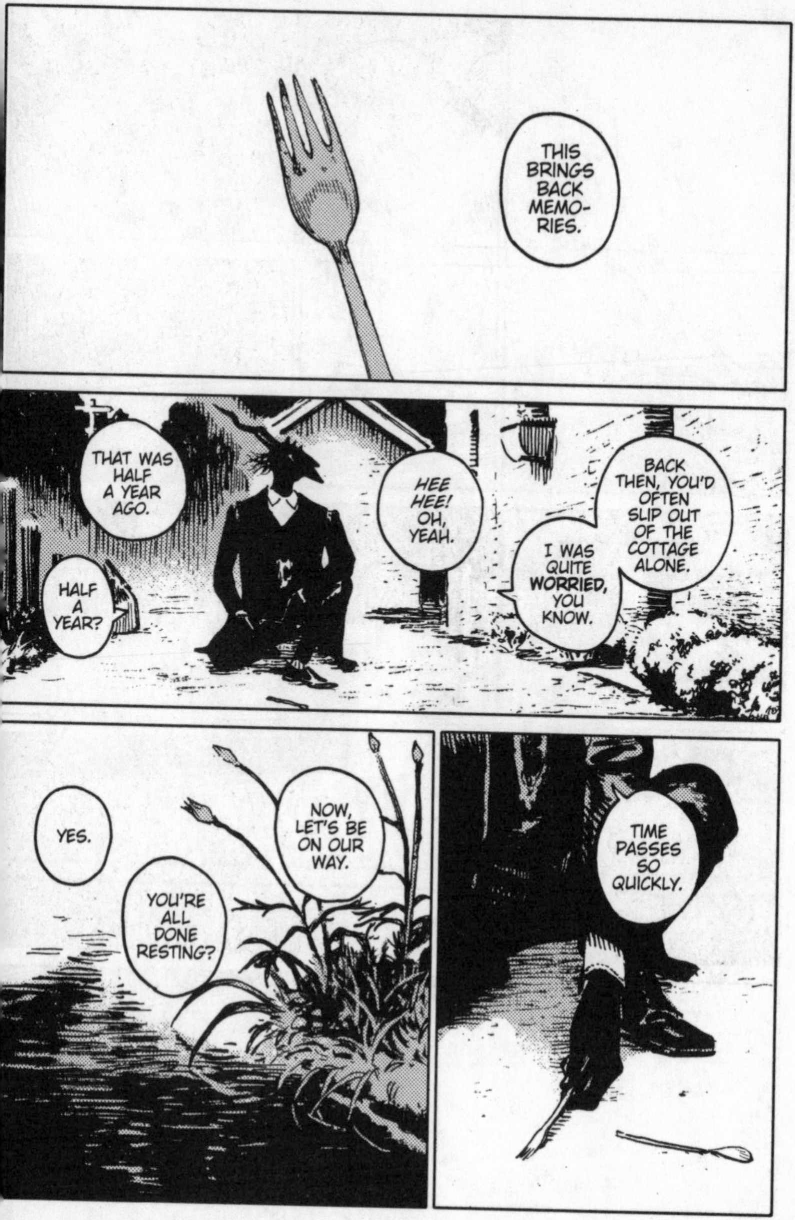
THIS BRINGS BACK MEMO-RIES.
BACK THEN, YOU'D OFTEN SLIP OUT OF THE COTTAGE ALONE.
I WAS QUITE WORRIED, YOU KNOW.
HEE HEE! OH, YEAH.
THAT WAS HALF A YEAR AGO.
HALF A YEAR?
TIME PASSES SO QUICKLY.
NOW, LET'S BE ON OUR WAY.
YOU'RE ALL DONE RESTING?
YES.

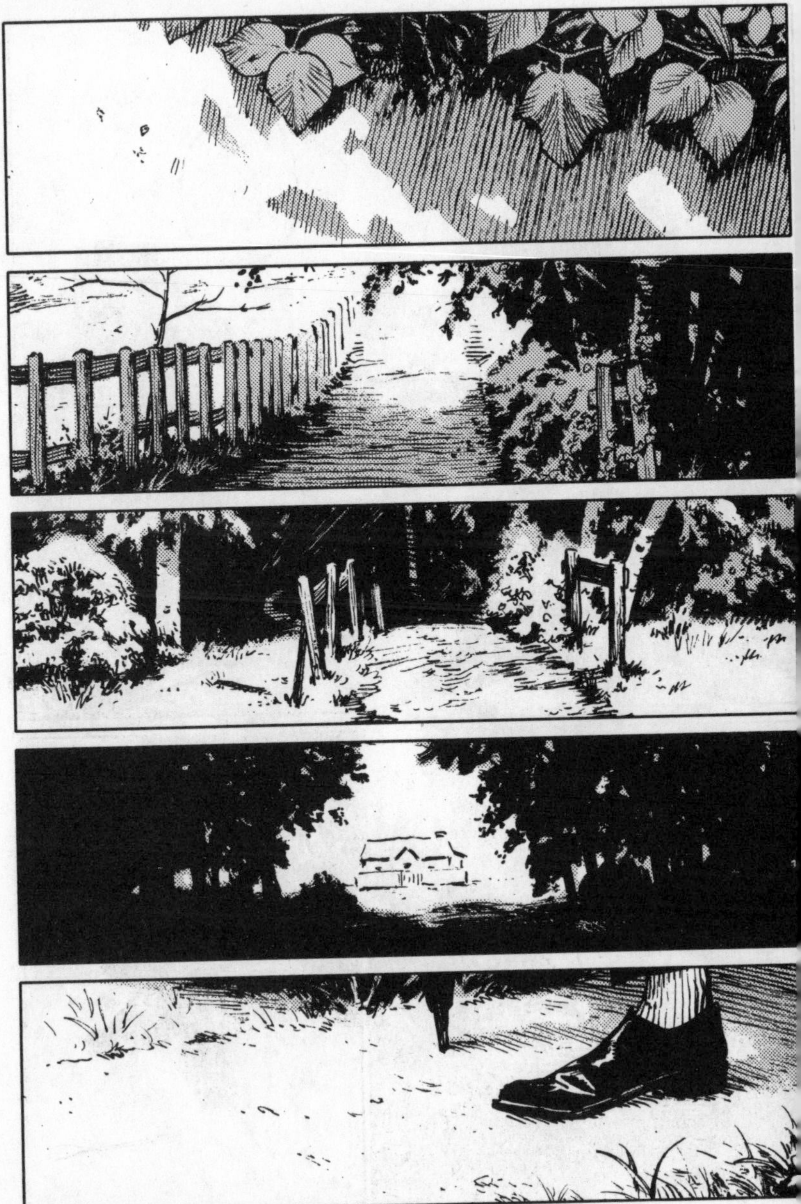

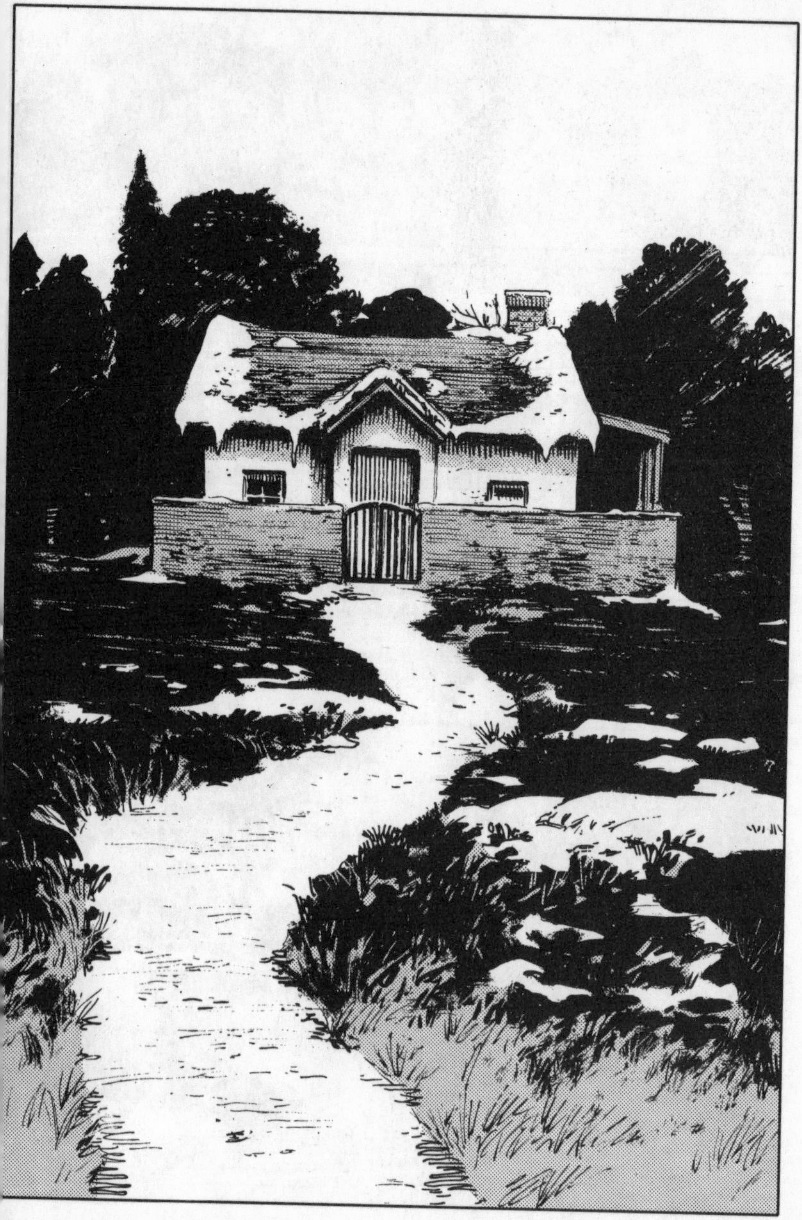

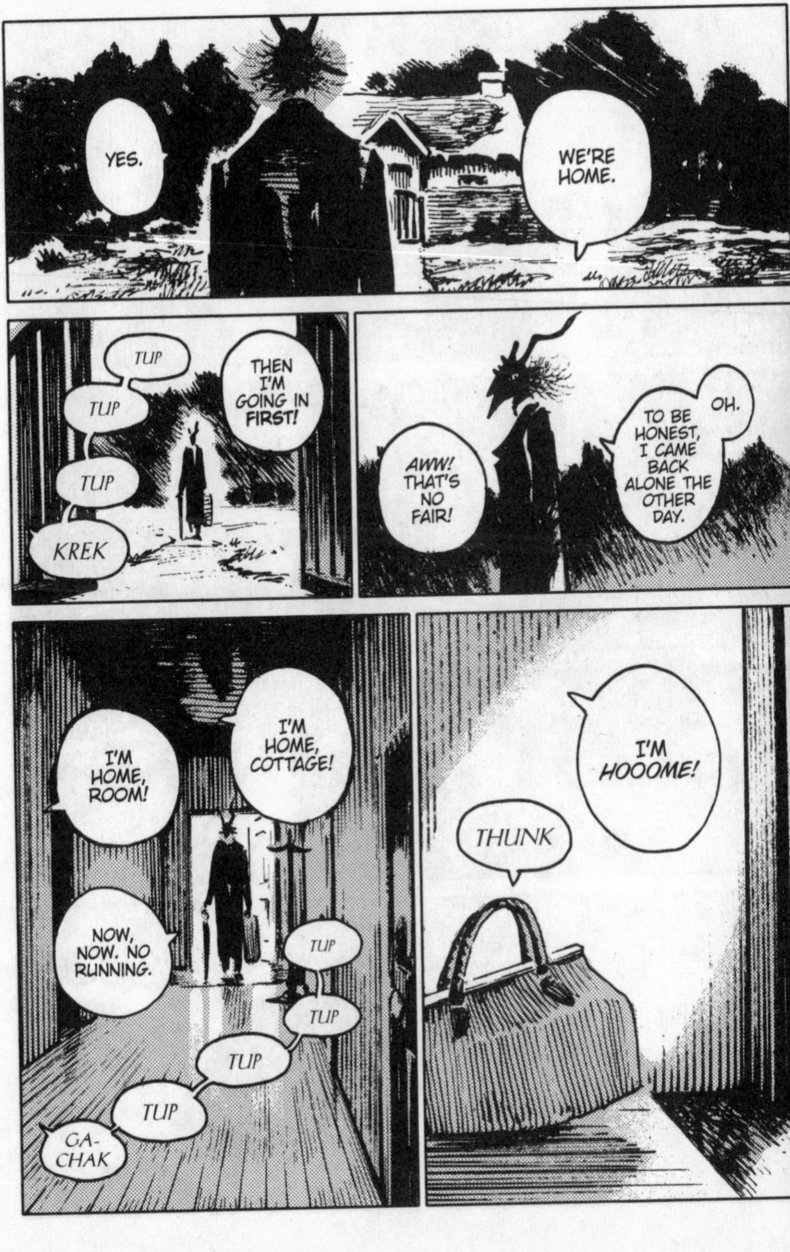
WE'RE HOME.
YES.
OH.
TO BE HONEST, I CAME BACK ALONE THE OTHER DAY.
AWW! THAT'S NO FAIR!
THEN I'M GOING IN FIRST!
TUP
TUP
TUP
KREK
I'M HOOOME!
THUNK
I'M HOME, COTTAGE!
I'M HOME, ROOM!
NOW, NOW. NO RUNNING.
TUP
TUP
TUP
TUP
GA-CHAK

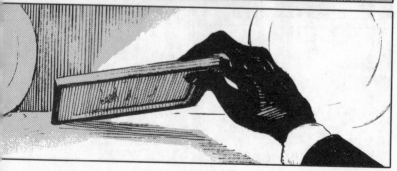

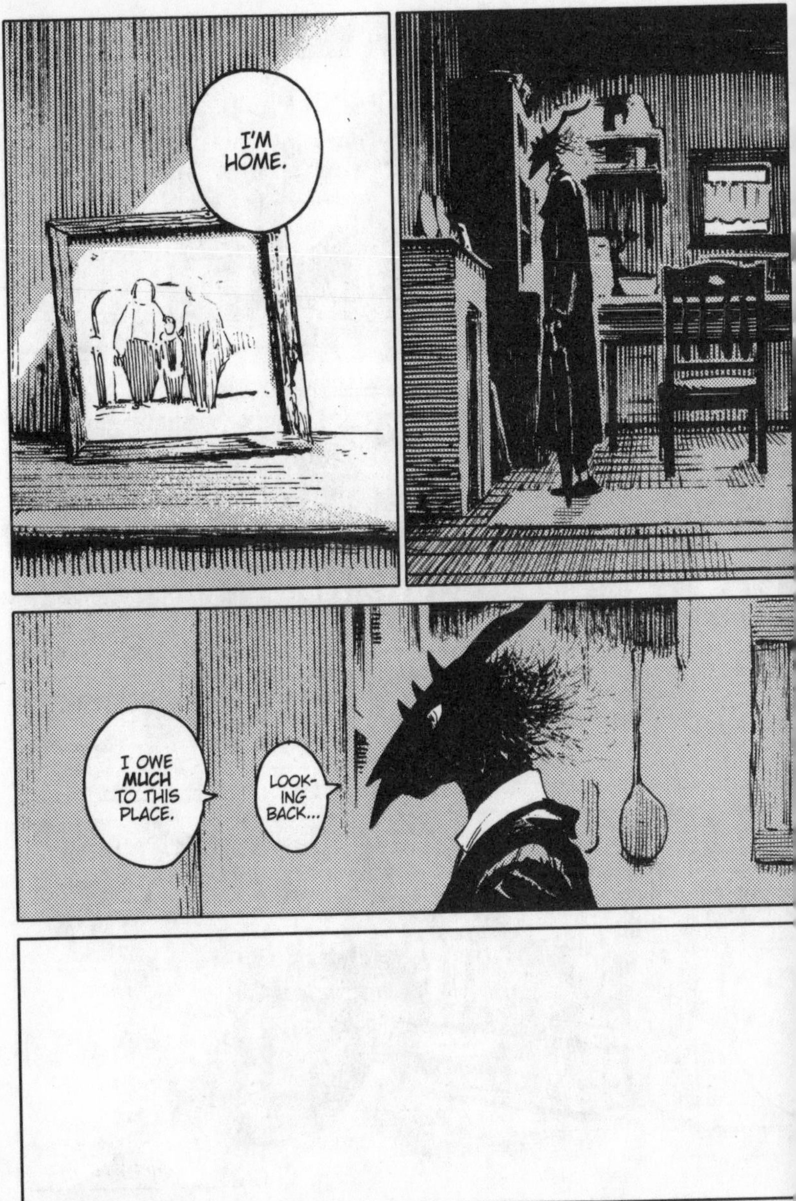
I'M HOME.
LOOK-ING BACK...
I OWE MUCH TO THIS PLACE.

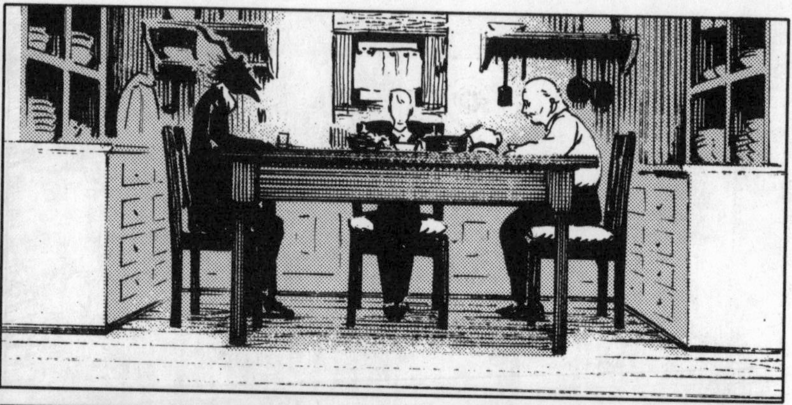
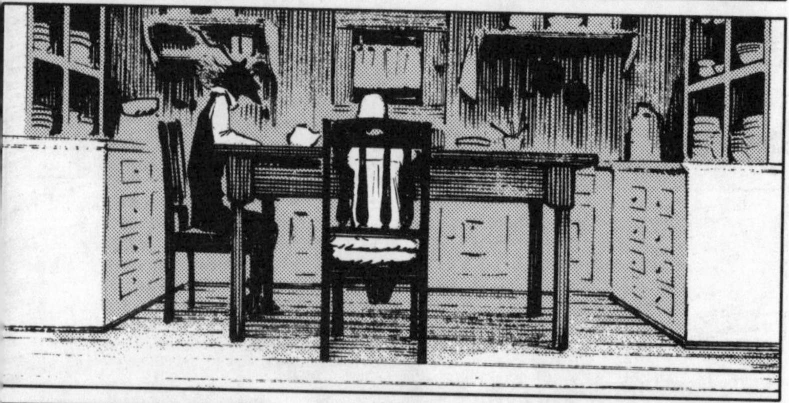
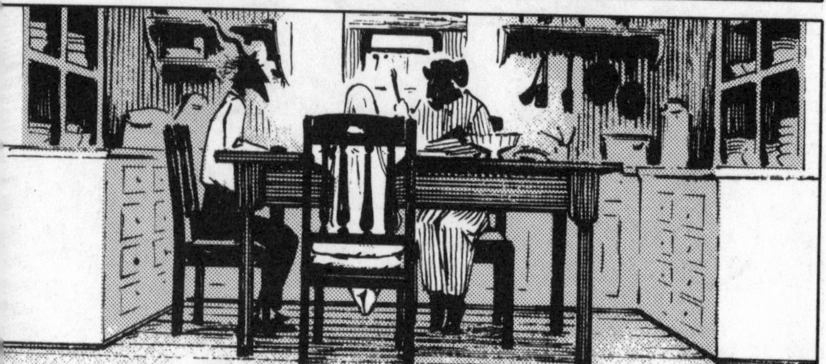

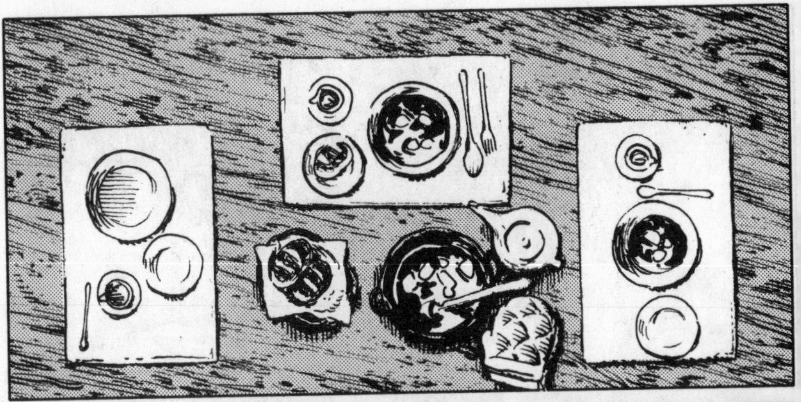
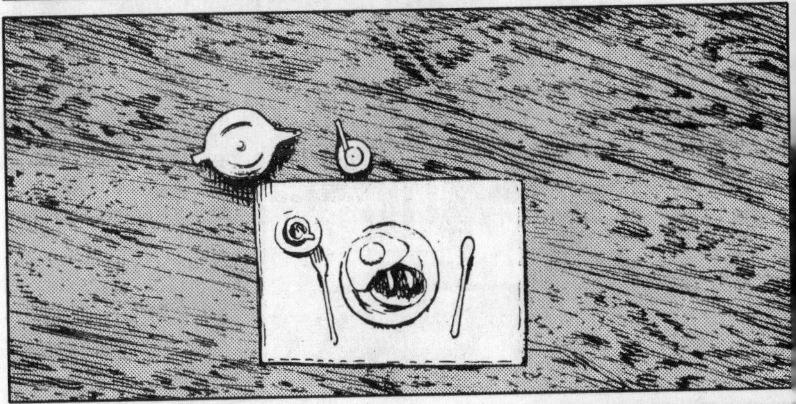
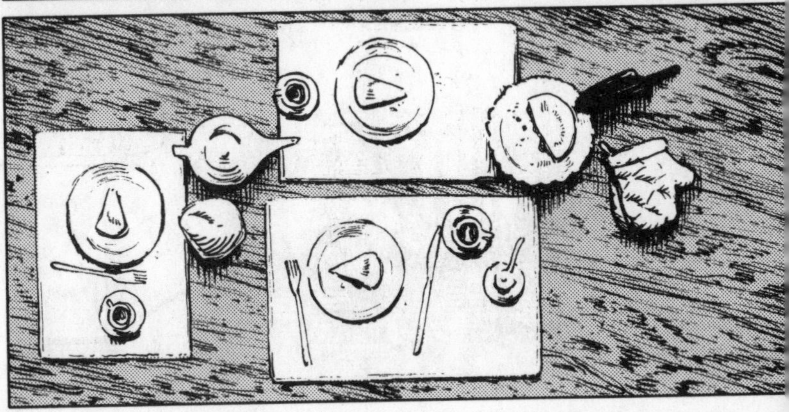

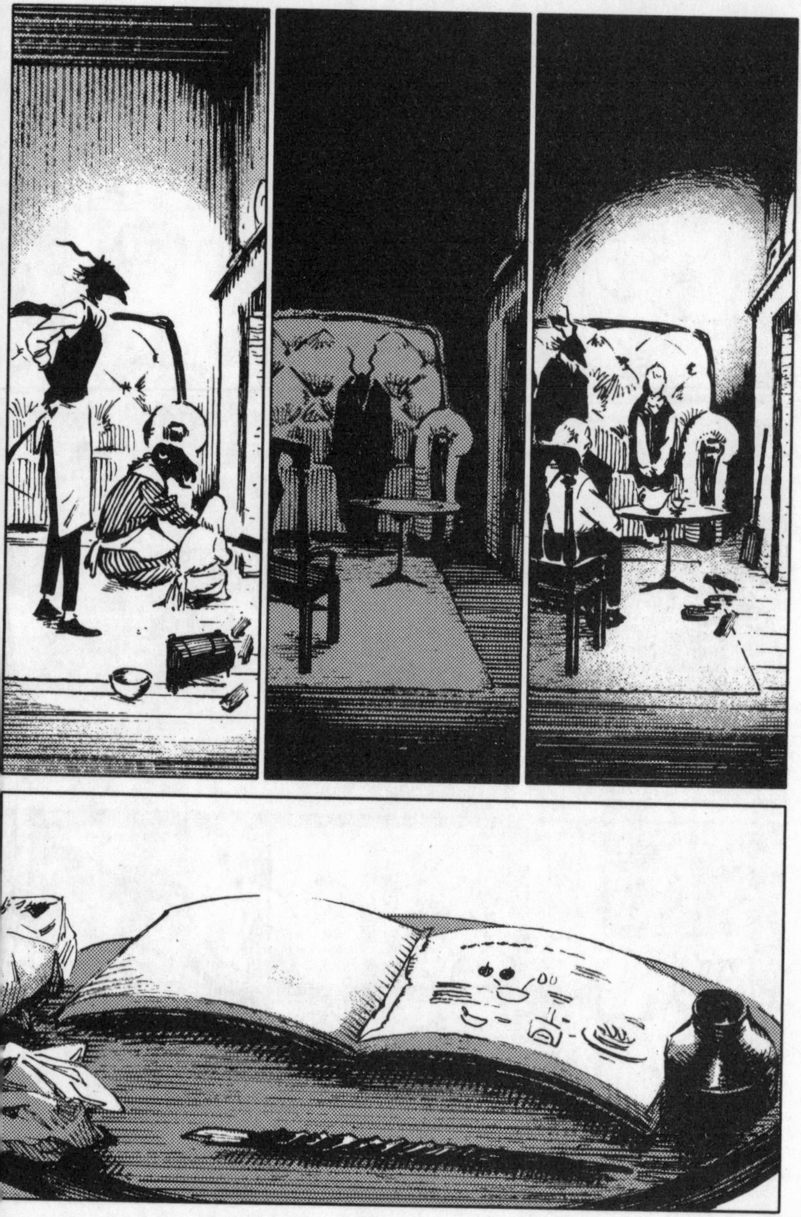

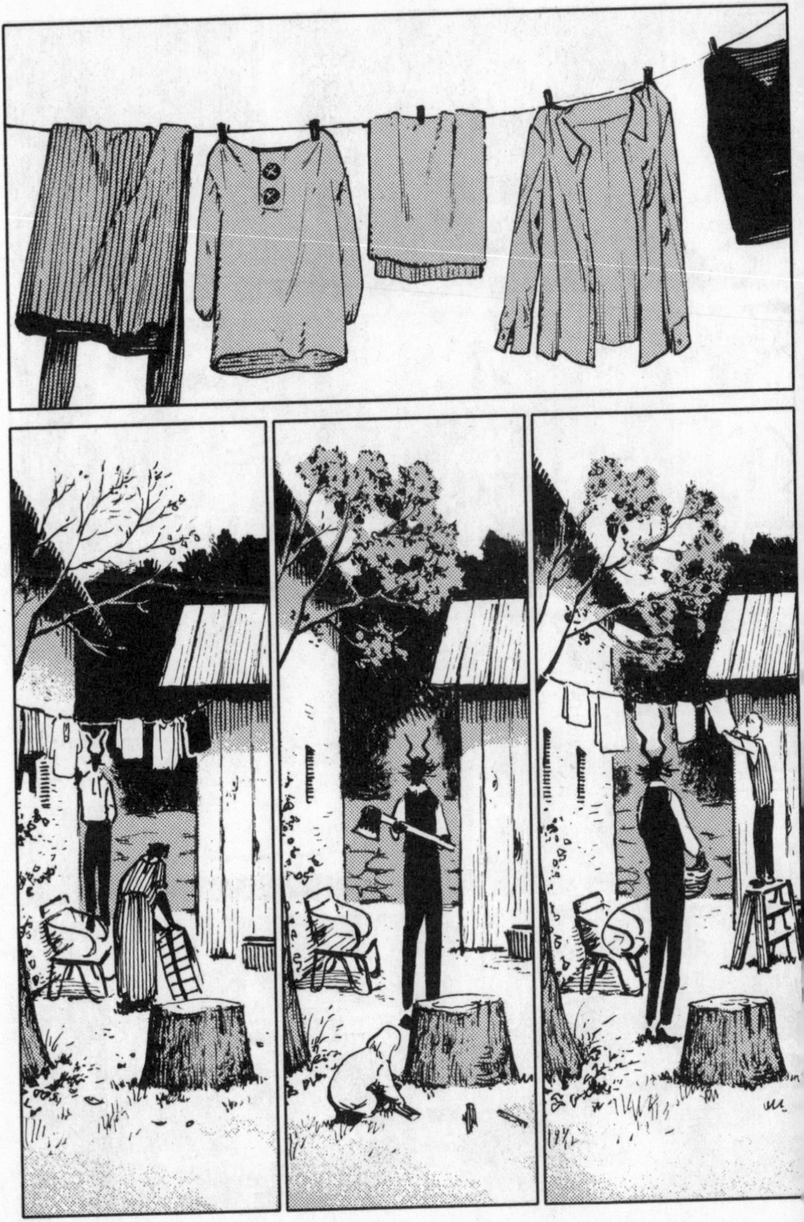

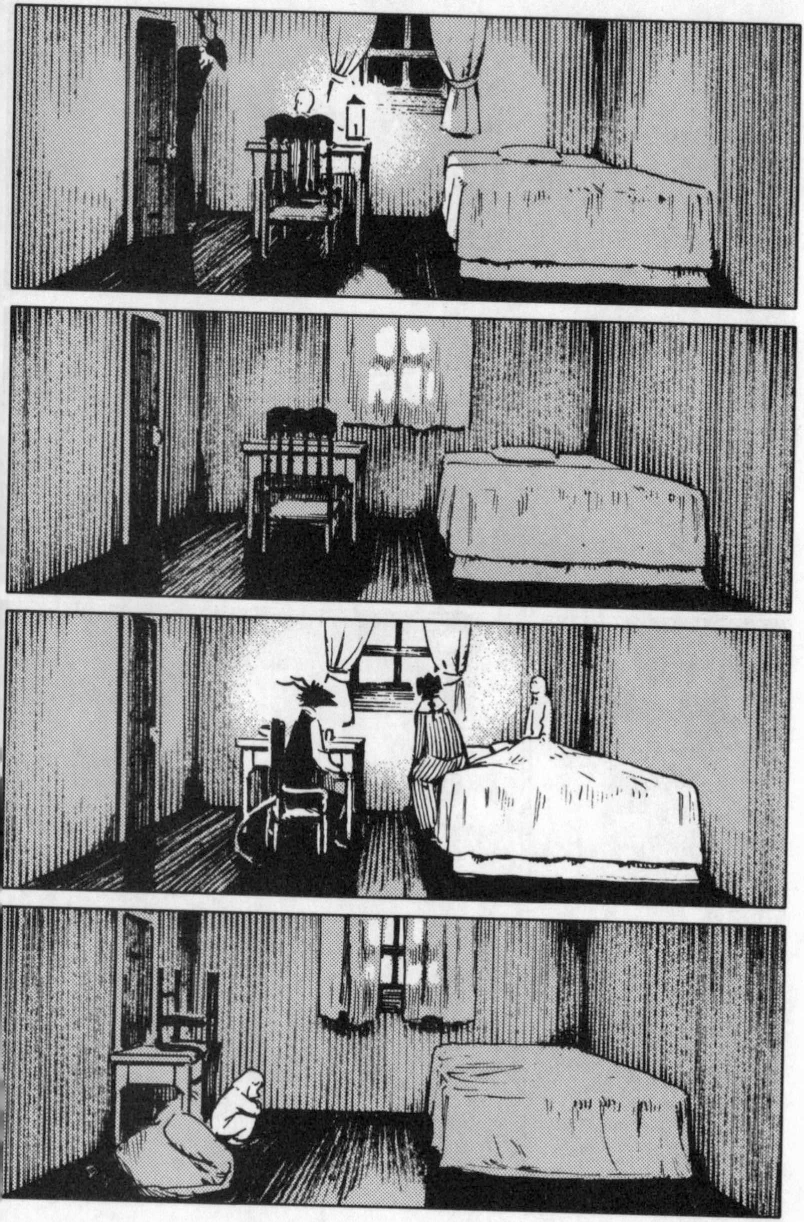

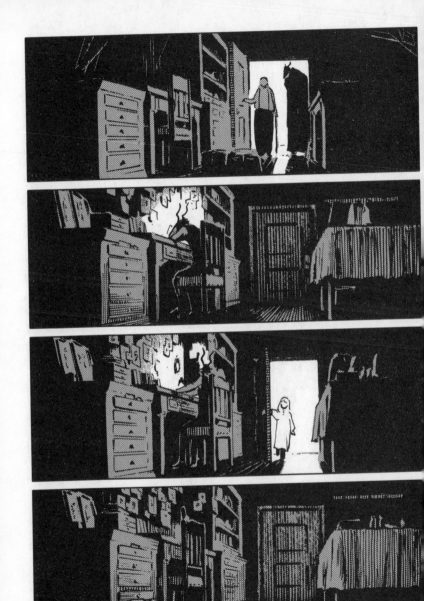

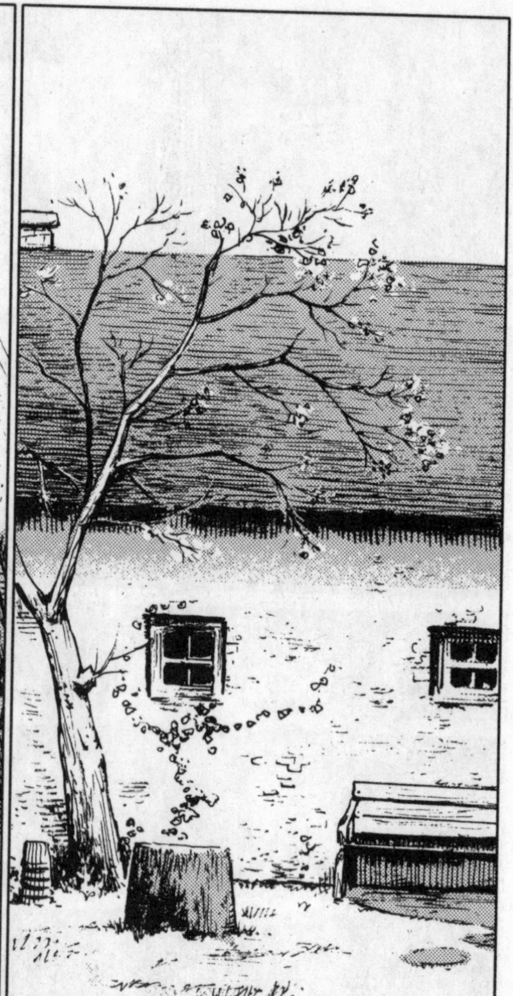
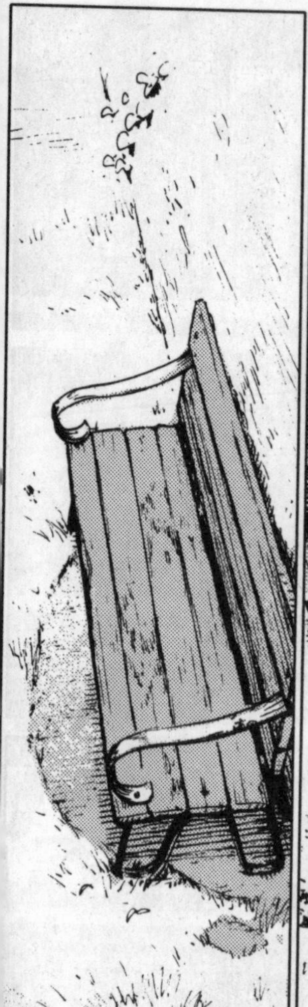

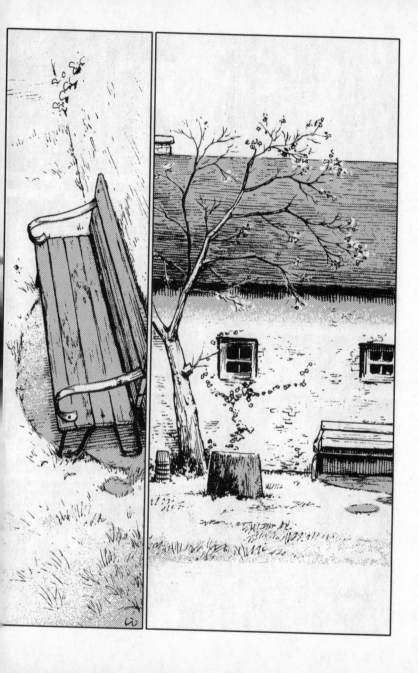

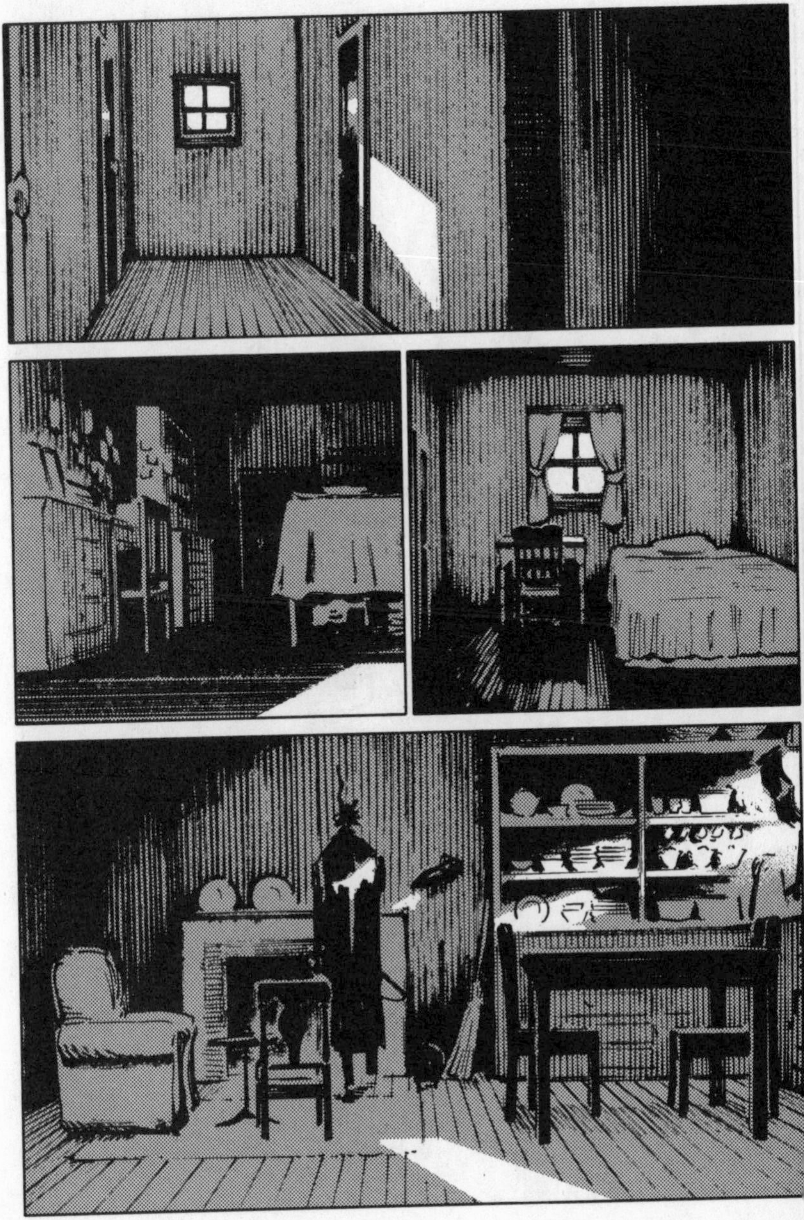

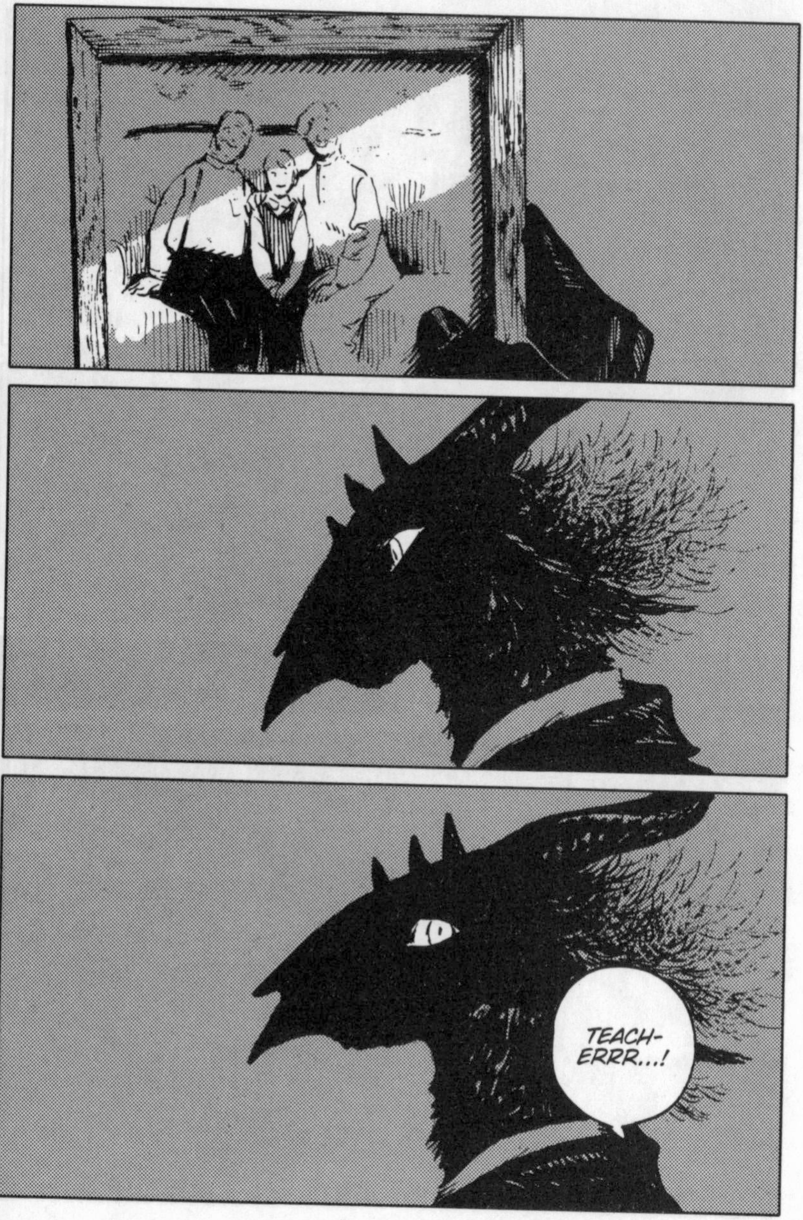
TEACH-
ERRR...!

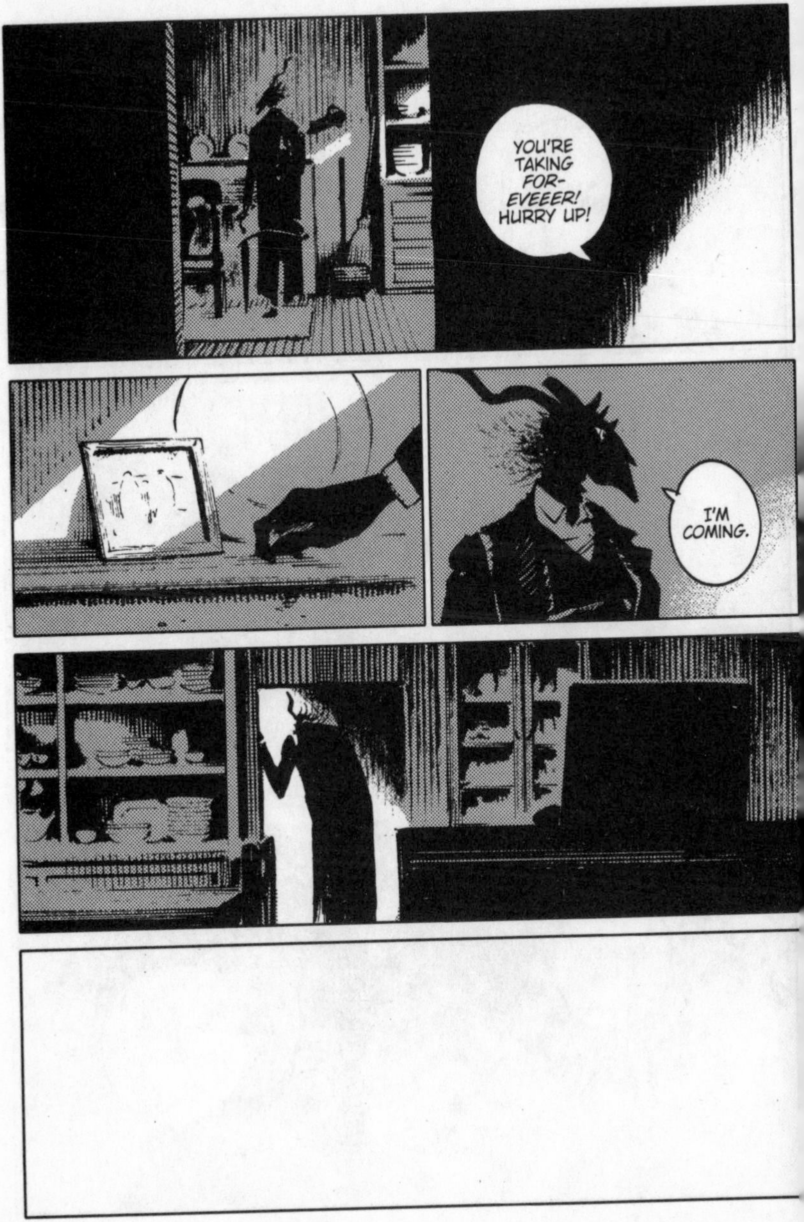
YOU'RE TAKING FOR-EVEEER! HURRY UP!
I'M COMING.

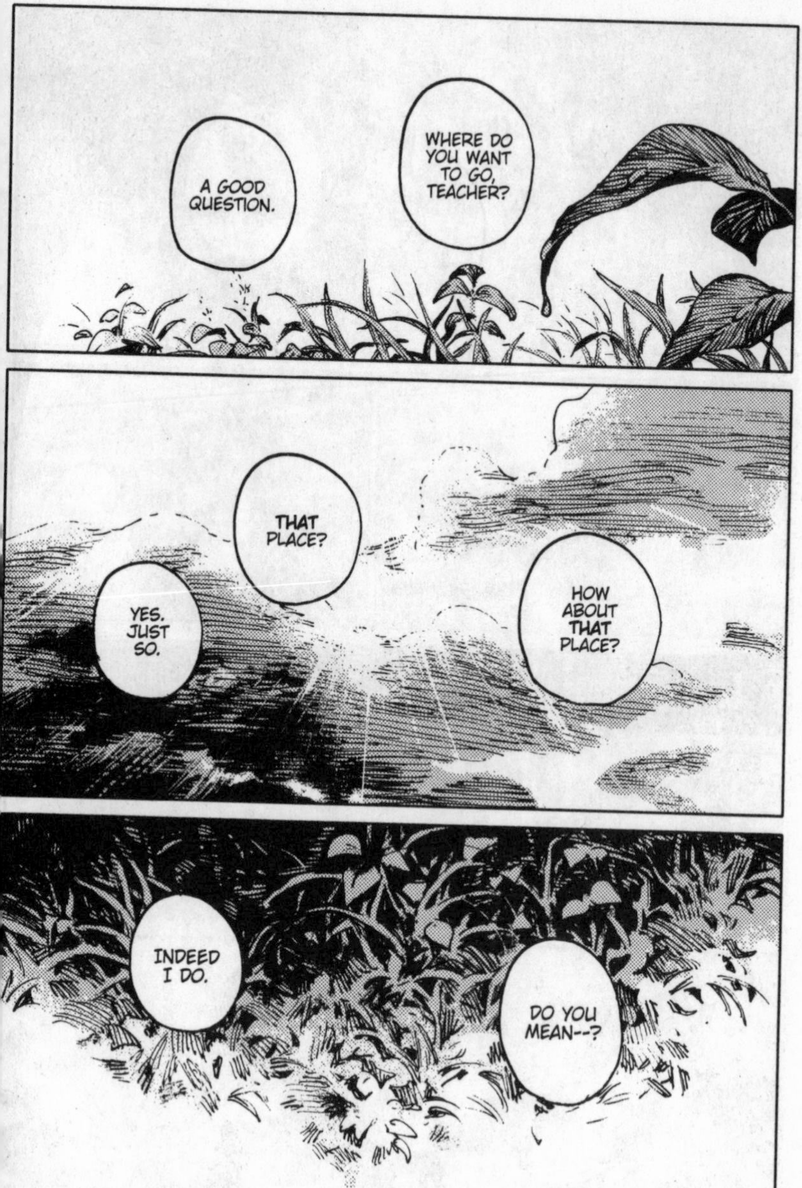
WHERE DO YOU WANT TO GO, TEACHER?
A GOOD QUESTION.
HOW ABOUT THAT PLACE?
THAT PLACE?
YES. JUST SO.
DO YOU MEAN--?
INDEED I DO.

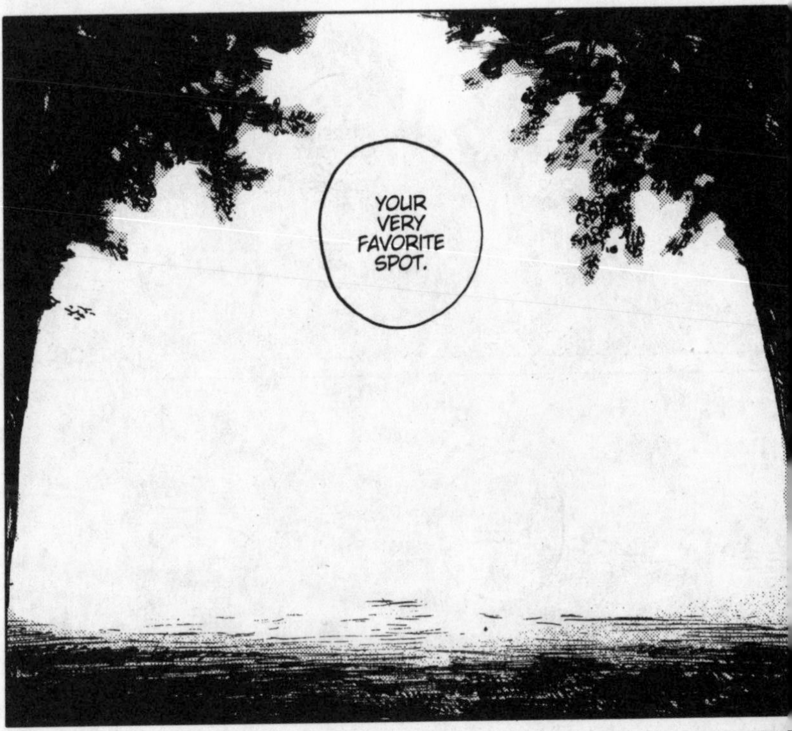
YOUR VERY FAVORITE SPOT.
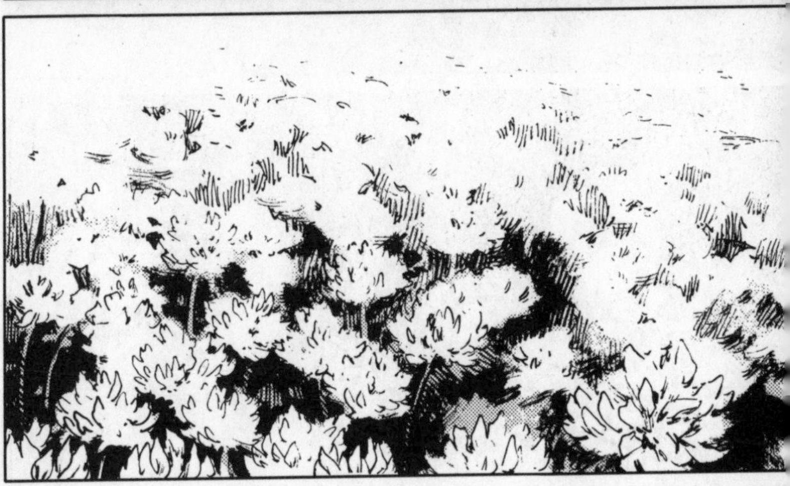

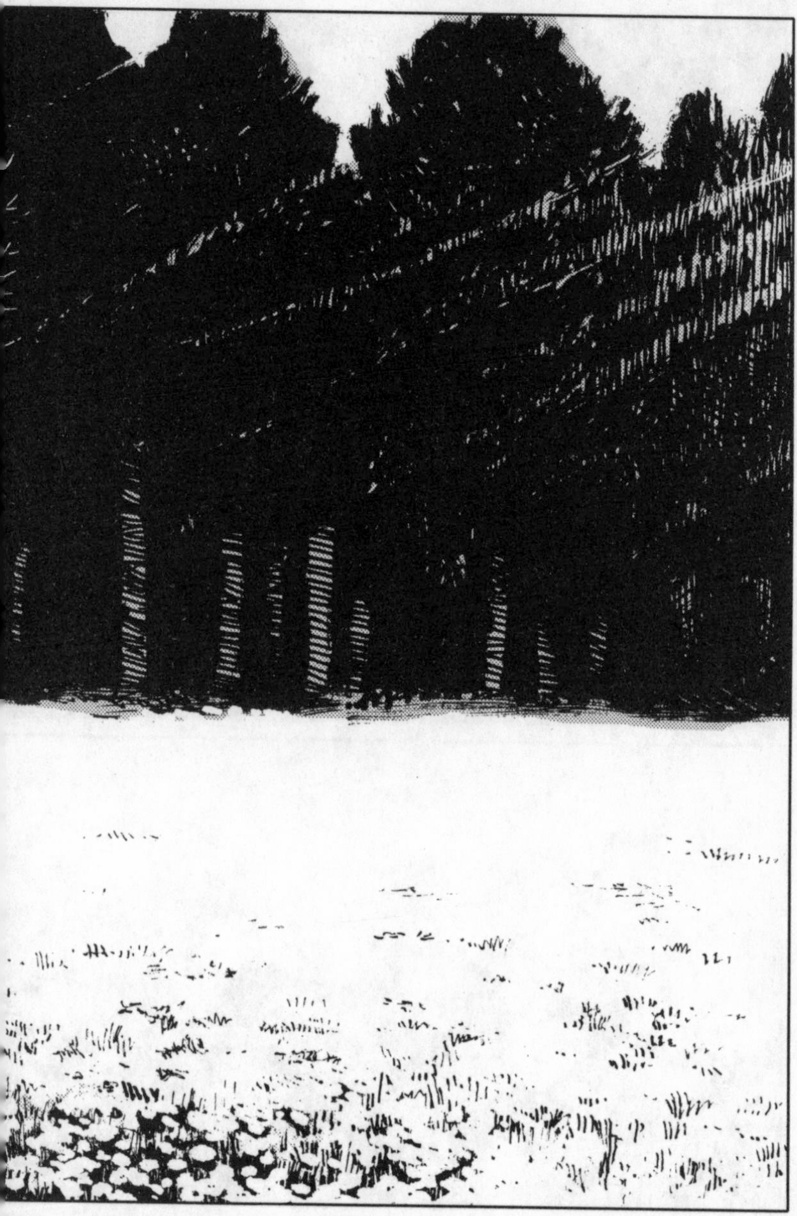

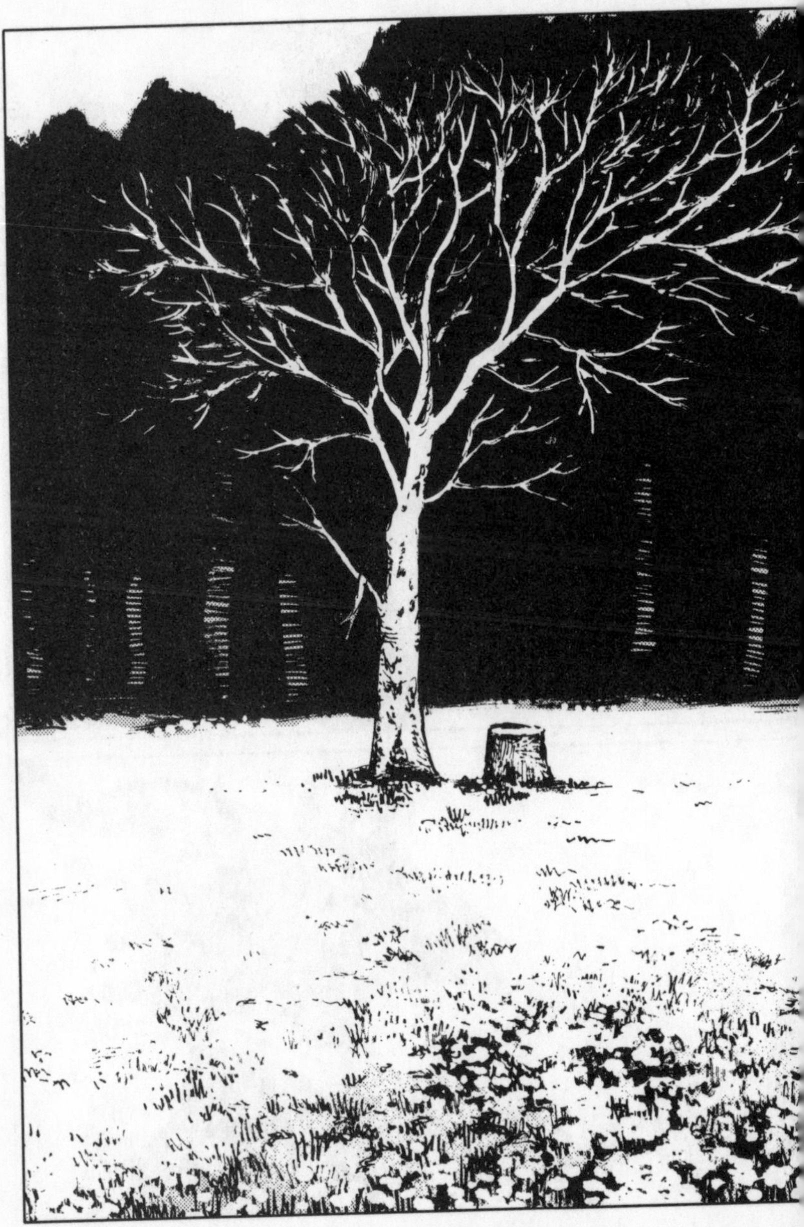

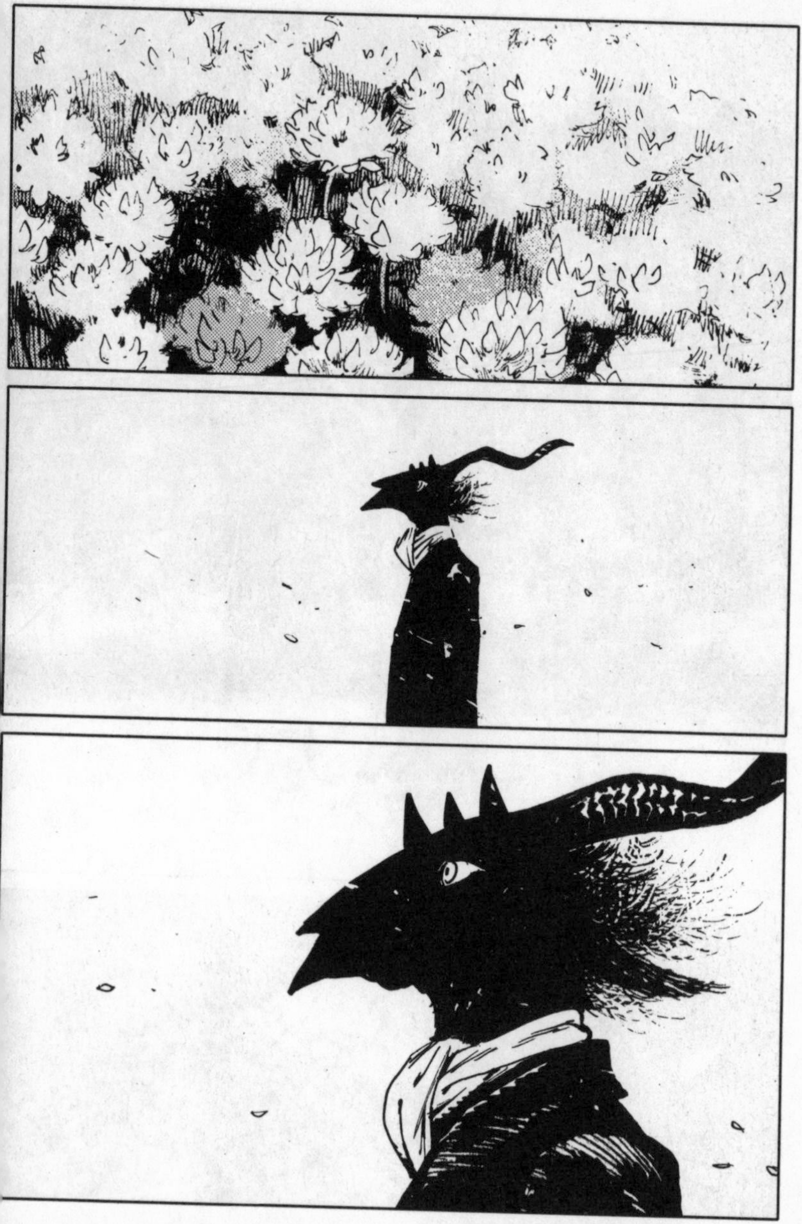

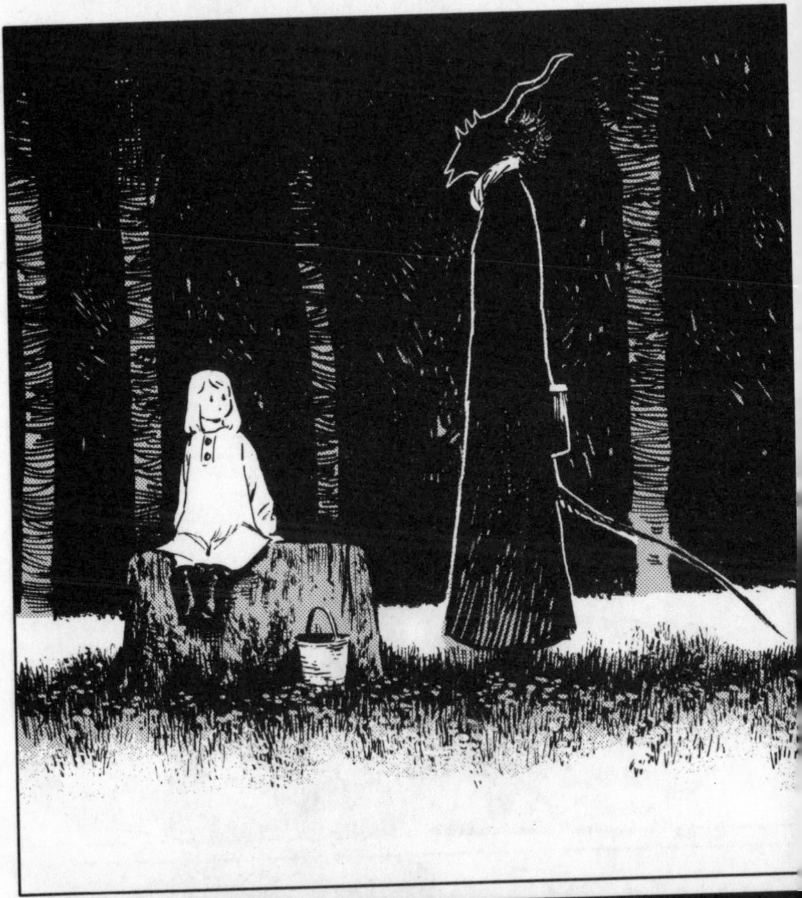
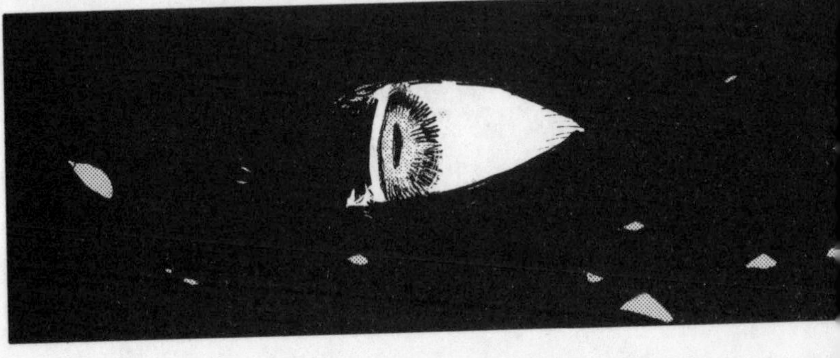

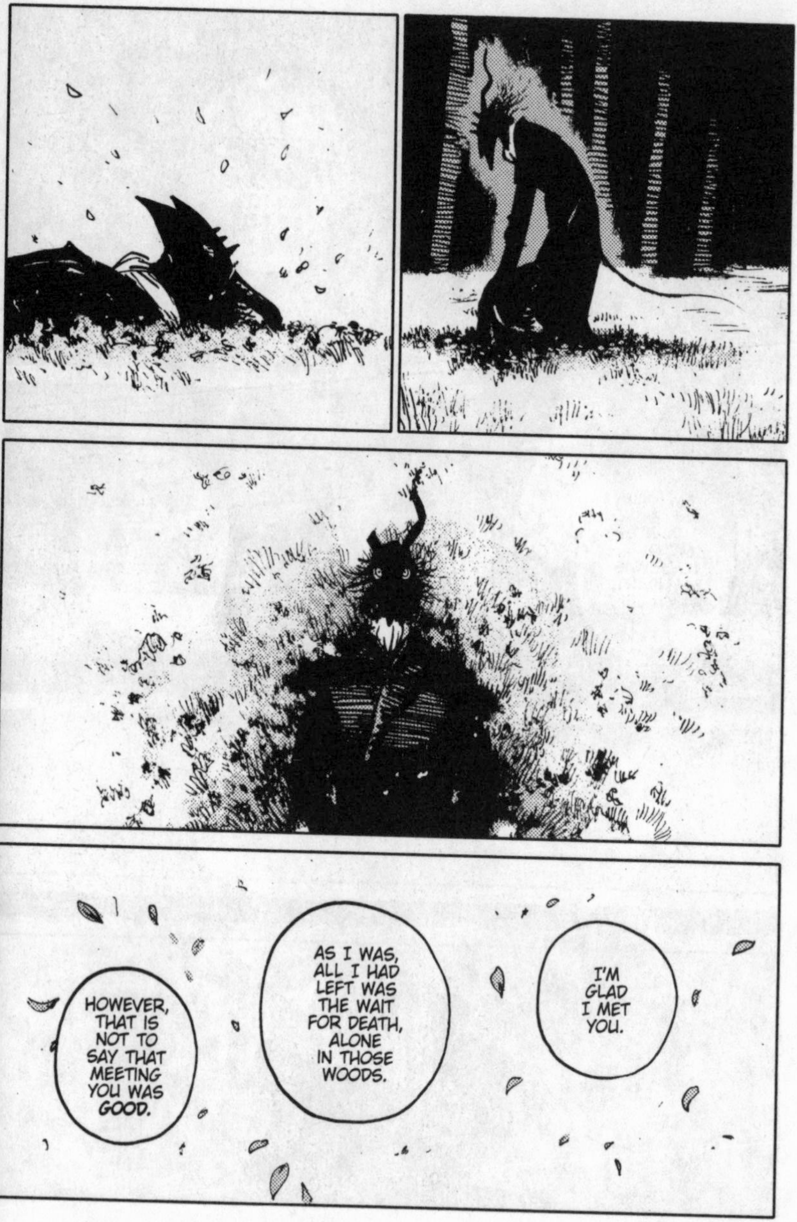
I'M GLAD I MET YOU.
AS I WAS, ALL I HAD LEFT WAS THE WAIT FOR DEATH, ALONE IN THOSE WOODS.
HOWEVER, THAT IS NOT TO SAY THAT MEETING YOU WAS GOOD.

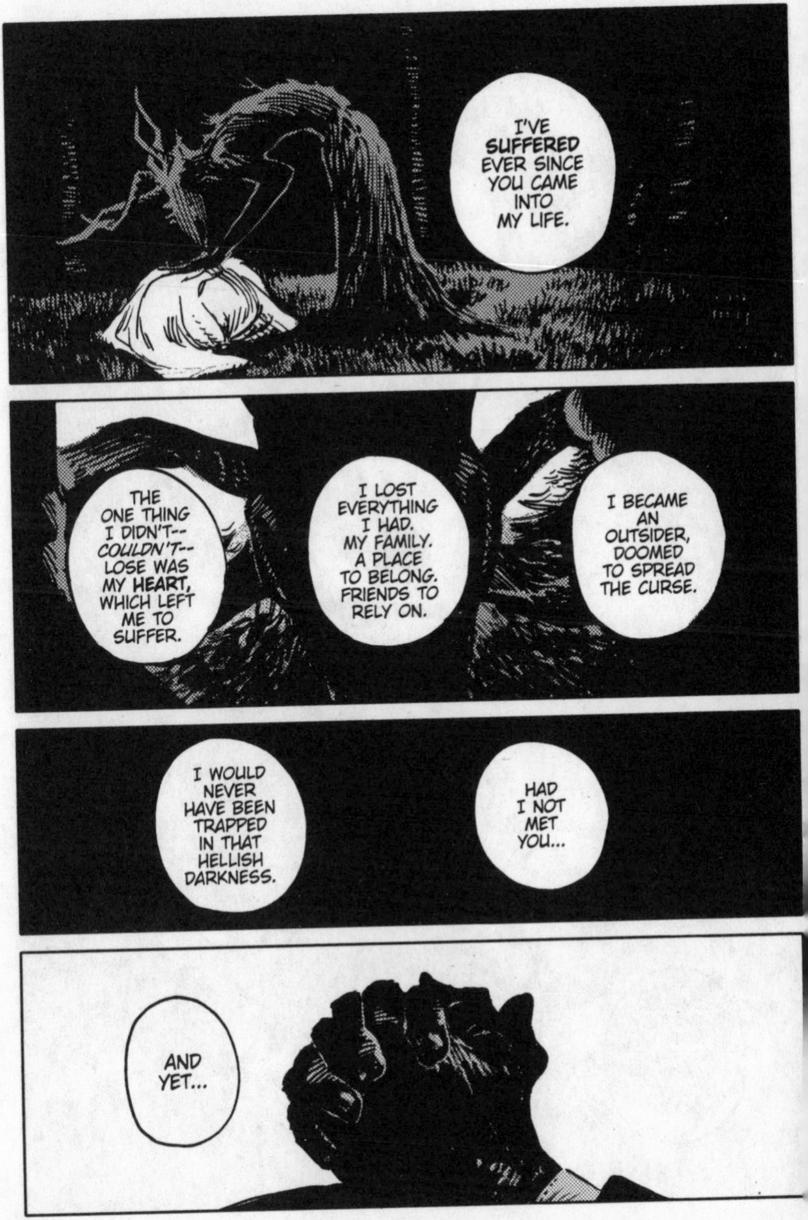
I'VE SUFFERED EVER SINCE YOU CAME INTO MY LIFE.
I BECAME AN OUTSIDER, DOOMED TO SPREAD THE CURSE.
I LOST EVERYTHING I HAD. MY FAMILY. A PLACE TO BELONG. FRIENDS TO RELY ON.
THE ONE THING I DIDN'T-- COULDN'T-- LOSE WAS MY HEART, WHICH LEFT ME TO SUFFER.
HAD I NOT MET YOU...
I WOULD NEVER HAVE BEEN TRAPPED IN THAT HELLISH DARKNESS.
AND YET...

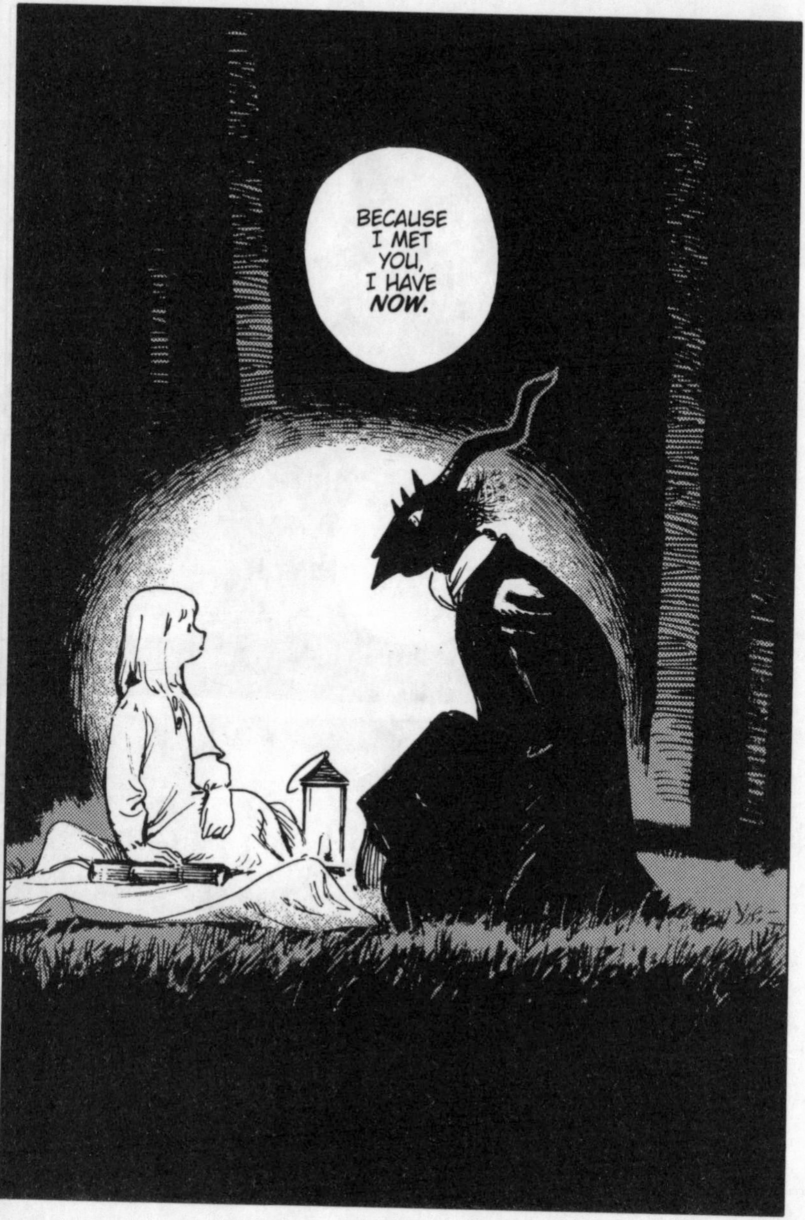
BECAUSE I MET YOU, I HAVE NOW.

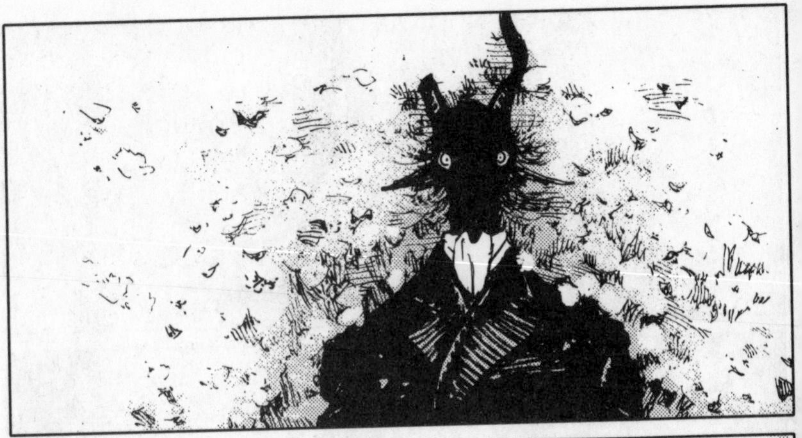

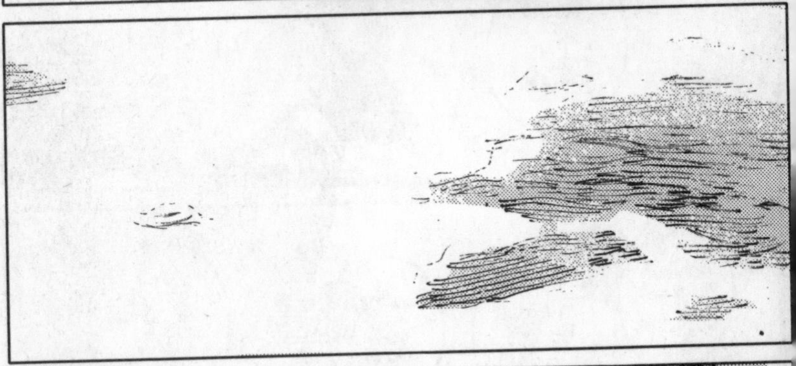

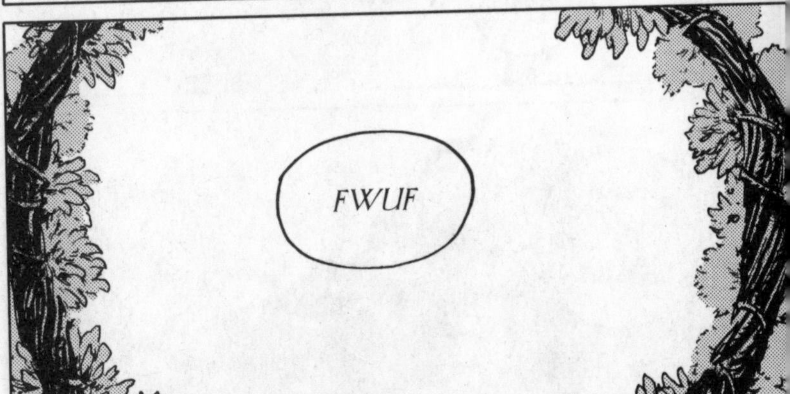
FWUF

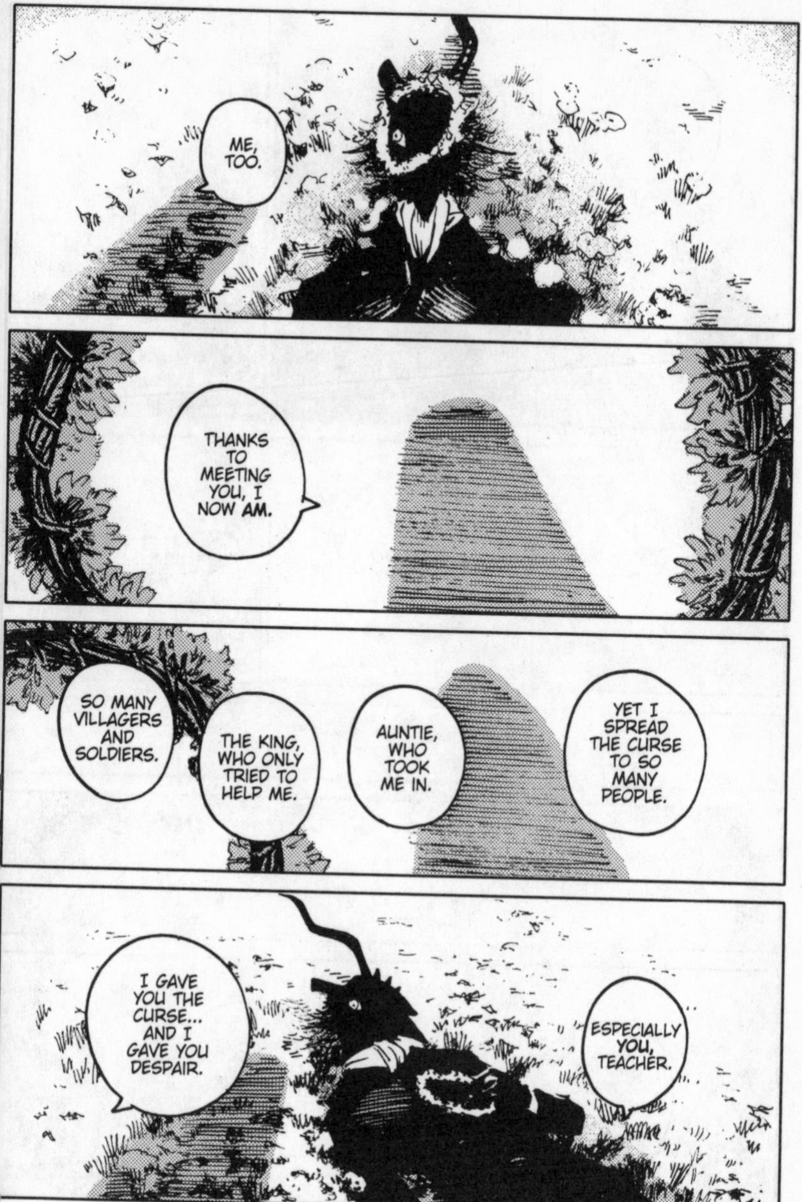
ME, TOO.
THANKS TO MEETING YOU, I NOW AM.
YET I SPREAD THE CURSE TO SO MANY PEOPLE.
AUNTIE, WHO TOOK ME IN.
THE KING, WHO ONLY TRIED TO HELP ME.
SO MANY VILLAGERS AND SOLDIERS.
ESPECIALLY YOU, TEACHER.
I GAVE YOU THE CURSE... AND I GAVE YOU DESPAIR.

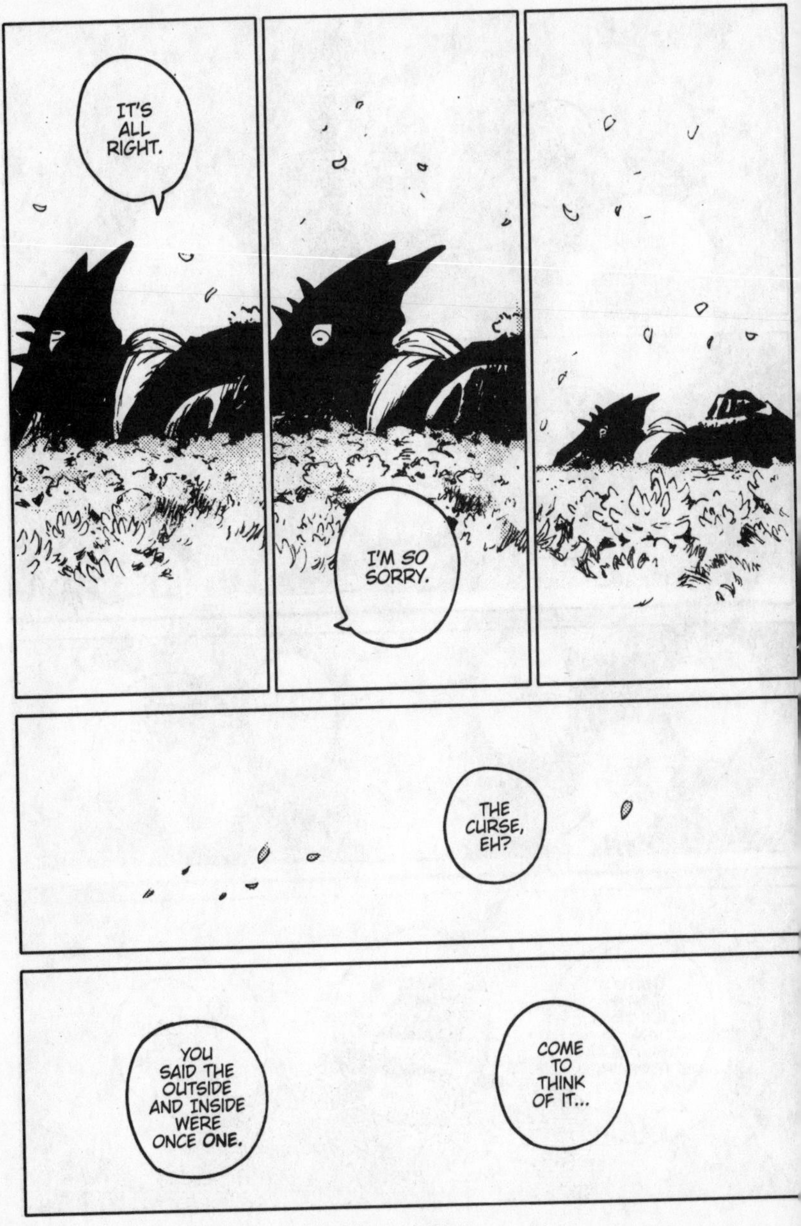
I'M SO SORRY.
IT'S ALL RIGHT.
THE CURSE, EH?
COME TO THINK OF IT...
YOU SAID THE OUTSIDE AND INSIDE WERE ONCE ONE.

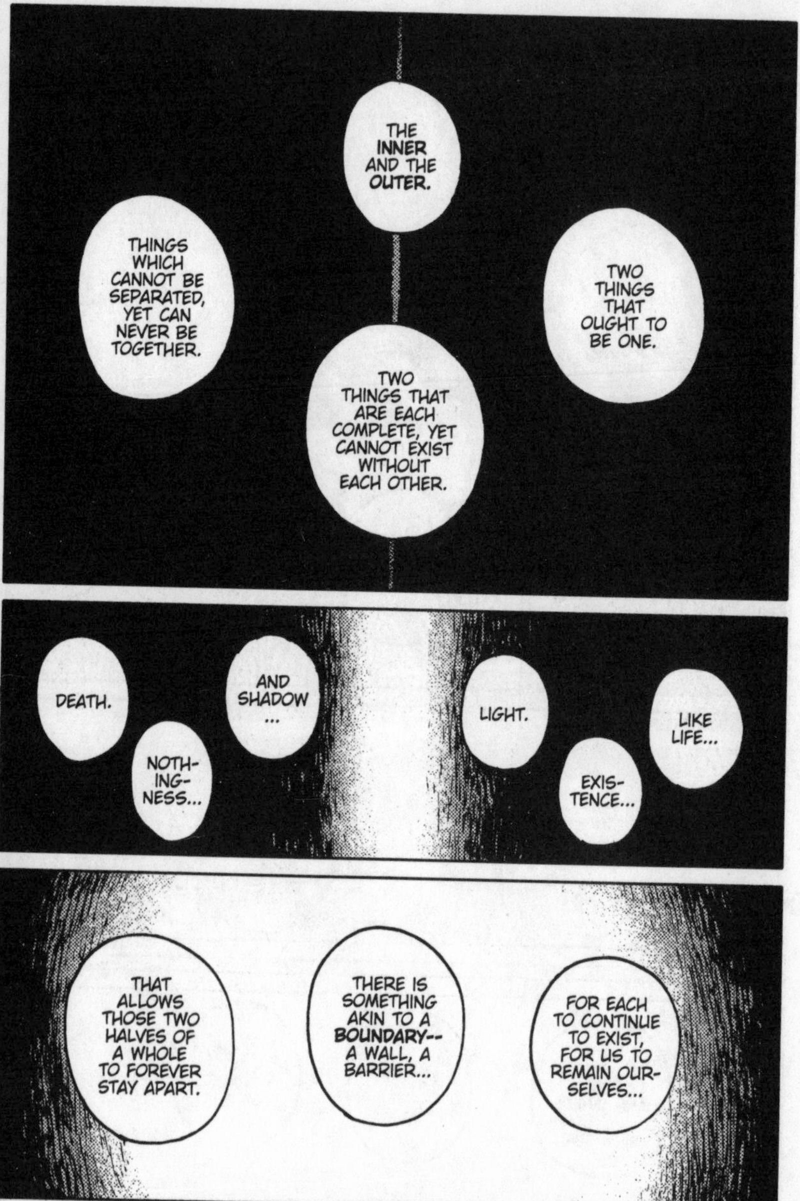
THE INNER AND THE OUTER.
TWO THINGS THAT OUGHT TO BE ONE.
THINGS WHICH CANNOT BE SEPARATED, YET CAN NEVER BE TOGETHER.
TWO THINGS THAT ARE EACH COMPLETE, YET CANNOT EXIST WITHOUT EACH OTHER.
LIKE LIFE...
EXISTENCE...
LIGHT.
AND SHADOW...
NOTHINGNESS...
DEATH.
FOR EACH TO CONTINUE TO EXIST, FOR US TO REMAIN OURSELVES...
THERE IS SOMETHING AKIN TO A **BOUNDARY**-- A WALL, A BARRIER...
THAT ALLOWS THOSE TWO HALVES OF A WHOLE TO FOREVER STAY APART.

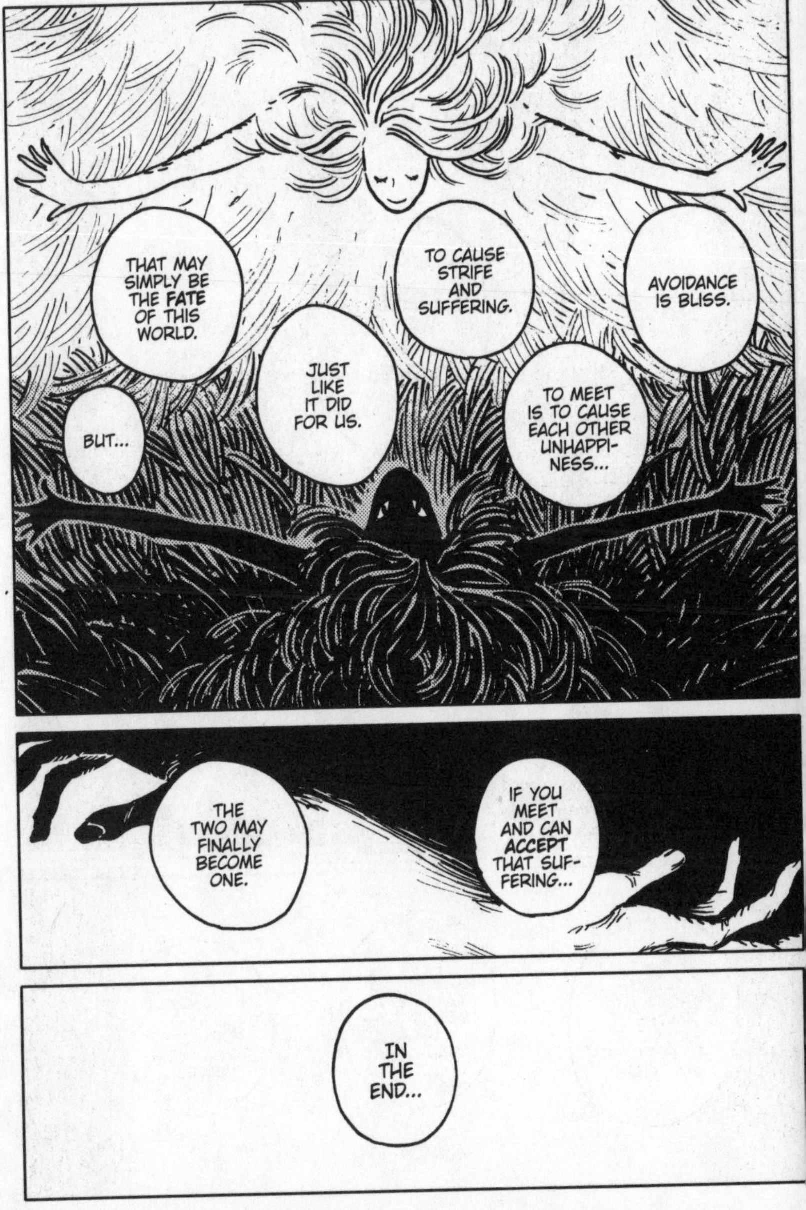
AVOIDANCE IS BLISS.
TO MEET IS TO CAUSE EACH OTHER UNHAPPINESS...
TO CAUSE STRIFE AND SUFFERING.
THAT MAY SIMPLY BE THE FATE OF THIS WORLD.
JUST LIKE IT DID FOR US.
BUT...
IF YOU MEET AND CAN ACCEPT THAT SUFFERING...
THE TWO MAY FINALLY BECOME ONE.
IN THE END...

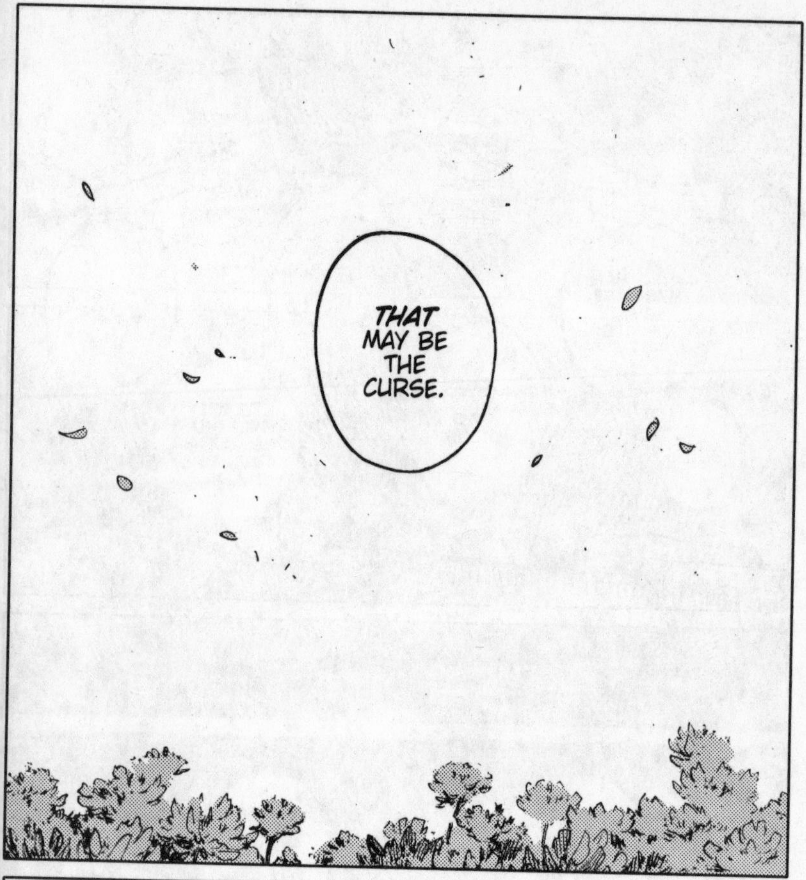
THAT MAY BE THE CURSE.
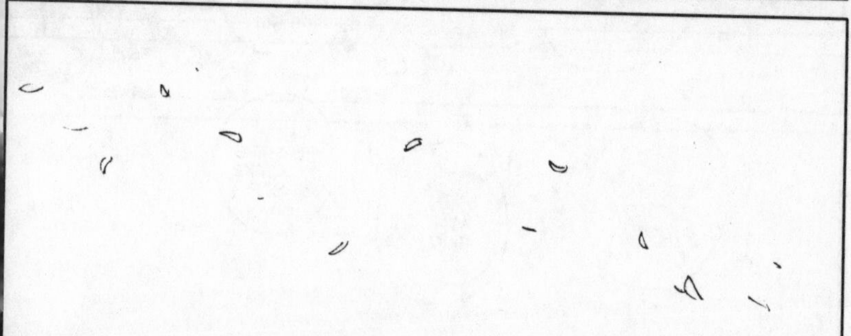

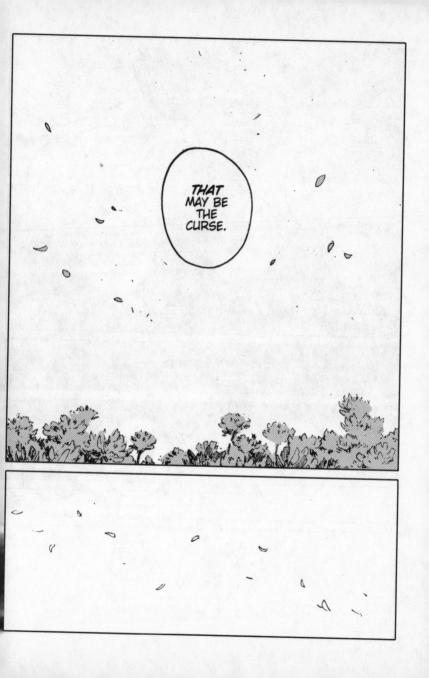

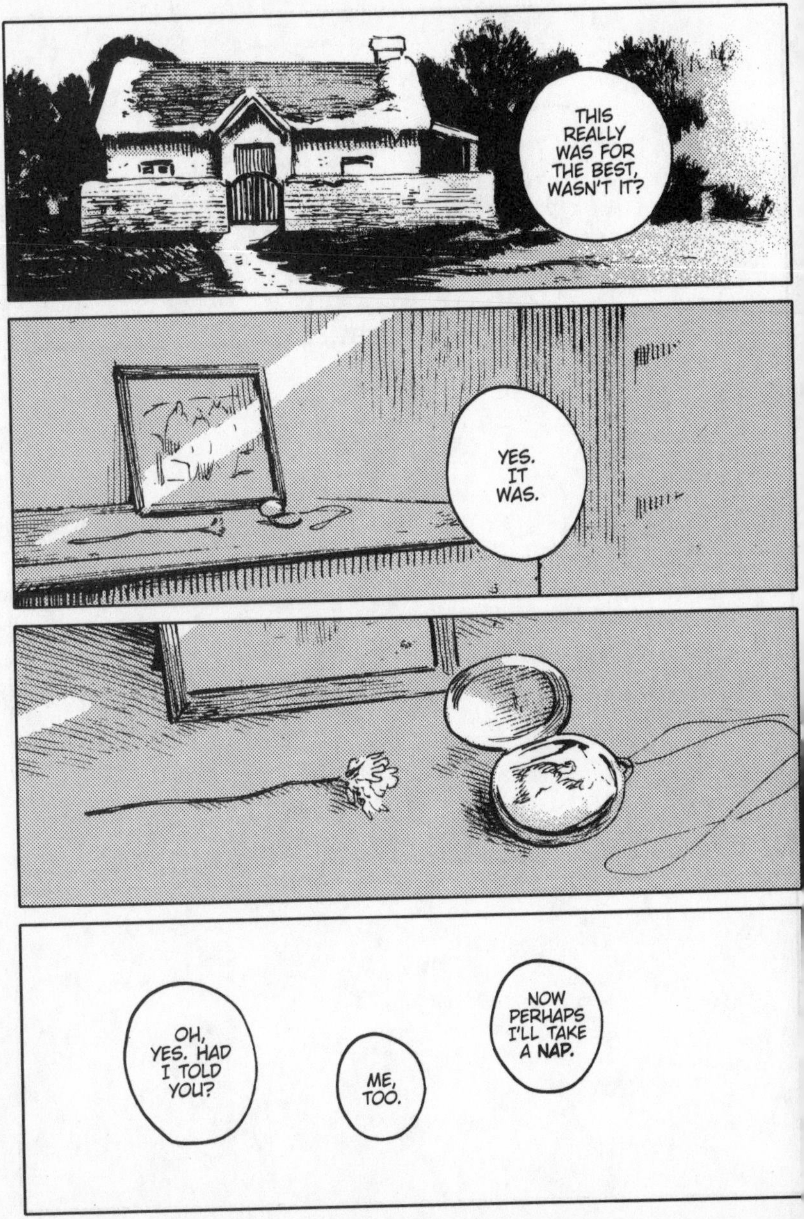
THIS REALLY WAS FOR THE BEST, WASN'T IT?
YES. IT WAS.
NOW PERHAPS I'LL TAKE A **NAP.**
ME, TOO.
OH, YES. HAD I TOLD YOU?

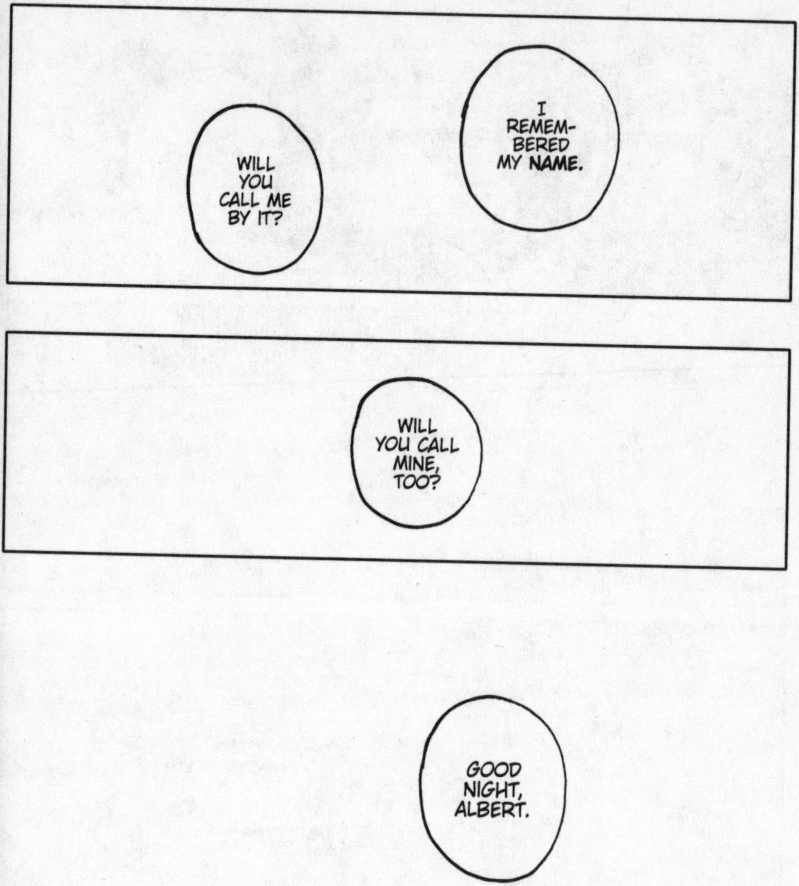
I REMEMBERED MY NAME.
WILL YOU CALL ME BY IT?
WILL YOU CALL MINE, TOO?
GOOD NIGHT, ALBERT.

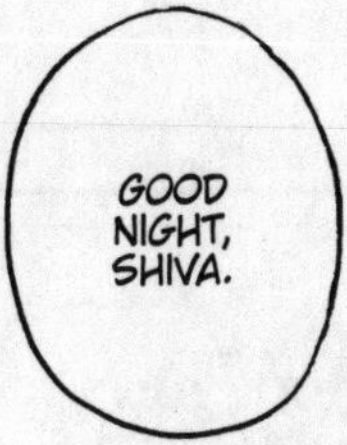
GOOD NIGHT, SHIVA.

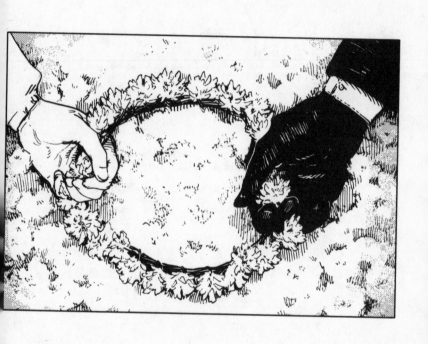

The Girl From the Other Side: Siúil, a Rún

THE END

Siúil, siúil, siúil a rún

Siúil go socair agus siúil go ciúin.

LINGERING IN THE HAZE BETWEEN THEIR JOURNEYS, DAYS OF QUIET PEACE.

JULY 9, 2022

Living in the haze between day and night
set the two on a difficult path. Yet along
the way, there were days that glowed
with peace. Days of quiet tranquility
in between the storms. Ordinary days,
where little of note happened.

Day and Night.
These are the bonus
stories of two people--
one human, one inhuman--
who lived in the stark
divide between them.

The Girl From the Other Side:
Side Stories
A special twelfth volume
featuring brand-new material.
COMING SOON

SEVEN SEAS ENTERTAINMENT PRESENTS

Siúil, a Rún
The Girl from the Other Side

story and art by NAGABE vol. 11

TRANSLATION
Adrienne Beck

ADAPTATION
Ysabet Reinhardt MacFarlane

LETTERING AND RETOUCH
Lys Blakeslee

INTERIOR LAYOUT
Sandy Grayson

COVER DESIGN
Nicky Lim

PROOFREADER
Dawn Davis

EDITOR
Alexis Roberts

PREPRESS TECHNICIAN
Rhiannon Rasmussen-Silverstein

MANAGING EDITOR
Julie Davis

ASSOCIATE PUBLISHER
Adam Arnold

PUBLISHER
Jason DeAngelis

THE GIRL FROM THE OTHER SIDE: SIUIL, A RUN VOL. 11

Originally published in Japan in 2021 by MAG Garden Corporation, Tokyo. English translation rights arranged through TOHAN CORPORATION, Tokyo.

Seven Seas press and purchase enquiries can be sent to Marketing Manager Lianne Sentar at press@gomanga.com. Information regarding the distribution and purchase of digital editions is available from Digital Manager CK Russell at digital@gomanga.com.

ISBN: 978-1-64

Printed in Cana

First Printing: N

10 9 8 7 6 5

7-18-22
MEVLER
0

FOLLOW US ONLINE: *www.seven*

READING DIRECTIONS

This book reads from ***right to left***, Japanese style. If this is your first time reading manga, you start reading from the top right panel on each page and take it from there. If you get lost, just follow the numbered diagram here. It may seem backwards at first, but you'll get the hang of it! Have fun!!

1
2
3
4
5
6
7
8
9

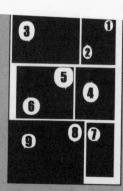